WALKS THE SKY

Ron Habeck

To my wife, Jaynanne, S.H.M.I.L.Y.

To my daughters, Bekah and Jaryn, I am so proud to be your father.
I love you.

CONTENTS

PROLOGUE

June 1836, Eastern Florida Territory

It's amusing when inferior-minded people accuse me of insanity.

Colonel Jeremiah Morse smiled and snapped his monocular telescope closed.

"There's your proof, Lieutenant," he said as he stood and began to brush the dirt off his stomach and legs.

"What proof are you talking about?" Lieutenant Arthur Hatten lowered his telescope and looked at the colonel. "We've watched the settlement for an hour and hardly seen anyone milling about in this heat."

Colonel Morse laughed. "That's your problem, Lieutenant, you need to see something before you believe. I know I'm right by what I *didn't* see."

Lieutenant Hatten snorted before rolling back onto his stomach and peering through his telescope at the settlement once again.

"Look closer," Colonel Morse said. "Do you see any guards? Are there any lookouts or a sentry of any kind?"

"No, there's none of that," Lieutenant Hatten replied. "But that doesn't mean—"

"The United States is at war with the Seminole Indians," Colonel Morse said. "A ruthless enemy that's been known to raid villages and settlements throughout the Florida territory, killing innocent women and children. And here sits this settlement carved out of the very woods the Seminoles call home. A bit suspicious if you ask me. Those settlers shouldn't even be there. Be that as it may, they should, at the very least, be armed to the hilt, with guards, lookouts and, if it were me, I'd cut down a few more trees and fortify the area. They have no protection of any kind."

Colonel Morse duck walked to his horse and secured his telescope into one of his saddlebags as if tucking the Mona Lisa in for the night. "It appears to me they're quite comfortable living smack in the middle of the Seminole territory."

He grabbed the reins of his horse and started walking to where he stationed his men leaving Lieutenant Hatten in the dirt behind him.

"They're missionaries, Colonel." Lieutenant Hatten replied. He closed his telescope and stood. "That would explain the lack of protection."

Hatten jogged up next to the colonel. His bright red hair and freckles were offset by his innocent green eyes however, his fair skin was a detriment in the Florida summer sun. The colonel had heard stories of how Lieutenant Hatten was often invited to parties with dignitaries while he was at the Academy. Apparently, he fit the image West Point wished to portray to the public, but it sometimes made the colonel wonder if the lieutenant didn't belong behind a desk somewhere. Still, the lieutenant was one of the top students in his class and the best field leader the school had produced in years. He wasn't impulsive in the slightest, making him a master strategist. His unfailing poise frequently infuriated the colonel who, more often than not, chased success on the battlefield by making hasty decisions.

"Did you hear me, Colonel? They're missionaries. That would explain—"

"Even missionaries have enough sense to protect themselves," Colonel Morse replied. "On the frontier like this, most missionaries live within the walls of a fort or fortified settlement. Not out in the open like that."

"There has to be some explanation as to why they don't have any defenses. Maybe they—"

"Why can't you just see it for what it is?" Colonel Morse asked.

"I just can't accept—"

"You can't, or you won't?"

"I...I..."

Colonel Morse turned and faced the lieutenant. "I told you an hour ago. They're helping the Seminoles. The enemy of the United States. *Our* enemy! Helping them by giving them food, supplies and telling them of our whereabouts. And we must put a stop to it. We must cut the legs from under the Seminoles. And it starts with that village."

"You're insane, Colonel."

Gratified his assessment of Lieutenant Hatten's inferior mind was correct, Colonel Morse continued walking towards his men. "What's insane, Lieutenant, is not altering our tactics after six months of failures. We must change our approach."

"We need to stay the course, Colonel," Lieutenant Hatten replied as he caught up to the colonel. "We cannot go—"

"What we cannot do is fight the Seminoles like we would the British. It will not work." Colonel Morse handed the reins of his horse to one of his men as they finally reached his platoon, who were still standing in formation just as he left them. "The Seminoles are savages, and they fight like savages. They attack and retreat only to attack again. They go after unsuspecting troops and supply wagons. They look for our weaknesses and exploit them. And we must do the same."

"Attacking villages and farms cannot be the way," Lieutenant Hatten said.

"We must strike at their heart," Colonel Morse said. "Take away their supplies."

"Let's burn their crops then," Lieutenant Hatten said.

"That's not enough!" Colonel Morse replied. "We must hit them hard and fast where it hurts."

Lieutenant Hatten shook his head and exhaled. "But what does all of that have to do with this village of white settlers?"

"They have everything to do with it," Colonel Morse replied. "They're the reason the Seminoles know our whereabouts."

"How's that even possible?"

Colonel Morse gritted his teeth and rubbed the handle of his saber but kept it sheathed. Lieutenant Hatten's constant questioning of his tactics in front of the men was maddening. When they first arrived in Florida six months ago, the lieutenant would pull the colonel aside and ask questions. The colonel took the queries as a young officer trying to learn how to command. However, Hatten became more accusatory as time went on and no longer waited until they were alone.

"My scouts told me they've seen Seminoles come and go out of that settlement as of late," Colonel Morse replied.

"That could mean anything," Lieutenant Hatten said. "If they're missionaries it would only make sense for Seminoles to feel free to come and go."

"I disagree," Colonel Morse said. "We were never ambushed until those visits to the settlement started."

"You're suggesting they've been telling the Seminoles our whereabouts and operations?"

Colonel Morse nodded. "That's precisely what's happening."

"That's impossible!" Lieutenant Hatten said. His voice was louder and laced with more venom than the colonel appreciated. "How would they even know? They're civilians."

"Doesn't matter. They need to be punished."

Lieutenant Hatten stepped forward. "You can't do that!"

"They are enemies of the United States government, and I am ordering you to attack that village."

"This is not what we are here for, Colonel."

"You are here to follow orders, Lieutenant." Colonel Morse nodded towards his First Sergeant, Donald Clark, who stepped forward and stood directly behind the lieutenant with several other men. "Now, Lieutenant, order your men to change into their Seminole disguises and attack that village."

"I refuse to—"

"Are you disobeying a direct order, Lieutenant?" Colonel Morse asked.

Lieutenant Hatten glanced at the men looming behind him. He stared at the ground for a few moments before looking back up at the Colonel.

"I cannot, in good conscience, give those orders."

Colonel Morse looked at Clark. "Sergeant, get him on his knees."

Clark dropped Hatten with a rifle butt to the back of the knee.

The lieutenant's voice echoed through the forest. "Women and children are in there! You're a lunatic!"

Colonel Morse smiled and ambled towards Lieutenant Hatten. Three soldiers held the younger man on the ground with his arms pinned behind his back.

"Don't do this," Lieutenant Hatten said. "You have no proof, you paranoid—"

"Six months, Lieutenant! We've been down here six months. And after all we've seen and been through you still want to question my orders?"

"When the lives of civilians are involved, yes."

"You're refusing to obey a direct order, Lieutenant!" The colonel pulled his saber out of its sheath, slow and deliberate. "A punishable offense I may add." Even Clark flinched a little with the cold sound of metal abrading metal. "Especially a direct order from *me*."

Colonel Morse stopped two feet in front of the lieutenant. He could see fear in Hatten's eyes, but he saw something else – defiance.

"He's not fit to wear an officer's uniform. Get it off him!"

The soldiers ripped off the lieutenant's coat and shirt.

"They're settlers!" Lieutenant Hatten said. "Not warriors! Innocent women and children are in there! We can't—"

"Innocent?" Colonel Morse chuckled. "Who's innocent? They're traitors!"

"You don't know that! You're ordering the slaughter of defenseless people!"

Colonel Morse placed the flat side of his blade under the young man's chin.

"I won't allow traitors in my midst." He lifted Lieutenant Hatten's head with the sword. The two men's eyes met. "Nor will I tolerate disobedience!"

With a flick of his wrist, the colonel's saber sliced the lieutenant from his suprasternal notch down to his belly button. Lieutenant Hatten collapsed in a heap as the other soldiers stepped away to avoid the crimson pool.

Morse seemed mesmerized by the aimless rivers of blood snaking away from the lieutenant's body. He did not move until one of the red streams almost touched his boots.

"He'll live," the colonel said. "Not the first time I've sent that message." He looked around. "Anyone else have a problem with my orders?"

A handful of men glanced away. Colonel Morse grinned.

"Good," he said. "Lieutenant Watkins!"

"Yes, sir!"

Lieutenant Elias Watkins sprinted over and saluted. Even at attention, Elias exuded an aura of arrogance and danger. The junior officers loathed him; the soldiers avoided him at all costs.

"You know my orders," Colonel Morse said. "Make it look like the settlement was attacked by the Seminoles."

"Yes, sir," Lieutenant Watkins replied before turning to the other soldiers. "Alright men, get out of your uniforms and make ready."

The soldiers changed into the clothes they'd taken from dead Seminole warriors in the past. They painted their faces garnet red with a black stripe ear-to-ear over the eyes.

The colonel wiped Lieutenant Hatten's blood off his saber and placed it back in its sheath.

"Might want to have him attended to," he said before stepping over the young officer on his way to his horse.

The colonel rode over to the crest of the small hill overlooking the settlement. He made sure to stay hidden amongst the trees. A moment later, dressed in a blue calico shirt with a decorated pocket, red leggings, and a red print turban on his head, Lieutenant Watkins rode up and cleared his throat.

"May I ask a question, sir?"

Colonel Morse assessed the lieutenant's disguise. Except for the lieutenant's intense, angelic blue eyes he could have easily passed for a Seminole warrior.

"You look horrible, Elias."

The hint of amusement in his voice made Elias smile.

"Is it too much, sir?"

"No. It's fine. Just don't get too comfortable in it, that's all."

"Don't have to worry 'bout that, sir." Elias looked out over the settlement. "I didn't want to question you in front of the other men, but I'm wonderin' why you want to raid this village tonight."

Colonel Morse studied the lieutenant for a moment, making sure he didn't have another soft-hearted officer in his midst.

"These people have been helping the Seminoles. Telling them our whereabouts or giving them food or telling them about the good Lord, it doesn't matter. They're assisting the enemy and I can't allow that."

"Why would they help the Indians if they know the savages are gonna be relocated?" Elias asked.

Colonel Morse looked back at the settlement. "Some people have a soft heart when it comes to the Indians. They think we're too hard on them. A lot of folks think we should just let the Indians be and live alongside them."

Elias nodded.

"What if we went to the settlement and made some arrests?" Elias asked. "Surely that would send a message to anyone thinking of helping the Indians. Not to mention savin' a bunch of lives."

"You're right, Lieutenant," Colonel Morse replied. "Simply arresting them would send a clear message to anyone thinking about helping those godless savages. However, I have…*we* have a job to do. And part of that job is to stop the Indians from uprising. And if they're being emboldened by someone's help, white or not, we have to see those people as our enemy as well."

Elias frowned. "But why make it look like the Seminoles killed these people?"

"If we make it look like the Seminoles are the ones who attacked this village," Colonel Morse replied. "and we let a scant few survive to tell the tale, word will spread that the Seminoles are still attacking settlements unprovoked. That'll scare the wits out of any settlers in this area, creating more allies for us. They'll be less willing to help the Indians and more likely to take up arms against them. And if Washington hears of it, they'll continue to see the Seminoles as our enemy. Other people's fear is a powerful weapon, Lieutenant. Remember that."

Elias nodded and looked out at the gray outline of the village disappearing into the darkening sky.

"Are the men ready?" Colonel Morse asked.

"Yes, sir."

"Good. You lead the raid. Remember, no shouts of charge or barking orders. Just ride like a bat out of hell and do your worst. My men know what to do."

"Yes, sir."

Ten minutes later the colonel heard the thundering sound of hooves headed towards the settlement. Gunfire and shouts bounced across the hills. When the first screams from the villagers echoed in the darkness, and fires from the burning settlement lit up the night, he looked up at the darkening sky and smiled.

CHAPTER ONE

TWO YEARS LATER

MAY 25, 1838, EASTERN GEORGIA

Captain Thomas Edwards shifted his weight and stared at the two-story white house at the end of the lane. His back, legs, and butt ached after days in the saddle. The deluge he rode through earlier had only added to his discomfort.

Only three hundred yards to go, he thought. *Three hundred yards after thirty-six months shouldn't be this difficult.*

The columned plantation house looked pristine in the post-storm moonlight. A single candle burned in each of the eight front windows, welcoming beacons in the night for would-be visitors. Thomas's mother, Louise, insisted on the small lights for as long as Thomas could remember.

As a boy, he enjoyed helping her light the candles. He followed her from room to room. She'd sing a hymn or a favorite song from her childhood. Every night she encouraged her son to sing along even though his father thought it was a distasteful thing for a boy to do. Thomas and his mother shared a few laughs on those evenings and sometimes danced if they thought they could avoid his father's watchful eye and subsequent chastisement.

13

Where did all the time go? he wondered. *Seems like all that happened to someone else.*

Silo nickered and tossed his head.

"Easy, boy. We've had longer rides than this."

Silo stomped his hoof and swiped his wet tail against Thomas's leg.

"All right, we'll go."

Thomas guided Silo towards the barn when a figure emerged from the darkness. Horse and rider flinched at the same time.

"Master Thomas, it is you."

A wizened black man jogged through the mud. Thomas slid to the ground and seized the elderly man's proffered hand.

"Rigton, I should've known you would greet me. It's mighty good to see you, my old friend."

"Old." Rigton wheezed out a laugh. "You right 'bout that. Oldest one left here. Lemme take your horse there."

Rigton flashed a partially edentulous smile. "It's good to see you, sir. Let's get you outta this mess."

Thomas handed Silo's reins to the best groom he'd ever known. When he turned toward the house, he was enveloped in a bosomy hug.

"Thomas! Welcome home."

Even in his soaked condition, Thomas could feel hot tears running down his neck.

"It's good to see you too, Clarebelle," he said.

"Aw, Lord, Master Thomas." She rocked the two of them from side to side. "They said you was comin' home, but I wouldn't believe it 'til I saw you with my own eyes. I prayed for you ev'ry day. For the Lord to bring you home safely. An' here you are. Thank you, Jesus!"

Thomas held tight as she continued to sway and pray. They hugged until thunder cracked in the distance. They scurried for the barn with Silo leading the way.

Once inside, Silo whinnied, then shimmied like a sodden retriever. His deep eyes glared until Thomas began a brisk rubdown with a blanket. Thomas, Rigton, and Clarebelle laughed.

"Quite a character, ain't he?" Rigton said.

The barn was warm. A fireplace blazed in the corner and filled the barn with an oddly pleasant odor of smoked manure.

After hanging the captain's coats up to drip dry, Rigton grabbed some towels and herded everyone to the fire. Thomas stood with Clarebelle; Rigton tended to an impatient, scowling Silo.

"I can't believe you are home, Thomas," Clarebelle said.

Thomas looked at the woman whom he had known all his life – solid as a stump, more precise in her appearance than any military cadet, and – as she often described herself – "tougher than a pine knot." The hair he always tried to muss when he was a youngster was slicked back in a tight knot at the base of her neck. Her apron was tied in a precise bow.

Clarebelle stepped away to inspect the young man she hadn't seen in three years.

"Don't they feed you in the Army? And what you doin' ridin' out in this weather?" Clarebelle asked as she wiped her head and face. "Didn't they teach you a thing? Even your father's cows have the sense to come in out of a storm like that."

My father.

Thomas felt an involuntary shiver. "I was trying to get here in time to dine with Senator Lumpkin like my father requested."

"Uh huh," Clarebelle replied shaking her head. "Well, you only missed it by...let's see (she glanced around the barn as if searching for a clock) ...six hours. The dinner was at seven. Lord in heaven, you always this late in the Army?"

Clarebelle exhaled with exaggerated disgust.

Thomas hung his head in mock shame. "I am never late in the Army, Clarebelle."

"C'mon to the kitchen when your horse is settled. There's plenty left over."

Clarebelle peered out of the stable to ensure it was not raining, then grabbed a small piece of canvas and put it over her head anyway before heading for the house.

"She hasn't changed a bit, has she?" Thomas asked. "Same ol' Clarebelle."

"No sir," Rigton replied. "A woman like that don't need to change."

Thomas smiled.

I wonder if anyone else knows how much he adores her, he thought. He put a hand on Rigton's shoulder. "It's truly good to see you again."

Rigton smiled. "'Tis good to see you too."

Thomas patted Rigton on the shoulder then walked to Silo. He rubbed the horse's neck.

"This here's Silo," he said. "One of the most courageous, smartest, fastest, pain in the ass horses anywhere."

Silo grunted and swung his tail at the captain.

"Missed me that time," Thomas said with a smile.

Silo snorted.

"Well, hello, Silo," Rigton said. "Yes, suh. You's one fine animal."

Silo bumped Thomas, then whinnied when the young captain staggered.

"Flattery will get you everywhere with this one," Thomas said.

Rigton stood in front of Silo and stroked his nose with care before leaning in and whispering things only a horse would understand.

"Yes suh, Silo," Rigton said standing upright. "You's in my barn now. An' I'm gonna take good care of you."

Thomas smiled and went to survey the rest of the barn. He noticed a mare in one of the guest stalls.

"Rigton."

"Yes, sir?"

"I am afraid to ask. That mare. It's Grandmother Miriam's, right?"

Rigton reached out to pet the animal. "You know it is. Miz Miriam rode all the way from her home."

"Long ride," Thomas said.

"Over three hundred miles," Rigton said. "Said she wanted to see you – very particular about that."

"Oh."

"She told me she ain't seen you since her husband's...since yer Grandpa Madison's funeral."

Thomas hung his head. "That sounds about right."

"Yes indeed, this is another fine animal. Not as fine as Silo over there, but fine as they come."

Silo snorted and showed his teeth. Rigton went on about all the horses in the barn, but Thomas wasn't listening. Instead, he was trying to conceive a way to avoid seeing his grandmother.

"You all right, Thomas?"

Thomas raised his head. "Guess the long ride's finally getting to me. I'm going to go on into the house. You going to be okay?"

"Oh, yes sir. I'm gonna get Silo fed and watered right quick. Get him settled in fer the night." Rigton looked up at the ceiling of the barn as if he could see the sky. "That storm's movin' through as fast as it came upon us." He looked back at Thomas and smiled. "You have a good night."

Thomas looked at the man who had taught him to lace a boot, to fire and clean a shotgun, to jump a galloping horse over a hedge. Despite all social convention, he loved Rigton – hated it on the public occasions when the groom called him "Master." But they had come to an understanding. Rigton would employ the social conventions when required at gatherings and Thomas could employ a nickname when they were alone.

"You too, Rigs," Thomas said.

Rigton chuckled. "I ain't heard Rigs in three years." He shook his head and smiled. "Sure's good to have you home."

Thomas stopped and scanned the old barn before nodding towards his friend. "It's good to be back. Good night."

"Good night, *Master* Thomas."

Thomas could hear Rigton's hearty laughter all the way to the house.

§§

Finally, in dry clothes, Thomas sat with his back to the kitchen table, mesmerized by the flames flickering inside the oven. Road weariness and the weight of old memories forced him to slump even lower in his chair.

Clarebelle brushed past and opened the door to the oven. She checked the biscuits she'd insisted on making.

"Was my father angry?" he asked.

Clarebelle chuckled as she used her apron to pull the biscuits out of the oven.

"You know Master Edwards," she said.

She placed a couple of biscuits on the captain's plate alongside warmed-up chicken, potatoes, and greens. When he grabbed his fork to devour his food, Clarebelle slapped him on his arm.

"Ain't you gonna pray?"

Thomas hesitated, put his fork down, and folded his hands. He hadn't prayed in such a long time he wasn't sure what to say. Finally, the simple prayer his father said before every meal came back to him, so he repeated it with little conviction.

"Sorry," he said. "Dear Heavenly Father…we thank…I thank you for this day and for this food. We…I ask that you continue to watch over us, um…guide us…me, and direct us. In Jesus' name we…I pray, Amen."

When he finished, he looked at Clarebelle for her approval. She frowned.

"I've heard better," she said. She continued cleaning up. "As to your father, he kept apologizin' to the Senator – how embarrassed he was by you not bein' there. He blamed the storm."

"So, he was angry then," Thomas said with his mouth full.

"I'd say he was. But the Senator never knew it."

"The morning should be interesting."

Clarebelle laughed. "I'm sure yer pa will be in a fine mood when he sees you."

CHAPTER TWO

MAY 9, 1838, NORTHERN GEORGIA, CHEROKEE TERRITORY

The crock of molasses shattered at Catherine's feet and wrenched her attention away from the assembly of soldiers gathered in front of the saloon across the street. The other customers inside of the general store looked around for the source of the noise. Catherine let her long black hair dangle over her face while she studied the mess at her feet. One by one, people resumed inspecting the many boxes, barrels, crates, and tables spread across every available inch of floor space. A man in the corner went back to turning the handle on the coffee grinder. The aroma of freshly ground coffee mingled with the alluring smell of smoked meat and the stale odor of dirt and mud perpetually tracked in from the street.

Catherine knelt down to pick up the pieces of stoneware. "I'm very sorry, Mr. Andrews."

Andrews, as skinny as the mappe in his hand, scurried from behind the counter. A toothy grin fractured his angular face.

"No worries, dear. Accidents happen. Just step back, careful now, an' I'll get it cleaned up in no time."

Catherine moved away from the broken crock and watched Mr. Andrews kneel and begin to clean up the mess. A fastidious man, he was very specific about the way things worked in his store, which included how spills were cleaned up.

Self-conscious, Catherine looked up in time to catch a pair of frumps staring at her. Pillars of the local church, they clucked and shook their heads with disapproval at the Indian girl whose luxurious hair hung nearly to her waist without a single finger wave or pin curl like a "proper, Christian" woman. She stared them down until they turned their attention to the neatly organized bolts of cloth on the shelves in the dry goods section.

"Is your father still bringin' in his asparagus and strawberries this month?" Mr. Andrews asked, glancing up from the mess. "Already have a few ladies waitin' on the berries. Guess they use 'em to make jam." He pushed his glasses back up and refocused on the broken crock and molasses. "Not sure how he does it year in and year out, but your father sure grows the best fruits and vegetables."

Catherine nodded and smiled.

"He does," she said. "I believe he will have them ready to bring in sometime next week. He said there will be some radishes and onions for you, too."

"Good," Mr. Andrews said. "Don't have much in the way of onions so far this year. And radishes will be a nice addition."

Mr. Andrews had done business with Catherine's father for as far back as she could remember. Mr. Andrews and his wife, two of the five white faces in an otherwise all-Cherokee church, sat behind Catherine and her father each week at church – over twenty years without fail. Every Sunday he belted out the hymns with little care

for how far off-key he usually was, an endearing quality – at least to
Catherine.

Across the street, a crowd of soldiers whooped and hollered.
Catherine walked to the window and saw them harassing two young
women with catcalls and whistles. The women scurried away
exchanging horrified looks.

Mr. Andrews joined Catherine at the window. "Rough lookin'
bunch."

Catherine nodded.

"What're they doin' here, you reckon?" Mr. Andrews asked. "All
they do is make a mess of things."

Catherine knew the rumors.

"Everyone says we will have to move," she said. "The
Cherokees. Everyone says the government wants our land and is
going to relocate us."

Andrews only "tsked" and continued his clean-up.

Forgetting about Mr. Andrews and the mess she'd created on the
floor, Catherine stepped outside. Staying in the shadows, she made
her way to the corner of the store. She stood just short of the corral.
She was certain someone would hear her heart pounding, but no one
seemed to notice. She jumped when a male voice slithered over her
shoulder.

"May I offer some assistance?"

She turned, expecting to see a young militiaman standing there with his tongue hanging out like a dog. Instead, she was taken aback by a weather-beaten man leaning forward on a wooden fence. The stranger was dressed in black from head to toe. He spun an abnormally tall top hat around in his hands. His coal-black hair was cut short. A pronounced widow's peak lent a ghoulish air to his appearance. Thick, black eyebrows angled over each eye – bushy housetops. His fastidiously groomed beard formed a perfect triangle below his chin.

"Hello," he said. His mouth formed a smile but there was no kindness in his expression.

Catherine didn't respond. She was transfixed by the fiendish man's angelic eyes. The blue was so intense it made her question if she were staring at a painting instead of an actual person. In spite of his dark presence, the stranger's eyes were quite beautiful. Catherine realized she was gawking and looked away.

The stranger chuckled. "The name's Elias. Elias Watkins. Used to go by Lieutenant Elias Watkins."

Angry for having gaped at the man's eyes, Catherine refused to react.

"May I ask yer name?" he asked.

Catherine held still, hoping he'd lose interest and leave.

"No name? Pity. A beautiful woman such as yourself should have a name."

Everything inside of Catherine screamed for her to run away, but she couldn't move.

Elias pursed his lips. "You're Cherokee. Ain't ya?"

Catherine refused to look at him.

Elias spun the top hat around on his right hand several times before looking at her again.

"Do you speak English?"

Catherine's facial expression changed enough to let him know she understood English quite well.

"Since you know English, I hafta tell you that I find Cherokee women irresistible. Yer eyes are truly beautiful."

Catherine's skin crawled.

"Listen, I'm on yer side," he said. "It ain't right what the government's tryin' to do to yer people."

His random comment surprised Catherine. She looked at the devil of a man who was studying her – a child with a new pet – or a predator eyeing prey?

"I'm a good person to know," Elias said.

He leaned toward Catherine and held the position until she finally looked into his eyes. They stared at one another for a few moments.

"Nothin'?" he asked. "Nothin' at all?"

With a slight lift of her chin, Catherine held her ground. Elias shook his head in disbelief, stood upright and put on his top hat.

Catherine couldn't take her eyes off of him. Everything about Elias, the way he moved, his clothes, voice, and eyes, came out of a dark tale written in an ancient language she didn't understand but knew to be obscene.

He walked to a black Marsh Tacky hitched to a post inside a corral. Catherine knew the South Carolina breed – smallish, sturdy, fearless. A splendid animal.

Was that there the whole time? Catherine wondered.

Elias untied the horse and guided it out of the corral. He turned back to Catherine and gestured towards the soldiers who'd disappeared from her consciousness.

"I can think for myself, I ain't like them saddle bouncers over there. Idiots, ever' last one. I used to be an officer down in the Florida Territory fer a spell. Should you require any assistance, I am at yer service."

Despite his kind words, something about his tone turned Catherine's insides stone cold. She showed no emotion; Elias refused to lose eye contact.

"Still nothin'?" he asked.

He waited for a few moments to see if Catherine would respond before he laughed and turned to leave once again. Catherine stood, rooted in place. Horse and rider oiled their way around the corner and were gone.

When the church bell rang, Catherine jumped. Breath she had not realized she was holding exploded from her lungs. She turned to see two soldiers stacking crates.

The church bell sounded again.

It's not Sunday – it's not Christmas Day.

A crowd gathered, bit by bit. An Army officer in a full-dress uniform conspicuously out of place in the rustic setting stepped atop the crates and waited. Elias appeared from around the corner of the saloon. He placed his shoulders and one foot against the wall and tipped his chimney of a hat forward. He was accompanied by a group of several men also dressed in black.

Catherine heard a voice from the platform. "Excuse me. Indian girl. Hey!"

Catherine looked around. It was the officer. She pointed to herself with an unspoken question on her face.

"Yes, you," he said. "You may want to step forward so you can hear me better. This pertains to you."

CHAPTER THREE

MAY 25, 1838, EASTERN GEORGIA

Thomas sat in the parlor outside of his father's office and stared at
the enormous oil painting. `

He spent hours studying the clash of anonymous warriors as a
kid, memorizing every detail, and fantasizing what it would be like
to be in such a battle. He imagined leading his men to a glorious
victory. Perhaps someone would paint a picture depicting his heroics
for all eternity to remember. Now, after having fought in battles, he
saw little use in painting anything that had to do with war.

The office door snapped open.

"The Colonel will see you now."

Thomas knew Tobias's deep voice. The man had been the butler
since Thomas was knee-high to a pup. Thomas stood and adjusted
his already immaculate uniform before following Tobias into his
father's office.

The room hadn't changed. It still smelled of fine, leather
furniture, firewood, and cognac. The office was large; the walls were
barren save for shelves sagging with the weight of hundreds of
books.

An enormous oak desk dominated the room. It, too, was clean and tidy. But what demanded the most attention was the man to whom the room belonged, Colonel Clinton A. Edwards.

The colonel was a bull, well over six feet with the presence of three angry men.

Pushed by his own father, Clinton enrolled in the first class at the newly-opened United States Military Academy at West Point. Upon graduation, he distinguished himself and rose rapidly through the ranks. He met and married Louise Madison, the daughter of a Methodist missionary. Shortly after meeting his future wife, Clinton left to fight in the War of 1812. He vowed he'd return to her without a single mark, a promise he managed to keep in spite of seeing a great deal of action.

The colonel stood with his back to the door and stared out the window. It looked as if he was enjoying the beautiful morning light filter through the trees just outside of his office, but Thomas knew better. His father didn't pay any attention to things like that. No, his father was always at work. He was surely calculating something, working out his strategy, anticipating the exchange they were about to have.

"That'll be all, Tobias," the colonel said without turning.

Tobias bowed his head and closed the door behind him without making a sound. Thomas remained at attention and waited for his father to speak. It was a game they often played, although neither would ever admit to its existence. Thomas refused to break the silence out of respect. The colonel, when the mood suited him, liked to see how long his son was willing to stand without speaking. One afternoon the silent tug-of-war lasted until well over an hour after dinner had been served.

Thomas could smell the macassar oil his father used to smooth his hair. No matter where Thomas was or how far away, the smell of bergamot would bring the captain back to this exact spot.

Thomas remembered his last time in the office – just before his assignment in the Florida Territories. The game of silence was brief that day and so was the conversation. The colonel simply wished Thomas good luck and reminded him that his time in Florida was a good first step towards future success. Being killed wasn't an option and Thomas knew better than to mention it.

I came close, Thomas thought. And still, he waited.

"You embarrassed me," Clinton said. "Senator Lumpkin traveled a great distance just to meet you. The least you could've done was get here on time."

Thomas's head swam with excuses, but he remained quiet.

"Or is that how things are done in the military these days?" his father asked still looking out the window. "It's no wonder we can't expand this country any farther than we have if that's the new standard."

Thomas clenched his teeth, feeling as if he was an impish, pubescent child once again.

"I set up these meetings for your advantage," his father said. "You need to make connections if you are to be the governor of Georgia. Senator Lumpkin was once our governor, and it would have benefitted you to have met him."

Clinton turned and surprised Thomas with a look of satisfaction upon seeing his son in uniform.

"You could be governor someday. Perhaps even President, if you make the right connections," Clinton said before walking over and inspecting his son. "I see those savages in Florida didn't get the better of you. It's good to see you, son."

Clinton held out his massive hand. Thomas grasped it.

"It's good to see you too, father," he said, letting his hand be swallowed up by his father's bearlike paw.

"The beard looks good on you," Clinton said. "Makes you look regal." He gestured to a seat in front of the desk before walking around to the other side. "I, myself, can't grow a decent beard even if I wanted to. Never could."

Thomas waited for his father to take his place behind the desk before he sat down. He squirmed then remembered comfort would remain elusive. The legs of the chairs in front of the desk were sawn one inch short at Clinton's instructions. Colonel Edwards never looked up at anyone. He never wanted any questions about who ruled the room.

"Mother wrote in her last letter that you had news for me," Thomas said. He tried to cross his legs.

"Ah, yes," his father replied looking up from the pile of papers in front of him. "And if you had made the effort to be at dinner last night, you would know it by now." He returned his attention to the documents.

Thomas stared at the lawn over his father's shoulder and waited. The colonel looked through several more documents before speaking again.

"I understand they are sending you to Fort Newnan."

"Yes, sir."

"That's too bad. My aim was to get you to a larger fort, a more prominent position. Alas, it appears Fort Newnan was the best they could do."

"What do you mean? That was the best *who* could do? Father, what have you done?"

Clinton sat even taller in his chair. "I simply did what was best for my son. After almost three years of fighting the Seminoles in the swamps of the Florida Territory it was time to get you out of there. You did yourself proud down there. Made a name for yourself as a soldier and as an officer. Now, the time has come to make a name for yourself politically."

With his knees higher than his waist, Thomas felt like he was shrinking.

"Let me see if I understand this," he said leaning forward the best he could. "You had my *entire* company transferred to Georgia to enhance my political career?"

The colonel's attention was back to the papers on his desk. "That is correct."

Thomas yielded to the force of gravity and slumped into his chair. The amount of political influence it must've taken for his father to achieve such a thing was unimaginable. Thomas watched his father with a strange mixture of appreciation and fear. He was thankful to be out of Florida, but it was startling that the man across the desk possessed enough gravitas to make it happen.

"Why?" Thomas asked. "Why get me reassigned to be a part of the relocation of the Cherokees?"

"It is a great opportunity," Clinton replied without looking up.

"For whom?"

"For you. For me. For the state of Georgia."

Clinton signed something, then straightened a small stack of papers.

Thomas tried to sit up straighter in his uncomfortable chair.

He's leaving something out. He never does anything for someone else's benefit.

"You can play a part in this historical moment," the colonel said once he was satisfied with the appearance of his desk. "We are finally acting on the Treaty of Echota the Cherokees signed almost three years ago. They gave up their lands here east of the Mississippi. They get new land in the Indian Territory."

"I'm aware of the treaty."

"Then you are also aware the treaty stipulates the United States will escort them out west. We will provide food, water, transportation, and protection in exchange for their cooperation. And the land they are to receive out west will be equivalent to what they are giving up here."

The colonel sat back in his chair and folded his hands across his stomach.

"The eyes of the nation are on us right now. That is why it is imperative for you to be a part of such a historical event. You will help escort the Indians out of Georgia once and for all. In essence, you will be seen as a hero here in Georgia for doing something pretty simple and straightforward."

"You think it'll be that simple?"

"Without question." The colonel sat up and leaned on his desk. "The time has come. The treaty clearly states they had until May of this year to move voluntarily. Now, the government is going out of its way to make the relocation as easy as possible for them. The Georgia Militia is preparing to escort them to different forts as we speak. That part will take a month or so. Then you will help guide them out west. Easy. You are looking after them, nothing more."

Thomas's brow wrinkled.

"Once they are safely out west and settled, you will return to Georgia, retire from the military, and start your path to the Governor's mansion. The people here in Georgia will see you as a hero, a war hero for having fought the Seminoles and, a political hero for being part of the successful removal of the Cherokee. No one could run against that kind of success. You will have demonstrated your burning desire to look out for the best interest of the citizens of Georgia."

His father's plans intrigued Thomas but there had to be more to it. "Earlier, you said *you* would benefit from this. How?"

The colonel chuckled. "Having a son as governor, of course."

Thomas smiled, mostly at his father's weak attempt to put his son's success ahead of his own ambitions. Clinton's smile broadened knowing what his son was thinking.

"You want to know how else I will benefit. Well, there will be a lot of money. The Cherokee land is extremely valuable. Not only is the land fertile, but there is a great deal of timber—"

"And gold," Thomas said.

The colonel looked at his son without expression. He held the gaze for a few moments before offering a slight smile.

"And gold. Yes. By escorting those savages out west, you will be making many important men extremely rich." He saw a stray corner and fidgeted with a stack of papers for a moment. "You will start out as a state Senator, get to know the state politics. While there, you will make sure the federal government cannot get its hands on the land…or the gold, thereby making you a hero here in Georgia once again. Then, when you run for governor, victory will be certain."

The colonel leaned forward. His face grew stern.

"And with the powerful people behind you, I see nothing standing between you and the presidency."

Thomas sat up in his chair the best he could. He was surprised to find himself wrapped up in his father's plans. However, instinct told him to pull back on the reins a bit.

"I do want to follow in your and grandfather's footsteps," he said. "You both fought in wars for a noble cause, but I have to be honest with you. I'm struggling to see the nobility in forcing unarmed Indians off their land."

"You are not forcing anyone off their land. Remember, they signed the treaty—"

"I'm aware of the treaty. It's just that I know how sacred the land is to the Cherokee people. Can you sit there and tell me that *all* of the Cherokee people are willing to move out west?"

"They *have* to relocate," the colonel replied. "Or else they will disappear."

"What do you mean, disappear?"

"Like Old Hickory says, the Indians are surrounded by a growing white population. They are doomed to 'weakness and decay' and eventual extinction if they do not leave now. Squatters come in, sit on their land, and when the Cherokees try to remove the squatters, it always ends up in court. In court, the Cherokees have no rights at all. So, they eventually lose the land to the squatters and get nothing in return. And the cycle continues. So, for their own sake, they have to see the wisdom in relocation."

Thomas decided not to break in on another of his father's epic monologues.

"And what was the noble cause your grandfather and I fought for?" Clinton asked. "We fought so we could have a country of our own. We wanted to foster the American way of life, to watch it grow and develop without an aristocracy controlling it. Our way of life draws foreigners from all over the globe. Thousands of new faces arrive on our shores every day. And where are they going to go? The United States needs to expand its territories so our way of life can survive."

The colonel took a deep breath. "By escorting the Cherokee off the lands *they* signed away, we create the opportunity for America to grow. I fail to see how your role in all of this is any less noble than what my father or I did. And when you become a politician, you can make sure all of our causes are noble."

Thomas looked down and tried to absorb his father's words. Clinton got up from his chair, walked around the desk and leaned against it.

"I remember three years ago when a bright-eyed young man full of vigor and patriotism headed off to the Florida Territory to do his part in taking it from the Seminoles. You were going to liberate Florida from those savages, come back to Georgia, and set the nation on fire as a politician."

Clinton studied Thomas for the first time since he'd walked into the room. "Do you remember that, son?"

Thomas looked up at his father and nodded.

"I can see in your eyes that war has changed you," the colonel said. "How can it not? Soldiers see some god-awful things. So, no, you are not as bright-eyed as you were back then. But I doubt you lost your patriotism. Son, this relocation gives you the opportunity to do something you could not do in the Florida Territory. You can expand the American empire without spilling a drop of blood. No one has to die. Or suffer. You can see to that. You have a chance to right what was wrong about the war in Florida. Relocate the Cherokee, something they have already agreed to do, and make sure they are treated well in the process. I cannot think of a nobler venture than that."

A bell ringing in the hallway broke the moment.

"Ah, breakfast is ready." The colonel stood and adjusted his suit jacket. "Your mother will be happy to see you." He walked to the office door leaving his son in stunned silence. "Her mother is here as well. She will be glad to see you, too." He turned and waited for Thomas to move or speak. "Surely, you are not willing to miss another chance to dine with your mother."

Tobias opened the door.

Clinton paused. "Son, are you coming?"

"Oh, um…yes, sir."

Thomas stood, adjusted his uniform, and followed his father out of the office and down to the dining room where his mother Louise was waiting with open arms.

Thomas held her close. He never allowed himself to miss her until the moment he saw her. It felt good to hold her again. Somehow her embrace relieved some of the misery he'd witnessed over the past three years.

Louise pulled away and cupped his bearded face in her hands. The tenderness in her eyes made him want to tell her everything and hear her say all would be all right. But how does a man tell his mother her son faced his death more times than she'd ever want to know.

"It's so good to see you, darling," she said.

Thomas smiled and pulled her to him once again. Mother and son hugged for several moments until the colonel cleared his throat.

"Are we going to eat or hug one another all day?"

Louise turned her head to wipe her eyes. "Of course, of course."

Thomas put his hand on her shoulder at the same moment he felt a hand on his own. He heard a quiet voice from behind.

"Thomas?"

Thomas involuntarily stood at attention and wished he could be anywhere else. He pivoted to see the one person he'd hoped to avoid.

"Grandmother Miriam."

CHAPTER FOUR
MAY 14, 1838, NORTHERN GEORGIA

The wagon bucked and rocked over the broken trail, jostling the supplies a bit more than Clarence Jenkins liked. He looked back to check on the load and caught a glimpse of Elmer Jones guiding his wagon through the same ruts and holes with more ease. Elmer gave an all-knowing smiled and gestured toward the ruts. Clarence checked to make sure the supplies in his wagon were still secure before turning back around to face forward.

"It's bad enough we gotta meet up with that blue-eyed devil, Elias," Clarence said. "But why we hafta meet him all the way out at Frank's old cabin is beyond me."

Grover Murphy shifted his rifle from his right leg to his left but didn't utter a word. He preferred to keep his eyes on the surrounding woods and let Clarence do all the complaining.

"Don't make no sense to me," Clarence said. "Elias must have some connection to the place we don't know 'bout."

Frank Thomas built the cabin decades before in the foothills of the Appalachian Mountains in Northern Georgia. It became a popular stopping point for travelers in search of food and furs in the late 1700s and early 1800s. The business exchanged hands several times after Frank died and as time went on, the road past the cabin became less traveled. By the early 1830s, only locals and what few trappers were left in the area knew about the place. They turned it into a place for drinking and gambling, a broken-down dwelling few dared to enter.

Clarence stopped his wagon directly in front of the rundown cabin and wondered how it was possible for the building to have deteriorated even more since the last time he was there. Elmer pulled to a stop on the other side of Clarence and let the reins drop to his feet.

"This place looks worse than the last time we was here," he said then spat tobacco juice and wiped his mouth with his sleeve. "I'll stay here an' watch the wagons while ya'll go in," he said with a twinkle in his eyes.

Clarence stared at Elmer for a moment then chuckled. "Go 'head and untie our horses," he said, wishing he didn't have to go in himself. "It'll save time an' who knows…we may need a quick getaway."

Long shadows fell across the front of the building. The gloom only added to Clarence's dread.

"Let's not dilly dally in there," Clarence said to Grover as they jumped down off the wagon. "Let's get the money, an' get out of here."

Grover nodded and checked his pistol one last time before grabbing his rifle off the seat. Clarence led the way up the stairs and through the squeaky front door, stopping once he was far enough in so Grover could step in and stand beside him. There was barely any natural light inside the place. It took a good minute for their eyes to adjust to the gloomy room that offered little in the way of hospitality.

The room smelled of years of stale cigar smoke and beer. The small fire in the fireplace gave off a little light that danced on the floor in front of it. A few undersized tables and mismatched chairs were along the wall but there was little else to the place.

Five men, all with hats drawn over their eyes, glanced up from their cards. Tobacco smoke hovered above the table. Cash in the middle – small jugs of moonshine – a typical day at Frank's. With little interest in the newcomers, the gamblers refocused on the hands with less enthusiasm than they did twenty-six hours before when the game began.

Clarence could make out the shape of a man behind the bar. He took a step forward when he heard the vile sound of Elias's voice.

"Over here."

In the darkest corner of the room was a silhouette of a man sitting at a small table. He took a drag off a slender cigar. The glow shed just enough light for identification. With one final glance at Grover, Clarence strode over and sat down. Three empty glasses sat on the table. Elias filled each one with moonshine, no doubt made in the same still Frank operated.

"How was the ride?" Elias asked. He raised his glass in salute before throwing back the shot.

Clarence took a sip of the liquor to calm his nerves. The moonshine burned his throat on its way to his churning stomach.

"Trip was fine," Clarence replied and looked about the place. "Why'd we have to meet here again?"

Elias poured another drink and shot it down. "I like this place. I always come here if I'm within a half days' ride. I can sit and drink in peace."

Clarence didn't think anyone needed to ride for half a day just to find peace and quiet, but he kept his opinion to himself. Elias looked over at Grover who made no effort to reach for his drink.

"What's wrong with ya? I paid for that drink. Ain't it good 'nough?"

Clarence's heart sank when Grover's eyes became thin slits locked onto Elias's every move. Grover didn't drink nor did he take kindly to anyone trying to bully him. Clarence doubted Grover was a match for Elias, but he knew Grover wouldn't back down if he felt his manhood was being challenged.

"He never drinks while on duty," Clarence said. "Been workin' with him fourteen years, ain't never seen him take a drink."

Clarence counted sixty-three agonizing seconds before either Elias or Grover blinked.

"No kiddin'?" Elias asked finally, without taking his eyes off Grover. "That's a shame."

Elias reached over and took the shot glass from in front of Grover. Without looking away or blinking he drank the contents in slow, deliberate gulps. Clarence grew more nervous with each passing moment. When he finished the drink, Elias set the glass back down directly in front of Grover and waited. Clarence held his breath when he noticed Grover's knuckles turning white.

"Yer missin' out my friend," Elias said when he grew tired of the staredown.

Elias looked over at Clarence, whose forehead was covered in sweat.

"So, what did ya bring me this time?" Elias asked. "More buildin' supplies?"

"No, actually," Clarence replied. "Food this time. My understandin' is that Fort Newnan has all the buildin' supplies it needs or is ever gonna get. The shipments should be food from here on out."

"That's fine," Elias replied. "What are we talkin' about?"

"Well, you got yer cured pork, salted beef, cornmeal, and some ground wheat from last season, I guess. Oh, plum forgot…got 'bout two to three hundred blankets in there too."

Elias frowned. "It's gettin' mighty hot out there. Them Cherokees don't need them blankets."

Clarence agreed that the blankets weren't important, but the Cherokees would no doubt need the food. It didn't sit well with Clarence that the food meant for the Cherokees at Fort Newnan was being sold off for profit. However, he had a family to feed. Ever since he got involved with swindling the government years ago, he had not always slept well. When his wife Carrie would ask what was wrong, he told her he had an unsettled stomach or an old war wound. He couldn't bear to tell her what he was involved in and every night he prayed his eight-year-old daughter Helen would never know her daddy was taking part in such a racket.

"You givin' *me* the money, or are you settlin' up with my boss?" Clarence asked.

Elias didn't respond right away, which meant anything could happen. Clarence held his breath and wished he could hide behind his whiskey glass. He often wondered if he'd be shot while delivering in the black market and dealing with the shady fellows that lingered there. He didn't want to be killed by a man like Elias in a place like Frank's.

"Got the money right here," Elias said. He put a bundle wrapped in butcher paper and secured with twine. "You boys want to count it?"

"Naw, neither one of us can count too good," Clarence replied. "Besides, if anything comes up short, I don't want to be accused because the twine was cut. I know that's a special knot. Question is, are we gonna make it back alright? I mean, that's a lot of money, an' this ain't the safest neck of the woods. Know what I mean?"

Elias snorted in contempt. "I understand. But, don't you worry none. Anyone inclined to rob the likes of you knows yer workin' with me. From here to the main roadway will be the safest trip of yer life. I hop guarantee you that."

Elias sat back and took a drag off his cigar.

Clarence nodded. He'd heard rumors about a few years back when a young man tried to rob a delivery driver. What the man in black did to the would-be robber was so gruesome, the would-be bandits now acted as Elias's guards.

Clarence drank two more shots with Elias, one for himself and the other for Grover, thanked the man in black then nodded that it was time to go.

"Maybe next time you don't bring that old cuss in with you, lest he's willin' to have a drink with me," Elias said.

Clarence clicked his tongue and stepped in between Grover and Elias.

"Let it go," Clarence whispered in Grover's ear. "He's just tryin' to goad you."

Clarence glanced over at the men playing cards, several of whom made like they were going to stand. They seemed a little too interested in what was happening with Elias. Clarence gripped

Grover's elbow and ushered him through the door. Elmer had the horses positioned for a quick departure.

"What in tarnation?" Elmer asked. "Grover's red as a beet an' you're white as a ghost."

"Never mind," Clarence said. He swung into the saddle. "Let's just get outta here."

They were at the main road before Clarence's heart began to beat normally again.

CHAPTER FIVE
MAY 25, 1838, EASTERN GEORGIA

Even as a child Thomas was not allowed to step foot inside his father's office after supper. Every evening Clinton insisted he be left alone so he could tie up any loose ends from the day and prepare himself for the business he would attend to the next day. Even Thomas's mother respected her husband's wishes in the matter, interrupting him only a handful of times in the eighteen years they lived in the house.

So, it came as a complete surprise when Tobias appeared shortly after supper and informed Thomas he was wanted in the office. Tobias led the way without any explanation; neither did he announce their presence upon entering the room. He simply gestured towards the tall back leather chairs angled towards one another in front of the fireplace. Once his task was complete, Tobias shut the door and went to prepare the master's room for the evening.

Feeling somewhat abandoned, Thomas tried to take in the entirely different ambiance the office held at night. The treasure trove of books lining the walls faded into the shadows along with his father's massive desk, making the fireplace the unmistakable focal point of the room.

Thomas made his way over to the tall back leather chairs and found his father already seated. Clinton held a glass of cognac and stared into the fire as if mesmerized by the flames. He didn't seem to notice or care he was no longer alone. Unsure of what was required, Thomas considered clearing his throat but when saw a glass of cognac awaiting him next to the empty chair, he realized he was expected to sit down and wait for his father to speak first.

Thomas eased into the empty seat and was enveloped by the plush leather.

Nothing but the best for father, Thomas thought.

He wondered how many others had sat here, intimidated by the surroundings, impressed by the ridiculously expensive cognac. He relaxed a little and marveled at the difference between the silky texture of the French liqueur and the rough, liquid fire he consumed in his Army tent. The tension eased as the cognac slipped down his throat.

Surely, he doesn't invite me for a drink if there is bad news, Thomas thought. He took in the surroundings. *The fire…the chairs… the cognac…he's inviting me into his world.*

"Can I interest you in a cigar?" Clinton lifted the lid on an ornate humidor.

"No thank you, sir," Thomas said.

"Still have no taste for them, do you?" Clinton asked. "Pity – they are better than the cognac."

"I'll take your word on it, sir."

The colonel trimmed and lit his cigar, fussing with matches until the ash was uniform. Then he settled back and gazed into the fire.

"You are leaving in the morning?"

"Yes, sir."

"I think that is a wise choice. Get back to your men. Although I know your mother will not be happy about it."

"No, she won't."

A small smile flicked across the older man's face. He gestured towards the firelight with his glass.

"May I give you some advice?"

"It's always appreciated."

"When you get to Fort Newnan, no matter what you find there, keep your tongue. Do your duty to the best of your ability. Do not bring unwanted attention to yourself and before you know it, you will be back home."

"What do you think I might find when I get there?"

"I do not know. Probably nothing. But relocating the Cherokees is a nasty business. A big undertaking. There is bound to be a rogue commander or officer here and there. I have seen how dangerous a man can become when given absolute power in any situation. I know I said the relocation process would be simple, but that doesn't mean there are no chances of pitfalls along the way." He savored his brandy. "Just be careful."

"I will."

They sat in silence for a few moments.

"I assume you realize the exact location of Fort Newnan," Clinton said.

"I know it's in Pickens County, close to the Talona Mission and school where Grandpa Oscar used to work."

"It is not *close* to the old mission, son. It *is* the old mission."

Thomas almost dropped his glass of brandy.

"About a year after you left Talona, the government forced all the missionaries off of lands belonging to the Indians," Clinton said.

"Yeah, I remember," Thomas replied. "That's when Grandpa Oscar and Miriam moved to Dahlonega."

"Correct," Clinton said. "Talona stood empty for several years. Not too long ago, the military came in and fortified the area, and converted the buildings, even the church, and school, into dwelling places."

Thomas put his head back and remembered. At the age of fourteen, because his mother had fallen ill, he was sent to stay with his grandparents at the Talona mission. Although he did not feel the need for someone to care for him, Thomas went without question. The plan was for a stay of a few months; his father came to take him home after two years.

While at the mission, Thomas helped his grandparents serve and minister to the Cherokee people, an experience that had a profound impact on his life. After witnessing the powerful connection his grandparents had with the Cherokee, Thomas considered forgoing

West Point and becoming a missionary, however, his father's plans prevailed.

"Do me a favor, will you?" Clinton asked.

"Of course."

"As soon as you are able, let me know what route you will be taking out west to the Indian Territory. I have heard talk of using the Tennessee, Mississippi, and Arkansas Rivers all the way but there is also discussion of going by land. They would trek as far north as Kentucky and Illinois then drop down through Missouri and Arkansas." Clinton waved his hand. "No matter. Whichever way you go, let me know. I will ensure you are looked after, and you can meet some important men along the way."

"I appreciate that."

"Trying to help you make connections, son, just like I was trying to do last evening with Senator Lumpkin." Clinton took a drag off his cigar. "Business is all about whom you know. If you can meet some key figures along the way, it will help when you take over the family businesses. You will already know with whom it is you are dealing – putting a face to the name sort of speak. If your political career goes the way I think it can, you will be running for president one day. The more connections you can make outside the state of Georgia the better for you."

You have a lot of expectations, Colonel. I hope I can live up.

"You have a great family name," Clinton said. "It will open

many doors for you. After these men meet you, you will have them in the palm of your hands."

Thomas shrugged. He didn't know what else to do.

"You are a charming young man," Clinton said. "Consider it a gift from your mother. I barely know what the word 'charm' means."

His laugh lacked any trace of mirth. He inspected the burning tip of his smoke, tapped the cigar with the precision of a watchmaker, then took a few puffs. He talked with the cigar clenched in his teeth.

"You are not like me," he said. "I am a hard man. I tend to bully folks to get what I want but you have a way with people. I have watched you my entire life, son. People gravitate towards you. Grown men, children and…women…" He cut his eyes toward Thomas who thought he saw a hint of jealousy. "Everyone glows when you walk into a room. I doubt you ever notice, knowing you. You are humble – also like your mother. A good quality, I suspect, one destined to make you a great leader."

If people are so all-fired drawn to me, why aren't you one of them?

Thomas let the question fade into the dark corners of the room, unasked. Instead, he settled into his chair, sipped his cognac, and basked in the glow of the firelight and his father's attention.

Thomas let his father's words dance around in his head. What the old man said made perfect sense. Helping relocate the Cherokees was a great opportunity to get his name known, to make the connections everyone needed for success.

Maybe it was the cognac. Maybe it was the bliss triggered by his father's words, but whatever the reason, all the reservations Thomas had about relocating the Cherokees retreated like an early morning fog at the rising of the sun. Only the promise of his bright future remained.

"I noticed you did not talk much to your grandmother this morning," Clinton said.

Thomas shrugged. "Why would I do something like that?"

His question held little conviction. He managed to sidestep conversing with her at every meal, though they sat across from one another, and he'd been hiding from her the entire day.

"Well, she came here just to speak with you," Clinton said. "According to your mother, the two of you have not spoken since Oscar's funeral."

"She's written me a few times," Thomas replied,

Only I never opened any of them.

"That is not the same as talking," Clinton said. "You should make time for her." He tossed the stub of his cigar into the fire. "It is a shame what happened to Oscar, gunned down alongside a road like that. Shot like a dog. Your poor mother, it has been close to four years, and I do not think she has gotten over it."

"Is there any more news about who could have done it? Any new clues or ideas?"

"No." Clinton's eyes narrowed. "I put my best man on it, and he has turned up nothing. It was probably a couple of vagabonds who happened upon your grandfather. If they intended to rob him, there were not very adept. They left his guns and his horse."

"Have you given up the search?"

"Not on your life. We will catch those reprobates and they will hang, rest assured."

"I'd like to find them myself," Thomas said. "Not sure I'd hang them right away. Maybe tie them to Silo and drag them down the road for a while."

Clinton sat forward. "We will let the law do its work."

Thomas raised a hand in surrender and the subject passed.

Father and son sat fireside well into the morning, drinking cognac and swapping war stories, both the humorous and the tragic. They discussed the future of Georgia and the United States as a whole and what part they could play in it.

The first twinkle of sunlight filtering into the room was bittersweet. Thomas didn't want the evening to end even though he was increasingly excited about the days to come. After a single evening with his father, the first-ever, the world felt like a different place, full of promise and possibilities. He wondered if his father had enjoyed the evening as much.

When Thomas opened the office door to leave, he realized it was the first time he departed his father's presence and didn't feel like a bothersome child. He was a man now, one with a purpose and goal. He was ready to get on with his life and make his father proud. He knew they would pass more evenings together like the one they just shared.

He turned to say something. Clinton was already back at his desk, his nose in a pile of papers. He looked for all the world like a man totally lost in his own concerns.

Thomas doubted his father even heard the latch click.

CHAPTER SIX

MAY 9, 1838, NORTHERN GEORGIA

Jishnu took slow, deliberate steps through the tall grass just outside the front window of the dwelling house. His bare feet made no sound. It was something Catherine's father did every evening, a ritual he began many years ago. If he listened close enough, he could hear when to plant and when to reap, how wet or dry the season was going to be, and when to let a field recover.

Jishnu could hear the voice of the Great Spirit in everything. He bore witness to how the animals and plants praised their creator and listened to what they had to say. He could also hear the voices of his ancestors. He tried to teach Catherine how to listen to the land, but she didn't have the patience for it. His daughter, like most Cherokees her age, was influenced by the European way of life, meaning the role of a woman was to stay inside and cook and sew. Foolishness.

However, not all was lost. He still had a pupil who listened to his wisdom. Ayita, Catherine's six-year-old daughter, trod behind him, silent as a stalking cougar.

Watching Ayita follow her grandfather brought some comfort to Catherine's troubled heart. She had been trying to sort through the events in town, but she felt helpless, muddled. Whenever she closed her eyes she saw the blue-eyed devil, Elias.

"I can help you," he had said, but the offer seemed malevolent. His words had taken on a whole new meaning after the officer on the makeshift platform made his announcement.

The officer read a proclamation from someone named General Winfield Scott. The decree stated he was in Tennessee under orders from the federal government to oversee the westward relocation of the *entire* Cherokee Nation. General Scott claimed no harm would come to those who cooperated. All citizens of the Cherokee Nation had two weeks to give up their lands and homes as agreed upon in the Treaty of New Echota, something she and many like her never consented to do. They were to report to the nearest federal camp for relocation out west. "Recalcitrant" Cherokees would be forced off their land by the militia and marched to the nearest relocation fort.

Catherine did not exactly understand "recalcitrant," but she got the idea. Still, she had never heard of any Cherokee being forced from the land. The thought of leaving the farm was unimaginable. It was the place of beginnings. Her mother was born there along with her many aunts and uncles. Catherine drew her first breath in the house, so did Ayita. And it was the place of goodbyes. Her grandparents, her mother, and Onacona, her beloved husband, had died in the simple dwelling.

Catherine dried her hands, went out to the porch, and sat in her favorite chair.

"What is the land telling you tonight, father?" she asked in her native tongue.

Jishnu's face lit up. He loved when his daughter showed any interest. "It will be a long, hot summer, a summer unlike we have ever seen."

"A hot summer, Mamma," Ayita said.

Jishnu smiled and patted her on the top of her head before refocusing on the land beneath him. Catherine imagined a long, hot summer and thought of General Scott's decree. She took a deep breath to calm her racing heart.

"Father, I have to ask you a question."

Jishnu continued to look down at the ground.

"You have not said anything about what I heard in town today," she said. "Are you not a little concerned?"

Jishnu turned his face to the west. "This is *our* land. Our people's land. We have given too much of it away to the white man. It does not belong to them." He looked back down at his feet. "The soldier spoke empty words."

"How can you say that? The government has forced many nations off their lands already. What will stop that from happening to us? They have the treaty signed by Major Ridge and his son John."

Jishnu's dark eyes reflected weariness and pain. "Major Ridge and his son are good men, but they are not our principal chiefs," he said. He took Ayita's hand. "They do not speak for all of us. The white government must know this. John Ross is our chief. He is still fighting for our sovereignty. He told us to plant crops this year and to prepare for the coming winter. If he did not believe we would still be on our land, why would he say these things?" When Catherine said nothing, he continued. "We have fought with the American soldiers against their enemies many times. We have taken on their culture. Our own government is the same as theirs. Our towns are the same. We are an educated people. They have to recognize our rights as a nation."

Ignoring all decorum, Catherine bolted from her seat. "But they say our laws no longer mean anything. They say we must abide by the laws of the state of Georgia. We cannot even hold council anymore without soldiers breaking it up or trying to influence who is there and who is not."

Jishnu walked over, Ayita in tow, and guided Catherine back into her seat. He sat next to her and pulled Ayita up on his lap.

"Chief Ross was chosen by the Great Spirit to be our leader. He has wisdom that we do not. If he believes we'll keep our lands, we must believe it as well no matter how much the white man roars at us." Jishnu looked out at the forest just a few yards from their front porch. "The Great Spirit gave me a vision during the last full moon. I was a spirit dwelling among these trees and the woods all around us. I saw your mother and many of my brothers and sisters. They told me I was never going to leave the lands of my ancestors."

He turned to look at Catherine.

"And because of that vision, I planted corn this year. Many others have as well. We would not have done so if we did not believe deep in our spirits that we would be here when harvest time comes."

Catherine looked at her father's reassuring face. His faith in all things good was too strong to resist. She kissed his cheek and settled into her chair to watch the light of the evening give way to the darkness.

Over the course of the next two weeks, Catherine tried to forget about what she had heard in town about the relocation. Although the European culture infiltrated her people's lives, she tried to keep some of the traditional responsibilities of Cherokee women, fetching water for the household and gathering wood. Every morning she prepared food for whenever someone was hungry throughout the day. Whenever possible, she had her father's favorite, a simple combination of bread and bear grease for dipping.

On cool mornings, she helped Jishnu look after the crops, and during the afternoons, mother and daughter would take long walks through the woods, gathering wood and searching for wild plant seeds, leaves, roots, and stems to add variety to their diet. Although Catherine thought Jishnu was being naïve about Chief Ross's ability to broker a deal to keep their lands, she took solace in his words, nonetheless. She held onto the possibility she and her family would be forgotten about out on their little farm in the woods.

The weather was unseasonably warm just like the land told Jishnu and Ayita it would be. So, after working in the hot sun all day, sitting on the porch in her rocker and reading became Catherine's favorite evening pastime. She read while her father and Ayita walked barefoot in the tall grass.

On a particularly hot and muggy evening, Catherine opened her Bible, a gift from her mother, and began to read. She was in the habit of reading the Psalms of David as he praised God in the midst of battling for his kingdom against his son Absalom. She was always moved by David's faith and wondered if her own faith could withstand being removed from her home and pursued by her enemies.

Maybe it was the heat of the evening or simply fatigue, but whatever the reason she had difficulty concentrating. She closed the Bible, placed it on her lap, and watched her father and Ayita as they listened to the land.

Ayita was a beautiful girl with a quiet temperament, much like Onacona, who died suddenly when Ayita was two years old. It broke Catherine's heart knowing Ayita didn't remember him, but she took comfort seeing her daughter had his spirit. Despite her soft demeanor, the girl spoke her mind; she was determined and brave. Catherine could see Onacona's face in her daughter, particularly when Ayita smiled.

"What do you hear tonight?" Catherine asked.

"There is a storm coming," Jishnu said.

Ever the little echo, Ayita said. "A big storm."

Catherine and Jishnu laughed. Ayita's natural curiosity and desire to be as wise as her grandfather were hard to resist. Their faces beamed while they watched her before looking at one another. Then Jishnu went back to listening to the land and his ancestors. Catherine said a short prayer of thanks. It had been a long time since she felt so content.

Jishnu stiffened and looked towards the forest. He touched Ayita on the shoulder and guided her gaze. When he crouched down, she followed suit.

"What is it Pawpaw?" she asked.

Jishnu lifted for quiet but never took his eyes off the trees. Catherine sat up. Bears and large cats frequented the area. A few days ago, a big sow had wandered out of the woods trailed by two cubs. The Mamma bears were rarely aggressive unless they thought their babies were threatened, Still, Catherine's tension increased the longer she watched her father's unmoving figure.

Just before she asked if a bear was near, thirty or so mounted militiamen trotted from the trees, guns drawn. They fanned out is a menacing array – and said nothing.

Catherine's breath came in dry gulps. Jishnu moved Ayita behind him and placed his hand on the bone handle of his skinning knife.

Fierce horses…glistening sabers on the hips of too many soldiers to count…the shiny gray tubes of death pointed not at the ground, but at them – at Catherine – at her father – at her baby.

The silence was broken by occasional snorts from an impatient horse. Jishnu held Ayita still. The soldiers neither smiled nor lowered their weapons.

After an intimidating interval, a smirking officer nudged his midnight black stallion forward. "I have a message," he said. His lips curled in arrogant disgust as if speaking to *these people* was somehow beneath his considerable station. "I am Colonel Angus Smith, and I am here by direct order of the President of the United States."

He produced a scroll from a saddlebag and began to read, flat-toned, emotionless, devoid of compassion. "This property, and everything on it, on the twenty-third day of May 1838, now belongs to the citizens of the state of Georgia. We are here to remove you from the premises. Forcefully if necessary. We will escort you to the nearest relocation facility until such time as you are escorted to the Indian Territory."

Colonel Angus Smith lowered the paper and glared at Catherine. "I would ask your name, but I do not care. You and everyone else here, whoever you are, are hereby ordered to vacate this property forthwith!"

He wheeled his horse, primarily for effect, then looked back over his shoulder.

"As God is my witness, this will be your only warning."

CHAPTER SEVEN

MAY 27, 1838, EASTERN GEORGIA

"Don't give me that look, now," Thomas said. "You can't stay here. We're soldiers. We have our orders."

Silo snorted and turned his head.

"Good Lord. You weren't here long enough to be that spoiled."

Silo stomped his foot.

"My, you're an ornery ol' cuss when you don't get your way."

Silo grunted and dipped his head to eat while the captain tried to adjust the girth. Once the saddle was secure, he took inventory of his equipment.

No good riding into the future unprepared, he thought.

Slightly hungover and still a little unbalanced from the surprising, cognac-fueled conversation with his father, he could not shake the feeling something about the whole relocation didn't feel right.

Maybe I'm overthinking things and I should just be happy father believes in me enough to get me this assignment.

He knew his mother was not happy with his scant thirty-six-hour stay, but he had to get back to his men – and to his duty. He was cinching his saddlebag when a voice tapped his ear.

"Thomas?"

Grandmother Miriam. Damn.

He fiddled with the bridle. "I need to get going, ma'am," he said.

"I know," she said. Her voice was calm and sweet. "I just need a moment."

"There's nothing you can say that'll change things."

"Maybe," she said, "but heaven only knows when I'll see you again."

He closed his eyes and let out a slow breath.

"Go ahead and say what you have to, then," he said, still keeping himself busy with his bags.

"I don't want to keep you. I just haven't spoken to you since Oscar's funeral and...I wanted you to know that I love you."

Thomas stopped fiddling with his bags but did not turn around.

"Your grandfather loved you more than you will ever know," she said. "Do not blame yourself for what happened."

Thomas forced himself to turn and face his grandmother. Tears ran down his cheeks, hot streams of agony he'd held back all through the breakfast he'd rushed through in silence – tears he'd refused to shed when they lowered his grandfather's body into the ground a little over three years ago.

"How can I *not* blame myself?" he asked through clenched teeth. "If I hadn't sent him that letter, he wouldn't have come...he wouldn't have been on that road...and he'd still be alive. It's *all* my fault."

He choked off a sob. Miriam reached out and touched his cheek with a soft hand. "You can't think that way."

Thomas snapped his head back. "What am I supposed to think? If he hadn't been on his way to come get me, he wouldn't have been ambushed. Those murdering degenerates would've picked someone else to rob!"

"Oh, sweetheart—"

"What? It's true! I might as well have killed him myself! What can you say that'll make it go away? What?"

Miriam studied Thomas for a moment before speaking. "You're right. There's nothing I can say to ease your pain. You'll have to come to terms with it by yourself. But one thing I do know. Your grandfather wouldn't want you to carry this guilt around."

She took a deep breath. "He gladly went after you. He would've walked through hell itself for you. I know he died with no regrets, save one, that he couldn't help you. Don't let his death embitter you, dear. He wouldn't have wanted that."

Thomas gritted his teeth and looked away toward the woods surrounding the plantation. He tried to absorb her words.

"If I'd been stronger," he said, "if I hadn't been such a scared little rodent wanting out of the Academy, he wouldn't have died. My cowardice killed him!"

"No, the bandits killed him. No one could have known they were going to be there."

Miriam pursed her lips.

"I'm sorry, dear. I didn't want to upset you," she said. "I simply wanted to give you a couple of things before you left."

She handed him a handkerchief. The embroidery read: OTM. Thomas unfolded the cloth.

A leather-bound Bible lay inside. Brown and held closed by a worn leather strap, the book was battered from regular use. Thomas could see his grandfather's hands working the clasp and opening the book from which he read in a sonorous and reverent voice.

"I can't take this," Thomas said.

"Oscar wanted you to have it."

Visions of bloody battles in the Florida swamps, memories of atrocities he would never forget, flooded Thomas's head. He tried to hand the Bible back.

"I'm not worthy to touch this, let alone own it."

"Your grandfather told me on more than one occasion that he wanted you to have it. It's yours as far as I'm concerned."

The book felt inexplicably heavy. "Thank you."

"I have something else for you." She pulled a wooden flute from her shoulder bag. "Do you remember this?"

Thomas nodded.

"Oscar and I carved it out that first summer I came to the Mission to help you," he said. He inspected the crude instrument. "Pretty good job actually."

76

He heard his grandfather's voice, his patient instructions, his constant reassurance that the piece of variegated walnut would yield a musical instrument.

It's in there, Thomas.

A smile fought its way onto Thomas's face.

"Of course, when we finished, neither one of us knew how to play it. We were pretty awful."

"Yes, you were." Miriam's smile grew bigger. "You scared away the horses with your…ah… talent. Even the chickens hated it."

The two of them burst into uncontrollable laughter. It was the first time in three years Thomas had thought of his grandfather without the pain of guilt. He laughed until his sides hurt and he was gasping for breath.

"Thank you for this," he said.

"You're more than welcome, my dear."

Miriam lifted her arms and Thomas squeezed her.

"I'm so sorry," Thomas said. "I miss him so much."

He buried his head into Miriam's embrace and wept, a cleansing cry three years past due. Miriam held his head and stroked the back of his neck until he stood upright and wiped his eyes. He straightened his jacket and sniffed. Miriam placed her palms on his cheeks.

"That's the end of it, my dear," she said. "Now, you must find peace."

She let him gather himself a little longer, then asked, "Where to?"

"Talona," he said. "They've converted the Mission into a fort. When the Cherokee report in sufficient numbers, I am assigned to escort them west."

A knowing look flicked across the old woman's face. "That might be difficult for you."

"Just doing my duty," he said. "They won't be there long, and I'll be busy. Besides, I like the idea of being able to watch over them, protect them as much as I can."

"The relocation won't be that easy, dear, you must know that."

"What do you mean?"

"Most of the Cherokee people don't recognize the Treaty of Echota as law. There have been protests and arguments in court over this."

Thomas looked away. He didn't want to think about any other possible future than the one his father painted for him.

Miriam touched his arm and smiled. "You might see some people you know."

Thomas looked puzzled for a moment. Then, recognition dawned. "You mean Catherine."

Miriam nodded.

"I don't want to think about her," Thomas said. His jaw protruded and his lips tightened. "We were just foolish kids. Puppy love. Have not thought about her until this very moment."

Miriam opened her mouth to speak but stopped.

"What are you going to do, Grandmother?" he asked.

"I'm returning to our home near Dahlonega," Miriam said.

"Only a day or so ride east from Talona, right?"

Miriam inclined her head.

"Feels like it's been a long time since I've been there. Do you still have all that land?"

"Close to a thousand acres. You can come visit any time."

"I'd like that. Not sure I can before I leave for the Indian Territory, but I will on my way back."

They talked for a while, sharing memories both joyful and poignant. When he was ready to go, everyone came out of the house to say goodbye. Clarebelle and Rigton stood to the side.

No, he couldn't stay another night. No, he didn't need anyone to ride back with him. Yes, he would write more often than he had. After more than a dozen "last" hugs, he mounted Silo and wheeled towards the road.

When he passed the outer gate, he encountered an unfamiliar emotion: sadness about leaving.

CHAPTER EIGHT

MAY 23, 1838, NORTHERN GEORGIA

"If she ain't gonna move, drag her hide down off there!"

Colonel Smith's face glowed an overripe tomato. "It's too darned hot and I'm too tired to be messin' about."

A couple of soldiers leaped onto the porch a few feet from where Catherine was frozen in her chair. Her brain said, "Run!" Her body would not respond.

The first soldier, a bulldog of a man with whisky on his breath, grabbed her wrist. His calloused fingers dug into her skin. "Move!"

When the second soldier seized her other wrist, he knocked her mother's Bible to the ground. The sight of the beloved book bequeathed by her beloved mother roused Catherine from her petrification. She wrenched from side to side.

I have to pick it up…it doesn't belong in the dirt.

The farther the men dragged her from the Bible, the more desperate Catherine grew. One of the soldiers tripped on her flailing leg. The three of them tumbled off the porch.

Ayita ran forward. "Mamma!"

A nearby militiaman scooped up the child. "Oh, no you don't. Your Mamma can walk on her own."

Enraged by the treatment of his family, Jishnu rushed forward. He took three steps before a rifle butt struck him in the head and drove him to the ground. No one moved to help him.

Catherine shrieked and fought her captors with newfound fury. "No!"

"Damn, she's a hellcat! Hold on to her now!"

"I'm tryin'! I'm tryin'!"

The other soldiers burst into laughter.

"Look at that." It was the man holding Ayita, "Your Mamma's a crazy woman."

Tears formed in Ayita's eyes, but she refused to whimper.

Catherine, dress in shreds, kicked one of the soldiers in the groin. He crumpled. She wriggled away from the other soldier, sprinted to her comatose father, and covered him with her body. She was surrounded by a gaggle of soldiers, all uttering vile threats for her insolent "attack."

Colonel Smith's voice cut through the babbling. "That's enough! Return to your duties."

One of the soldiers booted the ground and sent a spray of dirt into Catherine's hair. "Lucky bitch," he said.

"Mamma!" Ayita continued her struggle.

Catherine looked at Smith, her eyes pleading. "Please, let my daughter go."

"Well, what do ya know," Colonel Smith said. "The wild woman can speak English."

He studied Catherine for a moment, then beckoned to the soldier with Ayita.

"Let her go, son."

Ayita raced to her mother. The two of them embraced and attended to Jishnu. He had not moved.

The soldiers went about their business. They paid no attention to the Indians huddled together on the ground. The ranking men carried furniture and home items from the house – they scavenged the smokehouse for meat and the corn crib for vegetables. The officers assessed every item, putting some in one area and slipping anything they thought might be of intrinsic value into a saddlebag aboard their mount. Catherine took care of her father.

Jishnu moaned. His eyes flicked open.

"Easy, father," Catherine said. She helped him sit up the best he could.

Ayita yelped when she saw the blood running down her grandfather's face.

"Look away, sweetheart," Catherine said but Ayita was transfixed.

Horror and fear painted her face. Catherine tore a strip of cloth from her hem and bound the gash on the back of Jishnu's skull. Ayita ran to the horse trough and brought back a tin cup full of water. Jishnu sipped, then poured the rest on his head. He winced, then braced his hand on Catherine's shoulder and stood.

Catherine's adrenaline faded, replaced by fear and revulsion. She sat in the dust, her father's palm on her shoulder, and looked at the discarded Bible still on the porch where it had fallen. She pulled Ayita to her chest and sobbed.

A group of men on horses approached along the same route the soldiers had used. Catherine recognized one of them right away.

"It's Mr. Andrews," she said. "He'll fix everything." She struggled to her feet. "Mr. Andrews! Mr. Andrews!"

Andrews glanced in the direction of the noise, then joined the others who looked like they were on a prospecting trip. Catherine took a deep breath to yell once again; Jishnu placed his hand on her arm. Catherine turned to argue but when she saw the look in his eyes she understood.

When the group exited the barn, Catherine could hear them.

"What about livestock?" one of them asked.

"Four horses, a cow, two pigs and a spattering of chickens," Colonel Smith said.

Catherine's jaw fell open when the men walked into the only home she'd ever known. In her head, she saw them touching her spindle, standing next to her bed, inspecting the fireplace where she'd made so many meals. She wanted to run inside, to scream until they left, to whoosh them out of the house with a broom like she would an invading squirrel, but she knew she could not. So, in her terror and confusion, she stood, covered in dust, and tried to comfort her terrified and confused child.

84

"So, where should we start?" Mr. Andrews asked.

"Start what?" Colonel Smith asked.

"The auction, of course."

Colonel Smith looked confused. "Shouldn't we wait until we post—"

"No need for that," Mr. Andrews said. "We'll be the only ones who'll show up, so might as well get it over with."

Colonel Smith nodded and gestured towards Catherine's home, the dwelling house. "Might as well start here."

The men went inside. With one foot over the threshold, Colonel Smith noticed the Bible on the ground. He picked it up and slapped it against his leg and carried it inside.

It was all over in less than an hour. The white man's gold bought everything from the building and land to hairpins and hunting knives. When the last of the items were sold, the men walked outside and shook hands. They smiled – the "savages" stared in disbelief. Everything they owned, everything they knew, everything they were not wearing was gone.

Colonel Smith assembled the men and issued orders. Catherine could not understand a word; the blood pulsing in her ears made everything unintelligible. Someone struck her in the face – someone bound her hands. Catherine and her family were tied to a long rope like a string of ponies.

A bugle blew.

Smith said, "March," and the order filtered from one platoon commander to the next. The human chain lurched forward. The rope burned Catherine's wrists. The sun seared her neck. She realized she had not had any water in…she could not remember. Her tongue swelled in the back of her throat. Dust invaded her nostrils and stung her eyes.

Jishnu staggered along, his wound still trickling blood.

Ayita cried and stumbled. Catherine reached for her.

A soldier yanked the rope attached to Catherine. "Keep in line, woman."

"Please, at least let me get my daughter some shoes," she pleaded with one of the men riding closest to her. "She's just a little girl."

Much to her relief, the soldier looked down at her with a crooked grin. "Sure, my dear. How 'bout a little kiss first?"

The soldiers nearby laughed.

"Hell, if you lift your skirt. I might even let ya get an extra blanket."

The militiamen erupted in laughter, whistling and hollering, hoping Catherine would oblige them.

Catherine did not allow any expression or reaction. She just stared straight ahead and marched towards a distant land and an uncertain future.

CHAPTER NINE

MAY 30, 1838, NORTH CENTRAL GEORGIA

Thomas ran his fingers through his hair. The verdant mountains spread out before him. A light wind, growing in intensity, carried the promising smell of rain. He hoped the approaching clouds would bring a few days of cooler weather along with some relief from the drought.

It's going to be a long, hot, miserable summer.

Thomas wiped his brow and put his hat back on before spurring Silo. He hoped to rendezvous with his men before the rains came and night fell. He kept a watchful eye on the storm but enjoyed the occasional flashes of lightning and the distant silver strings of rain that hung down from the dark clouds.

Two hours later, still debating his part in the relocation plan, Thomas crested a small hill. On the plain in front of him, he saw several dozen canvas tents in perfect rows. Small fires dotted the ever-darkening landscape.

Silhouetted figures of men and horses moved about the camp. He spotted several drummers moving between the tents selling everything from blankets and clothes to alcohol (technically contraband) and tobacco. Dogs barked their secrets to one another while men talked, laughed, and ate.

He'd driven his men hard before leaving to visit his parents. He gave his lieutenants the coordinates for the rendezvous point and orders to put as much distance between them and the Seminoles as possible. The command was exactly where he'd instructed. Thomas smiled with self-satisfaction and rode into camp.

Thomas made his way over to the first cooking fire. Three men were dressing a stag.

"Good to see you're not slacking off while the captain's away," he said.

A corporal with a knife didn't' look up and said, "Go to hell."

The other two did double takes and leaped to attention. The first man continued to mutter curses while he hacked away at the deer.

"At ease," Thomas said.

The "butcher" froze at the familiar voice, then slowly put down the knife and rose to his feet. He left a smear of blood on his face when he saluted.

"S...s...sorry, sir," he said, "Thought you was Kildaire from 'cross the way. He's been raggin—"

"As you were, Corporal," Thomas said. He suppressed a laugh. He disliked the part of military bearing that erected a barrier between him and those who might die next to him at any minute. They were brothers in blood. Though he understood the need for discipline and decorum, he wasn't about to rip someone who had been unintentionally disrespectful.

The men relaxed and returned to their work. Behind him,

Thomas heard a rippling message: "Captain's back."

One of the men, Private Dawson Bates, looked up. "Been a couple good days of huntin'," he said. "Look yonder."

He pointed to a massive bear hide hanging over a smoky fire.

Thomas smacked his forehead in exaggerated amazement. "Holy smokes, where did you get that beast?"

"'Bout an hour after you took off, sir," Bates said. "That means you've missed a few days of biscuits and bear grease gravy."

"Any left?" Thomas asked.

"Sorry, sir," Bates said. "The men scarfed it up pretty damn fast."

"Too bad," Thomas said. "Might have been a few days off for the man smart enough to save some for his C.O."

The men laughed. There were no days off in the frontier, but they appreciated the captain's banter.

"All's not lost, sir," Bates said. He held up a small pan of meat. "Fried bear's pretty tasty."

Thomas bit into a strip. The succulent meat melted in his mouth.

"Oh my, that's good," he said.

"My paw taught me how to do it just right," Bates said. "How 'bout them days off?"

Thomas shook his head. "That was only for the gravy, and you know it." He slapped Bates on the shoulder. "Thanks for the snack. Well done."

Bates beamed. "Pleasure, sir."

Thomas took another strip and nodded his approval. "You men keep up the good work." He raised the meat in a salute and walked away.

"Yes, sir," they replied in unison.

Thomas worked his way through the camp towards his own tent. He stopped at every fire, sampled every offering, laughed at every joke, and complimented every man.

With a belly full of wild game, Thomas made it to his tent. The site was immaculate and orderly.

Typical Roe, Thomas thought.

First sergeant, Dearborn Rowland Bickford III, "Roe" to the captain and to those with whom he'd served for a long time, was an enigma. He was a career soldier whose uniform and effects were in perfect order but whose face was always dirty. Roe valued the chain of command – to a point. In the heat of battle, he wasn't afraid to bark orders at anyone, including those of a much higher rank. Discipline was one thing – saving your butt was another matter.

Roe looked up from his fire. By silent agreement, he did not rack to attention or salute when he was cooking.

"Evenin', Captain," he said. "Hotter than a billy goat's ass in a pepper patch, ain't it?"

Roe was shirtless and drenched in sweat.

"Better wash up. Supper be ready purty soon."

With almost three decades in the military, Roe had seen the entire country. Almost everyone in his family had served. He could trace his fighting kin back to the French and Indian War. Roe had a friend or relative in almost every fort or outpost where an American flag flew.

Though he spoke in a high-pitched, southern drawl and often used colorful colloquialisms, Roe was intelligent and, though he'd never attended school past the age of nine, possessed an extensive vocabulary.

"Well, hello to you, too," Thomas said,

He set his saddlebags on the ground. Roe offered no response.

Thomas glanced at the meat hanging over the fire and regretted having eaten so much. Roe was the best cook in camp. Undeterred, Thomas went into his tent, poured water into a washbasin, and cleaned the grime from his face and hands. He stepped out and took a seat on a log. Roe loaded two plates with potatoes, grits, and deer meat.

"Wasn't sure you'd make it on time. Thought I might be forced to eat all this on my own."

"I appreciate that you waited"

"Sure thing," Roe said.

He handed the captain a plate before grabbing his own and moving to a spot away from the flames.

"Feels good to get away from that darn fire, let me tell ya." He raised an eyebrow at Thomas whose fork was already traveling mouthward. "We eatin' or prayin'?"

The fork hit the plate.

"Bless this food, O Lord, and those who receive it through Christ our Lord." Roe looked up. "Short enough for you, Captain?"

"Good job," Thomas said. "I can tell you're not a Baptist. Food's still warm."

"Ain't nothin' but Scotch Presbyterians in Mecklenburg County, North Carolina and you know it, sir."

The religious duties observed, Roe's sole interest was consumption. He ate like a man who'd been locked in a prison for months, arms crooked around his plate, head down, fork shoveling food as fast as he could work it.

Thomas, already more than stuffed, took his time.

"You know," he said, "for a worthless coot, you're a pretty good cook. May have to keep you around."

Roe never broke his rhythm. "You'd starve without me, sir. I ain't exactly filled with trepidation." Another mouthful disappeared into his maw. "And I can knock the spots off a ladybug at fifty yards and you damn well know it."

They ate in silence for a while. "Well," Roe said, "you ain't much for revelation, so I guess I'll have to make my own inquiries. How was your visit?"

"Good."

"House still standin', I assume."

"Yes."

"Everyone alive and well."

"Sure."

Roe swallowed some coffee. "Well, Captain Monosyllabic, are ya gonna give me the skinny or do I have to pry you open like an oyster and wrestle the pearl out of you?"

"Huh?"

Roe hurled a biscuit at Thomas's head, which the captain caught and ate.

"Now you're just being a contrarian. What was so important that you're pa called you home?"

Thomas shrugged. "He wanted me to meet Senator Lumpkin."

"How was his royal lumpiness?"

"Didn't make it on time."

-"Bet yer pa didn't appreciate that."

"Not really, no." Thomas shrugged and smiled. "Visit would have started better if I'd made more of an effort to get there."

"There's never any harm in placating the patrimony," Roe said. "But it's good to keep 'em guessin'. Can't always have his way, can he?"

"Not for a lack of trying," Thomas replied.

He got me transferred out of Florida easily enough, Thomas thought. He decided not to reveal that information. "Looks like a storm's heading our way. Saw the clouds on my way in."

Roe waved off the prediction with the back of his hand. "Nothin'
to it...a short frog gagger just like the other night. It'll just muddy
the path and make the hair sticky for a few days." He tossed his
long, gray hair in a coquettish fashion. "Won't be able to do a thing
with my coiffure until next week."

Thomas shook his head but smiled in spite of himself.

"What'd your pa have to say 'bout our mission with the
Cherokees?" Roe asked.

"The Tsalagi people," Thomas replied.

"The who?" Roe ignored the grease staining his army trousers.

"The Cherokee. They call themselves Tsalagi. It's the word
'Cherokee' in their language. The word 'Cherokee' is actually a
Muskogee word meaning 'speakers of another language.'"

Thomas cut off a piece of venison then looked at Roe who had
stopped eating and was staring at him.

"The Tsalagi prefer to call themselves Aniyunwiya, but they've
come to accept Tsalagi."

"Okay," Roe said, "my edification is complete. I have no idea
what you said, but it sounded erudite as hell."

He smacked on a piece of meat and studied his friend. "How do
ya know all this?"

"Remember, I lived with my grandparents for a couple of years.
They were missionaries to the Tsalagi people at the Talona Mission."

"The Talona Mission? Where in tarnation's that?"

"About a half day's ride from here."

"So, it's close to Fort Newnan then?"

"It *is* Fort Newnan."

"What?"

"Yeah. The government converted it into an Army fort."

"Well, I'll be. Some ol' stompin' grounds fer ya then."

Thomas nodded.

"So, you know the Cherokee people?"

Thomas held both palms up. "A little. My grandparents were really close with a few of them. I even…"

Thomas saw a momentary vision of Catherine, smiling, laughing, beautiful.

"What?"

"Nothing," Thomas said. "Believe it or not I can speak some Cherokee."

"No kiddin'."

"Well, at least I used to. Haven't spoken it in a while."

Roe studied his friend for a moment. "So, it's possible you'll see folks you know?"

Thomas nodded. "Yeah, maybe. It's been seven years and I was, what, sixteen when I left. I may not recognize anyone."

"So, back to my original question, what did your pa have to say about our mission with the *Tsalagi*?"

Thomas pursed his lips and shrugged. "Not much really." He didn't have the energy to explain everything his father shared with him.

"So, you think them Tsalagi are gonna just pack up and move out west?" Roe asked.

"Don't see why not." Thomas cut off another piece of venison. "Don't think they have much of a choice at this point. Why? You worried they'll start shooting at us or something?"

"It's possible. We just came from Florida. Look at the Seminoles. Who's to say the Cherokee won't do the same?"

"The Cherokee aren't that way. Besides, I don't think they could even if they wanted to."

"How you figure?" Roe asked.

"Three years ago, when I was sent to Florida," Thomas said, "a few friends of mine were sent here to the Cherokee Nation under General Wool to enroll them for this relocation. Not only that, but my friends had to disarm them in the process."

"Bet that didn't go over too well."

Thomas shook his head. "On the contrary. Smooth as silk. The Tsalagi gave up their weapons—"

"All of 'em?"

Thomas shook his head. "Doesn't matter though. They've been beaten down so much by the government over the years. I don't think they have much of a choice. Out west, they can live however they want. Keep their laws and government. They won't have to worry about white people settling in on their land. So, the whole thing makes sense."

Roe tossed a stick on the fire. "Not to me, it don't." He laughed with the manner of someone who didn't believe a word he was hearing.

"What?" Thomas asked.

"You really believe *we're* gonna leave 'em alone? Oh, Captain! I thought you was smarter than that."

Roe cut loose with a belly laugh, caustic and irritating.

Thomas edged closer. "What's so damn funny?'

Roe choked for a moment on a biscuit, spit on the ground, then stared at his commander.

"C'mon, Captain. You've been 'round long enough to know better. We will negotiate, renege, fabricate a new agreement to push the Indians into someplace we will eventually want for ourselves – then repeat the whole process. We ain't gonna leave them poor folks alone until we've driven 'em into the Pacific." Roe took a drink of water.

"The Cherokee already got their own land right here," Roe continued. "Why do they need to go anywhere else? They've done learned how to farm. They're merchants, and teachers. Heck, most of 'em is more civilized than *I* am, certainly more cultured. So why do they gotta go out west? Just don't seem right, that's all."

Thomas munched away.

"Besides, if the land out west is so great, why ain't we keepin' it?" Roe asked. "Why's the government so quick to give it away? The Cherokee ain't nomads. It makes more sense for white frontiersmen to go out there, don't it?"

Roe looked down at his plate and shrugged. "Heck. I'm just a dumb ol' country boy. What do I know 'bout these things?"

Thomas laid his empty plate on the ground, sat back, and thought about Roe's diatribe. He had to agree that the Cherokees had always tried to live amicably with the white people around them. They'd based their civic structure on the government of the United States. They had schools, towns, and European-style farms. Some of them had very successful businesses.

"Well, what I *do* know is that our orders are to report to Fort Newnan in Pickens County Georgia," Thomas said. "We're to help escort the Cherokee peacefully to their new lands out west."

"Peacefully, huh?" Roe took another bite of food. "Who's in command?"

"Captain John Dorsey."

Roe choked.

"Dorsey? The good *Reverend* Dorsey?" Roe wiped his mouth with a handkerchief. "He's a drunken waste of a captain's uniform. More worthless than nipples on a boar. And *you* have to report to *him*? Good lord!"

"But he's a parson, right? It's not just a nickname."

"Oh no. And he'll be happy to remind you of his sanctified ecclesiastical rank 'tween swigs of whisky if you doubt him."

"Sounds like you know him."

"Not personally, no, but I've heard the stories. My cousin served under him a while back. Said one day the *Reverend* is upright and sanctimonious and the next, his aides are scrapin' him off the floor, drunk off his rear."

Thomas felt a tingle on the back of his neck.

"My cousin said that most of the men under his command lost respect for him right quick," Roe said. "If there ain't any strong officers under him, things can go to hell in a handbasket quicker than all get out." Roe looked over. "He's darn lucky to be gettin' an officer like you, that's for sure. Heck, I remember clear as day how you became our commander. Remember that?"

Thomas offered a halfhearted smile and rested his elbows on his knees. "How could I forget?"

It had been less than a year since Thomas was promoted. At the time, he was a lieutenant in charge of a small platoon under the command of Captain Alfred Young, an arrogant and bullheaded man. Young was afraid to make decisions, so he relied on written orders to justify his actions regardless of the situation.

Captain Young and his men were positioned less than a half-mile north of a small settlement along the border of Georgia and the

Florida Territory. Their orders were to prevent any attack by Seminole warriors. Young was ambivalent about the assignment and knew little of strategic troop placement. A few days after arrival, the soldiers heard screams coming from the settlement just before noon.

Thomas hopped on Silo and rode to Captain Young's tent.

"Sir, we need—"

Young spoke into the novel he was reading. "Lieutenant Edwards requesting permission to enter, sir. Come in, Lieutenant."

"Sorry, sir," Thomas said. "Requesting permission to enter, sir."

"Permission granted."

"Sir, the village—"

Young peered over the top of his book. "Has there been a change in the Manual of Operations, Lieutenant, or is the lack of a salute your idea?"

Thomas snapped to attention and saluted. Young flipped a haphazard hand across his brow.

"Now, Lieutenant, about the village."

"They are under attack," Thomas said.

"You mean 'it,' don't you Edwards?" A smug grin curled across Young's lips. "You are an Academy man. I thought they taught English there. The village is an object, not a person – the village is an 'it.'"

"Yes, sir—"

"So, is the village under attack, or are the villagers being assaulted individually?"

Thomas was about to say something about a distinction without a difference when Young held up a hand. A steward entered the tent with a tray bearing a silver teapot, a sugar bowl, a spoon, and one cup. The steward poured a cup of tea.

"That will be all, Phillips," Young said.

The captain dropped three sugar cubes, more sugar than Thomas had seen in several weeks, into the cup and stirred in slow figure-eights. He sipped a little tea from the spoon and bobbed his head in satisfaction.

"Perfect," he said, "tea is so much more civilized than coffee, don't you think?"

"The village, sir. *It* is under attack. And, I assume, the villagers therein."

Young stared at his cup with the rapt attention of a starving man eyeing a rump roast.

"Thank you for the report, Lieutenant, however sarcastic it might have been. You are dismissed."

"But, sir—"

"We're here for the sole purpose of prevention," Captain Young said. "We're not here on a rescue mission."

"But—"

"In addition to your grammar lessons, you also apparently bypassed military discipline. You have been dismissed. I, on the other hand, am well aware that I have orders from higher up the chain."

"Damn your orders, sir," Thomas said.

He was racing away on Silo before Young recovered enough to respond. Having wasted time with Young, Thomas didn't stop to give orders. He hoped the men would see him and follow.

The screams grew in intensity the closer Thomas got to the settlement. Men and women ran towards the woods. They clutched terrified children. Flames from inside the gate reached for the sky. Heavy smoke made breathing difficult. Still, Silo charged ahead.

Thomas saw the outline of a mounted Seminole at the gate. The sound of rifle fire split the air and a bullet whizzed past Thomas's head.

The guard at the gate fell.

That came from behind me.

Thomas turned and saw Roe lower his rifle and continue to lead the charge toward the settlement.

With Thomas in the lead, the soldiers quickly secured the settlement. Though the buildings had been severely damaged, only two of the settlers suffered wounds. While they were serious, neither was life-threatening.

When they returned to camp, Thomas saw Phillips packing dirt around a post he'd obviously just set into the ground. Before Thomas and the others put away their horses and equipment, Young appeared from his tent in full dress uniform.

"Lieutenant Thomas Edwards," he said, "you are hereby accused of insubordination and inciting a mutiny. Until such time as we can convene a proper court-martial, you will be confined to the stockade."

Thomas resisted the temptation to tell the captain to go to hell. "We don't have a stockade, sir," he said. "We are in the field."

"I am well aware of our primitive conditions, Lieutenant. In lieu of proper confinement facilities, I have made other arrangements. Phillips, secure the prisoner."

A tide of angry murmurs rippled through the men. Roe put his hand on the butt of his pistol. Thomas shook his head.

"Send them to their tents," he said. "We don't want to make things worse."

Phillips told Thomas to strip to his skivvies, then chained him to the post using both wrist and ankle restraints. Once a day, Phillips gave Thomas a few sips of water from a ladle, then poured the rest over his head. Young announced that anyone giving food to Thomas would be shot on the spot.

The July sun blistered Thomas's skin. By the time they unshackled him, he was nearly mad from dehydration and hunger. He'd been chained for five full days. His recovery took two weeks.

Not once during the entire ordeal did Thomas complain, nor did he speak ill of his commander.

A month later, Captain Young was recalled to Washington. Roe always claimed he'd been assigned to "duties that didn't include thinking." Thomas Edwards received a citation for meritorious service and was promoted to the rank of captain.

Roe stood and gathered their plates. Thomas grabbed his sketch pad.

"You ever gonna tell me who that Indian woman is?" Roe asked. He gestured to the sketchbook.

"What do you mean?" Thomas asked. He felt heat rise in his cheeks.

"You draw in that thing pert-near ev'ry night. And ev'ry one of 'em is an Indian woman – same beautiful eyes in all of 'em."

Thomas looked down into the stunning eyes he'd drawn the previous night. Eyes that sustained him. Eyes that haunted him. Eyes he imagined every day for the past seven years though he'd told Miriam otherwise.

"Who is she?" Roe asked.

Thomas didn't respond.

"Captain. C'mon. I promise, I ain't gonna tell a soul."

Thomas looked at the storm clouds. He watched the darkness consume the light and wondered if the same storm was rolling in on the woman in the drawings.

CHAPTER TEN

They'd tied the rope at the end of the human chain to a sturdy horse whose pace never slackened. Catherine stumbled, then set Ayita down.

"I'm sorry, sweet girl," Catherine said. "Mamma can't carry you any farther."

Ayita never lost a step.

Jishnu collapsed in a heap. One of the soldiers tugged on the horse's bridle. The horse stopped.

Catherine knelt.

"Father, please get up."

Ayita grabbed one of his arms. "Please, Pawpaw."

His voice croaked a response. "I'm sorry. I…I can't."

His face was bloodied, swollen, and ashen, the light in his eyes long since faded. Catherine tried to shoulder him upright, but his dead weight was too much. She looked around unsure why they were not moving.

A soldier walked past and kicked dirt into Jishnu's hair. "You made it to the rally point, ol' man," he said. A half-dozen other soldiers laughed. One of them spit and said, "Now you can just waller in the dirt."

Mother and daughter collapsed next to Jishnu. The scorching evening air was stagnant and heavy with moisture. They'd trudged over five miles without a break, without food, without so much as a sip of water. Jishnu's shirt was black with blood. The scalp wound continued to ooze.

Catherine cleaned the gash as best she could. She positioned Jishnu's head in Ayita's lap. When the young girl crossed her legs, Catherine gasped.

"Oh Ayita, your feet."

Ayita shrugged. "It's okay, Mamma, they stopped hurting a long time ago."

Ayita's smile was thin but determined.

"Rest with father," Catherine said.

His skin was dry and warm, his breathing labored Jishnu gave her a feeble nod, but Catherine wasn't sure he recognized her. Ayita stroked the side of Jishnu's face. He glanced up at her and smiled, then his eyes rolled up into his lids and his breathing grew shallower.

Catherine snapped to her feet. She didn't want Ayita to see the tears. The day had been a nightmare. When she wasn't carrying Ayita, she was fending off sexual advances from the militiamen. After they tired of tormenting her, they prodded Jishnu with sticks and bayonets and screamed for him to pick up his pace. They struck him with their fists whenever he stumbled, but the old warrior remained on his feet until the very last minute.

"You mean to tell me you rode all that way jus' fer three of 'em?" asked one of the officers who'd been waiting. "What a waste of time."

"If we'd rounded 'em up a week ago, like I suggested, it wouldn't have been just three of them," Colonel Smith replied. "Every farm we stopped by was empty except theirs." He gestured to Catherine and her family. "Can't decide who's the biggest fool, the people who ran, these three, or me for gallivanting the woodlands of Georgia for nothing."

Twenty yards away, Catherine saw over a hundred Tsalagi people in a small, makeshift pen. They wore the faces of the condemned, blank expressions of people abandoned by hope. Most of them were barefooted; some were nearly naked. Most sat in the dust. The few who walked around threatened to fall over at any moment. Sadness and loss saturated the little corral. Colonel Smith gestured toward Catherine and the rest. "Throw 'em in with the others."

Jishnu and Ayita collapsed the moment they were shoved into the makeshift pen. Catherine stood over them, a mother wolf on guard for her brood. Everywhere she looked she saw the same heartbreaking story. Most tragic were the confused and terrified eyes of the children.

Ayita tugged on her hem. "Can we go home? I'm tired."

"Me too," Catherine replied. She sat down next to her daughter. "But we can't go home…yet."

How do I tell her we no longer have a home?

"I'm scared, Mamma."

"Me, too, sweetheart."

Catherine brushed Ayita's long black hair back over her shoulders and looked into her deep, brown eyes. "Why don't you put your head on my lap and get some rest?"

Tears welled in the child's eyes. She scooted over, put her head on her mother's leg, and cried without a sound until she fell asleep. Catherine stroked her daughter's hair.

I promise you, little one, everything will be all right.

She moved Jishnu's head onto her other leg and listened with increasing dread to his labored, rattling breath.

If he dies, I will never forgive myself, she thought. *We should have packed up and left the minute I heard the proclamation in town. If we had cooperated, the soldiers might have been nicer.*

She did not know how long she sat. No one spoke to her. No one said anything – to anyone – not until a soldier stood at the gate.

"Colonel says it's time to go," he said.

Catherine was jolted awake. She was still seated with her loved ones in her lap.

Colonel Smith rode up on his horse. "Corporal, move it. Get 'em separated and let's go!"

The soldiers began issuing orders like barking dogs.

"Listen up!"

"…two groups of wagons…"

"…Fort Newnan…"

"…Fort Hetzel…"

"…move or we'll move you!"

Catherine nudged Ayita who blinked awake and sat up. Jishnu stirred. His eyes registered no understanding of the situation. It took two full minutes to hoist him into an upright position.

No one moved fast enough to suit the soldiers. The corral became a sea of blue uniforms, flashing cudgels, crying infants, screaming women, and groaning men. A young man helped Catherine hoist Jishnu to his feet.

A soldier stood over a mother and father whose three small children huddled close.

"Here, let me help you."

His voice was anything but kind. He grabbed a boy and began dragging him towards one of the wagons. Mother and father suddenly energized, scrambled up and hurried along with their other children in tow. Catherine could hear the mother's pleading voice.

"Where are you taking our son? Give him back."

"Let go of my son," the father said. "He's only a boy."

109

The soldier ignored them until he got to the wagons.

"Get in and I'll give yer kid back," he said. The boy's parents clambered into the wagon. The soldier tossed the boy in behind them and turned back to the corral.

Following his lead, other militiamen grabbed the nearest child and headed for the wagon. Chaos erupted. One man pushed a soldier only to be beaten bloody with a rifle butt. Screams and curses lumbered through the oppressive evening air.

Too afraid to move, Catherine pulled Ayita closer to her as she watched a woman struggle against three soldiers. The beating she received was so brutal Ayita had to cover her eyes.

Jishnu, determined to avoid separation, grabbed onto Catherine's hand with a weak and trembling grip. When Catherine looked at him, he gave her a reassuring smile. Suddenly,-Catherine was jerked forward, almost falling to her knees, from the force of a soldier ripping Ayita from her mother's arms.

"Mamma! Mamma!"

Catherine charged after the soldier. A lanky, pimply-faced private stepped in her path.

"Where are you goin'?"

"That's my daughter!"

"Don't care," he replied.

He shoved her into the mayhem behind her. Catherine was instantly swept up into the frenzy. She lost sight of Ayita, but every mother can hear her frightened child.

"Mamma! Mamma!"

People fell on all sides of Catherine. They fought soldiers and one another, desperate to escape the nightmarish fracas. Catherine shoved her way through the sea of people, stumbling over bodies and squinting into the dust. She spotted her daughter.

"Ayita!"

But the more she fought, the slower her process became. She was in a quicksand of humanity. People swirled all around her.

Two soldiers tackled a young man who was trying to climb the fence. They knocked Jishnu to the ground. The older man tried to stand but could not.

There was a line of Cherokees standing to board the wagons. Some of them realized Catherine's plight and took up her cause.

"Don't take that girl from her mother!"

"Let her go!"

"She's just a little girl!"

Sensing a rising tide of resistance, soldiers began to shove the protesters.

"Sit down or suffer the consequences."

"It doesn't matter," another said. "You'll all end up in the same place."

The closer Catherine drew, the more Ayita struggled. The soldier, unsure why he'd picked up a baby wildcat, flung the child in the back of one of the nearest wagons, then said something to the attending officer. The officer nodded, stepped to the side of the wagon, and yelled to the driver.

"Fort Hetzel, move 'em out!"

The wagons lurched forward. Over the groans of the wheels, the crack of whips, and the cries of frightened passengers, Ayita's voice soared like a screeching hawk.

"Mamma!"

Catherine willed herself forward, but the wagons were picking up speed. She screamed as she ran.

"I'm here, Ayita, I'm here!"

"Mamma!"

Suddenly, Catherine's shoulder hit the ground. Her face skidded through the dirt. Her lungs collapsed. She could not refill them because of the two soldiers on top of her. She wheezed out a protest.

"Ayita..."

The reply began to fade. "Mamma! Mamma!"

Catherine kicked with the fury of an enraged mule. The soldiers pinned her bucking torso to the ground.

"Damn she's strong," one of them said.

The other called out. "We need help over here!"

Someone pushed Catherine's face into the ground. She could not yell without eating a mouthful of dirt. Her lungs screamed for air; her eyes burned. Her weary legs began to cramp but nothing else mattered. Her voice oozed out in a paroxysm of grief.

"Ayita."

She heard a low voice, an older man, someone kinder than the others.

"Sorry, ma'am. Wagon's gone. Nothin' you can do."

The men got off of her. Slowly, she rolled into a sitting position, lifeless and forlorn. She did not notice that the top of her dress had ripped open until one of the men leaned over and reached for her exposed breast. Before she could react, a gunshot split the air.

Colonel Smith sat astride his horse and reloaded his pistol. "That's enough," he said. "You are U.S. Army soldiers, not barbarians. Get that damn woman on her feet and into a wagon. If we're not loaded and on our way to Fort Newnan in the next twenty minutes, you're all on report. You'll walk post until the Lord Jesus himself returns and forgives you. Now move it!"

He turned to the remaining Cherokees, all of whom had stopped to watch Catherine's struggle.

"Get your backsides onto one of those wagons. Next one who gives us any trouble gets a bullet in the brain – man, woman, or child. Am I understood?"

Dejected, the Tsalagi boarded the wagons for Fort Newnan. The heartier adults helped the elderly and the children before climbing on themselves. Several young men lifted Jishnu aboard.

Catherine did not move.

Colonel Smith dismounted. He walked to her and held his flintlock pistol to her forehead.

"You going to move, or do I need to put you out of your misery?"

CHAPTER ELEVEN

MAY 30, 1838, FORT NEWNAN

Fort Newnan stood in the Hickory Log District of the Cherokee Nation, the central portion of northern Georgia. It was a heavily wooded area surrounded by mountains. Several rivers fed close to a dozen creeks that trickled their way through the area. The shambolic fort was a blend of new and old buildings, most of which were used for storage or quarters for the officers. In the center stood an old horse corral.

The corral was a little more than half an acre and designed to hold around thirty horses, short-term. A split rail fence enclosed the area.

The barren patch of earth was more of an eyesore than a landmark. Under normal circumstances, the sun-drenched corral would go unnoticed, just a lonely patch of hard dirt. However, riding up on it, Thomas could not ignore the several hundred empty faces of Tsalagi Indians inside the enclosure.

There's barely enough room to move, he thought.

He saw a few small fires but no food. Hardly anyone had shelter from the blistering sun. He flinched when he saw a woman relieving herself less than a foot from three children cowering on a threadbare blanket.

The corral was heavy with the distinctive smell of human waste and death. Swarms of flies swirled around and on the occupants.

Thomas felt his pulse quick. His nostrils flared. "This is a disgrace!"

Thomas guided Silo closer to the fence line. A handful of people glanced up at him. Most looked away in defeat. A few stared in quiet resentment. Thomas turned to Roe.

"Find Dorsey!"

Roe did not move. His eyes were locked on a child withering in a mother's arms.

"Roe," Thomas said. "Now."

Roe continued to stare at the tableau of death even as his horse trotted away.

Despite his curdling stomach, Thomas forced himself to look at the people in the enclosure. He *knew* these people.

Any one of them could have sat next to, in front of, or behind him at church on the Sunday mornings he went with his grandparents. They could have been to one of the get-togethers at his grandparents' home and broke bread with them. He'd probably spoken to dozens of them at one point or another during his two years with Oscar and Miriam.

Thomas heard Miriam's words swirling in his head about the relocation. *That might be difficult for you.*

Disgusted for letting his father's vision of an opportunistic venture overshadow the possibility of hardship for the Cherokee people he knew and loved, Thomas was turning away when a Cherokee girl about the age of fifteen caught his eye.

Catherine?

She was fifteen when Thomas met her nine years ago.

His throat tightened. His pulse increased. He felt the veins in his temples pounding. His eyes darted left...right...back to the left.

Is she here?

Thomas searched the faces in the crowd for Catherine. Part of him did not want to find her. Inspecting every person, he was overcome by the memory of another voice – Clinton's.

The United States will escort (them) the Cherokee people safely out west. We'll provide food, water, transportation, and protection. The government's going out of its way to make the relocation as easy as possible for them.

As the words spun round and round, Thomas grew angrier – angry with the government – angry with the military – angry with his father for involving him – angry with Dorsey and everyone else in charge of this mess. But most of all he was angry with himself for being gullible enough to believe the lies. He'd seen awful things in the Florida Territory, but nothing like what was in front of him.

He stopped looking for Catherine and saw the Cherokee people as a whole once again. *They don't belong in there.*

He dismounted and grabbed the gate closure. He slid it to one side and was about to open the gate when Roe returned with another man.

"Excuse me, sir," Roe said. "This is Private Ratliff, sir. He's Captain Dorsey's clerk."

Roe's voice brought Thomas back to reality – a bucket of cold water poured over his rising rage. He stood with the top rail of the gate in his hand and scanned the faces of the Tsalagi. They were confused and curious. Was the deranged man going to harm them – or set them free?

Thomas dropped his shoulders and slid the closure back in place.

Letting them out will only make matters worse. Someone will get hurt. I need to protect these people.

He looked at Ratliff.

I need to protect Catherine.

"A *private* is the best you could do?"

Roe moved closer and spoke in a low voice.

"Only one who seems to have any idea of what's going on 'round here."

Moving deliberately, Thomas mounted Silo and turned him to face Roe and the private who might have been seventeen.

"So, you're the one I need to talk to about…this?" Thomas asked. He gestured toward the corral.

Ratliff cleared his throat. "I can answer any question you may have, sir."

Thomas glanced back at the Tsalagi. "*Any* question?"

"Yes sir." Ratliff paused. "Less you ask me something…you know…that only smart people know."

"I'll keep it simple, Private. Where in God's name is Captain Dorsey?"

§§

Captain Dorsey was in charge of seventy men, most of whom walked around aimless, shirtless, and unwashed. Many of them were either drunk or well on their way to becoming so. Their tents were scattered throughout the fort without any discernable pattern. While Thomas was not surprised to see a raft of drummer hawking their wares, he'd never seen prostitutes openly soliciting customers inside an Army facility.

The fort was in obvious disrepair. Stacks of unused lumber rotted in the sun. Buckets of paint and crates of nails lay unopened. Sentries napped at their posts, at least the few that had bothered to report for duty.

Someone attacking this place could take it singlehanded.

By the time they reached the command post, Thomas had learned more than he needed. Not a single morsel of food has been passed out to the Cherokees; save for one cup of water a day, the only liquid regularly made available to the captives was corn liquor.

Thomas stood outside of Dorsey's office and stared at the captain's horse. He'd seen better animals pulling trash wagons. The mare's mangy coat had not been curried in months. Her ribs were as prominent as her rail-thin snout. For a cavalry officer, refusing to care for a mount was unforgivable.

"Roe, attend to that animal right now," Thomas said.

"Yes, sir."

Thomas adjusted his uniform jacket.

"Tell Captain Dorsey I have arrived."

The young man tapped on the door. There was no reply.

"A bat couldn't hear that, Private," Thomas said.

Ratliff shuffled his feet, blew out an exaggerated breath, and knocked louder. Again, no response.

"Again, Private."

This time, Ratliff pounded on the door with an open palm. The report echoed through the fort like a cannon shot. A smoky voice slurred from the other side of the door.

"Who the hell is that?"

The private looked back at Thomas for reassurance.

"Cap…Captain Dorsey, this is Private Ratliff. There's a Captain Edwards here to report for duty, sir."

"Who?"

"Captain Edwards, sir."

"Private Ratliff, come in – alone."

Private Ratliff shot Captain Edwards a nervous glance before reaching for the door latch. He took his time opening the door, then stepped in and closed the door behind him.

Thomas tried to listen through the door but all he could hear was muffled conversation. He heard a lot of scrambling and clinking.

They're cleaning up.

To keep his anger in check, Thomas inspected his uniform one more time. He couldn't find a single flaw.

Finally, a sweaty Private Ratliff emerged and stood at attention.

"Captain Dorsey will see you now, sir."

The inside of the cabin smelled like a saloon and looked like a monk's cell. The only furniture was a cot, a shaving station, and a field desk behind which Dorsey was attempting to sit straight. The captain appeared to be busy pouring over paperwork, but Thomas noticed half the papers on his desk were upside down.

Thomas swallowed his disdain for the disheveled and obviously hungover commander and stood at attention. "Captain Thomas Edwards, reporting for duty, sir."

Captain Dorsey stared at the sheet in his hands. He finally looked up and attempted to focus through bloodshot eyes.

"Captain Edwards," he said. "Where are you coming from, Captain?"

This sorry excuse is going to keep me at attention, Thomas thought.

"The Florida Territory," Thomas said. He left out 'sir' on purpose. "My men and I fought the Seminole Indians. And now we —"

"The Seminoles are still there, aren't they?" Captain Dorsey asked.

He sat back in his chair and inspected Captain Edwards with contempt.

"Excuse me?" Thomas said.

"The Seminoles. They're still living in the Florida Territory, aren't they? Giving our troops fits from what I understand. I just don't see the need for you here, is my point. Perhaps you needed to remain in the Florida Territory and finish off the Seminoles, once and for all. We have the Cherokee under control here."

Thomas snorted. "I've only been here ten minutes or so but I'm not sure you're in control of anything, *Captain*."

Private Ratliff struggled not to snigger. Thomas locked eyes with his counterpart until Dorsey looked away.

"Do you have your papers?" Captain Dorsey asked.

"I do," Thomas replied.

He reached into his bag, pulled out his orders and handed them to Captain Dorsey, who took his time opening and reading through them. Thomas remained at attention.

"Private Ratliff, you may leave," Captain Dorsey said without looking up.

"Yes sir."

Before leaving, the young man locked eyes with Thomas and unleashed a crooked grin. Once the private was gone, Thomas assumed he'd be told to stand easy. Instead, Dorsey meandered through the orders without acknowledging Thomas at all.

"And where's the rest of your men?" Captain Dorsey asked.

"I had them set up camp about a half-mile down the road."

"Why'd you do that?"

"Before arriving, I sent my scouts ahead. They reported substandard conditions for both military and civilian personnel. I determined to have them bivouac outside the fort until I had made my own determination."

"Which is?"

"Having seen Fort Newnan, my men will stay where they are."

The veins in Dorsey's neck bulged. "You will bring them in forthwith," he said.

Thomas took an uninvited step forward.

"No, they'll stay where they are," he said. It was all he could do not to snarl. "My men, *good* men, maintain military bearing at all times. I will neither expose them to the poor excuse of soldiers I've seen outside nor require them to report to an officer who has so little self-respect he can't even feed or water his own horse."

Dorsey recoiled just enough to encourage Thomas to continue.

"Should there be any charges brought against me or my men as a result of my actions, I will submit a full, written report of the deplorable conditions here to the Secretary of War, the Honorable Joel Roberts Poinsett."

Dorsey recovered a little of his equilibrium.

"I don't like your tone, Captain."

Thomas kept his eyes locked on Dorsey. "Frankly, I don't give a shit, *sir*."

Captain Dorsey neither moved nor spoke. Thomas decided on something else.

"I will require the services of Private Ratliff while I am at Fort Newnan."

Dazed by the full frontal assault, Dorsey nodded.

"Yes, he…he can show you around."

"Good," Thomas dropped his foot back a step to pivot, but Dorsey interrupted the about-face.

"Before you go, I suggest you make yourself known to Lieutenant Colonel Morse."

"I wasn't told about a Colonel Morse being assigned here."

"Neither was I," Captain Dorsey answered with a sigh. "But he showed up a couple of days ago, out of the blue. Ol' Colonel Jeremiah Morse was sent here by General Eustis to help relocate the Cherokee. So, I guess Fort Newnan will have *three* commanders – just like Ancient Rome."

"We all know how that ended," Thomas said. "That doesn't make any sense."

Captain Dorsey picked up a jug from the floor next to his desk and poured a shot of viscous, brown liquid. "A lot of things don't make sense 'round this place," he said.

He raised the glass.

"Welcome to Fort Newnan."

§§

When Thomas slammed the door, the concussion sent several sheets of paper to the floor. No longer concerned with the appearance of his cabin, Dorsey fell back in his chair and turned the glass of whiskey in his hand, studying the reflection of the sunlight. The silence in the cabin filled with the sound of women and children begging for help. Real or imagined, Dorsey could hear them – night and day – awake or asleep.

Studying the amber liquid, Captain Dorsey chuckled. He remembered being young once, full of piss and vinegar just like Captain Edwards. At one time he was prepared to risk life and limb for his country. He had not realized his biggest sacrifice would be his soul.

Captain Dorsey proposed another toast.

"Welcome, Captain Edwards," he said. "Welcome to Fort Hell."

§§

When Thomas exited the cabin, he saw Roe and a couple of other men attending to Captain Dorsey's horse as he had ordered.

"Sergeant Bickford, come with me," he said without stopping. "Let's head back to camp. We'll talk along the way."

Roe gave the other men some instructions before climbing on his horse, Ticket, and following after Thomas.

"What's gotten into you?" Roe asked as he caught up with the captain. "You look spooked."

"That was a strange encounter."

As they rode back to their camp, Thomas told Roe everything that happened inside Captain Dorsey's cabin.

"Wow, that's quite a story," Roe said. "I'll make some coffee. Sounds like you might need it."

Roe fanned the flames on the cooking fire. Thomas sat with his back against a tree and thought.

Everything about Fort Newnan feels wrong. The longer this goes, the more cracks there are in Father's picturesque scenario.

"Here ya go, sir." Roe handed Thomas a cup and sat.

"Thanks," Thomas said. He took a sip. "You're right. Exactly what I needed."

Roe had worked with Thomas long enough to know when to keep quiet. So, with the patience of a wise parent, he waited for the captain to break the silence.

"There's one more thing," he said. "When I was leaving, Dorsey said I should introduce myself to a colonel who showed up a couple of days ago."

"What?"

"Yeah.   A Lieutenant Colonel Morse."

Roe spit out his coffee.

"Colonel Jeremiah Morse?"

"Well, it's *Lieutenant* Colonel Morse."

Roe cursed.

"What?" Thomas asked.

"You've never heard of Cutthroat Colonel Morse?"

CHAPTER TWELVE

MAY 23, 1838, NORTHERN GEORGIA

Catherine shot up gasping for breath.

"Ayita?"

She scoured the shadows for her daughter in the sea of faceless figures jostling back and forth in the dark.

Am I dreaming?

The sound of the wagon's wood creaking and vibrating as it rolled down the uneven road brought Catherine back to reality. The featureless shadows were still all around her, sitting shoulder to shoulder, moving in unison to lurches and jerks.

When did I get on?

"Father, where's my father?" She felt around.

A male tranquil voice, out of place in the hell of sticky sweat and stinking fear, rose from the darkness. "He's here, resting. I see firelight ahead; we'll be stopping soon. You can wake him then."

Something about his speech allowed Catherine to calm down enough to lie back on her elbows and try to catch her breath. She strained to see what was up ahead and made out the shape of another wagon leading the way toward what looked like a soldier's encampment.

Ayita's wagon must be miles away by now.

Catherine lay in isolation and despair.

The wagon creaked to a halt. A soldier lowered the tailgate.

"Everybody out!"

The dark world splintered with the sound of people complaining, crying, groaning when they hit the ground with legs drummed into numbness by the long ride. The soldiers glared, obviously resentful of their "special assignment." They were paid to fight Indians, not to herd them like cattle.

Catherine moved along with the crowd – not a single familiar face. And then…

…she was embracing her father. Neither could speak – and neither would let go. They held onto one another and slowly lowered to the ground where they wept silent tears with the foreheads touching.

The Tsalagi were in a makeshift, rope pen. Slipping under the rope would have been easy – and fatal. A sharpshooter stood at regular intervals and warned anyone who got within five feet of the boundary. The captives stood for a few moments afraid to say or do anything that would garner attention from the guards. Eventually, exhaustion won out over fear and the people collapsed in heaps of sadness and fatigue.

A man touched Catherine's shoulder.

"We…we have food," he said, "and a little water." He opened his arms as if welcoming guests into his home. "Please, come join us. My name is Waya. This is my wife, Leotie, and our daughters, Deepika and Charudutta."

Everyone nodded in acknowledgment.

This is the man who spoke on the wagon, Catherine thought.

Waya's face reflected gentle strength. His long hair and the shape of his nose were unquestionably Cherokee. His clothing was a different matter. He and his entire family were dressed in a mix of current European fashions and accented with traditional Cherokee accessories.

"I'm Catherine—" She stopped, cleared her throat, and switched from English to her native language. "I am Kasewini, and this is my father, Jishnu." She longed to ask about Ayita but knew no one knew more than she did. "Forgive me for asking, but how is it you were able to take things with you?"

"I don't know," Waya replied. "The soldiers told us to take only what we could carry," Waya replied. "No one inspected our things."

Catherine could see her mother's Bible lying in the dust where she had dropped it. She fought back tears.

"They…they didn't even give us a chance to grab my father's shoes," she said.

Everyone looked at her father's feet. Her mind screamed.

My daughter doesn't have shoes either…

…but she could not speak Ayita's name aloud.

The group nibbled on elk jerky and dried berries. Waya passed around a small flagon of water. No one took more than a few sips.

Another family was in the small circle. The father looked like an old bull – a creature once strong, mighty, and feared, now a shadow of his glorious past – proud but broken. His face was crisscrossed by wrinkles and scars – the marks of age and the testimonials of battle.

Catherine jumped back with a start when she realized he caught her gawking at him.

"I'm Jeevan," he said. His voice was resolute and dry. "This is my wife, Manjusha, my son Sahen and my daughters Rupa and Laboni."

Manjusha looked up through swollen, hollow eyes. "We have two more children, Kavi, another son, and…"

She broke down into tears and buried her head in her blanket. Her children sniffled and snuggled close to their mother. Jeevan reached out and stroked his wife's hair.

"They dragged us out of our home and put us in a wagon with three other families. We rode for hours until the soldiers met up with a larger group of white men who were heading north. Some of us were forced into the other group. They did not trouble themselves to keep families together."

Sadness washed over Jeevan's proud face. He looked at Catherine. "It was the same as when they took your child. They pulled Kavi and our youngest, Harsha, off the wagon and shoved them onto a different one. I...I shouted at the soldiers. I told them they were making a mistake. I told them those were *my* children." Jeevan took a deep breath and looked over at his wife before continuing. "I jumped off the wagon to get my children. The soldiers beat me."

Catherine looked closer and realized some of what she originally thought were battle scars from the past were fresh wounds, raw and wet.

"My wife and children screamed but the white men wouldn't listen. They didn't care. Even the people in the other wagon tried to give our children back. I could hear Harsha—"

He broke off for a moment to compose himself. His face showed an eerie mixture of indignation and helplessness.

"She...she kept screaming for her daddy..."

Jeevan looked down at his empty hands.

Catherine shifted over to be closer to her father as tears streamed down her cheeks. Waya and his family said nothing.

After a few moments, Jeevan looked up with eyes reflecting the rage of a thousand fires.

"When the soldiers forced me back into the wagon one of them said 'What difference does it make? She's just another worthless animal.'" Jeevan shook his head. "What kind of man can feel that way about another human being?"

He took a deep breath.

Catherine realized she'd been holding her breath. She placed her head on her father's shoulder. He flinched just enough to betray his pain.

"I'm so sorry, father," she said. "Let's have a look."

Waya helped take off Jishnu's shirt. The older man never uttered a sound, but Catherine could tell he was in pain. The shirt came off and with it, what little healing had taken place. Jishnu's wounds oozed. Ugly welts covered his abdomen and back.

Deepika brought Waya's small medicine bag. Waya crushed some herbs and applied the paste to Jishnu's wound with a skilled hand.

"This wound on the back of your head needs to be closed," Waya said. "Perhaps tomorrow we'll be fortunate enough to find a needle or tiny bone of some kind and I could close it up. Until then, we'll just have to keep it bandaged and clean the best we can."

"Thank you," Catherine said.

They all ate a little more, then said goodnight.

"Make sure your father rests," Waya said. "We have no idea what tomorrow may bring, and he'll need his energy. Hopefully, they'll put him in the wagon again."

Catherine thanked Waya and Deepika then helped her father to a quiet spot for the evening.

Clouds covered the moon as if hiding the night's eye in embarrassment. The familiar sounds of the woodlands began to filter across the camp as it quieted – the screech of a hawk, triumphant in the hunt, an owl asking its perpetual question, brother wolf calling for his mate, the wind filtering through the forest. Catherine watched her people. They were at ease with the land. The white men flinched at every noise.

Guilty men are jumpy, she thought.

Catherine lay a bit away from her father, fearful she might jostle him in the night. She forced herself to stay away until Jishnu's heavy breathing turned into familiar snores. She stared at the blackness and wondered if she'd seen her last happy day.

Ayita's face swirled in Catherine's mind, sometimes laughing, sometimes screaming in distress. She heard, "Mamma! Mamma! Mamma!" in every utterance of animal, bird, and wind. Catherine closed her eyes and forced the terrible doubts out of her mind. She imagined Ayita lying on a soft blanket. Perhaps someone was stroking her hair or holding her tight until she fell asleep. The peaceful image of her slumbering daughter consumed Catherine's final thoughts as she surrendered to sleep.

A hand slammed over Catherine's mouth, smashing her lips into her teeth. Catherine was airborne, lifted off the ground. She kicked and flailed but could not scream. Someone had stuffed a rag in her mouth. She heard a rough whisper.

"Told ya she was a hellcat."

The clouds moved for a moment and allowed the moon to open its eyes. Catherine counted three…no four men…all soldiers.

"Drop her here."

Impact with the ground knocked all the air from Catherine's lungs. Her head bounced off the hardpan. Blinding pain flashed through her temple. She wondered if one of her wrists had been broken in the struggle.

She felt part of her dress tear away.

"You kicked me earlier, bitch," a voice said. "Now yer gonna soothe my aches and pains."

Catherine screamed for all she was worth. The gag was so deep in her throat she barely made a sound.

"Yell all you want, no one's gonna hear you. And if they do, ain't nobody gonna come help you."

Catherine felt the wind run its cold fingers across her naked body. She looked toward the sky and cursed its vast emptiness.

CHAPTER THIRTEEN

MAY 30, 1838

"He killed one of his own men?" Thomas asked.

Roe stared into the fire and picked at his teeth with a whittled toothpick. "A while back, Ol' Cutthroat was up in Ohio somewhere. My uncle John wuz up there with him. They were relocatin' the Seneca Nation out west. They were at a relocation camp like this one for a couple of months before they started the big march. 'Bout a week into it, Ol' Colonel Morse went an' hung one of his own men. Then the crazy ol' coot left the body to rot for three days, so everyone could see it."

"Who hangs one of his own men just to send a message?"

"Someone bereft of his total fiduciaries."

Thomas did not correct the malapropism.

"Uncle John said this soldier, a sergeant Hall I believe his name was, had relations with a Seneca squaw. They met at the relocation camp and fell in love, I guess. She went an' got pregnant. Hall thought it'd be best to try an' hide it. I guess they was plannin' on gettin' hitched once all the hullabaloo of the relocation was over."

Roe threw his toothpick into the fire.

"They never got a chance to, though," he said. "When the colonel got wind of everything, *vvvvvvvvtttttt*!"

Roe yanked his fist up next to his ear and cocked his head like someone being hanged.

"Strung him up, just like that?" Thomas asked. "No court-martial?"

"Well, not immediately. Morse knew all about the pregnancy and how Hall was planning on marrying the woman, so he slit her throat and made Hall watch. When the sergeant screamed, the colonel slapped the horse Hall was perched on and let him swing in the breeze."

Thomas almost dropped his cup of coffee. "Holy Mother of God!"

"I'm tellin' ya, Captain, Morse is a sadistic piece of work."

"Most horrible thing I've ever heard," Thomas said.

"Well, that ain't all. Two days later, the company's marchin' along with the Indians. They look over and see the girl's body hanging from a tree – well, what's left of it. Buzzards had enjoyed her pretty good by that time."

"You're telling me that a commanding officer in the United States Army had someone transport a dead body fifteen miles or so just so he could display it to his men?"

"Exactly," Roe said. "Morse was not one to countenance…ah… what's that word…fraternization. Soldiers in his command might rape the occasional Indian, but they damn well better not fall in love with one." Roe looked over at Thomas to make sure he was listening before gazing back into the fire. "Uncle John said it was horrifying and he fought against the British in two wars. Said that purty young thing didn't hardly assimilate a human being."

"I think you mean 'resemble.'"

"God Almighty, Captain. I'm tellin' you this horror story and you're givin' me a vocabulary lesson?"

"Sorry, Roe," Thomas said. "I couldn't think of anything else to say." He stared at the fire. "How does Morse keep his commission?"

"Best guess? He'll do what the folks in Washington want done but don't care to vocalize. They want the Indians gone. They don't worry about how – and they can always say someone got out of hand. You know, a spasm of over-enthusiasm for the assignment."

The coffee suddenly tasted like blood. Thomas poured it on the ground.

"There's more," Roe said.

Thomas put his face in his palms. "Go on."

"Story is that Morse murdered an entire village in Florida during the Seminole business."

Thomas blew out a deep breath. "That's horrible, but I've heard close to a dozen stories about villages being attacked."

"Not like this," Roe said.

"How's that?"

"The village that the soldiers wiped out wasn't Indian, they was white. And when his lieutenant objected, Morse cut him from his Adam's apple to his tallywacker."

§§

Thomas watched a group of dirty-faced children playing in the filth of the old horse corral. His oath to follow orders and Roe's accounts about Colonel Morse held a wrestling match inside his head.

Thomas turned his back to the corral and studied a large, newly erected, canvas tent standing twenty yards from the holding pen. It was big enough for a dozen men.

"Odd place for a command tent," he said.

"Ain't no command tent, Captain," Roe said. He listened to his spittle sizzle in the fire. "That's Morse's personal abode."

The wind shifted. Involuntarily, both Roe and Thomas covered their noses.

"Lord, that corral stinks," Thomas said. "Can't they let those people use the latrine?"

"Morse says pigs roll around in their own shit. Why should Indians have it any better?" Roe had not taken his eyes off a small boy whose legs were covered with sores. "Ratliff tells me not one of them's been out of that pen for over two weeks. Ain't been a food shipment neither." Thomas shook his head. "That's a disgrace to the Army and to the nation," he said.

Private Ratliff emerged from Morse's tent and headed towards Thomas like a man hurrying to find a place to pee. He saluted.

"The Colonel wants to see you now, sir."

Thomas motioned for Private Ratliff to lead the way.

"Don't start any trouble," Roe said.

"I can't promise anything," Thomas replied over his shoulder.

At the tent's opening, Private Ratliff cleared his throat before stepping inside. Thomas followed close behind, looking back at Roe one last time before entering.

Once Thomas's eyes adjusted to the low light inside, he was surprised how much the colonel's living space reminded him of his father's office back home. High-quality, ornate furniture crowded the space. Easels displayed half a dozen paintings. The one directly in front of the colonel's desk featured a family weeping at the feet of a man swinging from the hangman's rope. The tent was clean and organized. The dirt floor had been packed tight and swept. Other than the stench of sewage from the corral, everything reeked of military discipline.

Colonel Morse bald pate swept across a pile of papers while his quill scratched like chicken foraging a barnyard. Ink stained Morse's fingers.

"Colonel Morse, Captain Edwards reporting as ordered," Private Ratliff said.

Thomas glared at Ratliff.

I was not ordered and I'm not reporting until I know why Morse is here.

The colonel remained focused on the sentence he'd been struggling with for the better part of an hour, unable to capture the precise amount of rancor. He scratched out a word here and there, then dipped his quill into the inkwell and continued scrawling with more vigor.

When he looked up, Thomas nearly jumped. The colonel's immense face featured thick eyebrows set over beady eyes that were settled unevenly on either side of an enormous, flat nose. Jowled like a bulldog, the colonel could have hung pencils from the thick folds of skin below his jawline. Thomas had seen more attractive possums.

Trying to recover, Thomas focused on the colonel's pudgy hand as it placed the quill back into its holder. When Thomas looked back at the colonel, the shock of his unpleasant face caused the captain to recoil, something the colonel noticed and seemed to relish.

"That'll be all, Private," he said.

Morse fixed Thomas with a hard gaze, the same look Thomas had seen so many times as a child and young man, He was unintimidated – and unimpressed.

Colonel Morse let out a long, exasperated sigh. Without looking, he reached for his quill, dipped it in ink, and refocused on his writing. Thomas clenched his teeth to keep from saying anything, or, worse, storming out of the tent. To pass the time, he counted the twenty-four long, light-brown hairs lying across the barren plain of the colonel's scalp.

Sorriest head of hair in history.

Thomas studied the enthusiastic scribbler. As repugnant as he was, it was still difficult to believe the man was a progenitor of the terrible stories Roe had related. Thomas had envisioned a slender man of good build and vitality, someone who invoked fear by his sheer presence and personal energy. This jester of a man enjoyed pitiful little mind games and was homely to the point of absurdity.

When the colonel continued to write, Thomas counted the fourteen moles atop the colonel's head. Then he started naming them for figures from Greek mythology.

Apollo...Brizo...Castor...Dionysus...Eros...

He was glad when Morse looked up.

Good...can't think of a character with an F.

"Captain Thomas Edwards. I've heard of you."

Colonel Morse stood and waddled over to a small table. He muttered to himself while he poured a cup of tea. He did not offer any refreshment to Thomas.

The desk chair expressed displeasure when the colonel plopped down.

"So, tell me, Captain, is there a good explanation as to why you're just now reporting to me? I understand you've been here for several days. Isn't it customary to report to your post as soon as you arrive?"

"I did."

"Yet I'm meeting you for the first time."

"I wasn't aware of your existence until yesterday morning. My orders were to—"

"You're reporting to me a full twenty-four hours after learning of my existence?"

"Oh no, sir. I think a mistake's been made."

"I agree."

"I'm not reporting to you at all. This is merely a courtesy call to an officer of higher rank. Nothing more."

Colonel Morse's eyes became impossibly smaller. A tiny smear of drool made its way onto his shirt.

"I'm the highest-ranking officer at this fort, Captain. My rank demands that you report to me."

"I recognize that you're the highest-ranking officer, sir, thus my extension of respect. But I'm not *reporting* to you."

"Is that right?"

"Yes sir. My orders stated I was to report to Captain Dorsey. To my knowledge, he has neither relinquished command nor been relieved of his duty as commander. Until I see the proper paperwork to the contrary, I will only report to him."

Morse thumbed the stack of papers in front of him.

"Let me get this straight, Captain. You're demanding 'proper paperwork' from a superior officer?"

"I'm just following regulations."

"Regulations?"

"Yes, sir. Regulations demand I follow written orders when it comes to reporting to a new duty station."

"Regardless of written orders, Captain, you're to show respect that my rank demands. Am I understood?"

"I believe I have, sir."

"How's that?"

"By introducing myself to you."

"My rank demands more than that, Captain."

"I'm confused, sir."

"What part of all this confuses you, Captain?"

"All of it, frankly."

"Excuse me?"

"May I ask a question?"

"If it helps you to understand who's in charge around here."

"Does Captain Dorsey have orders to report to you, sir?"

Colonel Morse sighed. "No. He does not."

"So, he's the commanding officer according to the written word. Not you."

"No, he's not the *only* commander at this fort!"

"Based on what?"

"My word as the highest-ranking officer!"

"You're telling me I have to simply trust you? That you're the commander here, regardless of what I've been told otherwise?"

Colonel Morse looked back down at his papers.

"Yes, you'll have to trust me," he said finally.

"I can't do that, Colonel."

"And why the hell not?"

"Are you telling me I should abandon the practice of following written orders when reporting to a fort?" Thomas asked.

"No."

"Are we at war?"

"No. And watch your tone, Captain. I don't like a smart aleck. Under my command or not, you *will* show me the proper respect."

Thomas rolled his tongue across the inside of his cheek and waited.

"Why are you and your men camped outside of Fort Newnan?" Colonel Morse asked.

"We will remain there until I figure out what's going on around here. Even you have to admit that things are a bit out of sorts. I felt it was best to keep them outside the camp until the proper chain of command was established."

"Well, I'm telling you to bring them into this fort under my command."

"I'm not doing that."

"That wasn't a request, Captain."

"Until I have clear orders from General Eustis or General Scott, those men are staying put."

"You're going to disobey a direct order, Captain?"

"I'm obeying the written order from a *General* over the verbal command of a *Lieutenant Colonel*. So, no, I'm not disobeying a direct order, *sir*."

Colonel Morse studied Thomas a while before he took a sip of his neglected tea. After setting the cup down, Morse took a piece of paper from his desk and glanced at it before handing it to the captain.

Thomas studied it – an order stating Colonel Morse was, indeed, in command of Fort Newnan. The orders referred to Captain Dorsey as in command of the fort's cavalry and overseer of "daily operations." In an odd specification, Colonel Morse was designated as "in charge of the Cherokees and their well-being."

Thomas lowered the paper and looked at the colonel.

"As you can see, Captain, the orders I just handed you have been signed by General Eustis." He sipped again. "The situation is a bit odd I'll admit, however, everything is legal and aboveboard I can assure you."

He handed over Thomas's original orders. Thomas compared the signatures – the same. "So, what now?" Thomas asked.

Morse snatched the paperwork out of Thomas's hands.

"Depends on you, Captain. I know all about you – your family's military legacy. Your paternal grandfather was an officer. And your father. I know how he likes to get involved in things, whether he needs to be or not. I understand he dabbles in politics. And I know all about his political plans for you, Captain."

Thomas could not stop the wince.

Dammit.

Morse chuckled.

"That's right, son. I know how you got yourself assigned here, and why. I know all about the plans your father has for you. As I see it, I can have a huge impact on your future goals, Captain. You're not the only one with connections and friends in influential places, you see. One letter from me, one bad word, and your future disappears like piss on a hot rock."

Thomas opened his mouth, but the colonel held up a cautioning finger.

"I'll be frank with you, *Thomas*. There are men in high places that doubt your commitment, your willingness to follow orders. They know about your tendency to do things your own way."

Again, a breath – again, the finger.

"A little incident down in the Florida Territory comes to mind."

He lowered his finger.

"I don't follow, Colonel," Thomas said.

"Captain Young," Colonel Morse said. "You remember him, I'm sure. He was under my command for a while before he received orders to fight the Seminoles."

The information lingered like the smell from outside the tent.

"He was a fine young lad," Morse said. "Had a bright future until he lost his command because your need to be a big hero. Now he's the second adjutant to some cumberworld who's overseeing potato purchases in Washington." Colonel Morse held the captain's gaze and slurped. "Want to tell me your side?"

Thomas was wary of the game. "He had absolutely no idea how to lead. The men and I considered him incompetent and dangerous."

Colonel Morse wobbled from his chair, his face the color of ripe eggplant. He pointed a finger at Thomas's chest and was about to speak when someone spoke from the door of the tent.

"You needed to see me, Colonel?"

It took a moment for Morse to return to the present. He looked over Thomas's shoulder.

"Come in," he said.

A man wearing all black slipped into Thomas's peripheral vision. When he took another step, Thomas saw a large top hat in the man's hands. Something about the man's blue eyes made Thomas's skin crawl.

He smiled with insincerity and stuck out his hand. "Since the Colonel won't, I guess I'll have to introduce myself," he said. "I'm Elias. Elias Watkins."

Thomas took the hand without enthusiasm "Captain Thomas Edwards."

"Nice to meet you, Captain."

Thomas gave a slight nod.

"Captain Edwards arrived a couple of days ago," Colonel Morse said. He retook his seat. His face returned to its normal color. "He and his men are camped about a half-mile southeast of here."

"Really?" Elias said.

Thomas guessed Elias knew exactly where they were camped and when they had arrived.

"We sure could use more help 'round here," Elias said. "We got close to five hundred head out there waiting to be sent out west. Hard to keep an eye on 'em all."

"Head?" Thomas asked. "You think the Cherokees are cattle?"

Elias laughed. "No, of course not."

"Didn't think so," Thomas said.

"But we do have to keep track of 'em," Elias said. "If one gets loose, it's my job to hunt 'em down."

"You mean if one of them escapes."

Elias did not reply. Thomas turned to Morse. "And what happens when you catch someone escaping?"

Elias answered for the colonel. "I make it perfectly clear they should stay where we tell 'em."

Thomas drilled Morse with his eyes. "I've heard you like to send messages."

Colonel Morse drummed on the table with his fingers. "Do we have a problem, Captain?"

"I'm just curious why you have a civilian doing soldiers' work."

"You don't need to concern yourself with the way I run things, Captain," Colonel Morse replied.

Thomas wanted to punch Elias in his smirking face but chose to ignore the man.

"If you don't require anything else, sir, I need to get back to my men," Thomas said.

"That will be all, Captain," Morse said.

Thomas was halfway to the entrance when the colonel added, "We can reminisce about Florida another time."

Elias and Colonel Morse waited until the tent flap settled.

"So, that was the infamous Thomas Edwards," Elias said.

"The one and only," Colonel Morse replied. "I thought the future president would be taller."

CHAPTER FOURTEEN

MAY 30, 1838, FORT NEWNAN

Catherine leaned her head against the fence post and closed her eyes, tormented by the feeling of her daughter being ripped out of her arms. A week of not knowing where the soldiers took her was maddening and the distance between them felt more insurmountable as time passed.

Catherine shifted her weight on the hard, unforgiving ground. The night before, the second time in a week, soldiers had raped her again.

The morning after the first time, before they arrived at Fort Newnan, Leotie found Catherine lying just inside the makeshift corral, naked and bleeding. Leotie gave her a dress and helped her clean up before anyone saw her. The women had not spoken of it since.

She'd been intimate with only one man, Onacona. He was gentle with her the first time they explored the mystery of love-making together; over time, they created their own rhythms and silent communication. Sex did not have the earth-moving passion she'd read about in books, but she felt safe and loved. Onacona cared for her, he cared about her. The intimacy was wonderful.

And now, the soldiers had taken that from her as well as everything else.

Feeling alone and ashamed, Catherine looked through the fence at the white men. Bitterness bubbled in in her heart. The soldiers strutted around like roosters, shirtless, trying to impress one another with what they thought were the qualities of being a man.

They aren't men, Catherine thought. *They aren't even human.*

For the first time since being forced from her home, Catherine was glad not to have her mother's Bible. She did not want to read about loving enemies. All she wanted was to hate.

"How's your father doing?"

Catherine jumped and let out a little shriek.

Waya held up his open palms. "I'm so sorry, Kasewini. I didn't mean to scare you."

Catherine put her hand over her pounding heart and swallowed.

"It's okay," she said, embarrassed. She looked at Jishnu.

"He's sleeping now," she said. "But he's still sick. The diarrhea's not getting better." She stroked the top of her father's head. "He's getting weaker."

Waya looked at Jishnu with concern. "I'm still trying to gather up some food and clean water for him…for all of us."

He looked out at the soldiers and grimaced.

"I want to yell at them, Kasewini. Tell 'em they are letting us die in here."

Catherine tended to her father. "They don't care. I know they don't."

"They can't all be so callous. Can they?"

"I haven't seen proof otherwise," Catherine replied. She looked back down at her father.

Waya studied her for a few moments before kneeling down next to Jishnu. "How are his wounds?"

"His back's healing nicely," Catherine replied. "Your medicine helped a lot. But the back of his head is still festering. I just used the last of the medicine."

"I'll make more as soon as I can find the roots." Waya examined the gash on Jishnu's head and frowned.

Waya sat down. Without thinking, Catherine moved away a little, afraid he would sense what had happened to her.

"I need to get out of this corral," he said. "There's just nothing I can use in here to make medicine or help your father. When they built this fort, they stripped the area of vegetation. I need to get to the forest." He wrapped his arms around his knees. "But, that's a long walk from here." He pointed to the others. "A lot of people are vomiting and have diarrhea like your father. Being around this filth is killing them. Many have already died." He looked at Catherine. "I do not mean to frighten you. I am sorry."

"I understand," Catherine said.

I know what is happening. I do not understand why.

He stood and touched Catherine's head in a fatherly way. "I'll be back to check on you."

Catherine watched him go then took in her surroundings, the improvised shelters, the naked children, the tattered clothing on the adults, the leering soldiers, the nauseating odor.

She wanted to turn away and cover her face when a young Cherokee girl caught her attention. The girl was standing near the fence talking to one of the soldiers. Catherine started when the man touched the girl's hair. The girl did not move. Catherine did not understand until the soldier handed the girl a package.

The young girl let the soldier kiss her hand, then scurried away. When the girl got close, Catherine stood.

"What are you doing?" Catherine asked.

The young girl tried to pass. Catherine blocked her way. "What's in the package?"

The girl's voice was soft, humiliated. "Food."

She tried to dart past. Catherine spun her around by the arm. She had intended on calling the girl out, to reveal her lurid behavior to the others, but then Catherine saw that the girl, though stunning, could not have been more than fourteen. Except for dark bruises on her arms, her skin was smooth and unblemished, her hair long and thick. When she blinked, her eyelashes looked like reeds on the riverbank blowing in the breeze.

Catherine let go of the girl's arm.

The youngster looked down in shame. "I'm sorry," she said.

Then she walked away.

Dumbfounded, Catherine watched the girl stumble through the crowd to rejoin her family – an older couple and four more children the eldest of whom was no older than nine or ten. The girl knelt down, opened the package, and put food into outstretched hands. She pulled a canteen from around her waist and let the little ones drink before she passed it to the woman.

The young girl neither ate nor drank.

Catherine shook her head at her own ignorance.

A beautiful soul in a terrible place, she thought – just another of the sixteen thousand Tsalagi people whose dignity continued to erode every minute of every day.

Catherine was faced with the truth of her situation.

What am I willing to do for my father – for Ayita.

"Well, hello again."

Catherine froze. She has not heard the voice often, but it was burned into her memory – just like the enormous top hat.

Elias smiled – a wolf perusing its dinner.

"Given any more thought to my offer of help?" he asked.

CHAPTER FIFTEEN

Thomas was awakened just before dawn by a report that several
Cherokee captives had escaped during the night. He dressed and
raced to Fort Newnan hoping to get there before Colonel Morse
would send Elias on the hunt.

Before entering the fort, Thomas slowed Silo to a trot. He found
Elias and his men already on their horses outside of the colonel's
tent.

"Why, Captain Edwards," Elias said. "What're you doin' here so
early in the mornin'?"

"I heard about last night," Thomas replied.

He inventoried Elias's men, most of whom he'd never seen. An
even twenty, they were dressed similarly – looked like they'd been
outfitted at the same place.

"I'll lend a hand," Thomas said.

Elias clucked his tongue. "That's very kind of you, Captain. But
as you can see, we've got everything under control. Why don't you
stick around here and get yer men moved into the fort like the
colonel ordered?"

Elias's men laughed.

"I'm one of the officers in charge," Thomas said. "I want to
make sure the Cherokees get back here safely."

Elias exchanged glances with his men.

"Besides, it's a chance for me to learn how you and your men work," Thomas said. "Maybe I can learn a thing or two. Don't worry, I won't get in the way or try to take over. I just know tracking the Cherokee won't be easy when we begin to head out west, so it would be good to watch someone as skilled as you while I can."

Elias rubbed his beard and studied the captain.

"That ain't necessary, Captain. Trackin' escaped Cherokee is why me and my men are here. We'll be along for the whole trek out west; don't you worry none. If anyone wanders off, well, *we* will take care of 'em. You can spend your time learnin' about soldierin'. I hear you have a few things to catch up on in the following orders department."

"I'd rather take advantage to learn from an expert such as yourself," Thomas said. "Really, I insist."

Elias hocked and spit. "Okay, Captain. Come along. But if you get lost, we ain't responsible."

He turned his horse and addressed his men.

"We got nineteen on the run. They got a good head start. Footprints are headin' northeast toward the forest – prolly there by now. We ain't got time to lose."

Elias shot a suspicious glance at Thomas, then spurred his horse. Thomas let everyone clear, then followed along. He never mentioned the tracking skills he'd picked up in Florida.

The pack met up with a couple of advance scouts at the edge of the forest. The grislier of the two bobbed his head at Elias.

"Looks like five different groups entered the forest at different times," he said. "Can't be sure how long ago, but they shouldn't be too hard to find. Not making much effort to cover their tracks."

"All right, listen up," Elias said. "Gabe, Cooper, Johnny, and Captain Edwards will go with me. The rest of you split up into groups. Find 'em...bring 'em back here. We'll meet before sundown."

The men wasted little time dividing into hunting parties and rode away. Thomas trotted over the Elias.

"What happens when we reconvene with the Cherokees?" he asked. "We taking them back to Newnan?"

Something akin to a grin snaked across Elias's face. "They'll get what's due," he said. "Don't worry none." Before Thomas could reply, Elias shouted to his group. "Head out, boys. Let's find us some runaways." Once again Thomas settled into the rear. He kept careful track of the other four who moved with surprising speed through the trees. After a mile or so, Elias pulled up and dismounted. He studied the ground for a few moments before motioning for all of his men to dismount. They huddled around him.

"Looks like our group decided to split up here," he said. "Johnny, follow that trail heading due north. See it there? Take Gabe and Cooper with you. Me and Captain Edwards will go east."

The men departed on foot, leading their horses by the reins. Elias watched them go, then turned and studied Thomas – a curious cat surveying a mouse.

"Lead the way," Thomas said, hoping he didn't sound anxious.

Elias said nothing. He finally grabbed his horse's reins and headed east. He moved deliberately. His head moved from side to side. Nothing escaped his attention…a partial footprint…a broken branch…a speck of cloth clinging to a tree.

Thomas never took his eyes off Elias.

Elias froze, knelt, and motioned to Thomas who lay Silo's reins over the saddle. On his way to Elias, Thomas jiggled his pistol to make sure it was not stuck in the holster. He knelt.

"Look here," Elias said without looking up. "They split up here. Looks like a single male went this way, while the rest went more to the east."

One of the footprints belonged to a child. Thomas's heart sank.

Elias was whispering. "These tracks are fresh. I'll follow the single. He'll be faster and more likely to fight back. You go after the rest. I'm willin' to bet the single is just a decoy – wants to help the rest of the family get away."

"How many are there?"

"No more than four or five," Elias replied as he stood up. "They've got at least one little one with 'em, so they should be easy to find."

Without another word, Elias led his horse away. Thomas watched until Elias was out of sight, then grabbed Silo's reins and went east.

As he began to make his way through the dense foliage, Thomas felt more and more conflicted about finding the escaped Cherokees. Finding them meant he'd have to take them back to Fort Newnan, but, if he didn't find them, how long could they survive in the forest, especially the children?

Thomas crept along distracted by his internal debate. After a while, he realized he hadn't seen any signs for quite a while. He stopped and heard…nothing. The silence was unsettling.

Frustrated and tired, Thomas decided to lead Silo to a creek not more than a hundred yards away. Silo plunged his nose into the water.

Thomas laughed. "You were thirsty."

Thomas stroked Silo's buckskin and decided to let him rest a bit and snack on what could be found on the forest floor. Thomas set off to explore.

Thomas followed the creek for several minutes before coming on a small cluster of broken branches. The breaks were fresh, less than twelve hours old. Convinced he was on the right trail once again, Thomas hurried back, climbed aboard Silo, and set off in the new direction until he came to the base of a small ridge.

He dismounted and moved ahead with caution. Each step awakened the battlefield soldier inside. Before he realized it, his pistol was in his hand, primed and ready. When he came to a clump of trampled grass. He froze.

When people are looking back, they sense someone is close.

When he knelt, hand feeling the earth for vibration, eyes up, he heard something… something unmistakable – the sound of another human breathing. The hairs on the back of his neck bristled. He looked around.

There!

Staying low, he moved towards a fallen log. When still ten feet away, he lowered himself and looked.

Eyes – the wide, brown, frightened eyes of a child.

He was about to say, "Show yourself," when—

"Whatcha got there, Captain?"

Thomas whirled – gun extended. Elias's hat was a little cockeyed but the man in black's stare never wavered. He was sitting on his horse and holding a rope. The other end was tied to the hands of an aging Tsalagi man. Elias secured the rope to his saddle horn and slid to the ground.

"Good way to get shot, Elias," Thomas said.

"Not worried 'bout getting' shot by you, Captain," Elias said. "You think too much – makes you slow." He took a step. "So, like I said, whatcha got there?"

"Raccoon," Thomas said. "Took one look at him and he skittered away. What are you doing here?"

"Looking for you, Captain," Elias said. "Been leadin' this bastard through the trees here for the better part of an hour. You ain't real stealthy-like. Sounded like a buffalo thrashing through the trees there. I thought you might be a bear. Was hopin' to shoot me a little dinner – somethin' special." He straightened his hat and tilted his head. "Ain't you supposed to be a bit more east of here? That's where the trail's at."

"Dies out," Thomas said. "When I couldn't find anything, I took Silo to the creek."

Elias scratched at his groin. "Fine lookin' animal there. Ever lookin' to get another one, I'll take him off your hands."

Hell will freeze over first, Thomas thought.

"I'll keep that in mind," he said.

Thomas scanned the ridge above their heads.

"There's a lot of good hiding spots here," he said.

Elias examined the ridge. "You sure you followed the trail all the way out?"

"I did."

"Well, shit," Elias said. "Figured I'd have me some little Cherokees by now – ain't got nuthin' to show for this afternoon but a sore ass." He looked at the ridge again. "You ain't looked up there?"

"Have not. Getting ready to. Head back to the rally point at the edge of the forest. I'll cover the ridge."

Elias smirked. "Tell you what, Captain. You look a little tuckered out. I'll sweep the ridge." He paused. "That is, if you don't mind takin' this one along with you." He motioned to the older man who had sat down.

"I think I can manage," Thomas said.

He walked over and untied the rope from Elias's saddle. The man, not nearly as old as he appeared from a distance, had obviously been beaten.

"You abuse this prisoner, Elias?"

Elias put his hand to his chest. "You wound me, Captain. I ain't no officer now, but I used to be. Do you think I would harm someone in my custody? Fella fell a couple of times. Probably been drinkin' – you know how they do."

Elias swung his right leg over the saddle. "See you later, Captain."

After Thomas was sure he was gone, he spoke to the man in Cherokee.

"Do you speak English?"

The man did not move.

"What's your name?"

Silence.

"I am Thomas Edwards, Captain Thomas Edwards."

Nothing.

"Look. I can't save you. But I can do something for the others. You have to let me help." Thomas pointed to the fallen tree. "They're hiding over there. I sent that man away. You have to trust me."

The man studied Thomas's eyes. He spoke in nearly perfect English. "My name is Rupesh," he said. "We will use your tongue. Your Cherokee is terrible."

Thomas could not resist a smile. "Done," he said. "Who are they?" He pointed to five children of various ages who were shimmying into the open.

"My children," Rupesh said. He pointed to the tallest. "Falcon, my son. He is seventeen."

"Can he survive in the wild?"

Rupesh squinted in disbelief. "Only a white man would ask if a Tsalagi youth can survive in his natural home."

"Sorry," Thomas said. "I cannot let you go. The man in the hat – Elias – he will know I helped your children if you disappear."

Rupesh said something to his children. The conversation was so fast, Thomas could not follow it, but he knew sarcastic laughter when he heard it.

"What did you say?"

"I told my children that only an arrogant white soldier would think a Tsalagi warrior could not escape from him. But I understand.

I agree to remain your prisoner." He waited for a moment. "Where should my children go?"

"East," Thomas said. He started to point, then thought better of it.

They know which way is east, you idiot.

"My grandmother has land," Thomas said. "It is about a day's walk—"

"So, silly hat man will just hunt them down there."

"Once they get to my family's land, they'll be safe. No one can take them from a private property – not even a soldier."

Bitterness spread across Rupesh's eyes. "They came onto *our* private land...they took our home...they killed my wife in the process...but they cannot violate the land of another white?"

Thomas had no answer.

"What's to keep your family from turning them in?"

"My grandmother, Miriam, lives on that land. She's a full-blood. Not Tsalagi, but Oneida – the turtle clan. She will take care of your children as if they are her own until you can return for them."

The suspicion never left Rupesh's eyes, but he gave instructions to Falcon. Thomas handed over his second canteen and two parcels of dried meat. He relayed directions through Rupesh.

"I do not understand why you are doing this, but I thank you," Rupesh said.

Thomas hung his head. "We are not all bad men."

Rupesh embraced his children, one by one. The little ones moved off in the direction Rupesh pointed. Just before he departed, Falcon turned.

"How will the Miriam lady know you sent us?" His English was as good as his father's.

Thomas reached into his breast pocket and took out a handkerchief. "She would take you in regardless, but I understand your concern." He handed Falcon the handkerchief his grandmother had given him. "Give this to the first person you meet on the land. They will take you to Miriam. It has my grandfather's initials on it. No one else would have it so she'll know I sent you."

Falcon bobbed his head and trotted away after his siblings.

§§

Twenty minutes later, they met Elias.

"Waste of time, Captain." he said. "Any luck on your end?"

"Nope. Let's head back."

Elias sucked his teeth and counted on his fingers. "Saw Bert a minute ago. Nineteen of them critters tried to escape. Only five of 'em got away – all children. You wouldn't know nothin' 'bout them, would you, Captain?"

"You saw what I saw."

"Did I?"

They rounded a bend and came on several of Elias's men. A group of Cherokees sat at the edge of the forest. Thomas counted thirteen. Each one of them had been abused.

"Looks like a lot of those people had issues with falling down, Elias," Thomas said.

"Guess they're a clumsy lot, Captain," Elias replied.

"I will report this when we get back."

"Do whatever you want," Elias said. "Your words 'gainst mine – and my men."

Thomas untied Rupesh and sent him over to the others.

"Okay," he said. "Back to the fort."

He heard a disturbing chuckle. Elias and his men all grinned – savage, vile, a show of missing teeth and sun-cracked lips. Elias slid to the ground.

"Got another idea," he said. "Got to make a little example, first. Bert – you pick 'em."

"Yes, sir."

Bert ambled back and forth in front of the captives, a man assessing livestock before an auction. He hoisted two men off the ground. Elias pointed to the older of the pair.

"Not him," he said. He turned and jabbed a finger at Rupesh. "That one."

Bert shoved the older man down. "Your lucky day, Pops," he said. He jerked Rupesh to his feet. "But, it ain't yours."

"What's going on?" Thomas asked.

Elias spiraled a rope over a tree branch. "Got to make sure these savages know they can't waltz off whenever they take a mind to it. I figger a couple of …ah…road signs might deter their wanderlust a little. Bert, string 'em up!"

Thomas's hand was on his pistol. "Like hell you will!"

Elias looked at Thomas with something akin to pity. "Look, Captain," he said, "I know all about your reputation for softness – how you couldn't bring yourself to do what needed to be done in Florida. Why don't you head on back to the fort for a cup of tea and let the men here do what needs doin'?"

The moment Thomas pointed his pistol at Elias, five pistols were pointed at him. The youngest, Gabe, aimed a rifle.

"Give me a reason, Captain," he said.

Thomas felt no fear.

"My orders from General Winfield Scott are to give safe conduct to these people all the way to the Indian Territory."

Elias exploded in a fit of laughter. "Don't see the good general anywhere in sight, Captain. He's too busy drinkin' whiskey at fancy parties to bother with what goes on out here."

Thomas squeezed his knees into Silo who walked closer to Elias. "I will blow your head off unless you order these men to stand—"

Something behind Thomas moved. He raised his arm in self-defense just before everything went black.

CHAPTER SIXTEEN

The pain in Catherine's empty stomach clawed at her, a constant reminder of Elias's visit before the sun had a chance to rise in the sky. He'd said good morning, then presented her a full canteen of water, several bundles of food, and some ointment and bandages for her father's wounds.

The sight of the supplies startled her. Unloving and expressionless, Elias held out the offering for a while. When she did not move, he tossed everything into the corral.

Catherine let them land at her feet.

He watched her for a few seconds then smiled when she made no effort to pick up the packages or thank him.

"I admire your stubborn spirit," he said with a chuckle.

Elias waited for a response. When Catherine refused to offer one, he shook his head.

"Let me know when you want more," he said then rode off towards the big white tent.

Once he was gone, she could hear the parcels calling to her. Elias had not asked her for anything so maybe accepting his help carried no obligation.

But that look in his eyes.

She stood all alone, looking down at the packages when the question came back to her. How far was she willing to go to see her daughter again or save her father?

The daily heartbreak of watching Jishnu fade away was wearing her down. He grew weaker by the hour.

It would be so easy to pick up everything Elias offered.

No one would know.

Well, almost no one.

Flashes of the young girl taking supplies from the soldier in exchange for something Catherine did not want to consider kept running through her head. She had been angry with the young girl, looking down at the supplies, she understood.

Elias stood in front of the large white tent talking with a bearded soldier who'd just arrived by horseback.

Elias had never tried to touch me. Maybe he's not like the other men. Maybe he won't ask for anything.

Jishnu rolled over and groaned.

Father needs so much.

She felt her nails digging into her palms.

Take the food and water and pay the cost later. Or refuse the help...

She refused to finish the thought.

She looked at her father, his pain-filled face still a portrait of resolute integrity. Without a word, she bent over, picked up the packages, and tossed them over the fence.

Elias mounted his horse. His men followed him to the gate at a full gallop. The soldier was with them. Catherine watched until long after the dust settled behind them. She looked at the supplies on the other side of the fence once more to see if the temptation was still there.

She felt nothing.

Why did that soldier seem so familiar?

§§

The sound of Silo's high-pitched whiney was far off but still managed to stir Thomas. The black abyss slowly gave way to light – then to blazing pain. Thomas's hand tapped his thigh for his sidearm.

It wasn't there.

He sat up, vomited, and lay back down. Gasping for air, Thomas looked at the sky and tried to remember what happened.

Thomas mumbled what he thought was "Silo, come," but the horse did not appear. He could hear him grunting and stamping the ground. Bleary-eyed and double-visioned, Thomas pushed to a sitting position, swallowed back the bile attempting to rise from his stomach, and squinted. He could make out the silhouette of a horse,

Silo he assumed, standing next to a tree about thirty yards away. Silo stared over, then tossed his head and snorted.

"It's okay, boy. I'm okay." Dizziness overwhelmed Thomas once again. He slumped back to the ground. "Maybe not."

He closed his eyes to shut out the excruciating light. He touched the back of his skull. His hand came back covered with blood. After a few deep breaths, he rolled onto his knees and staggered to his feet. All the while, he concentrated on a solitary, low-hanging cloud.

The sun was behind him to the west.

Odd, it was noon, last I remember.

With his hands on his knees, Thomas turned and studied the large white pine tree next to his horse. The details came into focus slowly.

Small branches near the top.

Leaves.

The towering crown rising from a sturdy trunk.

Branches.

Then something else. Two shapes suspended from a branch some fifteen feet up. Thomas's subconscious recognized the objects before his brain registered the horrible reality of a pair of bodies swaying like gruesome lanterns, rocked in eternal sleep by a gentle breeze.

"Oh God, no!"

He heard hoofbeats.

Horses.

The morning came into sharp focus.

Elias!

No matter how many times he pounded his hip, his pistol was not there, Thomas looked for a weapon. He picked up a stick about four feet long. While it helped balance him, he knew it wouldn't do much to stop a rifle ball.

The horses broke into the clearing. Thomas saw Roe's dirty face and collapsed again.

Roe slid from Ticket before the horse quit moving. "What in tarnation happened?"

"He did it!" Thomas said. He raised a weak arm and pointed toward Rupesh and another man hanging from the tree above Silo. "That son-of-a-bitch killed 'em."

"Who?"

"Elias. Elias hanged them." He looked at Roe, his eyes red with anger and grief. "Cut them down. For the love of God, cut 'em down."

Roe gestured. Several men raced to the tree. They let the bodies down with care while Roe tended to Thomas's head.

"Might need to cauterize this," Roe said.

He helped Thomas up. It was several minutes before the captain could stand without being overcome by the urge to vomit.

Roe pointed to Silo. "Someone get him loose."

The moment he was let free, Silo trotted to Thomas, Silo spun in circles and whinnied. The men backed up a few steps.

"Never saw him this worked up," Roe said.

"He saw everything," Thomas said. "Not sure what he understands, but I promise he knows it wasn't right."

Silo stomped on the ground as if in agreement.

Thomas hoped he didn't look desperate. The only thing keeping him upright was his grip on Silo's bridle.

"Easy, boy," he said. "It's okay. I'm okay."

It took several minutes for Silo to calm down enough for the captain to inspect him. The horse was fine, but he was breathing heavily, and his heart pounded like a drummer signaling battle.

Thomas leaned his head against Silo's and whispered. Silo's heart slowed, then returned to normal.

"That's a good boy," Thomas said. "You're a good horse." He stroked Silo's flank.

When Thomas pulled himself into the saddle, he found his pistol looped around the saddle horn.

"We need to find that degenerate," he said. He checked his pistol – loaded. The same was true of his rifle, still in the sheath. "Roe, give these men a proper burial. I'll take a few men and go on ahead."

"Where you going?"

"To find Elias. I figure Colonel Morse's tent is a good place to start."

When Silo moved, Thomas almost fell out of the saddle.

"I'm not so sure that's a good idea," Roe said.

"Why not?"

"Yer certainly in no condition fer an imbroglio."

Thomas did not feel like pointing out the misused, but impressive, word.

"I'm not looking for a fight, Sergeant. I just want some answers."

"Captain, did that blow to your head make ya forget you're a soldier? He's your commanding officer. You can't demand anything."

Thomas looked off into the direction of Fort Newnan. "Elias and his men killed two innocent people.

"They escaped," Roe said. "They weren't innocent—"

"They escaped from a hell of Colonel Morse's making!"

"The fort was a hell before Morse even arrived. Don't forget that."

"Why are you defending him?"

"I'm not. I'm lookin' out for *you*."

Thomas sat back in his saddle.

"Don't let yer emotions override yer brain, Captain. There's a lot of folks watchin' you."

Thomas thought of his father. "People *are* watching. That's exactly why I have to do this!"

Silo responded to the spurs with a leap forward. Thomas was halfway into the trees before Roe could respond.

"Dagnabbit!" Roe grabbed the two nearest soldiers. "Go after him. Try to keep things from escalating into a gun battle."

The men raced off after their captain. Roe unlashed a shovel from his saddle.

§§

Though an expert horseman, Thomas clung to the saddle horn with one hand to avoid being tossed aside by Silo's maniacal charge. The horse knew the way to the fort. All Thomas had to do was hang on long enough to get there.

There was still a little bit of light left in the evening sky when Thomas arrived. He slowed Silo down to a trot, settled the reins in one hand, rested the other on his thigh, sat with a ramrod back as he bounced through the gate.

Dorsey's men were no less disheveled than usual – no threat. Thomas kept an eye out for anything suspicious but arrived at the colonel's tent without incident. Except for an occasional shout from a card game, the place was eerily quiet.

Two soldiers stood post at the colonel's tent. Thomas dismounted and strode for the entrance. The guards crossed their rifles in his path.

"You can't go in, sir."

"You'll have to shoot me to stop me," Thomas said without slowing down.

"Sir, you don't understand—"

He walked inside with the guard on his heels.

"Where is he?"

"That's what I was trying to tell you, sir. He's not here. He said you'd be coming, sir. He instructed me to tell you to come for a drink in his parlor."

"Excuse me, soldier?"

"His parlor, sir."

Thomas stomped out of the tent, throwing the flap into the guard's face behind him. He looked around for a light – any sign of life. The guard caught up to him.

"It's the second building on the other side of the corral."

Thomas peered through the encroaching gloom and spotted a light shining through a window at the far end of the fort. He pointed.

"His parlor?"

"That's what he said, sir."

Thomas swung onto Silo and clicked.

"Let's go, buddy," he said.

Thomas felt like everyone in the world knew what was waiting for him inside of the building except him. Even the Cherokees inside of the corral were quieter than usual. They stared as he rode by, spectators of his impending demise.

Several scenarios flashed through the captain's mind. They all ended with a knife in his back or a bullet in his brain. He was beginning to doubt his decision when the two men Roe sent cantered through the front gate. He motioned for them to join him.

Thomas hitched Silo to a post outside of the colonel's parlor. The ground spun for a moment, but he took in some air and righted himself. Once his thoughts cleared and his stomach settled, he adjusted his belt and checked his pistol.

Satisfied, he turned his attention to the parlor.

The whitewashed door was chipped – bare in some places, just like the other buildings. Thomas grabbed the metal knob. The click echoed like a gunshot. With a hand on his pistol, Thomas stepped through the doorway and into an odd military wonderland.

Whale oil lamps, bright and relatively smokeless, hung from the walls and stood on various tables. Their light cast a wicked shadow on the wall as Thomas walked across the room. Like the colonel's tent, there were various pictures scattered about the meticulously appointed room, which encompassed the building's entire first floor. It was as elegant as any museum Thomas had ever seen. Thomas paid little attention to the paintings; they were not the primary attraction. Scratching the back of his head in amazement, Thomas pivoted to take in the astounding assortment of weaponry on display.

Twin sets of armor, completely intact, stared at each other from opposite corners. There was a line of small cannons against one wall.

Twelve pounders, Thomas thought. He remembered naval warfare class at the Academy. *Quarterdeck guns.*

Neat pyramids of cannonballs stood sentinel beside each gun. Thomas continued to gawk. There were firing armaments of every kind. He saw a wheellock pistol and recognized a Japanese Tanegashima rifle, flintlocks, even an arquebus. Thomas stepped to a glass-fronted case and admired what he recognized as Colt Paterson's revolver. With a five-shot cylinder and a gleaming ivory grip, it was the most beautiful handgun Thomas had ever seen.

The room overflowed with stunning displays of knives, swords, axes, maces, shields, helmets – a world-class collection of artifacts of death and destruction.

Dumbstruck, Thomas holstered his weapon. He stepped over to a table and noticed a war club, white and gleaming. Unable to resist he picked it up and swung it.

"Gorgeous, isn't it?"

Thomas whirled. Colonel Morse stood in the stairwell, a contented smile on his face.

"I imagine it could cause a lot of damage," Thomas said.

Morse nodded. "I suppose if handled correctly."

Thomas tested the weight in his hand. It was perfectly balanced for mayhem, heavier in the head, tapered to the grip.

"What is this, ivory?" he asked.

Morse shook his head. "Bone," he said.

"Must have been a big animal," Thomas said.

Morse's caustic laugh rattled off the walls,

"Indeed," he said. "The Seminole whose leg that was stood over six feet tall. I killed the red bastard with my own hands."

CHAPTER SEVENTEEN

"Don't ever do that again!"

Leotie hit Waya on the arm. He laughed and hugged his wife, who buried her head into his chest. His daughters wrapped their arms around his legs while Jeevan and his family greeted Waya. Catherine helped Jishnu sit up a bit taller, but she knew if she let go, he would collapse.

"We were worried about you," Catherine said after Leotie regained her composure and pulled away from her husband.

Waya looked at her and smiled. "Everything is fine."

"You could have been hurt," Catherine said. "Who would take care of all of us?" She blushed at her outburst. Waya squinted as if just realizing his recklessness.

"I'm sorry. I didn't mean to worry you all." He hugged his wife again. "Causing you grief was not my intention."

She kissed him softly.

"When we saw the others return and you were not with them, we thought... Did the others get away?"

A cloud settled over Waya's brow. He picked up his youngest, Charudutta, and gestured for everyone to sit down.

"I have much to tell you."

"How'd you get out of the corral?" Deepika asked.

Waya spoke in a strong, quiet voice – a master storyteller. "I waited until everyone was asleep. When the moon was at its highest, even the guards were asleep. I snuck through the fence and out of the fort."

"The guards were asleep?" Deepika asked.

"They were," Waya replied. "Most of their horses were asleep as well."

His daughters laughed.

"Weren't you afraid to go into the dark forest by yourself?" Charudutta asked.

"I know the ways of the forest, Little One," Waya said. "Much less terrifying than the ways of the white man."

Waya described how he hid in the shadows of the forest until early morning. After gathering all the healing roots and herbs he could carry, he found a hiding spot by a pool of water. His plan was to wait until nightfall then sneak back into the fort. His plans changed when he caught the smell of a horse and heard footsteps.

"Was it one of the trackers?" Jishnu asked, revived by a good story.

"Or the man with the hat?" Catherine asked.

"Believe it or not, it was a soldier, an officer," Waya replied. "I followed him and witnessed something remarkable."

Waya told them how the officer kept the man in black from finding Rupesh's children.

"He told the children how to get to his land, somewhere east of here," Waya said. "Then he gave them food and water."

Leotie's face grew stern. "You should not tell such tales, husband," she said.

"I do not believe a white man – a soldier – would help the Tsalagi."

Without rancor, Waya looked at his wife. "Have you ever known me to lie?" he asked.

"No husband," she said. "Please, continue."

Waya smiled and kissed her hand. "Rupesh said goodbye to his children and sent them off. So, once the captain and Rupesh left the area I decided to follow the children and make sure they were going to be okay. When they got far enough away from the white men, I made myself known to them."

"Were they scared?" Deepika asked.

"The little ones were at first," Waya replied. "But when I told them I had two daughters of my own (Waya reached out and messed his girls' hair) they were no longer afraid."

Deepika and Charudutta looked at each other and giggled.

"So, this soldier, he just let the children go on, alone?" Catherine said. Her voice was harsh. "They'd been better off coming back here where we could take care of them."

"Their father, Rupesh, was right there," Waya said. "He even *thanked* the officer for what he did."

"It was a foolish thing to do," Catherine replied.

"But they were trying to escape from here," Waya said. "Why would they want to come back?"

"To be with their father," Catherine said.

Waya looked down. "Ah, yes. Their father."

"What happened?" Charudutta asked.

"It is a bad thing," Waya said. "When I left Falcon and his brothers and sisters, I tracked the white men back to the edge of the woods. All the white men had their guns drawn. The officer was pointing at the man in black; the others were aiming at the officer."

Ever inquisitive, Charudutta blurted out another question. "Why would the white men fight each other?"

"The officer did not want anyone punished," Waya said. "But one of the men snuck up behind the officer and hit him in the back of the head. While he was unconscious, the other white men…the other white men hanged Rupesh and another man."

Everyone gasped.

Catherine snarled in her anger. "If the officer made the children go back, the white men wouldn't have killed their father."

"How could he have known, Kasewini?" Waya's voice was stern. "I think the man in black might have killed Rupesh *in front* of his children."

"Poor children," Leotie said. "They are probably lost."

Waya grinned, but only for a moment. "Falcon knows the forest better than I do. He had his father's knife and the supplies the officer gave him. The children will be fine. If I had not thought so, I would have brought them back to the fort myself."

"Even if they do make it to the officer's land, what good does it do?" Catherine asked. "The soldiers can just find them again."

Jeevan spoke for the first time. "It will not matter. Soldiers will not take something from another white man's land. The children will be safe."

Without a word, Catherine got up and walked away. Both Waya and Jeevan made to get up, but their wives stopped them with a look. After a while, Jeevan's spouse, Manjusha, wandered into the darkness along the line of Catherine's departure. She found Catherine with her elbows on the fence and her face in her hands.

"May I join you?" Manjusha asked.

Catherine jumped. She wiped the tears from her eyes. "Of course."

"You probably don't think much of me," Manjusha said.

"Why would you say that?"

Manjusha moved over and stood next to Catherine. "I've done nothing but dwell in my own self-pity and fear since you've met me. I haven't been much help to my husband, to my...children. Or to you."

"You've every reason to be sorrowful. We all do. Besides, you have no obligation to me at all. I'm not your family – "

"Oh, but you are," Manjusha said. "We're all family. We may have different mothers and fathers but we're all one."

Catherine didn't know what to say.

The two women listened to the drone of quiet voices within the corral.

Manjusha looked straight ahead. "They hurt you, didn't they – the soldiers?"

Catherine could not look at her.

"I can see it in you," Manjusha said. "A woman knows when another one has been wronged."

"I don't…I can't — "

"You have nothing to explain. But you must do something. You must forgive—"

"I can't forgive those animals."

"Not them." Manjusha touched Catherine's arm. "You must forgive yourself. You did nothing wrong."

Silent tears of bitterness, shame, and anger stained the ground at Catherine's feet.

Manjusha took Catherine's hand into hers. "If you don't forgive yourself, you will never love again – not anyone – not your father, not your daughter, not yourself. Your future depends on forgiving yourself."

"There's no future!"

"If you believed that, you would not weep. You would not feel. Do not let the darkness here conquer your spirit. Your loved ones need you."

Manjusha's eyes glistened even as she smiled. "We are both separated from our children, but the Tsalagi are a wonderful people. I know in my heart our children are being taken care of. I can *feel* it. We will see them again. So, who are you going to be when you see Ayita again? Are you going to allow bitterness to make you unrecognizable to your own daughter?"

Catherine could not speak. Mahjusha's soft voice penetrated her heart.

"Ayita is old enough to remember everything. She will have her own struggles. You will be powerless to help her, she will never find peace, unless you forgive yourself."

Catherine looked at Manjusha and saw a woman much wiser and stronger than she had imagined. She squeezed Manjusha's hand, and the two women walked back to the ones they loved.

CHAPTER EIGHTEEN

Thomas moved the club to his left hand and reached for his pistol.

"No need for that," Colonel Morse said. "We're the only ones here."

The colonel ambled over to a table and picked up a crystal decanter. He pointed to the club.

"He was a fierce warrior. He died a good death."

"If you say so," Thomas replied.

"God only knows what he would've done with *my* corpse." Colonel Morse poured himself a drink. "You know how those savages are. They use every part of the animals they kill." He gestured toward the bone. "Seemed like a good practice to me. Would you like a drink?"

Thomas blinked a few times, then replaced the bone with great care.

"Captain, a drink? Best bourbon you'll ever taste. I have it brought in from Kentucky from time to time. An old friend of mine makes it. Name's Elijah Craig – Baptist minister of all things." He cocked his head and looked at Thomas for a moment. "Oh well, suit yourself. The man's not much of a preacher but makes a hell of a whiskey."

Thomas clenched his fists. "I know what you're tryin' to do, and

Walks The Sky

it won't—"

"What do you think of my collection?" Morse asked. He gestured around the room with his glass. "Impressive, is it not?"

"Look—"

"You're lucky." The colonel held his glass near a lantern and checked the color of his drink. He turned the glass several times. Satisfied, he drained its contents, set it on a table, and strolled towards the captain like a man in a park on a lazy afternoon.

"I haven't been able to display my entire collection in a room like this for quite some time," Morse said. "It takes a lot of work to set everything up, you see. Don't have room for it everywhere I'm assigned. So, when I get a chance to see it all at once, I like to enjoy it as often as possible."

He paused in front of a painting of a proud Roman soldier sitting on a horse.

"I've been collecting these things for years," he said. "It was something I started to do when I was a young man. Younger than you even. Didn't consider myself a collector for a long time. I just appreciated fine art…and fine weapons."

Colonel Morse moved on from the painting with the same casual pace.

"A lot of what you see here was used against me or my men at some point. Every time I conquered an enemy, I kept a little souvenir. Eventually, as I found myself blessed with sufficient

194

capital, I began to acquire more exotic pieces. I didn't have a master plan...but here we are."

"Where's Elias, Colonel?"

Colonel Morse walked past Thomas without looking at him.

"That's the only downside of having such a large collection, finding a suitable place in which to appreciate it. I don't have a home, you see – too much travel. I think homes are cumbersome when you're a soldier. Much like a family can be. Wouldn't you agree?"

"Elias? Where is he?"

Colonel Morse meandered away from the captain towards an easel.

The easel faced away from the captain. It held a canvas, about three feet wide and two feet tall and covered with a gray sheet. Paintbrushes of different sizes and shapes sat on a small table next to the easel as well as rags spattered with a variety of colors. Everything had been arranged on what Thomas recognized as a regulation U.S. Army tent (unassembled).

Interesting drop cloth.

The colonel lifted the sheet.

"May I share something with you? A piece I've been working on. No one else has seen it. You are a man of parts; I would value your opinion."

Curious, Thomas scanned the room once more then walked over

to where the colonel was admiring his creation. Expecting a battle scene like the one hanging outside of his father's office, Thomas was surprised. A thin red line ran vertically through the center of the painting. The rest of the composition was a garbled mixture of black and white, broken here and there by various shades of gray.

"I've been working on it for months," Morse said. "Can't seem to get it quite right."

Morse's face reflected angst. He appeared on the verge of tears. Thomas studied the painting again.

Once he quit focusing on the distraction provided by the scarlet line, Thomas could see a small boy, five or six, kneeling all alone in an open field.

A field of flowers? Hard to tell with no color.

Muted clouds dotted the sky. Dark, shadowy trees loomed in the background.

The boy's arms hung by his sides; his hands, empty and open, lay just in front of his knees on the ground. The boy's head was down, so Thomas couldn't see his face, but he didn't need to. It was obvious the boy felt helpless and had been crying.

What is the red streak? It bisects the child's chest.

"I can't remember if the trees had leaves or not," Colonel Morse said. He rubbed the center of his chest as if massaging an old wound. Then he closed his eyes and shook his head.

Thomas took a step back. He palmed the butt of his pistol.

"Very interesting, Colonel. But my initial question remains unanswered. Where's Elias?"

"Ah," Morse said. He looked at Thomas for a moment with no expression then cocked his head. "We return to the inquisition."

He waddled away, forgetting about the painting or the captain's opinion of it. His pugnacious arrogance returned.

"Did I ever tell you about the first battle he and I were in together?"

"I don't care. Where is he?"

"I'll never forget it. We were in Florida, fighting those godless savages. They are like children, really. Innocent and trusting at first – eager to please. But the moment they do not get what they want, they unleash a hell of uncontrolled emotions. They are, all in all, a deplorable lot, as you well know." He refilled his glass and took a sip. "We were on the last leg of a five-day march, dog-tired, thought we were safe when we were ambushed. We were hopelessly outnumbered."

Colonel Morse strolled to a table and fingered a wicked-looking dagger.

"It was madness at one point," he said. He stared at the far wall, his mind lost in the gore and glory of days past. "Close quarter combat – hand-to-hand. I'm sure you can relate."

He did not wait for a response. "Though they had a great number of men, they were not well organized. So, when the cowards turned and ran, we gave chase. Apparently, Elias got separated from the main group. We rounded a copse of trees and there he was in all his sartorial glory – Elias, complete with his idiotic hat, surrounded by six Seminoles."

"So, you saved his life?" Thomas hoped he did not sound too interested.

"On the contrary. We abandoned him to his fate. We were engaged up to our eyeballs, outnumbered. Still, my men made a brave stand, and we repulsed the godless heathen even though we took heavy casualties."

Morse swirled his bourbon and appeared to offer a short prayer. Thomas, weary of the theatrical performance rolled his eyes.

"Out with it, Colonel."

"About thirty minutes after the last of the Indians skittered away like cockroaches, Elias emerged from the swamp covered in blood – crimson and black from head to toe, I tell you. I wasn't sure how he kept walking given his blood loss."

Colonel Morse polished off the bourbon and smacked his lips.

"Upon closer examination, however," he said, "I realized all he needed was a washbasin and some soap. Save for a few scratches, he was unscathed. The blood all belonged to the six Seminoles he dispatched single-handed."

Thomas was impressed, despite his disdain for Elias. The colonel shook his head.

"To this day, I have no idea how he did it. He had no shot, no powder. To my knowledge, his only weapon was a small pocketknife. But since that day, I have made sure he remained under my command."

"Impressive story," Thomas said. "Bravery aside, he is still without morals. And since he works for you, I am sure you know where he is."

Morse's expression mixed confusion with pity. "I'm not sure you want to find him, Captain."

"Because?"

Morse reached for the decanter, thought better of it, and lowered himself into a nearby chair. "My dear boy, did you not listen to my tale? What do you think will happen when you find him? Are you going to arrest him? Take him prisoner? Kill him? For what, injuring your sensibilities?

"He killed two innocent men."

"He executed a pair of dangerous escapees," Morse said. "They were men who undoubtedly attempted to involve others in their seditious and dangerous enterprise."

"Our job is to escort *all* the Cherokee." Thomas felt the heat rising in his neck. The pistol on his hip whispered, *This man needs to die. You'd put down a mad dog.*

The colonel chuckled. "You are precisely like all pigeon livers in Washington." He adopted a mocking tone. "Don't hurt the Indian.

Treat them humanely." This time, he succumbed to the temptation for a third bourbon. "Hell, if I had my way, we wouldn't be escorting them anywhere. We would simply wipe them off the face of this earth."

"Pretty much your stock in trade from what I hear."

Morse's head snapped back a little. "Soldiers kill when necessary."

"By reputation, you have a broad interpretation of 'when necessary,'" Thomas said.

Time to ease back a little, he thought. *Scoring debate points will not help the ones left in the corral.*

Thomas let silence fill the room. He looked at one art piece, then another. He picked up a sword. He appreciated the fine Spanish craftsmanship. The heft and balance were perfect. He imagined what it would look like buried up to its hilt in Morse's chest. Then, he put it down.

"Why'd you invite me here, Colonel?"

"I know everything that goes on in my camp. I heard you visited the company surgeon yesterday evening."

"I did."

"I also heard you suggested he ease up on his whiskey consumption."

"My exact words were, "Quit drinking and start helping the Cherokee, or I will shove that bottle so far up your backside that you'll need a twenty-mule team to pull it out.'"

The corner of Morse's mouth twitched. "My, my, Captain. You do have a way with words."

Thomas stood and looked around the room one last time before addressing the colonel.

"You tell that piece of trash Elias to stay out of my way."

Morse fired off a mock salute. "Oh…you can be sure I will."

Thomas slammed the door on his way out and Morse walked over to his painting. He admired it one more time, covered it, and began extinguishing the lanterns. Elias stepped out from behind a suit of armor.

"Let's just kill him and be done with it," he said.

"Not yet," Morse said.

"I can have it done before he pulls off his boots tonight."

Morse placed a hand on Elias's shoulder, saw the withering gaze, and removed it.

"Elias," Morse said, "you are a blunt instrument. I think of myself as a virtuoso performer. You use force; I employ finesse."

"Only because I play the hammer to your carpenter."

"Point taken. I promise, if the young captain strays too far afield…well, it's the wilderness. Accidents do happen."

CHAPTER NINETEEN

Three men shouldered their way through the crowd of stultified Cherokees. Instinct took over and Jishnu pushed up on one elbow – anything to protect his daughter.

"It's okay, father," Catherine said. "There's nothing we can do to stop them."

The old man moved as close as he could, and Catherine took his hand.

It's not you they want, she thought.

These were the men she'd seen with Elias outside the General Store. It seemed so very long ago. They said nothing at first but stood over Catherine and Jishnu like vultures waiting for a wounded animal to die.

After a while, the youngest, a grown man with the face of a twelve-year-old, knelt. The stench from his torch was a fetid as his breath. But his soft voice was kind and genuine.

"You Kasewini?" he asked. "Catherine?"

Catherine looked at the other men holding torches and said nothing.

"Am I saying it wrong?" the young man asked. His tone remained kind and curious. "Kasewini? That's you, right?"

Catherine looked at the young face for a long time and finally nodded.

"Wonderful," he said. "The name's Gabe." He stood and extended his hand. "We need you to come with us. Someone wants to speak with you."

Catherine shivered despite the muggy air.

"Please don't be scared." Gabe bobbed his head a grinned. "No harm will come to you. I promise."

Catherine glanced at Leotie, Waya and the others. Her fear was reflected in their worried looks but she knew she didn't have a choice in the matter. Catherine said a quick, silent prayer, took Gabe's hand, and stood. "This way, ma'am," he said. He stepped into the middle of the other four men, all of whom carried torches and pistols.

One of the men barked orders. "Out of the way. Stand clear!"

Catherine's eyes darted back and forth at the partially lit faces. She saw concern but she noticed something else. Every last woman and girl had the same expression: "I'm glad it's not me."

This time she was not bound and gagged, but Catherine had no doubt about what was about to happen. She would return in several hours ravaged, beaten, and violated. At least this time, there were several hundred witnesses.

Elias's men treated her with gentle courtesy. Every last one of them tipped his hat. One of them held her hand and helped her climb through the fence. There were no groping hands, no lewd comments.

Once she cleared the barricade, they allowed her time to gather herself before continuing on the way.

The smudgy odor of charred lamp oil clogged her nostrils – she was partially blinded by the ring of fire surrounding her. She was vaguely aware of tents and other people. She caught a brief glimpse of the moon and a cooking fire, but she knew nothing of the direction they were taking or their destination.

No one hurried her. They were not marching; it was more of a stroll. Catherine saw a large gate rising up in front of them. Before she realized it, they had exited the fort and were walking into the unknown darkness. No one spoke. Their footsteps provided the only accompaniment to their journey.

They headed towards a light a short distance away. Catherine recalled a small grove just outside the fort. She'd seen it on the day they arrived – an oasis of beauty in the midst of desolation.

As they neared the grove, the source of the light became apparent: a series of small fires spaced evenly, like a pathway. Her curiosity stirred. So did hope…and immediate resentment.

There's nothing hopeful here – these small fires cannot get rid of the darkness.

When they reached the edge of the grove, Catherine saw a clear path through the trees. Evenly-spaced small torches marked a distinct route. Despite her trepidation, Catherine caught herself thinking, *This is quite lovely.*

Elias's men kept their distance and did not speak; Catherine had the momentary impression of being alone in a magical place where there were twinkling light and no pain.

The illusion deepened when she got to the end of the path and stepped into a glade. A crystal clear moon lent sublime light and was added by dozens of more lanterns, some on stakes driven into the ground, others hanging from trees at the edge of the small grove. The dreamlike surroundings made Catherine stop, mouth open and eyes wide.

The fantasy ended abruptly.

"How do you like it?"

Elias!

Catherine crossed her arms over her chest and stepped back so fast she stumbled a little.

"It's okay," he said. "It's okay." He showed her his hands. No weapon, only a bunch of wildflowers.

"Thought you might like these," he said.

She hesitated. He stretched his arm a little, proffering the blossoms. Catherine took a quick step forward, snatched the bouquet, and retreated.

Elias pointed to the decorations.

"So, do you like it?"

He surprised Catherine by keeping his distance from her.

"I did all of this just for you."

He ambled in a circle around Catherine, who turned in time with him, unwilling to turn her back on him.

"Yes," Catherine said.

She immediately bit her tongue in disgust.

Elias looked down, a shy schoolboy working up the nerve to ask for a dance. Feeling encouraged, Elias drew a little closer with each revolution.

"When I was a boy," he said, "my mother came home one day from whorin'. One of her men gave her a little puppy – he was gonna kill it 'cause it was the runt, but Mamma talked him out of it. She brought him home to me, so I wouldn't be alone at night while she was entertainin'. We lived way out of town – no one around for me to play with."

The tenderness in Elias' voice disarmed Catherine. He continued to circle, getting closer with every revolution.

"Cutest thing you ever saw. Little brown nose – all different color fur – a mutt just like me. I called him Joseph, on account of all his colors, you know, like the fella in the Good Book with the fancy coat. Joey, what a good little boy."

Although Elias was within an arm's reach of Catherine, he made no overt move.

"He was a spunky little thing, like you. We played all the time. He sat next to me while I fished. Then we'd swim together – good little paddler, that Joey. He liked to play fetch in the water. I threw a stick – he'd go and get it. I tried to keep up with him when he chased squirrels, but he was too fast. He loved to run."

Elias was face to face with Catherine. His hand stroked her arm. She shivered but did not move.

"He slept in the crook of my arm every night. I loved him. I can love, you know – just like I loved Joey."

Elias moved very close. He put his hand on Catherine's immediately rigid shoulder. His hot breath blew against her neck and ears. She expected to smell liquor on it, just like the soldiers who raped her, but his breath was clean with a light whiff of mint.

"Would you like to dance?" Elias asked.

Elias began to hum – a slow, eerie tune, one Catherine had never heard.

This is absurd.

She half expected someone to jump from behind a bush and yell, "Got ya!" All she heard was the chirping of insects and the faint buzz of Elias's voice.

CHAPTER TWENTY

"I can't believe Colonel Morse had the gall to set up the chuck wagon for his men right next to the corral where people are starving."

Roe looked at Thomas. "You're eyes are not prevaricatin'. The colonel's got the heart of a timber rattler."

Thomas fought the urge to set everything on fire.

"The doctor's going to start seeing patients today," he said. "Let's keep him away from Colonel Morse as long as we can."

"Will do."

Thomas and Roe walked towards the corral where they had agreed to meet Dr. Carlton Lambert.

"So, what about the sanitation?" Thomas asked.

"About as good as can be expected. I split the corral into sections like you suggested – one squad per section." Roe let out his patented "chipmunk titter" laugh. "The boys are something else. They've seen more blood and guts than most town butchers but the minute I put them on pee patrol, they acted like they were gonna die."

Thomas shrugged. "The logic of a soldier, I guess. What about water?"

"We'll start takin' the healthy ones down to the creek today. The old and infirm – another situation. We ain't got enough canteens but we'll figger something out. Everybody in there's ready to help."

"Do the best you can," Thomas said. "Organize some hunting parties. We need food for these people."

"Supply wagons are a day or so past due," Roe said.

"How often are they scheduled?" Thomas asked.

"Hard to say – but they should be here any time."

Once they reached the corral, Thomas leaned his elbows on the fence. "These people need a hell of a lot more than something to eat and a place to relieve themselves."

A tall, slender man balancing oval eyeglasses on the end of a hawkish nose approached.

"Captain Edwards?"

"Ah, Doctor Lambert."

Squinting against the sun, Lambert shook Thomas's hand.

"My aide, Sergeant Bickford," Thomas said.

"Nice to meet you, Doctor," Roe said.

Lambert offered a shy wave. Thomas motioned towards the corral. "How do you want to do this?"

"I've been thinking a lot about this. Is there a designated space for the sick and injured?"

Thomas resisted the urge for sarcasm. "No," he said.

"All right then. Let's do battlefield triage. Maybe we could start cordoning off the sick – to minimize the chances of an epidemic."

Too late for that, Thomas thought. But he said, "Good idea."

"Might I have a translator for those who do not speak English?" Lambert asked.

Roe was calling over his shoulder before Thomas asked. "I'll get Fitzwalter."

Thomas gestured towards the corral. "After you, Doctor. I'll do my best to translate until the expert arrives."

Thomas followed the doctor through the fence. On the other side, the dust seemed thicker, and the fog of misery made it harder to breathe.

Lambert spotted a mother rocking her small child. The little girl appeared lifeless. Almost as soon as he knelt, Thomas heard whispers of "medicine man" filter across the corral. By the time Lambert was finished with his examination, a crowd had gathered. They were friendlier than the doctor had expected, and most seemed aware of his efforts on their behalf.

When Roe returned, Thomas stepped aside and let Fitzwalter do his duty. Thomas and his aide remained. They helped as needed, moving patients, restraining a few who needed to have a boneset, and organizing the chaos as much as possible.

"This is a catastrophe, sir," Doctor Lambert said. "Do you have anyone experienced with battlefield wounds?"

"Sure," Thomas said. "Roe, get Sergeant Brooks and Sergeant Todd. Not sure why I didn't think of them."

The moment the two men arrived Lambert put them to work. Brooks and Todd handled triage. They separated the sick – those with the grippe, dysentery, smallpox, and consumption – and then ranked those who needed to see the doctor for injuries.

Fitzwalter and Roe went with the sergeants. Thomas stayed with Lambert to learn as much as he could in case Morse commandeered the doctor for his own men. After a while, the team found its rhythm.

Well into the afternoon Thomas forced Doctor Lambert to take a break and eat.

"You have to take care of yourself so you can take of them," Thomas said.

Doctor Lambert finally agreed and sat with Thomas against the split rail fence.

"You're a good doctor," Thomas said. "You've done a lot of good today."

"I'm ashamed of myself," Lambert said. "Should have been doing this long ago. Got caught up in feeling sorry for my lousy circumstances and tried to drown myself in a bottle."

"What's done is done," Thomas said. "Concentrate on what happens going forward."

Lambert took a long slug from a canteen. "How long before you move them out?" Thomas perused the sea of faces. "About a month. Think we can make a difference."

"The improved sanitation will help – so will more water. You've got to figure out how to get food for—"

Roe skidded to a stop. Dust showered Thomas and the doctor.

"Come with me," Roe said.

Thomas was on his feet before the dust settled. "What?"

"No time, Captain," Roe said. "Just bring the doctor and come on!"

CHAPTER TWENTY-ONE

Exhausted from her night of dancing with Elias, Catherine struggled to hold her father's head up enough for Waya to try and get him to drink some water. The spark of life in Jishnu's eyes was all but gone in spite of Catherine's constant vigil and Waya's efforts to treat him.

Waya shook his head and motioned for her to lay his head back down on her lap.

"I'm sorry, Kasewini," Waya said. "He's just not responding to anything we do." Waya sat on his knees and studied Jishnu. "If only I could have found something to close up that wound." He looked around and sighed. "Still, without a steady supply of food and water there's little hope of him regaining his strength."

Catherine thought he was about to cry.

"I'm not sure I can do much more for him," he mumbled.

Catherine held her father's head in her lap. She did not bother to wipe away her tears.

"That wound on his head is just too…" Waya trailed off.

"Maybe the soldiers' doctor can help," Jeevan said. "He climbed the fence earlier today down on the other end. He's been treating people all day."

"Maybe," Catherine said.

"Rumor has it the soldiers are letting people go down to the creek for water," Jeevan said.

"That'd be wonderful if it's true," Waya said.

"I'm sure it's just a rumor," Catherine said. "The soldiers don't care about us."

"I saw the white doctor myself," Jeevan said. "There's an officer with him. They will be here soon. Have faith, Kasewini,"

"Faith?" Catherine asked. "In what?"

Catherine saw something in Waya's eyes. Suspicion? Pity? She did not know. Her mind jumped back to the night before.

She had not told anyone anything. Surely everyone thought she'd been assaulted again. She saw no reason to say otherwise.

No one would believe me.

Elias kept Catherine until well past midnight. He did not make any advances, but his constant presence felt to Catherine like trying to breathe while someone was sitting on her chest.

In the glade, surrounded by the fires of dozens of torches, Elias placed his cheek on hers and danced. He hummed the entire time – a mournful tune – over and over. Whenever Catherine tried to pull back, Elias squeezed her harder.

"Don't fight me, darlin'," he said.

Her feet hurt, but Elias kept humming. Her body ached; he kept dancing. Catherine lost all sense of time. They danced until the torches burned out and the fires were reduced to embers. When there was barely enough light to see one another, Elias stopped swaying. He cupped her face in his hands and kissed her.

"Until next time," he said. Then he disappeared into the shadows.

Almost immediately four torches blazed on the pathway. Gabe and the others encircled her with their firelight and led her all the way back to her spot in the corral. They never said a word.

Once she was back inside, she fought her desire to curl into a ball – to hide from the world. She checked on Jishnu. His breathing was worse. She woke Waya who watched Jishnu while Catherine took a fitful nap until just after dawn.

Jeevan's voice brought Catherine back. "Have faith in yourself and in your people."

Waya left to search for food and water. After a while, he returned.

"I found a little food," he said. "It's not much but let's try to get him to drink first." He lifted Jishnu's head and held a mostly empty canteen to his lips. Jishnu struggled to chew the measly strip of jerky but managed to swallow it after a while.

Jishnu lay back, exhausted. Waya covered him with a blanket.

"The soldiers are working their way over here," Waya said. "The doctor is with them."

A wave of energy rippled through the corral. With it came the sounds of shuffling feet and pleading.

"Over here…"

"Do you have any bandages?"

"Help me, please."

When Catherine saw the folding caps of the soldiers weaving ever closer, she felt her throat tighten. She froze – a deer unsure whether to remain motionless or to bolt for cover. By the time she could breathe normally, the soldiers were within a few yards. She noticed they had no sidearms – no sabers – no pistols.

While Catherine quivered, Waya sprang into action.

"Come…please come. My friend needs help. His head is badly injured. Just a moment of your time, please."

Before Catherine could move, one of the soldiers was on both knees and looking at the back of Jishnu's head.

"My God," the man said.

Catherine closed her eyes and began to pray. When she opened her eyes, a dirty face stared at her from no more than two feet away. She yelped.

The face laughed, then spoke. "It's all right, ma'am. All women tend to react that way when they see me in close proximity. Don't worry. I'm as harmless as I am homely,"

The man attending to Jishnu spoke. "Roe, look at this," he said.

The dirty-faced soldier moved towards Jishnu.

"Look at the back of his head," the kneeling soldier said. "They said the militiamen did this when they rounded him up. Looks like someone poked him right regular with a bayonet. See here?"

To Catherine's surprise, the dirty-faced soldier scowled and turned red. "Bastards," he said. "What can you do?"

"Not a damn thing," the kneeling man said. "Ain't got the learnin'. Get the doc over here – pronto!"

"Got it," "Roe" replied. "And the captain needs to know."

"Yep."

After the dirty-faced soldier ran away, the other man looked at Catherine.

"I ain't no doctor," he said. "I just look at people and figger if they need help. You understand?"

His words tried to penetrate Catherine's confusion, but most of what she heard was garbled – a voice coming through wads of cotton batting. Before long, four men walked through the parting sea of curious bystanders. A man carrying saddlebags stood over Catherine.

"I'm Doctor Lambert," he said.

Catherine registered no response. The doctor looked at Jishnu's head.

"Oh, my." His eyes locked onto Catherine. "How long has it been like this?'

Waya answered the question. The doctor waved his hand in front of Catherine's face.

"Miss…miss?"

When Waya spoke to her in the native tongue, Catherine snapped back to the present. "Kasewini," Waya said. "the doctor needs you to get out of his way."

Feeling outside her body – as if watching everything from above – Catherine stood and shuffled a little way. Her gaze never left the doctor's hands. She watched him probe at Jishnu's scalp, pour sips of water down his throat, check his forehead for a fever – all with a delicate, concerned touch.

Once again, the dirty-faced man was inches from her nose.

"Excuse me," he said. "Miss?"

Catherine looked up from the doctor's hands.

"My name's Sergeant Bickford," he said. "Everyone calls me Roe."

Why are you telling me this? All I care about is if my father is going to be okay.

"I want you to meet someone," Roe said.

He touched the shoulder of a bearded officer. "This is the captain."

She acknowledged the captain with a nod but didn't look at his face, her focus now returned to the surgeon's ministrations. In her periphery, she saw the officer step toward her.

"I'm sorry about your father," the officer said.

The voice.

Scenes flashed behind her eyes, scenes from a past so far removed from the present hell as to seem unreal – impossible...

...a handsome young man smiling under a cloudless, blue sky...

...sounds of laughter rising from a field of flowers and tall, green grass...

...quiet walks, hand in hand...

...was there a kiss?

Catherine's head snapped up.

"Thomas?"

CHAPTER TWENTY-TWO

Everything in Thomas's world stopped. He heard nothing but the
blood whooshing through his ears…he no longer smelled the foul
corral…the only thing he saw was the woman in front of him clad in
a sack of a dress three times too large for her petite frame.

Dirt caked her feet from her toes to her ankles. Her long, dark
hair gathered in dirty clumps around her shoulders was generously
salted with dust. Purple bruises covered her arms; her shoulders
drooped with fatigue. But her extraordinary eyes burned with an
intensity he remembered from long ago.

She had been – and still was – the most beautiful creature he had
ever seen.

The girl in the sketchbook, now the woman in front of him,
spoke only one word but it moved his heart to the point of breaking:
"Thomas."

He had not looked for her at the fort. Though he longed to see
her again, he loathed the possibility of finding her in this squalor.

"Catherine."

They stared at one another for an awkward beat or two.
Catherine was transported to another place and time – a happier, less
fetid location where the air was clean and the future promising. Then

her father moaned, and reality buried her fanciful memories under the avalanche of reality and anger.

Her smile disappeared. She was dirty, disgusted with herself and disgusting to others. What little humanity she'd possessed at the beginning of the long march to the fort had disappeared in the middle of a dark night along with her tattered dress. She felt foolish for being forced to dance with Elias in the clearing while he hummed a creepy tune until the fires of his manufactured magical moment burned out. She was certainly unworthy to harbor happy memories of past love and long ago kindness.

Forgetting about her father, Catherine ran away.

"Catherine!"

Thomas took a step of pursuit. Two Cherokee women popped to their feet and stood in his way. Once it was clear Thomas would go no farther, the women turned and walked after Catherine.

Oblivious to the exchange, Doc Lambert tugged on Thomas's trouser leg. "Captain, this man has to get out of here. Permission to move him to the fort's medical tent?"

Now on his toes and trying to spot Catherine, Thomas waved a dismissive hand. "Granted," he said.

Unable to see where Catherine had gone Thomas turned his attention to the injured man. When he dropped to his knees, all the air in his lungs seemed to disappear.

He remembered two old friends, a dignified Cherokee elder and Thomas's own grandfather, how they often talked into the wee hours of the morning. Thomas listened to them as long as he was allowed to remain. Jishnu was almost a part of the family. He took Thomas on long walks and showed the eager lad the wonders of the forest. He unveiled the ways of woodland creatures. He taught Thomas how to listen to the Earth, how to tell a rainstorm was coming hours before it struck, how to stalk a deer undetected, how to stay downwind of predators, Jishnu knew the secrets of life in the wild, and he shared them with a wide-eyed, eager Thomas Edwards.

In a matter of moments, the monstrosities of Fort Newnan had changed from a professional embarrassment to a personal affront.

"Um, no…no," Thomas said. "Colonel Morse would never allow a Cherokee to share space with his soldiers. Roe!"

"Captain."

"Set up a tent as far away from this…this sewer as possible. Use our company's equipment – nothing belonging to Fort Newnan. Understand?"

"Yes, sir."

He turned to Sergeant Todd.

"Keep triaging these people," he said. "I'm sure this man isn't the only one who needs a surgical tent."

He looked towards the place where Catherine had disappeared, then walked out of the corral in the opposite direction.

§§

Catherine ran until she made it to the other end of the corral. Out of breath, she turned to see if anyone was behind her. Overwhelmed, she collapsed in a heap against the fence and buried her head in her hands. Her splintered mind streamed in a million different directions. She could not stop the swirling thoughts, nor could she get rid of Thomas's voice echoing in her head.

Catherine…Catherine.

She bounced her head against the fence post hoping the stop the sound…to cleanse the memory…to forget what had just happened. She did not notice Leotie and Manjusha until they sat next to her.

"Kasewini?" Leotie asked.

Catherine jumped. Leotie put her hand on Catherine's shoulder.

"It's just us," she said.

Catherine leaned her head against Leotie's shoulder.

"I should not have left my father," she said. "I have to go back."

"Waya and Jeevan are with him," Leotie said.

Manjusha and Leotie exchanged looks as if each were prompting the other to speak. Manjusha cleared her throat.

"You ran from the white captain?" she asked.

"Yes."

"Was he one of the men…" Manjusha could not finish the accusation.

"No," Catherine said. The woman strained to hear her. "He would never..."

"You know the captain?" Manjusha asked.

"No." Catherine wiped her tears away. "I knew the boy he once was."

"So, you met a long time ago," Leotie said.

Catherine explained about Thomas's grandparents and the time he lived with them. She talked about Jishnu's friendship with Oscar and the tutelage of Thomas.

"At the beginning, I didn't go with my father," Catherine said. "I felt it was not my place to go. They fished or hunted. I stayed at home and took care of things. One day, my father suggested I come with him. He thought Thomas and I might be friends."

Catherine pushed out a weak smile.

"I didn't want to go," she said. "I had no interest in meeting a well-to-do white boy from Savannah, but my father spoke so highly of Oscar and Miriam, that I finally decided to go. I was convinced he would be a spoiled brat. Instead, I found a kindred spirit."

"Love?" Leotie asked.

Catherine shook her head. "No, not at first," she said. "There was a connection, but it was more like we were meant to meet. I knew the path of our spirits were supposed to intersect."

"But your feelings for one another grew," Manjusha said.

Catherine looked down at her dirty hands. "They did," she replied. "Over time. In the beginning, I don't think either one of us even knew what romantic love was other than what we read in books or heard in stories. We just enjoyed being together. Maybe part of it was we were close to the same age. Everyone else was much older or much younger."

The smile grew – broader – more genuine.

"He was funny," she said. "and smart. He wanted to learn as much as he could about me and our people. He wanted to know all about our traditions. He even begged me to teach him our language." Catherine laughed in spite of herself. "He was so bad at it. It was hard for him to say our words correctly, but…he never gave up trying."

She blew out an elongated breath.

"He didn't care how bad he was," she said, "and I teased him without mercy. To his credit, he never stopped trying. He wanted to know everything about the Tsalagi. I truly appreciated that about him. And he wasn't the spoiled brat I thought he'd be. He worked just as hard in the garden as anyone else. He never took advantage of his position."

Catherine put her hands over her face and coughed, mostly to hide the tears building in her eyes.

"He was a good person. After about a year after we met, I realized I'd fallen in love with him. It wasn't something I was looking for or trying to do. It just happened. I knew we were meant to be together."

She stared into the distance.

"How old were you?" Manjusha asked.

"I was fifteen, almost sixteen, when we first met," Catherine replied. "He was a year younger than me."

Catherine fidgeted with her dress. The other women could discern the anger bubbling just below the surface

"At least, I thought it was love," Catherine said.

"What happened?" Leotie asked.

Catherine shrugged. "I don't know. I never understood why he ended things with me. We had become so close. I thought…" The pain of memory began to unravel her composure. She took a moment before continuing. "We both knew Thomas was leaving. His father came to see what all Oscar was doing at the Mission and to escort Thomas back home. When Thomas brought me to the house, I could tell his father was not happy. He was cordial enough, but something in his eyes told me he did not want me in his son's life. After that, everything changed."

"How?"

"There was a distance between us – Thomas and me. He started talking about strange things. He suddenly wanted to go to West Point. His father had been in the first graduating class. Thomas said he had dreams of being an officer like this father and grandfather. I did not understand, but I told him we could work things out."

"So, you had talked about the future?"

"Oh yes. By this time, we'd discussed moving west, starting a farm, and raising a gaggle of children. We never – well, you know, but we were mad about each other. The moment he mentioned West Point it was like someone poured cold water on his dreams of a future with me."

Leotie daubed her eyes with her dress. "So, he broke it off then?"

"No."

"Thomas was set to leave on a Friday," Catherine said. "My father and I came to visit on the Wednesday before. Thomas was behaving strangely. I asked him if things were all right. He said they were, but I could tell something was wrong. He asked me to meet him at our spot down by the creek. He thought it would be a good place to say goodbye. I thought…I was ready…uh…I don't know how to say this."

"You were going to give yourself to him in love," Manjusha said. "It is okay to be honest. Trust me, we understand."

"Yes," Catherine said. "The next day, I rode to the creek. His father Clinton was waiting. He told me that Thomas sent him. He told me Thomas was already on his way home. He told… (her voice broke) …he told me Thomas never loved me – that I was a 'harmless distraction.' I felt like Clinton was lying but then he handed me the leather bracelet I made for Thomas and rode away. Neither Oscar nor Miriam ever talked to me about Thomas again. I wrote him at West Point, but my letters were returned unopened. Today was the first time I have seen him in seven years."

Catherine took in a quivering breath.

"I met Ayita's father, Onacona, not too long after that. He was a good man, a practical man. He wasn't a dreamer, a big talker, like Thomas. I trusted him. I knew he would never hurt me, so we got married."

She did not have the energy to sustain the smile she attempted.

"I watched you back there," Manjusha said. "You still care."

Catherine snorted. "I was overwhelmed by memories of a youthful folly. That's all. It didn't mean anything."

Leotie's hand was rough, but her touch resonated with firm tenderness. "No," she said. "That's not true. And there is more."

"What?' Catherine asked.

"I do not know everything about the world," Leotie said, "but I know enough to understand the white captain is still in love with you."

CHAPTER TWENTY-THREE

Doc Lambert could barely squeeze between the dozen or so cots in the surgical tent.

"Crowded in here," Roe said.

"At least it's clean," Thomas said. "You post the guards outside like I asked?"

Roe chuckled. "I didn't know captains *asked* anything. When you told me to post guards, it sounded a hell of a lot like an order."

"Just don't want Morse to think anyone is going to escape."

Roe pointed to the Cherokee patients. "Captain, if the Man from Nazareth came in here and said, 'Take up your pallet and walk,' those poor souls would ask for a pass."

"Don't blaspheme, Sergeant," Thomas said, but he was grinning for the first time in several days.

Jishnu was on the first cot. Lambert had the head wound cleaned and dressed but had not stitched it closed because of infection.

"How's he doin'?" Roe asked.

"Hard to tell," Thomas replied.

"Has the doc been by?"

"Yeah, about an hour ago. He said he'd check back before turning in."

"How are you doin', Captain?"

"Fine."

"You sure about that?"

Thomas refused to answer.

The two friends watched Jishnu sleep.

"So, that was her then?" Roe asked. "She's the girl in the drawings."

Thomas rubbed his face with his hands.

"Yeah. That was her."

"Catherine, is it?"

"Yep."

"No offense to your artistic proficiency, Captain, but you didn't do her justice."

"Nope."

"You listening, Captain?"

"Yep."

"Might I have a three-day pass?"

Thomas cut his eyes. "I told you I was listening."

"Can't blame a man for tryin', sir."

"Nope."

"And this is her father?"

"Yep."

"How long since you seen her?"

"Seven years."

"How did you do it?" Roe asked. "You drew her face from memory – you aged her and everything."

Thomas shrugged. "Not hard to remember something branded into your memory."

"She's quite beautiful," Roe said. "Even livin' in a hole like Fort Newnan for several weeks."

Thomas kept staring at Jishnu. "More to it than that."

"How do you mean?"

"The moment I met her at the Mission where my grandparents worked, I felt like I'd known her forever. Sounds corny, but it's true." Thomas told the back story including his mentorship by Jishnu.

"Jishnu thought we might be friends because there weren't many others around our age. He was right, we did become friends. Then, over time…we became more than friends. We even talked about getting married if you can believe that."

Roe's eyebrows arched.

"Never heard you talking about matrimonial bliss before, Captain," Roe said. "What happened?"

"My father."

"Thought that might be the case."

"The morning I was supposed to meet her at the creek, my father came back from a ride. He told me he'd run into Catherine on her way to see me. She told him to tell me goodbye – that she had enjoyed our time together but that it was only…I remember these words like I heard them yesterday…it was only a 'harmless distraction.' I thought he might be lying but—"

Lambert pushed back the tent flap. "How's Jishnu?"

Thomas shook himself as if coming out of a trance. "He's resting. Breathing is still weak."

Lambert sucked his teeth. "Not surprising. It's amazing he's still alive."

Lambert put one end of the wooden tube against Jishnu's chest and the other end to his ear.

"What are you doing?" Roe asked. "And what's that thing?"

"Called a 'stethoscope,'" Lambert said. "A doctor in France came up with it a while back. Helps me listen to a patient's heart."

"Well, I'll be damned," Roe said. "Another magnum opus in the field of medicine. What's it tellin' you, Doc?"

"What we already knew," Lambert said. "Tonight will tell the tale."

He stood and put the device in his saddlebag.

"Speaking of which," Thomas said, "you need to get shut-eye yourself, Doc. It was a long day; tomorrow will probably be just as bad."

"I know," Lambert said. "I just wanted to check on him before I turned in. Goodnight, gentlemen."

The tent flap was still moving when Roe squeezed Thomas's arm. "The doc ain't the only one that needs some sleep," he said.

"You honestly think I'll be able to sleep?"

"Either get some sleep or answer to me," Roe said. "You may be the captain, but right now, I am the boss. Okay, sir?"

"Okay"

Thomas reached out and grabbed Jishnu's hand.

I have missed you, old friend. Thought about you almost every day. There's so much I want to tell you – so much of your wisdom I need. And I have to tell you how sorry I am – about everything.

Thomas waited. He hoped Jishnu's eyes would open, but the old man never moved. Thomas gently folded Jishnu's hand across his chest, then turned to Roe.

"Sergeant, no one bothers this man."

"Yes, sir."

Thomas strode out of the tent and into the oppressive night.

I didn't become a soldier for this.

§§

When Catherine reached the medical tent, a young soldier escorted her through the maze of cots.

The place was clean – something Catherine had not seen for a while. All were elderly. Most were suffering from dehydration and a lack of nutrition. Most were asleep. All of them were alone except for her father. Two men stood sentinel by his bed. The dirty-faced soldier sat in a chair by her father's head.

He stood when Catherine approached and addressed her escort. "Good job, Ratliff," he said. "Now turn in."

The private saluted and left. "I'm Roe, remember?" the dirty-faced man said. "Captain Edwards will be relieved to know you made it."

Catherine's eyes darted around the tent.

"No worries, ma'am. He's attendin' to his other duties. Won't be back until after sunrise."

Roe slid his chair closer to Jishnu. "Please, have a seat."

Catherine sat, uncomfortable in the presence of the soldiers. But, the sight of her father lying on the cot made her forget everything but his condition. He'd been washed. Somehow without the dirt on his face, he looked worse. He had no color at all. She whimpered and inclined until her temple touched his.

"Doc's done everythin' he can," Roe said. "We gave him water, but we can't rouse him enough to feed him."

She took her father's withered hand in hers and whispered. "Thank you."

"We'll be leavin' you now, ma'am," Roe said. "We're just outside the tent flap if you need anything. No one will bother you." He took two steps, then turned back. "No one."

Lambert came to check on Jishnu in the middle of the night. At four minutes after two in the morning, with Catherine holding his hand, Jishnu breathed his last. Catherine didn't say anything. She stroked his hand and his hair until dawn.

CHAPTER TWENTY-FOUR

"Everything is set for Jishnu Sevenstar's burial," Roe said. "That's what I came to tell you. We'll head out for the forest this evening when it's a bit cooler."

"You a religious man, Roe?"

Roe nodded. "I am. Was raised in a God fearin' home. My Mamma read the Bible to us every night before bed."

"Do you pray?"

"Some days more than others. Never as often as I should. Why?"

Thomas pursed his lips. "I've tried. After all, I've seen and done. After all the awfulness. I just don't…"

He picked up a Bible from his table and waved it gently. "Belonged to my grandfather, Oscar."

"Never seen you with it before."

"Miriam gave it to me the last time I was home."

"Looks well used."

"Not on my account," Thomas said. He motioned Roe to a seat. "I was hoping to find…hell I don't know…something."

"Any luck?"

"Well, I got stuck in the Old Testament. Found out some weird things like we are prohibited from eating owls,[1] but nothing particularly helpful."

"I'll keep that in mind, sir."

Thomas replaced the Bible and stared at the far wall. "Oscar and Jishnu prayed. They were two of the most God-fearing men I've ever known. Both died in awful ways. How come they suffered and men like Morse and Elias sail along unscathed?"

Roe scratched his neck. "You don't think Colonel Morse and Elias suffer? Gotta be honest. I'd rather die like Oscar and Jishnu than live the lives those skunks endure."

"What are you talking about?"

"Deep down, Elias and Colonel Morse are broken. They ain't ever gonna admit it to anyone – can't even admit it to themselves. They've forgotten what it means to have peace in their lives."

"They're soldiers. We all are. That—"

"I ain't talkin' about the absence of war, Captain. I'm talkin' about peace in your heart." Roe rested his elbows on his knees. "Peace with yourself. Peace with God. You know what I'm talkin' about." He tapped his chest. "Until you came here you had peace in here. Even when we wuz down in Florida, in the middle of all that madness, you had peace in your heart. It's what helped you. And me. But even on the quietest of days, Colonel Morse and Elias ain't got it. They don't know the meanin' of the word. Don't kid yourself,

---

[1] Leviticus 11:13-19

those two are suffering every day 'cause they ain't got no hope."

"You think I still have peace in my heart?" Thomas asked.

"Not since you've been here," Roe replied.

"Why do you think that is?"

"I don't know," Roe said, "but you're smart enough to figure it out. And you better pretty damn quick, or your life's gonna be a mess for sure 'nuf certain."

CHAPTER TWENTY-FIVE

Surrounded by soldiers, the forlorn group of Cherokees trudged towards the forest. Catherine guessed the horsemen were under Thomas's command. They were respectful to her and the others, and they carried themselves with military bearing and pride – far different from the drunken buffoons strutting around the corral every day.

In spite of their courtesy, the soldiers' presence was a harsh reminder of why she was burying her father.

I guess I should be grateful. Most of the others have to pass their loved ones' bodies over the fence for burial who knows where.

It was a long walk to the forest, but the distance did not bother Catherine. She wanted Jishnu buried as far away from Fort Newnan as possible. She didn't want his spirit to live anywhere near the fort in the afterlife. She was reminded of the dreams he had, telling him he'd never leave the area. That was when she'd realized the same thing would happen to her – her spirit would be laid to "unrest" hundreds of miles from her father's.

Catherine reached out for Leotie who took her hand and squeezed before interlocking their arms for the remainder of the walk.

When they arrived at the edge of the forest, Catherine was

surprised to find two soldiers, hats in their hands, standing next to a hole.

Catherine looked to see if Thomas was close. He was not among those near the grave, and she had not seen him in the mournful march from the fort. Just as four soldiers manned the ropes to lower Jishnu's wrapped body into the ground, she spotted Thomas standing at attention near a big oak about a hundred yards away.

Catherine's heart flooded with mixed emotions. She wanted to beat the chest of every man in uniform, the ones who kept watch as one Tsalagi after another drifted away into the "place of no wants." But she also imagined flinging herself into Thomas's arms for comfort and reassurance.

She did not want the soldiers there; she was grateful for their assistance. She hated Thomas for being a part of the nightmare she was experiencing. She loved him because...

Because of Thomas, she did not have the freedom to hate all soldiers, to despise anyone with white skin. Life would be so much easier – and less confusing – if she could. Instead, conflict raged inside her heart and mind as she watched the body of the only person who might have been able to help her make sense of the situation disappear into the cold earth.

Silent tears meandered down her cheeks. Two soldiers poured mounds of dirt on top of Jishnu's lifeless form with deliberate and respectful movements until the earth was smooth and mounded.

Thomas disappeared into the trees. The little group headed for the fort.

Catherine waved away Manjusha and Leotie and walked alone back to the corral accompanied only by her bitter thoughts.

§§

Thomas watched her – alone and slightly separated from the group. His men knew not to rush her – not to touch her. His first impulse was to run to her with open arms, but the more people who knew of his past with Catherine, the more dangerous the situation would become – for both of them, however, he felt the sands of opportunity slipping through his fingers.

If I don't get to her before she reaches the fort, I may lose her forever, he thought.

Thomas rode up to the back of the pitiful procession and slipped out of the saddle. He walked as fast as he could without attracting attention.

"Catherine?"

He expected a thin smile – he saw outrage.

"My name is Kasewini!" she replied in her native tongue.

Thomas cleared his throat.

Great, she's going to make me speak Cherokee.

"Sorry, Kasewini."

Catherine resumed her walk, her head held high.

"Kasewini, can we talk?"

"We are talking."

"I don't mean like this."

Catherine spun.

"What do you want?"

Thomas searched his limited Cherokee vocabulary for an answer he didn't even have in English.

"I…I want to make peace."

"Are we at war?"

"It seems that way."

"I can assure you we are not. In a war, both sides have weapons, both sides have an equal chance to win. I have neither."

Catherine resumed her trek to the fort.

Thomas slipped a little bit as he tried to keep up. "I don't want to fight."

"Your uniform says otherwise."

Thomas began to unbutton his jacket.

"Do not embarrass yourself," she said.

"That's not what I meant."

"You are more full of manure than the corral."

Thomas stopped dead in his tracks. "Can we speak English, please?"

Catherine huffed and stopped as well. "Fine. In addition, you are full of contradictions. You want something but you do not know what it is. You want peace but you oppress my people. You begin to take off your uniform but it's not what you mean."

"And you're a leader of men?" She stalked toward Fort Newnan.

Thomas jogged after her. Silo trailed behind.

"I...I..."

Catherine did not slow. "It breaks my heart knowing my father died in your custody, that I am your prisoner"

"No, you're not—"

"Not what?" She stopped and turned to him. Her voice hissed through the choking dust.

Thomas looked into Catherine's eyes, searching for a way to reason with the girl he once knew.

"Well?" she asked.

"You are."

"I am what?"

Thomas looked away.

"Go on, say it," she said. "Say it!"

Others began to look in their direction.

Thomas shook his head.

"Just say it, you coward!"

Her scream made several of the detachment step in their direction. Thomas motioned to let them know everything was fine.

"All right," he said. He spoke in a low voice and hoped she would take the hint. "All right. Because I'm a soldier, you're in my custody. But you're not a prisoner."

Catherine's laugh was bitter and cutting. "I'm not a prisoner?" She pounded on his chest with both fists. "I'm not a prisoner?"

The dam broke inside her heart. Anger poured out of her like pus from a ruptured boil. She struck him on the chest with every word.

"Am I free to go? Can I return to my home? Can my father go with me?" Her palm slammed the side of his face. "Will you give me back my daughter?"

Thomas saw Roe standing between him and some of the other men.

Thomas stepped back. "You have a daughter?"

Exhausted and drained, Catherine shook with fury and desperation.

"Her name's Ayita."

"How old is she?"

"Six."

In his confusion, Thomas strained with the mental math.

"She was born less than a year after my marriage."

"You have a husband?"

"*Had* – we met shortly after you left for the Academy."

The pain shooting through Thomas's heart was the same as when his father said the words "harmless distraction."

I always suspected Clinton was lying, but she married so soon...

"What happened?"

"He died when Ayita was two."

"I'm sorry."

"Are you?"

"I truly am. I care about you, Kasewini. All I ever wanted was for you to be happy."

Catherine looked down.

Thomas searched the faces of the girls standing behind them.

"Which one's Ayita?" Thomas asked.

Catherine stamped her foot into the ground. "You are not listening. I asked if I could have her back. She is not with me. She was taken when we came to Fort Newnan."

"Taken?"

Catherine relayed the story. She pointed to the others, all of whom had stopped. The soldiers were looking at each other unsure what to do. They knew better than to interrupt the captain, but they knew they needed to return the prisoners soon.

Catherine motioned to a man who looked ready to charge Thomas at a moment's notice. The man walked over.

"This is Jeevan," she said. "Two of his children were taken."

"Captain Thomas Edwards, U.S Army," Thomas said. He extended his hand

With his eyes locked on Thomas's, the man shook hands. Though malnourished and haggard, Thomas recognized a warrior when he looked at Jeevan – a formidable adversary – a man unacquainted with fear.

"May I ask for your children's names?" Thomas asked.

"My son is Kavi," Jeevan replied. "He's four. My daughter Harsha is two."

Thomas looked away. "This can't be right."

"We are not soldiers," Catherine said. "We have no reason to lie."

Thomas looked at the group of children standing nearby. He saw sunken eyes – he saw protruding ribs – he saw the specter of impending death.

"Any idea where they were taken?" Thomas asked.

"Someone said the name of two forts before they began forcing families onto the wagons," Catherine replied. "But I wasn't listening when they announced the names. One was Fort Newnan, obviously, but I don't…"

"Would you know it if you heard it?" Thomas asked.

"Possibly."

"Fort Gilmer?" Thomas asked.

Catherine shook her head.

"Fort Hetzel?"

Catherine looked up but said nothing.

"That's the one," Jeevan said. "The soldiers said one group was going to Fort Newnan and the other to Fort Hetzel."

"Is that where your children were taken as well?" Thomas asked.

"I do not know," Jeevan replied. "They were taken from me at a different place than Ayita was from her mother."

"What about Fort Gilmer?" Thomas asked. "How far did you travel after your children were taken?"

"Not far. Maybe half a day."

Thomas looked at Roe and Sergeant Wallace.

"If he's right, it could be either Gilmer or Hetzel." He turned back to Jeevan and Catherine. "Okay, I'll send a couple of men to the forts to find out what is going on."

"Won't that cause problems?" Catherine asked.

"No one will care if my men are just looking around," Thomas replied. "However, if we find them, getting 'em back to Fort Newnan may prove to be a bit more difficult."

Jeevan nodded. Catherine looked away, but Thomas caught a glimpse of a small smile – until it gave way to dread.

Thomas turned in time to see a man riding away on his black horse – a man with a tall, black hat.

CHAPTER TWENTY-SIX

"East side of the corral's secure, sir," Roe said as he entered the captain's tent. "The men are all settled."

He found Thomas slumped in his chair staring at nothing. An open whiskey jug sat on his lap. Oscar's Bible rested on his thigh – unopened.

"Sir, you all right?"

Thomas did not move.

"Captain Edwards, sir!"

Thomas jumped and barely managed to catch the jug before it fell to the ground. He sat up a little but made no effort to stop the Bible from sliding onto the dirt floor. "She got married and has a daughter."

Roe reached out a hand to steady Thomas who was tilting towards the floor. "I assume you mean Catherine."

Thomas nodded. "She married him not long after I left."

"Where is he?"

"He died."

Roe frowned and patted his friend on the shoulder. "What about her daughter?"

"She was taken from Catherine during the roundup," Thomas said.

"Is that why you sent Sergeant Wallace to Fort Gilmer and Private Bond to Fort Hetzel?" Roe asked.

"It is." Thomas shook his head. "Her daughter is six years old. Taken from her mother at six years of age. Can you believe such thing?"

"Unfortunately, I can."

Thomas snorted and took a drink from his jug. "And we have to do something about that sorry waste of flesh."

"A lot of that going around, right now, Captain. Need a little more specificity."

Thomas took another swig. "Elias. We need to do something about him."

"Don't disagree, but what brought on this revelational disclosure?"

Thomas exhaled, long and slow. "That bastard was there today."

"Where?"

"When we were walking back to the fort after the funeral. When I was walking with her. When she pounded on me." He took another drink then stood – not very steadily. "That sneaky son-of-a-bitch was back off in the woods…spying on the funeral. Spying on us. On her!"

"Why didn't you say anythin'?"

"I didn't see him until she did," Thomas said. "He was too far gone by then. Besides, Catherine deserved a little peace on the day she buried her father. Right?"

The jug tilted. Thomas wiped his mouth.

"I suppose ye're right," Roe replied.

He sat down in one of the empty chairs and looked up at the captain who'd begun to pace like a man walking on a ship's deck during a storm.

"But, just 'cause she was spooked by seein' him don't mean he's done something. That black-wearin' fool would unsettle the Angel Gabriel his own self. Truth be told, he give *me* the willies."

Thomas shook his head "He should not have been there, today."

"I can think of half a dozen reasons he'd be there. Maybe he was watchin' to make sure no one escaped."

A stream of whiskey trickled down Thomas's chin. He didn't bother to wipe it away. He proffered the jug to Roe who waved it off.

"No," Thomas said. "My gut is telling me there is something else. He was watching her."

"You sure ye're not imaginin' things – maybe seein' something that's not exactly there?"

"I'm sure."

Roe rubbed the back of his head. "Seems to me vision ain't yer strongest suit at the moment."

"What?"

Roe glanced at the jug of whiskey.

"What? I can't have a drink? I'm the captain. I can have a drink when I damn well please."

"It's not that."

"Then what? I can't read your mind, Sergeant."

Roe sat up straight and cleared his throat. "Permission to speak freely."

"Granted."

Roe moved to stand. "Maybe now's not a good time."

"As good a time as any."

"All right." He sat back down and waited for Thomas to take another drink. "That woman's got you all twisted up inside."

Thomas snorted.

"You built a tent for her father. You've kissed the colonel's ass so he could have a proper funeral. And now ye're sendin' scouts out to find her daughter—"

"I'm supposed to ignore the fact her daughter's been taken?"

"She ain't the only one! There's dozens of kids out there who ain't got their parents with 'em."

Thomas stopped in front of Roe. "So, you're saying I should do nothing?"

"Not sayin' that. It's just…are you planning to join up *all* the families?"

"No! I don't know. Maybe. If that's what it takes."

"If that's what it takes for what?" Roe asked.

"To help...I guess. What's your point, Sergeant?"

"Just concerned, that's all. You ain't been the same since you got here."

Thomas rubbed his forehead. "You yourself said this place is a hell on earth."

"Yeah, it is. And I did say that. But you. You've let this place get to ya. As bad as it is, it's even worse since you've found out *she's* here."

Thomas brought the jug up to his lips, thought better of it, and set it on the ground. "You're tellin' me this place has no effect on you?"

"I ain't sayin' that. But...it's jus' another horrible set of circumstances. We're soldiers. This place ain't no different than the villages we've seen looted and burned out down in Florida. We've seen innocent people suffer before. Caught in the crossfire and killed for bein' in the wrong place at the wrong time. I have to ask why this place is different. And the only answer I can come up with is *her*. Tell me I'm wrong."

"You're wrong. Fort Newnan is nothing...*nothing* like any place we've seen before. Let's get that clear right now. Nothing. Down in Florida, when the civilians were caught in the crossfire ...during a battle ...it all happened so quickly ...there wasn't time to think

259

about it. And…as for the burned-out villages and settlements we saw down there, I rode in after the fact."

He looked at the jug. Roe blocked it with his boot.

"But *here* it's all happening right before our eyes. A slow death. I've got plenty of time to think about it. Those people out there are being crushed under military boot heels. And I don't like being the one wearing the boot. Sure, Catherine's presence makes it more personal, but even if she weren't here, I'd still have an issue with this place."

"What'd you expect comin' here?" Roe asked.

"I don't know. Certainly not this."

Thomas walked over to the open tent flap and looked out at the silhouetted figures milling about inside the corral.

"What'd you think?" Roe asked. "Were we all going to frolic in the grass and sip lemonade—"

Thomas's face swelled with fury. "Don't patronize me! I'm not a child!"

He kicked the jug across the floor.

"Ever since the day I got my orders, I've been lied to." His volume increased with every word. "When I got this assignment, I was told it was our duty to be kind to the Cherokees during the relocation. My father spoke of it as if it was a fact. Hell, it specifically says it in my orders, *and* the decree from General Scott."

He picked up a handful of papers and waved them. "The Cherokees are to be treated fairly and humanely!" He tossed the papers into the air. They fell like giant leaves, swishing back and forth before settling on the dirt floor.

"Lies! All of it!" He took a step towards the jug, then stopped. "I'm a man of my word. If I say I'm going to do something, I do it. I don't lie to get my way or to get others to do something for me."

Thomas glared at Roe.

"No, I didn't expect child's play or a fairytale coming here. But I can guarantee you I didn't expect to see people living…like that (he flailed his arm towards the corral) …people under my care dying every day."

He walked to the opening and glared into the gloom."

"And you and everyone else are crazier than hell if you think I'm going to sit back and do nothing."

§§

After arriving back at Fort Newnan following her father's burial Catherine kept to herself in spite of everyone else's attempts to get her to eat and talk. It didn't take long for her friends to realize she wanted to be left alone so that's what they did up to the point of going to sleep.

Catherine wept quietly while the others slept. Whether from sadness or bittersweet joy, she had no idea, but she could not stop the tears.

Her head was in her hands. She heard the distinct sound of boots and looked up to find Gabe standing next to her. He said nothing – just offered his hand. Once she took it, he hurried her through the maze of tents outside the corral where a group of men waited, torches in hand like before.

When they arrived in the grove, there was no sanctuary of light, just a solitary fire.

"I wanted to do something simpler this time," Elias said once the other men disappeared into the night.

He clasped his hands behind his back and took slow, deliberate steps around the edge of the bonfire, tantalized by the opportunity to hold his darling Catherine once again. His breath came in short bursts, the nervous pant of a hyperactive dog. His palms slicked with sweat; his pulse pounded in his temple. He'd been around women, plenty of them, mostly whores and the like. He was no gawking, innocent schoolboy, but this woman, the bewitching Cherokee, took away his capacity to think of anyone else.

Watching the firelight dance across her face made him wish he'd picked the wildflowers again. He thought she liked them the last time. He knew women liked gifts.

Next time.

Whenever he took a step, Catherine moved in the opposite direction, mirroring his every move as he stalked her around the bonfire. He tolerated her coyness. It prolonged the anticipation.

"All alone, for a second time," he said with a smile, "in our own special place."

The moon was all but disappeared. The woods presented an impenetrable wall of shadows. Catherine looked like a fawn, lost and looking for its mother. Elias wanted to protect her.

"This is our little oasis," he said, "our spot to get away from the misery of *that* place."

Elias quickened his steps a little, and when Catherine did as well, he gave her a look telling her she was wasting her time. He could see in her eyes that she understood. She slowed her pace, almost coming to a complete stop.

"Sorry about your father," he said.

He inched ever closer.

"Sorrier that I never got to meet him. I wonder – do you think he would approve of us, of our special relationship, I mean?" His smile reflected predatory hunger. "I think he would have. What about you?"

Catherine stiffened but said nothing.

"I'll take your silence as a sign that you agree," Elias said. "You're right, he would've wanted this."

Unable to withstand another second, Elias reached out and grabbed her hand. Catherine's face registered horror but Elis was too busy studying their intertwined fingers to notice.

His elation drove him to a song – another bout of humming while he stroked his thumb over her knuckles. Her skin was soft, especially compared to everything else in his life – a cracked saddle, a stiff holster – the cold steel of his knives, guns, and bullets – the unforgiving ground he lay on every night – the harsh loneliness of a savage man. She was a softness and warmth long overdue, a welcome haven in his brutal life.

Elias squeezed her hand. He ran his hand over the top of her head. He studied her face and patted her like a dog.

Without warning, he grabbed a fistful of her hair and yanked.

"I saw you talking to Captain Edwards today. Doesn't he know you belong to me?"

Catherine opened her mouth, but Elias put a finger over her lips before she could utter a sound.

"Hush, now. It's not your fault the captain was talking to you today. But you should tell him you belong to me." He studied the details of her face. "I'll forgive you *this* time."

He traced the outline of her lips, mesmerized by their alluring contours. His finger, smelling of bacon and dirt, continued its circling. It pressed harder with every revolution. His eyes grew wide. He licked his chapped lips.

Elias smashed his lips against Catherine's. The kiss was harsh and unsympathetic. His whiskers abraded her skin. Catherine tried to close her mouth, but her resistance had no effect. Elias circled his tongue around the edges of her mouth, unable to stop himself from making strange sounds as if he were tasting food for the first time.

Then, as quickly as it started, he stopped. Elias stroked her face with sandpaper hands.

"I can see how he looks at you," Elias said. "He wants you for his own, ya know? But he can't have you! You're already mine."

He slipped his foot behind Catherine's ankle and pushed. She tumbled to the ground.

"And now it's time to prove it to you."

He lowered himself on top of her and whispered into her ear. "Don't fight me, darlin'. You have to do what I say."

His movements were quick and deliberate.

"Joey didn't."

Catherine saw an opportunity to deflect Elias's intentions.

"Tell me more about him," she said.

Elias raised up and studied her for a moment.

Catherine held her breath, unsure.

Elias moved to the side and sat up, suddenly lost in a shroud of memory. His blue eyes focused on something neither of them could see.

"Loved that puppy," he said.

He stroked Catherine's arm. Though her skin crawled, she resisted the urge to yank away.

"Then he was bad."

"Did he chew up your shoes?" Catherine asked.

Get him talking about the dog. Keep his mind on the dog. If he thinks about the dog, he won't—

The blue eyes went cold and turned iridescent black. "Messed the floor," Elias said. "Every day – same time – same place – a pile of dog shit. Smelled to high heaven. I tried everything. No luck. A stinkin' mound of his excretion inside the house."

His hand traveled over Catherine's shoulder and towards her chest. She went rigid but did not move.

"Mom beat me every time Joey soiled the house. No matter how hard I scrubbed, I couldn't get the stink all the way out. She knew – she always knew."

His hand traversed her breast and encircled her waist. He pulled her close.

"She beat me until I couldn't walk. I had a long talk with Joey about it. He promised he would do better."

Elias leaned into Catherine until she toppled into the ground. She closed her eyes. He fumbled with this belt.

"But the next day, he did it again – same place…same time. I picked him up and scolded him. He yapped at me like he wanted to play – like everything was okay." He stopped talking and waited for Catherine to open her eyes. "I squeezed his neck. He kept yapping."

Elias arm-barred Catherine's neck. She was paralyzed by fear. She strained to breathe.

"I squeezed harder – he wouldn't stop is yammering. Harder... harder (the pressure on Catherine's throat increased) ...until – Joey didn't bark anymore."

Catherine coughed and wheezed. The light broke back into Elias's eyes – the startling blue returned – he jerked his arm from her throat.

"Sorry, darlin'," he said. "I get a little emotional when I talk about Joey. Now, where were we?"

Catherine resisted for a while but the burdens she had endured, and the physical hardship left her without either the will or the strength to put up a fight. She morphed into a lifeless ragdoll – and Elias misinterpreted.

She's giving herself to me, he thought. *She is truly mine.*

Catherine stared into the endless void disconnected from her body. She felt nothing – hoped for nothing – and heard nothing for a long time. When he was done, he kissed her on the forehead and said, "Until next time."

CHAPTER TWENTY-SEVEN

"No thank you, sir. A little early in the morning for me, sir."

"Suit yourself, Captain." Colonel Morse put the bottle in his bottom drawer and wiped his forehead with a linen handkerchief. "Damn beastly out there," he said. "Sweating like this before 0900 is unnatural."

Thomas eyed the officer with contempt. Morse's bulk barely fit into his chair.

The man hasn't moved over fifty yards a day in years, Thomas thought.

"I understand you and your men have settled into Fort Newnan," the colonel said.

"Not too settled, sir. We'll be leaving in a month or so."

Colonel Morse mopped flop sweat from the folds of his neck. "Yes. I suppose you're right. I don't want to be here any longer than I have to myself."

"I don't think *anyone* does," Thomas said.

"True, very true," Morse said with the gravity of someone trying to sound wise. "On another note, I saw your men inside the corral again this morning."

You didn't see anyone. Someone told you. Seeing my men would require you to walk twenty feet to your tent flap.

"Yes, sir. They're getting some of the people ready to go to the creek for water."

Morse wrinkled his brow as if lost in deep thought. "I know. I've been thinking a lot about that. Damn fine idea – water and all. It will help with my new plan."

"Sir?"

"We'll be marching them to the Indian Territory soon enough. And that will be an arduous—"

"Marching?" Thomas asked. "I thought we were transporting them. What about wagons, boats, that sort of thing?"

Colonel Morse laughed. "You're less savvy than I thought, Mr. Edwards."

The colonel shook his head and chuckled. Thomas clenched his teeth.

"Some will go by flatboat, yes. I imagine we will have to take the ill and infirm by wagon. But we're looking at relocating close to *sixteen thousand* Indians, Captain. The government cannot reasonably be expected to absorb the expense of mass transportation. No, Captain, most of them will walk."

"That's over eight hundred miles."

Morse looked bored. "Very good, Captain. You know your geography. They will cover twelve to fifteen miles per day to arrive in the Indian Territory before winter. "

Thomas looked at the map on the wall behind the colonel's head and assessed the magnitude of the forced migration. Morse was still talking.

"With that in mind, the Indians will need to be in better shape to travel. Starting today, you will assemble the savages and march them a minimum of ten miles every day."

Thomas waited for the smile – the grotesque belly laugh. Neither came.

"I'm quite serious about this," Morse said. "They need to get used to it."

"But they're starving," Thomas replied. "Many are sick and dying."

"The ones unable to march will stay in the corral, obviously. No need to drag them along. But the others, regardless of the lack or abundance of food and water, must march every day."

Thomas's first inclination was to refuse the command but had to reconsider.

They're going to have to march, he thought. *If I don't do it, the colonel and his men will. Worse, it could be Elias.*

"Is there a problem, Captain?"

"Um, no, sir. No problem at all."

"Good."

Thomas closed his eyes for a moment and tried to imagine what it was going to be like to explain everything to the battered people in the corral.

"You were planning on escorting them down to the creek, correct?" Colonel Morse asked.

"Yes."

"Well, include that in their march. Circle back there at the end of the march." The colonel wiped at his massive forehead again. "But I have to be honest, I have misgivings about assigning you to the detail."

Thomas refused to dignify the comment with a response. After a pause, Morse continued.

"There is always the possibility of escape. If anyone runs off, Elias and his men will find them. The punishment for everyone will be severe and you, dear Captain, will be held responsible."

"I'll do my best, sir."

"It better be good enough."

Thomas executed a textbook about-face and took one step before Morse's next comment glued him to the floor.

"Captain, tell me about the woman. You asked for permission to bury her father in the woods. Why is that?"

Thomas knew he could not ignore the inquiry. He made a less enthusiastic about-face.

"Just one of the Cherokees," he said. "I felt responsible for her father dying, so I—"

"So, you beseeched me to overlook every protocol, something we have not done for anyone else."

Thomas tried to look nonchalant, but his mind echoed with Roe's story of the pregnant Seneca woman that Morse killed then hanged in the sun like a buffalo hide.

Careful what you say, old boy, he thought.

"I beg the colonel's pardon," Thomas said. "I let my guilt cloud my judgment."

Morse steepled his fingers and shifted in his chair. "Not exactly sure why you would feel any guilt over doing your duty."

"I promised her that her father would be fine under our care," Thomas said. He prayed that he wasn't sounding defensive. "That was the only way I could get her to let us take him to the medical tent. She put her trust in me. I felt responsible."

Colonel Morse considered the answer for a moment. "You say she gave you permission to take her father."

"Yes."

"But I heard she was nowhere to be found when her father was brought to the tent."

"An erroneous report, sir."

"Perhaps," Colonel Morse replied. He scratched his ear, then his nose. "I know how rumors can be unreliable." He refolded his handkerchief before sopping up more sweat. "Or maybe you're lying."

Thomas stared at the map like a West Point cadet being inspected – no movement, no expression. Morse's eyes bored into him.

"You spoke to her on the way back to the fort, after burying her father?" he asked.

"I did."

"I understand the two of you had an argument."

"Excuse me, sir?"

"It was explained to me that the two of you talked for a while, then a disagreement ensued."

"Did Elias tell you this?"

"No, I haven't spoken to him in a couple of days. I'm keeping him busy chasing down Cherokees who run away in the middle of the night. He's not my only source, Captain. Like any good leader, I have eyes and ears everywhere."

Thomas exhaled.

"We didn't argue, Colonel."

"Oh, yes, you're right. I apologize, Captain. An argument requires participation by two people. The way I heard it, the woman did all the yelling before she struck you several times. Pounded on your chest – struck your face."

"She was letting out her—"

"You did not report the incident to me – to anyone. It all seems quite suspicious."

"There was no need—"

"It all seems so...*personal*, Captain. Smells like you know her on a deeper level."

"There was nothing to report. Besides, I don't think—"

Morse's face turned purple.

"I don't give a tinker's damn what you think, Captain. Putting aside the fact that a civilian – a prisoner – struck a U.S. Army officer, it appears she did so in the middle of a lovers' spat. Who is she, Captain?" He picked up a teacup at the side of his desk and smashed it on the ground. "And, on the blood of our sacred Lord – do – not – lie – to me, damn it!"

The colonel's apoplexy was almost comical, but Thomas recognized the lurking danger.

"Were you watching, Colonel?" he asked.

"Who *is* she?"

"Were you watching?"

Colonel Morse's shriek filled the tent. "You know damn well I was not."

Thomas's quiet answer was in stark contrast to the colonel's fulminations. "Then how do you know we were fighting like lovers, sir? Did you ever consider that maybe it was just a grief-stricken woman taking her frustrations out on the person she felt was directly responsible for her father's death?"

Morse took a moment to gather himself. His voice was more controlled when he responded.

"Captain, what is your estimation of the time frame required to fulfill your orders here?"

"Six months sounds reasonable," Thomas responded taken completely off guard by the change of subject.

"Do you think six months is a long time, Captain?"

"It depends, sir."

"I couldn't agree more. It is situational, and individual, I suppose. If one were waiting for a loved one to return from a long trip, six months would seem like a long time."

"Yes, sir."

"But if someone had only six months to live, the time would fly by."

"I would…have to agree, sir."

"Well, young man, regardless of what happens, when you look back on this time, these next six months will represent less than a half chapter in the novel of your life."

"I'm not sure I follow, sir."

Morse smiled like a man who'd just drawn the winning card in a poker game.

"Let me make it perfectly clear. It would be a shame for a mere six months to ruin someone's entire future."

Thomas could not think of anything to say.

"Good," Morse said. "You understand."

CHAPTER TWENTY-EIGHT

It was close to noon before Catherine stirred inside her small tent, awakened by the scorching heat of the day. She rolled onto her back and stared at the sunlight filtering through the heavy canvas over her head. Just on the other side, the thin fabric of life was continuing.

Can I?

She couldn't recall how she got back to the corral the night before and she didn't bother trying to figure it out.

Last night with Elias was only the beginning she knew.

She felt lifeless and disconnected from the rest of the world like she'd been asleep for days. However, the empty spot next to her was a cruel reminder that her father had been laid to rest just yesterday.

My slumber did not last long enough.

There was a wall – something inside of her – impenetrable, inexplicable. She knew her body hurt from what Elias had done but she couldn't *feel* it. Horrific images, shattering memories, cruel emotions rushed at her in a stampede, but as long as she didn't move, everything was kept at bay.

How long can I keep this wall up?

Catherine took a deep breath and let it out before she realized there was something else so strange, so still.

So quiet.

Catherine cocked her head and listened. There were no sounds –
no clatter of pans – no scuffing of feet – not a single baby cried – not
a single child laughed.

Either I have gone deaf or…

Breaking through the wall that isolated her from her pain,
Catherine sat up and stuck her head out of the shelter, unprepared for
what she saw.

Nothing.

No one.

Everyone was gone.

Frantic, she tried to get to her feet but her body wouldn't
cooperate, causing her to fall onto her side several times before she
finally managed to stand upright.

From a standing position, she could see the camp wasn't as
empty as she thought. There was an aging dog lying in the meager
shade of a tent's shadow.

Catherine turned in a never-ending circle looking for any other
signs of life.

Nothing.

No dogs barking. No horses or soldiers going about their day. No
men trying to peddle their wares over the fence line like buzzards
trying to get the last scrap of meat. No militiamen causing trouble.

She ran over to Waya and Leotie's shelter and almost tore it
down looking inside.

Empty.

Catherine placed her hand on her forehead unable to breathe. The feeling of being utterly alone was overwhelming.

Am I dead? Is this hell?

A slight breeze blew, stirring up little dust devils making the corral feel much larger than she thought possible and all the more empty. Many of the canvas shelters strung out along the fence line flapped in the breeze taunting her with the same message, "Everyone has left you."

Catherine struggled to breathe. She could feel her mind was on the verge of collapse, and just before it was about to shatter into a million pieces she noticed a pair of legs sticking out from one of the shelters just across from her.

The legs were covered in worn deerskin leggings and the feet were black from dirt and filth.

She immediately ran over.

"Help me," she begged. "Please."

The man stirred a little, mumbling something.

Desperate, she grabbed his legs and shook him harder than she intended to.

"What's happened?" she pleaded. "Where's everyone?"

The man tried to get away from her grasp but his movements were too slow and weak. He mumbled a little louder but Catherine had no idea what he said.

She stood to run to the next shelter but it was empty.

Unsure if she could trust her eyesight, Catherine jogged around in no particular direction, turning in circles.

Did they leave for the Indian Territory? Where is Ayita?

She stopped spinning and put her hand to her chest, unable to focus on any one object.

A hand landed on her shoulder. Catherine shrieked and turned, arms up, nails prepared to fight to the death.

"Are you all right, my dear?"

It was the soldiers' doctor.

"Please," was all she said before she fainted.

CHAPTER TWENTY-NINE

Two male voices crept into Catherine's unconsciousness drawing her back into the real world.

Lacking the energy to open her eyes, Catherine concentrated on breathing, grateful she no longer felt like the only person alive.

"She's utterly exhausted," one of the men said.

The doctor.

"She needed medical attention. I felt it was best to bring her into your tent, Captain. I didn't think she needed to wake up in the same tent where her—"

"You did the right thing."

The undeniable sound of Thomas's voice soothed her mind.

"One of your men guarding the medical tent helped me. I am certain no one saw us bring her in here."

"Good."

"With all she's been through, I can only assume when she woke up, she was confused that everyone was gone – marching. It was simply too much for her to handle so, her body just quit on her."

"Will she get better?"

"She needs to eat. She is severely dehydrated and starving, just like all the others. But if she gets the proper nourishment and some rest, she should be fine."

"Understood. I will make sure she gets what she requires. Thank you, doctor. By the way, have you had a chance to examine the people in the corral since we returned from the first march?"

"Yes, and I will renew my concern about such strenuous activity with Colonel Morse, though I doubt it will do much good. At least by being out, they will get a regular supply of water."

"And food. I plan on letting them hunt and gather."

"You got permission?"

"I did not ask. And until the supply line is up and running like it should, I won't."

§§

After the doctor left, Catherine remained with her eyes closed. She could hear the sound of water being poured, then felt a damp cloth soothing her face. She opened her eyes.

Thomas.

His touch was gentle and caring, just as she remembered it being.

He was sitting in a chair at the side of the bed, cloth in hand, eyes intent on his ministrations. She started to speak but could find neither the words nor the strength. Sleep laid its soft, firm hand on her eyelids and she slipped into quietness.

She awakened off and on over the next few hours but never sufficiently to acknowledge anyone or anything. The coverlet on the bed was soft, the cloth on her forehead cool and damp. For the first time in quite a while, she felt safe.

When she finally opened her eyes and had the strength to sit up, Thomas was still there – only now he was Captain Edwards. Even in the dust and squalor of the camp, he looked elegant in his uniform. The sounds of the camp had returned. However unpleasant they were, Catherine found the noise and clatter oddly soothing.

A small lamp flickered next to the bed. Thomas was leaning forward and reading, his elbows resting on his knees. She smiled, never imagining he'd grow and keep a beard, but she had to admit she liked the look on him. At that moment, she didn't see a soldier sitting there, but an old friend who was struggling to make sense out of the insanity that brought the two of them back together.

His vulnerability made her reach out and touch his arm.

His tired and vexed expression disappeared the moment he saw she was awake. His smile made her quiver a little.

"It's good to see you awake," he said as he engulfed her hand into his, kissing it with a tenderness she'd forgotten existed in the world. "Can I get you anything?"

"Some…some water," she said. Her voice was barely a whisper.

He set Oscar's Bible on the table and poured her some water in a tin cup. She struggled with the first few sips but soon drained the contents and held the cup out for some more. She pointed to the book.

"Oscar's Bible?"

"Yes." He squeezed her forearm. "I'm sorry we left you alone today. Your friends said you were not well. I did not want to wake —"

"Please, there's no need to apologize."

They squeezed one another's hand. Catherine pointed to the Bible.

"He always carried it with him," she said.

Thomas smiled. "He did."

"I cried when I heard about his death. My father and I, we…we mourned him."

Thomas studied her for a moment but didn't respond.

"What were you reading?" she asked.

"Nothing specific. Just looking. Trying to find an answer for…" Thomas looked over at the flap of the tent then back at her. "For everything that's happening."

. "I haven't read the Bible since…well, since I was taken from my home." She smiled, choking back the memory of all she'd lost. "I used to read it every day." She looked back at Thomas. "Do you?"

Thomas sighed. "I…I don't. I just got out the habit. War can do that."

"Oh," Catherine replied. "I'd assume that would be the best time to read the Bible…and pray."

"Perhaps." Thomas looked down. "Trying to find faith, looking for good to overcome evil – not as easy as preachers make it sound. The world just seems to be getting darker by the day."

He ran his hand through his hair. "Pretty cynical, huh?"

"I understand how hard it can be to believe."

"I'm sorry," he said. "I have little to complain about."

"It's all right."

For the first time, she saw Fort Newnan and the relocation fiasco through his eyes. If he was still the kindhearted person she had known – and she believed him to be – his current assignment had to be tearing him apart.

"Let's stop apologizing to one another," she said.

A voice came from outside the tent.

"Captain Edwards? Someone to see you, sir."

Thomas went to the flap and pushed it open. Catherine snatched her knees up to her chest and wrapped her arms around them. A young man in civilian clothes held the reins of a horse. Thomas stepped outside. The young man glanced at Catherine before stepping closer to the captain and whispering. He handed Thomas a folded piece of paper then mounted and rode away. Thomas stepped back inside before he opened the paper and read it.

"Do you know where Miriam and Oscar went after leaving the mission?" he asked.

"They had land just outside of Dahlonega," Catherine replied. "Several hundred acres I believe."

"Miriam still lives there. You could join her."

"What?"

"I've been thinking about this," he replied. "Just hear me out. I can help you escape. Even give you an escort of some kind."

"I can't," she said.

"Why not?"

Catherine swung her legs over the side of the cot. Pain shot through her torso, but she kept her face impassive. "I am very grateful, but no."

"I don't understand."

"Many reasons but the main one is I do not have my daughter."

Thomas sat and patted the bed. Catherine reclined. The pain eased back into its lair.

"I'm still searching for her," he said. "I'll find her and bring her to you."

If Elias finds out about Ayita... Catherine could not finish the thought.

Thomas's jaw went rigid.

"You're mad," she said.

"Yes," Thomas replied. "I don't want to see you in here."

"What do you want?" she asked.

"I want to save you."

"You can't."

Thomas exhaled. "Maybe not, but I can make things better for you."

"How? You can't undo what's already been done. You can't give back anything that's been taken."

"I'm not trying to change the past. I'm trying to give you a future, Catherine."

"I am Tsalagi, Thomas. We have no future in your world."

"I can't stand seeing you here, Catherine."

She touched his face. He was beautiful at that moment, causing her to pull her hand away as if she was touching something forbidden.

"I can't leave my new family," she said, looking away.

"Your new family?"

"You've met them. Leotie, and her husband Waya and their children. Jeevan, his wife Manjusha and their children."

"So, nothing I can say or do would make you want to leave this godforsaken place?"

"No. I never thought I'd say this, but I *can't* leave." She stared into his worried eyes. "My dear Thomas. You were always a romantic. Always with big dreams."

Thomas pulled away. "Don't patronize me."

He jumped up and began to pace. He punched his left hand into his right palm.

"I didn't mean to anger you," she said. "That wasn't my intention. It's just that running away isn't as easy as you're making it sound."

Thomas turned to yell at her but thought better of it.

"Maybe it isn't that easy," he said. "I just believe I can get you away from here."

"It means a lot to me that you care so much. But too much has happened. Too many bad things. I'm too afraid to lose what little I have left."

Thomas sat back down in front of her but didn't take her hands. He studied her for a moment.

"What are you thinking?" Catherine asked.

He shook his head, sorting through his thoughts.

"I'm wondering how many others would like to escape," he said. "I'm wondering if they would accept my offer to help." He looked down. "I don't know, maybe I am just a big dreamer."

Catherine was sure there were other people planning to escape.

"I could talk with Waya," she said. "He's helped so many. I'm sure he knows who's planning to run away. But there's something else."

"What?"

"How do you know Miriam will agree?"

Thomas handed her the piece of paper.

"Read it," he said.

Catherine unfolded the paper.

> *Received your handkerchief and packages*
> *yesterday. All is well. Nothing missing.*
> *You can send more if you like.*
> *Love, Miriam.*

Thomas took the note and held the edge over the lantern's flame. He dropped the burning paper on the floor. When it was fully consumed, he ground the ashes under his boot.

"I didn't send her any packages," Thomas said. "She's telling me that Rupesh's children made it safely."

"How did she know you sent them?"

There was movement at the side of the tent. The shadow wearing a towering top hat floated past. Catherine shot to her feet.

"I have to go!"

Before Thomas could react, Catherine bolted past him and out into the night.

CHAPTER THIRTY

Getting everything organized for a daily ten-mile march challenged logistics and strained tempers. Roe pulled no punches.

"If we can't pull this off, Captain, tryin' to get all these folks 'cross the country to Indian Territory will be laborious."

The comment was just the tension breaker Thomas needed. "Do you know what those big words mean, or do you just throw them in there for effect?" he asked.

Roe looked a little hurt. "Just 'cause I ain't matriculated someplace fancy like West Point don't mean I'm a savage…*sir.*"

"No offense intended," Thomas said.

Roe softened a bit. "None taken…I reckon."

Thomas looked at the men and women slouching their way toward the line at the gate.

"They look just like I did when my ma sent me to get a switch so she could tan my hide," Roe said.

Thomas understood.

It had been five days since Catherine's headlong charge out of his tent – one hundred and twenty long hours without seeing her face. Thomas continually ran the conversation through his mind and could not figure out why she'd bolted so quickly.

On top of that, not a single Cherokee had approached him about escaping.

Maybe I am nothing but a dreamer.

"Forward!"

Thomas clicked and Silo led the grim parade out of the fort. They walked for two hours before Thomas broke off from the lead and trotted along the line of shuffling men and women.

He decided to stretch his legs, so he dismounted Silo. As he was rubbing his sore thighs, someone spoke.

"Hello, Captain," Waya said. He looked around before he offered his hand. "I want to thank you for all that you've done for my people. You are an honorable man."

Thomas took Waya's hand. "Thank you, but I'm not sure any honorable man would find himself here."

Waya gestured to the trail, and they began to walk. Waya walked with determination and purpose – the stride of a leader.

"I can understand why you say that," he said, "but difficult circumstances expose who is honorable and who is not. We are all the same when life is easy."

Thomas walked along. He did not need to hold Silo's reins. The horse followed without prompts.

"Is now a good time to discuss your grandmother's land?" Waya asked.

Thomas's pulse quickened but he knew he needed to be careful in his response. He took his time to avoid attracting attention. No one seemed to be watching. The soldiers were scrutinizing the Cherokees. The Cherokees simply tried to take one more step without collapsing.

"Kasewini told me your idea. It's one with great possibility." Waya moved closer to Thomas and looked at his people. "We should only involve those already planning to escape – those physically able to make the trip."

"Agreed," Thomas replied. "And we cannot have a mass escape."

Waya nodded. "That will not be difficult. The number of people who have the strength to run is dwindling every day." Waya rushed over to help a woman who had stumbled. He attended to her, gave her a sip of water, then wandered back over to Thomas. "Your grandmother will be okay with strangers running to her land?"

"Yes. Especially when she hears of the horrors of this place."

"That's what Kasewini told me, but I had to hear it from you to believe it. Kasewini said Miriam is a full blood."

"Yes. Oneida Nation. Her people are from the New York area but are continually relocating to the Territory of Wisconsin to get away from—"

"From the white devils," Waya said. His tired eyes danced with laughter. "Sorry, that was too easy. No offense, Captain."

"None taken," Thomas said.

They walked for a while looking to all the world like two isolated individuals who happened to be side by side.

Waya broke the silence. "So, your grandmother understands what it means to be pushed out of the land of her ancestors." When Thomas nodded, Waya said, "Then we must honor her with a good plan to get people to her land safely. The soldiers are not our only obstacle."

"Meaning?

"People will do most anything to stay alive," Waya said. "I am saddened by the Tsalagi who are trading information for food, but I hold no grudges. Some people's hold on their honor is looser than others. From now on, we must communicate indirectly – to be safe."

The two men discussed times and places, then devised a scheme of signals. Waya turned to join his people.

"How is Catherine?" Thomas asked.

Waya stared into the horizon. "She is a strong Tsalagi – a proud woman, but she has suffered much, more than most, more than she will say. How do you know her?"

"She's a friend from a long time ago."

Waya's raised his eyebrows but said nothing.

"I knew her father, Jishnu," Thomas said, "He and my grandfather were close friends."

Waya studied the captain for a few moments.

"Jishnu was a good man," Waya said. "That makes me believe your grandfather was a good man as well."

"He was."

"Then he'd be proud of what you're doing here."

Thomas bit his lip. Waya noticed.

"You carry too much guilt for what your government's doing," Waya said. "You mustn't let it cloud your judgment. You are here now – and you have important work to do."

"I'll tell her you asked about her," Waya said finally.

"Tell her I said I'm sorry."

"But you have nothing to—"

"Just tell her. Please."

CHAPTER THIRTY-ONE

"Thank you," Salal said. "I can never repay you for your kindness."

Catherine felt oddly husky next to such a petite man. And though they were the same age, she also felt much older.

"No need to thank me," she said. "If we don't take care of each other, none of us will survive."

When Salal bobbed his head, his entire body moved. He scanned the corral and looked at the dozen or so people who were attempting to make the piece of cornbread she'd given them last as long as possible.

"I wish there was more," she said.

She looked at Salal. Small and delicate, Salal's skin remained lustrous despite the blistering sun and grim conditions. His long hair accentuated features that could only be described as feminine. His masculinity was further undermined by a total lack of facial hair, a high-pitched voice, and moves more akin to a deer than most women she knew. He'd been ostracized from his own clan at puberty and left alone for most of his adult life.

The first time she'd seen him, he was sprawled in the dirt having been tossed into the corral like a sack of grain. No one moved to help him as he lay face down and whimpering. He had no pack, no bedroll, no possessions of any kind other than the tattered buckskins he wore.

When Catherine touched his shoulder, he looked up and revealed split lips, a bruised cheek, and a right eye so swollen it looked ready to explode. He'd winced when she touched him, whether from pain or fright, Catherine never knew, but the moment she showed him the smallest morsel of decency, he bonded to her like a stray puppy to someone offering a meal.

"Your eye's looking better," Catherine said.

Salal picked a crumb of cornbread from his shirt and dropped it into his mouth. He closed his eyes and savored the flavor as he finished off the rest of the bread she'd given him.

Catherine brushed at his face with a damp cloth.

"It's still swollen, but it's getting better."

Salal flinched a little but did not make a sound. "How long have you been here?" he asked.

Catherine was taken aback by the realization she had no idea how long she'd been at Fort Newnan. She missed her home as if she had been taken away from it only the day before, however, the pain she's endured since then made it seem like life in the corral was all she's ever known.

"I'm not sure. Several weeks. A month maybe."

Neither spoke while Catherine finished her ministrations by applying an herbal paste Waya had concocted to Salal's eye. All the while Catherine tried to fix the exact date of her arrival in her mind. She could not.

"I ran," he said after a while. "When they began rounding us up, I ran. I lived in a shack in the hills not too far from here. I was out gathering wood when the soldiers came. Don't know how they knew I was there, but they found me. So, I hid in a tree. They just made camp outside of my home and waited. They never bothered to enter. The next morning, they made ready to leave. I saw a soldier pick up a shovel. I thought he would extinguish their fire. Instead, he smashed my door, then picked up a burning stick and tossed it inside. Everything I owned was gone in a matter of minutes."

Salal gave Catherine an unconvincing smile.

"I didn't have much in there, but it was my home."

Catherine understood all too well.

"I grew up with my great grandmother, my grandmother, mother and two siblings," he said. He made a furtive gesture with his hand and wiped away a tear.

"My grandmother was an outspoken woman – didn't like my father much and let him and everyone else know about it. He must have grown tired of it because I never saw him after I turned seven. I was told he visited my mother in the middle of the night from time to time but that was all. My mother and grandmother were traditional women. They did all the farming and gathering. Chopped wood and did repairs on our home as needed. They didn't hunt but would trade some of their crops for meat. They didn't need a man."

Salal looked down at his hand.

"When I turned twelve, I stopped growing," he said. "I am the same size now as I was then. My voice never changed – seems to me it had gotten higher. My family became increasingly embarrassed by my presence. My brother hated me because I looked and sounded like a girl. When I turned fourteen it was obvious that I wasn't going to be much of a man, so my mother kicked me out of the house. She said I brought too much trouble to her home, so I had to leave."

He looked out at the soldiers who were in various stages of sloth. "After they burned my house, I ran. I managed to elude everyone for quite some time. But one morning I woke up and found seven soldiers standing around me. Some of them thought I was a little boy; others thought maybe I was a woman."

Salal took a deep breath and looked up at the sky.

"Were they the ones who hurt you?" Catherine asked.

Salal pulled his knees up to his chest and wrapped his arms around his legs.

"Were they?" Catherine asked again.

Salal rested his head on his arms. "That's enough sad stories for one day."

CHAPTER THIRTY-TWO

For each of the six days since Catherine left Thomas's tent, she expected Gabe to show up and escort her to the woods. Whenever the sun went behind the hills to sleep, she prepared herself for another assault. The summons never came.

Every day, as ordered, Thomas marched the people through the surrounding countryside. His custom was to allow them to rest after seven miles. On the first day, the adults all collapsed. The children did not. They ran around, played, and explored.

Since most of the parents refused to move until Thomas gave the order, Catherine decided to watch the youngsters. She organized games and other activities, so the adults could rest without worry. By the third day, the children would gather at the edge of the group during the rest time and wait for Catherine's arrival. Sometimes Manjusha, Leotie, Waya, or someone else helped, but the children always wanted Catherine.

On the sixth day, with Salal watching in delight from a tree – as usual – Thomas approached.

"May I join you?" he asked one of the boys.

The child hesitated for a moment. White soldiers rarely, if ever, interacted with any Cherokee. Catherine almost objected but within seconds Thomas was tossing children into the air and catching them while they shrieked with delight. They played longer than the usual rest time from the march. Finally, when Thomas announced it was time to go, in unison the children asked if he would play with them tomorrow.

He promised he would.

The next day, when they were close to the stopping point, Thomas guided Silo near Catherine.

"We need another game," he said.

"Excuse me?"

"I can't toss one more child," he said. "I could barely get out of bed this morning."

Despite herself, she laughed.

"You are turning into an old man, Captain," she said.

"Maybe," he said, "but I'm a crafty old coot."

He called for a halt. When everyone settled, he and Catherine walked towards the children who were standing in what had become their traditional place. Thomas carried a bundle of rope over his shoulder.

"And those are for?" Catherine asked.

"You'll see," he said.

Thomas summoned the children. Once they settled, he selected one of the older boys.

"Stand next to me," Thomas said. His Cherokee was terrible, but the boy understood enough to comply.

Thomas moved until his side touched the boy's. He tied his right leg to the youngster's left at the thigh and just below the knee. Thomas leaned over and whispered. The boy smiled and nodded before the two of them wrapped an arm around the other and tried to run.

Three steps later, much to the delight of the children, Thomas and the boy collapsed in a jumble of limbs. The tethered pair staggered to a standing position and kept trying until they could establish a passable gait.

Thomas assigned pairs and Catherine did the "roping honors." The captain let the boys and girls practice for a while, then lined everyone up.

"One…two…three…*race!*"

By the third race, most of the adults were standing and cheering. Every child clamored for a chance to have the white soldier as a partner, which proved quite a challenge in the cases where Thomas was almost two feet taller. But he was as game as his young compatriots and before long, the hills echoed with a sound no one had heard for a long time – a rumble of joy.

Thomas had just collapsed with his most recent partner when Roe approached.

"Begging yer pardon, Captain, we'll be needin' t' move with some alacrity elsewise Colonel Morse will be thinkin' we've absconded along with the tribe."

The children groaned.

"Can we do it again tomorrow?" one of the boys asked.

"Yes, I promise we can do this again tomorrow," Thomas replied.

He chose to ignore Roe's disapproving scowl.

"Those who can, run down to the creek for water. Drink your fill, then bring some back for the rest. Hurry."

Catherine slipped up beside him "That was a great idea," she said. "The children loved it."

Thomas's heart danced a jig when he looked at her.

"Thanks," he said.

Catherine walked away to escort a toddler to her parents. Thomas watched her go, contentment in his heart and thoughts of the future in his head. Then, he looked at Roe.

"Now, Captain," the sergeant said.

Thomas's shoulders sagged with the weary burden of reality.

On the way back to the fort, Thomas slid off Silo and walked next to Catherine. She walked without conversation but made no objection. Three small children tugged on her dress. She bent over, so they could whisper in her ear.

Catherine stood up. "Why don't you ask him?"

The children giggled but scurried behind Catherine when Thomas said, "What?"

Catherine looked around her. "Well, are you going to ask him?"

When the only response from the children was a group giggle, Catherine feigned disapproval, then said, "They want to know if they can pet Silo."

"Certainly. Tell them to move slowly at first – not to rush at him."

Catherine issued instructions and the children approached the enormous animal like Moses walking towards the burning bush. They were tentative at first, but soon were rubbing Silo's coat while he nuzzled them.

Thomas dropped the reins and clicked. Silo walked next to him with a retinue of Cherokee children streaming alongside. Catherine's face lit up with delight.

"To be honest, I think they'd like to ride on him, too," she said.

"They would?"

"Oh yes. To ride the horse that belongs to 'Walks the Sky' would be an honor."

"Who's Walks the Sky?"

"You," Catherine replied. "That's what everyone calls you, 'Walks the Sky.'"

"What does that mean?"

"Does a name have a meaning?"

"You know they do, especially among your people."

Catherine kept walking.

"What does it mean?" Thomas asked again.

Her smiling face, something he remembered from long ago, made Thomas's pulse quicken.

"The elders say you are always looking up at the sky, searching for answers. They say you walk the sky looking for wisdom on how to help us survive all of this. Some even suggested your spirit walks the sky to protect those who have escaped and those who have ...died."

Thomas stopped.

Catherine continued for a few steps until she realized he wasn't beside her anymore. When she looked back, his face registered stunned surprise.

"Are you all right?" she asked.

"I...I don't know what to say."

"What do you mean?"

"How can I live up to such a name?" he asked.

Catherine motioned for him to keep walking.

"You don't have to live up to it. It was given to you because of who you *are*, not what the elders expect you to be. There's no living up to a name. You must live up to the spirit inside you."

The only sound was the shuffling of tired feet.

"Could you do me a favor?" she asked.

"I will do anything in my power."

"Would you let the children have a ride on Silo?"

"Of course."

Thomas picked the first child up and sat her upon Silo. Once she was comfortable, he tugged on the reins. The child squealed.

One after another, Thomas hoisted children onto his faithful traveling companion. Silo looked a little irritated by the constant stop and go, but never once resisted – never once retaliated against the youngsters who were jumping up and down in his saddle with excitement.

The longer they walked, the closer Catherine moved to Thomas. Neither of them pulled away when their hands brushed – more than once.

CHAPTER THIRTY-THREE

Before the horde reached Fort Newnan, Thomas sent a couple of his men ahead with instructions to set up "a proper grooming." Though he never neglected his most trusted traveling companion, Thomas had not spent any serious time dedicated to Silo.

Silo cut his eyes and nickered.

"Yes, I know," Thomas said. "About time, right?"

Silo neighed as if to say, "Get on with it."

Thomas grabbed a curry brush. He used a circular motion to remove the accumulated dust, dander, and scurf.

"Hold still, now. I can't get you cleaned up with you prancing all over the place."

Silo settled down, snorted, and swiped his tail at the captain.

Roe walked up from the other side. "Gettin' him ready for more kiddie rides tomorrow?" he asked.

"If you have a problem with my conduct, Sergeant, say so." Thomas shot a wary look at his aide. "Otherwise, stand down and let me take care of my horse."

"As you wish, sir," Roe said.

Thomas saw Roe assume parade rest, feet shoulder-width apart, hand clasped behind his back.

"It's not the parade field, Roe. What's on your mind?"

"Been askin' around. Found where Elias has been for the past week or so."

"Where's that?"

"Up north in Tennessee. I hear he's taking care of business for Colonel Morse."

"Did he take his men with him?" Thomas asked.

"Seems so."

"How'd you find out?"

"Did some checking. Also heard he might not be coming back here."

To Silo's irritation, Thomas stopped brushing.

"Quit being so coy and tell me what's going on."

Roe relaxed a little and slipped half an apple to Silo.

"Rumor has it we'll be sendin' all these people up north within the next couple of weeks. I figger that snake'll be part of the welcoming committee."

Thomas resumed his brushing. Roe cleared his throat.

"Any word on the little Indian girl?"

"Which one?"

"The one you been movin' heaven and earth t' find."

"As a matter of fact, there is," Thomas replied. "Just this afternoon. Sergeant Wallace returned from Fort Gilmer."

"What'd he have to say?"

Thomas grimaced. "Apparently, Fort Gilmer makes this place look organized. Makes finding anyone hard – much less a child. He said there are children there without families, but no one's heard of a six-year-old named Ayita. They didn't know anything about Kavi or Harsha either."

"Wallace is pretty thorough."

"True," Thomas said, "but it doesn't matter."

"Why's that?"

"Private Bond came back from Fort Hetzel."

"And?"

Thomas knew better than to interrupt the grooming again. "It appears Fort Hetzel is an enigma – neat as a pin – vetting process – all the names recorded."

"Well, there's a novel idea."

"Bond managed to get a peek at the list."

"You're kiddin'."

"Not at all, I'm happy to say."

"Bond didn't happen to find Ayita's name, did he?"

"Believe it or not, he found all three kids."

"Well, I'll be damned."

"He said every child who was alone was assigned to a family that will take care of them until they reach the Indian Territory."

"You gonna try to get 'em back here?"

"Don't know. Whatever we decide to do, we need to proceed with caution."

"Why do you say that?"

"Private Bond," Thomas replied. "One of the old-timers at Fort Hetzel told Bond he's been a part of several Indian relocations over the years. Every time it's the same thing as with the Cherokees, families taken from their homes, some separated along the way to the holding camps. He said in the past, a lot of children just disappear. He suspects they're being sold into slavery."

Roe nodded and looked down. "Yeah, I've heard that before too. I didn't want to say anything to you about it if I didn't have to. I didn't want to worry you none until we found the kids."

Thomas moved to the other side. The horse nodded his approval.

"Private Bond's story's got me thinking," Thomas said. "We need to keep a close eye on the children here. If ever there were two cold-hearted devils that could sell a child into slavery it'd be Morse and Elias."

"Ain't that the truth."

"When are you going to tell Catherine?" Roe asked.

"After I finish up here."

Roe studied the captain for a moment. "You sure what yer doin' is a good idea?"

"Brushing Silo?"

"You know what I'm talkin' about. Spendin' so much time playin' with the children. Talkin' with Catherine."

"What's wrong with it?" Thomas asked.

"You've been doin' it a lot lately."

Thomas laughed. "A lot? I have played with those children exactly twice." He rested his arms on Silo's back. "It takes, what, five, six hours a day to march those people. And I spend, maybe, twenty or thirty minutes with the youngsters."

"I'm spottin' an exponential increase, Captain. Yesterday, it was throwin' 'em around. Today, it was three-legged races and pony rides. What's tomorrow – lemonade and homemade pie?"

Thomas went back to brushing Silo without a response.

"I don't think it's very professional, sir," Roe said. "You're a soldier. Not a nanny."

Thomas looked at Roe. "I'm making a couple of dozen children smile. It's the only decency they have encountered in this godforsaken place. You have an issue with that, Sergeant?"

"Watchin' out for you, sir. Feeding and watering 'em is one thing —"

"Dammit, Roe!" When the brush hit the bucket five feet away, it sounded like a rifle shot. "They're not horses. They are human beings."

"Ye're just awfully personal, sir."

"Personal?" Thomas rubbed his temple before he continued. "We're not at war with these people, Roe, but they are being treated worse than we would treat an enemy. For almost a month, you and I have looked into their eyes while they starve. We have heard them beg for water. We have carried their dead, filth-covered loved ones to a mass grave while they wait to see if someone else in their families is going to die. It's about as personal as it can get!"

"I agree, Captain, but I think ye're lettin' yer personal feelings about the woman cloud yer judgment."

"So you've said."

"You seem impervious to my advice."

"That's because—"

Thomas broke off and walked over to the grooming bucket. He tossed out the water, then took his time stacking all the loose buckets. He stared into the distance and muttered for a while before returning to the conversation.

"Let me ask *you* a few questions, Sergeant. Where's it written that a soldier can't make a child laugh? What regulation prohibits us from helping them forget where they are, even only for a few minutes? Why do we have to bring misery? Is it our duty as soldiers to inflict pain on these people, or are we allowed to offer a sliver of hope? What is our damn duty, Sergeant?"

Roe shook his head. "I just don't see how this ends well for you. These people are gonna be driven from their lands. And Catherine along with 'em. She's Cherokee and yer a soldier. What good can come of that?"

Thomas sucked in his bottom lip. "How long do you think it's going to take us to get them to the Indian Territories?"

"Five, six months would be my best guess."

"That's roughly one hundred and eighty days. Are we supposed to go that long without speaking or interacting with these people?"

"Gettin' personal with 'em won't change what's gonna happen, sir."

"And neither will be keeping our distance!" Thomas bit his lip and looked over at the corral until his heart rate dropped enough for him to speak calmly. "Like you said, nothing we do will make a difference in the end. They'll still lose everything they've ever known. Knowing that, I can't look into their eyes and pretend they're not human beings in pain. I can't look at their faces and not want to help them. I can't be around them and not interact with them."

He looked at Roe.

"If I'm wrong, I'm wrong. But when all of this is said and done...when it's all over, I'll be able to look back on it and know I did the best I could do for another human being."

Roe stepped forward with his finger raised. "Captain, ya need to think this thing through."

"And you need to remember your place, *Sergeant.*"

Roe's head snapped back. In all their time together, Thomas, though a thorough and competent commander, had always treated him as more of an equal, a confidant…a friend. Roe very deliberately slid his feet together, assumed a position at attention, and executed a textbook salute.

"Sergeant Dearborn Rowland Bickford III requesting permission to leave, *sir.*"

Thomas closed his eyes and shook his head.

"I didn't mean it, Roe. I'm sorry."

With his eyes riveted at something in the distance, Roe held his position – fingers and thumb aligned…index finger an inch above the right eye… bicep parallel to the ground.

Thomas waved through a sloppy salute.

"Permission granted," he said.

CHAPTER THIRTY-FOUR

Catherine leaned against the fence post and watched Leotie with her family as they ate what little they could scrape together for dinner. They interacted with one another as if they were anywhere else but the corral, a product of Waya and Leotie's determination to see the good in everything. Catherine thought of Ayita and missed hearing her laugh…seeing her smile…stroking her hair at bedtime.

Catherine turned away before the anguish of missing her daughter became too much; she saw a figure approaching in the fading light.

Thomas.

He stopped in front of her.

"Can we talk?" he asked. "It's about Ayita."

Startled, Catherine sat up. "Is she safe?"

"Yes," Thomas said. "Let me fill you in."

He gave her Private Bond's report minus the part about children being sold into slavery. Catherine placed her hand over her pounding heart and struggled not to cry.

"Ayita's okay?"

"Yes."

"And she's being cared for?"

"Yes."

Catherine took several deep breaths.

"Sorry for the repetition," she said. "I just want to make sure I heard everything right."

"You did," Thomas said.

"Was this private…Private Bonds…ah…did he speak to her?"

"No. He was not allowed to speak to any of the Cherokees."

"Oh."

"Given the situation, he said she is doing well. She gets food and water regularly. She is relatively clean and safe."

Unable to hold back the tears, Catherine sobbed. Thomas reached for her, then stopped. When Catherine looked up, she was smiling.

Thomas met her smile with one of his own. "I can see about having her transferred here to Fort Newnan," he said.

Catherine's smile faded a bit but didn't completely disappear. Although wrapping her arms around Ayita was the one thing she desired most, Catherine wanted to keep her daughter away from Elias.

"I've thought about what to say or do if you found her," Catherine said. "If she was in a worse place than this one, I would beg you to bring her here. However, knowing she is in a better place I think she should stay there."

Thomas considered her answer and nodded.

"I know I'll see her when this is all over," Catherine said.

"Did Waya tell you that you will be relocated soon?" Thomas asked.

Catherine nodded. "He did. You think I'll see Ayita wherever it is we go to next?"

"I don't know," Thomas replied. "I would think so."

"Why do you say that?"

"With Fort Hetzel located so close, I have to assume our two forts will be combined."

Catherine took a deep breath. "Will you be going with us?"

When he hesitated, Catherine felt her stomach drop.

"Thomas?"

"I...I...don't know," he said. "Lots of changes since I got here. No guarantees."

"And Elias?"

Thomas said nothing but the look in his eyes was all the answer she needed.

§§

Thomas had been gone an hour when Manjusha arrived.

"May I join you?"

Catherine moved over and watched her friend sit down next to her. Manjusha looked at her children. They were huddled together, drawing pictures in the dirt, and telling stories about them.

"It's good to know Kavi and Harsha are safe," she said finally. "Thank you for telling me. It was good medicine."

"Of course," Catherine replied.

"Sahen and Rupa have asked about them almost every day since they were taken," Manjusha said. "And I have lied. Every day, I have lied to my children. I told them I knew where their brother and sister were. Every day I said that I knew they were well."

A quiet tear rolled down her cheek. "I was dreading the day I would have to tell them anything different."

Catherine reached out and took Manjusha's hand. "You told them what you instinctively knew to be true."

Manjusha shrugged and squeezed Catherine's hand. "What do we tell them now? When we get to the Indian Territory, what do we tell them? How do we explain what has happened to our people?"

Catherine had no answer to a question she'd asked herself many times.

"My heart has become filled with so much hate," Manjusha continued. "Such anger towards the white man. So, what do I tell my children? I do not want to fill them with the hatred I have."

"I...I do not know," Catherine replied.

"Do we tell them anything or just..."

"It will take time," Catherine said. "Time to heal. Time to gain a perspective that benefits our people."

"I am worried, Kasewini. I am worried that in generations to come they will forget all about what happened to us. People will forget we were forced to leave. That we had no choice but to abandon our ancestors. They will forget our ancestors are *here* and not in the Indian Territory." Manjusha pulled at a loose thread on her dress. "I am also afraid it will all happen again. Once we settle into the new lands. What will stop them from taking that land away? And when they do, what will prevent the white government from killing us all?"

"I have not thought about it," Catherine said.

"Sorry," Manjusha said. She waved as if shooing a fly. "I am full of fear and bitterness. Ever since the soldiers burst into our home, I have been afraid. I feel so helpless, so vulnerable. I know I told you to forgive yourself and guard your heart against bitterness but I'm finding it harder to see any light in the future."

Catherine squeezed Manjusha's hand. "I feel the same way. We are blessed to have each other. In time, things will get better."

Manjusha looked away. "I wish I still believed that."

Catherine watched her friend and realized how easy it could be to lose hope.

"We should have surrendered our property months ago," Manjusha said. "My family would still be together. We might already be in the Indian Territory with the others, building our new life and not here, starving."

"I thought the same thing when my father was dying," Catherine said. "I imagine everyone has. But that is all in the past. We cannot drive ourselves mad by speculating."

"It's hard not to think about it," Manjusha said.

They sat in silence for a few moments watching Manjusha's children.

"Jeevan told me Salal's been asking about escaping," Manjusha said. "He should not speak so openly about it."

"He approached me for help," Catherine said.

"What did you tell him?"

"Just that Waya told me how he is helping people escape," Catherine said. "There is a meeting place by a clump of trees. Somehow, they arrange for an escort who shows them to Miriam's land – Captain Edward's grandmother. I didn't mention Waya's name of course."

Manjusha nodded. "Jeevan told me about it," Manjusha said. "Dangerous business I feel. I think it is best left alone. The less we know, the better. If Salal wants to run, he doesn't need to get us involved."

Catherine drew circles on the ground.

"I don't understand why he wants to risk being hunted down," Manjusha said.

"Maybe he feels like he cannot make the trip out west," Catherine said. "He seems so fragile, so desperate. Maybe he *should* stay here."

"Do not get involved, Kasewini," Manjusha said. "Desperate people can be dangerous."

§§

The sun's rays were wiggling over the eastern horizon when Thomas opened the flap to his tent. He was just about to step outside when he was stopped short by the outline of a man on horseback waiting just thirty feet away.

Thomas reached for his sidearm.

"Good morning, Captain." Colonel Morse said.

Thomas checked both sides of his tent.

Colonel Morse chuckled. "I can assure you I'm alone, Captain."

The silhouette of an exceptionally rotund man sitting upon a ridiculously large and unattractive draft horse made the captain smile.

"To what do I owe this honor, Colonel?"

Morse snorted in concert with his chubby horse. "You, Captain. You're the reason for my being here."

"Oh?"

"I've heard a rumor about you."

"You came here before the crack of dawn to find out about a rumor?"

Colonel Morse looked up at the sky. His face bore a quizzical expression as if he could not remember what a sunrise looked like.

"I feel it's time for me to accompany you and your men while on your march," the colonel said once he was finally able to refocus.

"It's your command, Colonel," Thomas replied as he sauntered over to say good morning to Silo. "Who am I to stop you?"

"Who indeed." Colonel Morse watched the captain, trying to ascertain if the announcement had any impact on the young man. "The fact that I'll just randomly pick a day to accompany you won't cause any problems, will it?"

Agitated by the question, Thomas turned to face the colonel. "Let's cut to the chase, Colonel. What do you want?"

"I told you."

"We've been marching these people for over two weeks now and haven't seen hide nor hair of you. So, why would I care if you accompany us or not?"

The colonel's smile faded.

"Runaways, Captain. It's come to my attention that their numbers have increased since you've started marching those people. I told you I'd keep an eye on that."

"Not sure what you expected to happen when we started letting them out of that corral, Colonel."

Thomas walked over and grabbed his saddle and started to get Silo ready for the day.

"So, you don't deny it?"

"What's there to deny?" Thomas asked. "I haven't been taking a count before we leave the corral or when we get back, so yes, it's possible there have been some runners. But it's ridiculous to think

we can keep track of everyone. There are far too many people for us
to—"

"I don't think that's what's going on here, Captain."

Thomas made a grand gesture of turning and facing the colonel.
"So, what *do* you think's going on?"

"You are not sufficiently attentive."

Thomas scratched his morning beard. "Fine by me, Colonel.
Why not have Captain Dorsey march them?"

When Colonel Morse laughed, his jelly-belly swayed out of
control. He managed to grab onto the saddle horn just before falling
off his horse.

"Dorsey?" the colonel asked once he regained his composure.
"That man hardly knows which way's up nowadays. I doubt he'd
ever be able to get the people back to the fort. No, I have no choice
but to have you do it, unfortunately."

"There's always Elias," Thomas replied before refocusing on
Silo's saddle.

"He's busy right now, but when he gets back...perhaps."

"How do you know there's been an increase in runners,
anyway?" Thomas asked. "Neither you nor Captain Dorsey ever
bothered to take roll, so how would you know if anyone's
disappeared?"

Colonel Morse shifted in his saddle and glanced into the
direction of Roe's tent before answering.

"If you must know, Captain, an individual came to my tent with an interesting story. This person suggested maybe you're getting too close to the captives. They also said you've been taking them into the same easterly direction, almost the exact same path, every day. Perhaps you're doing this to make it easier for people to escape."

Thomas looked into the direction of Roe's tent.

"So, I thought I needed to get more involved and see things for myself," Colonel Morse said.

Thomas cinched the girth and then settled the bit into Silo's mouth.

"I don't know what to tell you, Colonel. People have their opinions. I can't control that, nor will I try. If you think I'm up to something, put someone else in charge. But as long as I am leading, we will use the same route because it is familiar and, therefore, less frightening for these poor people."

Thomas wasn't concerned about Morse. Thomas knew when and where the "steal aways" were taking place and still, he had never witnessed one.

"That's your decision, Captain. I'm just here to oversee everything."

"Does this mean you're going to shadow me all morning? Do I need to have some extra breakfast made for you?"

"No need, Captain. I must be on my way. I just wanted to give you notice I was going to pick a day to ride along with you. Might be today, might not."

Thomas rested his arm on Silo and watched the colonel disappear behind one of the buildings when Roe happened to appear with coffee in hand.

"What the hell are you thinking?" Thomas asked.

Roe stopped in his tracks. "What'd I jus' stumble into?"

"A mess of your own doing. What were you thinking going to Colonel Morse?"

"What are you goin' on about?"

"The colonel said he feels I'm getting too close to the Cherokees."

"Well, he's prolly right."

"So that's it? You don't like how I'm doing things, so you go to the Colonel?"

"I didn't—"

"I trusted you! If you have something to say, come to me and say it."

"I did come to you."

"And what? I don't agree with you, so you go runnin' to the colonel?"

Roe looked down at the cups of coffee in his hand. "I think you're losing your bearings, Captain. I've never seen an officer—"

"I don't care what you've ever seen an officer do or not do! There's no protocol for this place."

"There's protocol for how to conduct ourselves around captives, sir."

"Captives? So, now *you're* calling them 'captives'?"

"We are soldiers, sir. Our orders come from the United States government, the same government the Cherokees signed a treaty with. They had plenty of time to hand over their property and goods as was enumerated in the treaty. And when they didn't, our bosses trusted us to carry out the treaty. The Cherokees broke the treaty they signed, which is breakin' the law. So, yes, if ya wanna get literal about it, they *are* our prisoners, our captives. You can ignore that fact all you want. You can pretend yer all friends and neighbors, but it doesn't change a thing."

"Do I like how they're being treated?" Roe asked. "No, I don't. But there comes a point when we as soldiers have to take a step back and accept things for what they are."

Thomas was suddenly calm. Perhaps his rage had reached the point of a perfect boil – an intense, rolling temperature – constant and dangerous to touch. His voice was measured and emotionless.

"Then I suggest you keep your distance, Sergeant if that's how you feel. And maybe when we get to Fort Cass, you can get yourself reassigned."

CHAPTER THIRTY-FIVE

Salal slid closer to the fence post he'd been hiding behind for close to an hour. He was keeping his eyes on a group of soldiers talking and laughing around a cooking fire as they drank out of brown whiskey jugs. He always hated alcohol for what it did to people, how it changed them, usually for the worst. And if the individual drinking was as unpredictable as the soldiers at Fort Newnan, Salal shuddered at what might happen.

He was so intent on the soldiers he did not hear Catherine until she sat down.

"Is everything all right?" she asked.

When he turned, his face was almost white with fear.

"It's just me," she said. "Everything is okay."

Embarrassed, Salal put his hand on his heart for a moment, realizing his fears were getting the better of him.

"No worries," he said. "I'm just a little jumpy."

"You doing okay?" she asked.

Salal looked over at the soldiers.

"I'm scared, Kasewini," he said.

"Of?"

Salal shook his head and pulled his knees up to his chest all the while unable to take his eyes off of the men in uniform.

Catherine followed his gaze.

"Did they do something to you?" she asked.

Salal shook his head. "No, *they* haven't done anything." Salal realized the way he answered her question was too revealing. He looked at Catherine and gave her the best reassuring smile he could muster. "I'm fine."

"I don't know what's worse," Catherine said, "being in the corral or having them as a constant presence."

The expression on Catherine's face let Salal know she had endured something bad. She was a beautiful woman with no children or husband around. It was no surprise to him that she would be singled out for abuse.

"I don't think I can make it to the Indian Territory," he said.

Catherine reached out and touched his arm. "You can, Salal. We'll stay together the whole way."

Although Salal believed Catherine and the others would help him, the very idea of marching to the Indian Territory while being surrounded by the soldiers was too much to consider. "I appreciate that. But I can't."

"Why not?"

"The soldiers," Salal whispered.

"We can keep you safe," Catherine said although she trailed off at the end.

Salal knew she didn't believe it.

"Maybe Captain Edwards and his men will be the ones escorting us," she offered.

"If these soldiers here, the ones who walk around shirtless and drunk half the time, if they escort us...I just can't take the chance."

"Why are you so afraid of them?"

"I have heard them talking about me," Salal replied. "They know who I am, Kasewini. They know...*what* I am. I...I have to get out of here."

"What happened?"

Salal's face flooded red.

"I cannot tell you," he said. "Not right now, anyway." He looked back at the soldiers. "But I know the longer I am here, the more likely they will come and get me."

"What?"

"Please, Kasewini, help me get out of here."

Catherine looked over at the soldiers and thought for a moment. "What did they do to you?"

The calm tone in her voice let him know she believed the soldiers were capable of doing bad things.

"Can you help me?" he asked.

"Salal—"

"I can't stay!" He looked down, unsure why he was so abrupt with the only person in the entire world he trusted. "Nothing you say can change my mind."

Catherine pursed her lips, then relaxed her face. Her expression had a calming effect on Salal. He took a deep breath to settle his mind and watched her for a few moments. Her warm nature, which always felt like home to him in some strange way, made him realize if he escaped Fort Newnan he had nowhere to go.

"I'm sorry, Kasewini." Salal looked down at his shirt and played with its torn edges. "I need to get out of here, but…where can I run and not be caught?"

When Catherine did not respond, he continued – inexplicably emboldened. "Could you tell me more about this person who helps people escape?"

"Salal, I do—"

"I'm running, Kasewini, whether I get your help or not."

He wasn't sure if he meant what he said but the rising feeling of dread wouldn't allow him to take the words back. Catherine took his hand into hers.

"I know it is hard, but we will be leaving soon. We will be in our new lands within the next couple of months. We can *all* start a new life. You will be with us. We are your family now. We will not cast you out, Salal. You just need to hold on a little longer."

Salal smiled. Her vision of what things could be like in the new lands was beautiful, but like all beautiful things, he couldn't have them.

"No," he said as her idealistic future for him dissolved into a pile of ashes in his mind.

"We can help you make it," she replied in a calm, steady voice. "Waya, Leotie, and I will help you. Jeevan, Manjusha...the kids."

He let go of her hand. "I cannot..."

Salal stopped. He realized the conversation was going in circles and Catherine wasn't going to understand why he needed to get away from the soldiers.

"They put a dress on me," he said. His voice echoed in quiet humiliation.

"What?"

Her response validated the shame he felt.

"They put a dress on me. The soldiers."

"When?"

"Almost as soon as I arrived here."

"Go on."

Salal sighed. "Do you remember that first day when you found me face down in the dirt?" he asked. "That wasn't the day I first arrived. I got here the day before." Catherine had to strain to hear him. "The soldiers separated me out from the others. I was unsure why, what I had done to garner their attention." He gestured towards the buildings around the corral. "They took me to one of these buildings where some of them sleep and eat."

"Please, you do not have to tell – "

"No, I have to. I should…I should tell you the whole story otherwise, I am afraid I will go mad – begin to believe I imagined the whole thing. I have to tell someone I can trust." He looked directly at her. "I have to tell a friend."

He looked down at his hands.

"Can I call you my friend?" he asked.

"Of course you can, Salal."

Her affirmation made him smile for a moment. He looked over at the soldiers as one of them got up to go relieve himself not far from where he and his friends were drinking.

"As you know, the soldiers like to gamble," Salal began. "Some of them were already playing cards when I was escorted into the room. They told me I was to serve drinks to them. They all cheered when I agreed. I thought it was odd that they were so happy to have someone serving them drinks, but what did I know? Then they started to whistle and catcall. Someone came from behind me and handed me a black dress. They forced me to change into it and start serving them drinks. I didn't mind at first. To be honest. I was so thirsty after the long walk and as long as I took care of their drinks, they let me have water. They even gave me a little food. But the more they drank, the worse they treated me."

Catherine closed her eyes. She did not want to hear more, but Sala continued.

"They became more vulgar," he said. "They started grabbing me, pulling at me. If I spilled a drink, they hit me until I brought another one and cleaned up the mess. One of them wanted to know if I could sing like a woman since I talked like one. They put me up on a table and ordered me to sing."

Salal took a deep breath.

"I was so scared. I didn't know what to do…or sing, so I just stood there and did nothing. That's when they… (he sniffled) … pulled out their guns and fired at me. One shot every few seconds until I started singing. I couldn't think straight, so I sang the first song that came to me, a silly children's song. Then another and another. I couldn't tell you if I was singing the right words or not, but they didn't seem to mind. They whistled and hollered – they ordered me to dance."

"How long did it last?"

"I have no idea. Finally, a dark man. – not dark-skinned, but a vile soul dressed in all black and the tallest top hat I'd ever seen – came out of the shadows. The minute he appeared, all the frivolity stopped. But since he was behind me, I kept singing and dancing. When the man came around in front of me, he was smiling – in a way. He looked me over from my toes to my head. When he looked into my face with blue eyes like a frozen river, I could tell he knew I was not a woman."

"What did he do?"

"He cursed and yanked me from the table. He said, 'If you want to act like a woman, I will treat you like one.' That's when I got this."

Salal pointed to his still swollen left eye.

Catherine reached out and took Salal's trembling hand. He didn't pull away, nor did he resist her.

"I have blocked out whatever happened next," he said. "The next sure thing I remember is seeing your beautiful eyes looking down at me here in the corral."

Catherine took a deep breath. "I'm so sorry," she said and squeezed his hand. "I'm so sorry."

"They did something to me, Kasewini."

"What do you mean?"

"That day you found me, I didn't say anything to you, or to Waya, but…they did something. I hurt…I cannot sit properly. It hurts too much. Sometimes I bleed out of my…you know, back there. They…they…"

He broke off in convulsing sobs.

Catherine stroked his hair. "Let me take you to the doctor."

Salal's head shot up and he hissed like an angry copperhead. "Do not tell anyone. No one must ever know. Swear it."

"Sala—"

"Swear it or I will never speak to you again."

Catherine swallowed, hard. "I swear. But we must make sure this never happens again."

"How can you?" he asked. "How can any of *us* stop any of *them*? The only thing I can do is run. I can't stay here, Kasewini."

There was stillness.

There was darkness.

There was a pervasive sense of hopelessness.

Catherine finally broke the gloom.

"I know the place they take people who want to escape," she said.

CHAPTER THIRTY-SIX

"You were gone a few days longer than I expected," Colonel Morse said. "Surely that extra time wasn't spent drinking in a dark tavern in the middle of *nowhere*."

Elias stopped in the middle of taking off his coat and looked at the colonel. "I can assure you it wasn't." He finished taking his coat off and set it and his gloves on a nearby table.

"Need I remind you we have a mission—"

"Who do you think you're talkin' to, Colonel? I'm fully aware we have a mission. I *always* put duty first. You know that better than anyone."

"Perhaps, but when I send you out on an errand, I expect a quick return. No dilly-dallying around the countryside chasing your tail."

Elias shook his head. "Paranoia's getting the better of you, Colonel. It's starting to cloud your judgment."

Incensed, Colonel Morse looked down at the pile of papers on his desk. While he searched for the perfect response with which to shut down his subordinate, he saw the letter he'd been writing.

Forgetting about Elias, Morse scanned the document.

It's gibberish, he thought.

He wadded the paper and flung it across the tent.

"Someone's been fiddling on my desk," he said. "That letter makes no sense – barely a complete sentence in the entire document."

But it's in my handwriting.

Elias said nothing.

Colonel Morse cleared his throat. "You're right, Lieutenant. I apologize for my rudeness."

"I ain't been a lieutenant for a long time now, Colonel."

Morse reached for his tea. The cup rattled against the saucer. Morse set the cup down but not before Elias noticed the tremor.

"Yes, I realize that," Morse said. "But you were a lieutenant when we met – that's how I think of you."

Elias nodded.

"Please, have a seat and tell me what you found out," the colonel said.

Elias settled into a chair opposite the fidgeting colonel. "Quite a bit," Elias said. "Seems both Fort Hetzel and Fort Gilmer have a lot of children – young'uns separated from their parents during the roundup. Saw the paperwork m'self."

Elias pulled the cork on a pocket flask and took a deep drink.

"Ah…" He exaggerated the satisfying sound. "That'll grow hair on your chest." He tapped the flask with his fingers. "You know, if you were to say those little savages belonged to parents here, who would say otherwise? Seriously, who would care?"

"Excellent," Colonel Morse said. "And I know a few good, wealthy men that'll be more than happy to take them off our hands."

They measured one another for a moment, then laughed. Elias pulled out a thin, black cigar, bit off the end, spit it on the floor, then struck a match off his stubble. "I hear tell a few Cherokees have run off while I was gone."

Colonel Morse bolted from his seat. "What are you accusing me of?"

Elias leaned back in his chair and talked with the cigar clenched between his teeth. "Rein those horses in there, Colonel. No one's accusing you of anything. Just tellin' you what I heard."

"Where are you getting your information?"

"I have my sources. You think I'm gonna leave this place for more than a week and not keep an eye on things? This is the best money I've ever made." He blew out a smoke ring. "I just want to know who's the jackleg that's helping 'em escape."

§§

It had been ten days since Elias had seen Catherine. He could still feel her soft flesh underneath him and hear her moans of passion – at least that's the way he chose to remember it. But there was something else, a longing he'd never known – an eagerness to lay his eyes on someone. He understood what motivated men to write poems and songs about yearning for a woman and love, and though he could never compose something so unmanly, he was slowly developing an appreciation for the notion.

He began to mumble to himself. "O my love is like a red, red rose that's newly sprung in spring. O my love is like a...a... something else. Damn, forget it!"

An unfamiliar feeling of insecurity forced him to take inventory of the glade and wonder if he should have added more light. There were ten small fires, one for each day they had been apart and ten lanterns hanging from the trees.

Maybe I should have ten lanterns in every tree. Would that have been better?

He was still fretting when he saw lights bouncing through the small forest.

Too late now.

He adjusted his jacket several times and willed the butterflies in his stomach into submission.

It's like right before the first cannon shot.

He glanced over where he laid his top hat.

Do I look better when I wear it? More dashin' or something?

She was drawing near; every moment made him all the more nervous.

Should I run to greet her? Is it better to step from the shadows?

He decided to stand in the middle of the glade and let her see his silhouette as she approached. On a whim, he put his back to her approach.

I'll be able to see her eyes light up when I turn around. Yes... that's perfect.

He counted every agonizing second. Even when he heard footsteps, he concentrated on holding still.

Don't turn too soon – it'll spoil everything.

The light of torches cast his shadow in front of him. Just when he thought his heart was going to beat out of his chest...

"Um, Elias."

Elias cursed as he spun.

"Dammit, Gabe! You ruint everyth—"

Elias's head pivoted one way – then the other.

"Where's the girl?" he asked. "Where the hell is Catherine?"

CHAPTER THIRTY-SEVEN

"This is it," Catherine said.

She and Salal slowed their pace. The scene was just as Waya had described, a haphazard mountain of fallen trees taller than the average Cherokee. The mound stood in stark contrast to the otherwise pristine landscape.

Catherine stared at the botanical carnage. *I'm in the middle of nowhere…I have no idea where I am…I am having trouble catching my breath…and we might get caught at any minute. I should have gotten someone else to help Salal.*

Forcing herself to keep moving, Catherine circumnavigated to trees and spied the rock outcrop where Waya said the escort would meet them.

"You sure this is it?" Salal asked. "It just doesn't feel right."

"I'm sure," she replied.

Not sure how you will react when I tell you I am not waiting with you – but I am sure this is the spot.

In the original version of the plan, Catherine had agreed to stay until Salal was comfortable with being left all alone or until an escort came. But it had taken longer to find the meeting place than she expected, and she was starting to feel like she had been gone far too long. The resting time at the seven-mile mark was surely over and Thomas would be organizing everyone to finish the day's march.

"Kasewini, I don't like this," Salal said.

"I know it's a bit unnerving, but it'll be all right."

When they finally reached the makeshift shelter, they were greeted by footprints in the dirt.

"No one's here," Salal said. He began wringing his hands. He turned around, first in one direction and back the other way – a confused child looking for a familiar face. "Is this right?"

"Yes," Catherine said, "I'm sure of it." Catherine watched Salal search the woods. She'd never seen him act so nervous. "No one's here, true enough, but that's not a bad thing," she said. She pointed to some footprints. "Look, they're fresh. And this place is exactly how Waya described it. Whoever was here will return."

She looked around and took a deep breath. She felt satisfied she'd given Salal the best opportunity to escape from Fort Newnan, now she had to consider her own survival.

"If you still want to run, you'll have to wait until someone comes, or go on your own."

Salal's crestfallen expression sent a pang of guilt through Catherine.

"Someone will be here shortly," she said.

"Will you wait with me?"

"I have to get back."

"Please stay."

"I can't."

Salal grabbed her arm. "You have to stay with me." His tone was more threatening than scared. "It's important."

"I...I can't."

"You must!"

"Okay, for a couple of minutes," she said. She did not want a confrontation. "Then I have to get back."

"You can't, Kasewini. You have to—"

The sound of a stick being stepped on cracked like a small gunshot.

Catherine smiled, relieved she could finally leave. "See, your escort's here."

She turned and her blood ran cold.

Gabe stood at the edge of the trees only a few yards away. Behind him, the rest of Elias's men smirked and chortled.

Catherine gasped. "I...I don't understand. How—"

"Good work," Gabe said.

Catherine whirled and snarled at Salal. "How could—"

"I...I didn't!"

Gabe and the other men burst out in laughter. When one doubled over, Catherine saw Manjusha's face.

"I'm so sorry Kasewini. I tried to tell you—"

"She came to us last night," Gabe said. "She had an interesting little story to tell."

Catherine rushed the woman.

"I trusted you!"

Gabe held out a restraining arm.

"They know about my children." Manjusha moved out of Catherine's reach. "Harsha and Kavi. They know where my children are."

Catherine pushed Gabe away. "How could you do this?" She put her hands behind her head and tried to get a grasp on what was happening. "How—"

"They threatened to sell my children if I didn't tell them who's been helping people escape," Manjusha continued. "They're my children. I couldn't...I didn't..."

Manjusha collapsed onto the ground, sobbing. "Forgive me, Kasewini."

"Did you tell them anything else, Manjusha?"

Manjusha did not respond.

"What did you tell them?" Catherine's voice echoed like a wounded hawk. "What else did you tell them?"

Manjusha continued to cry.

"What did you say? Did you tell them about—"

A hand-spun Catherine around by her shoulder. She stared into a face topped by a ridiculously tall hat. Elias's eyes were slits, searching, probing.

"About what. Missy?" he asked. "Or is it about *who*?"

Never before had anyone looked so deeply into Catherine's soul. Elias's blue eyes revealed anger, inquisitiveness, and something else – profound sadness.

His cheek was next to hers, his stubble digging into her face. The embrace began with a deadly tenderness – a constricting snake of a hug. The intensity increased little by little until Catherine could hardly move...or breathe.

Elias whispered into her ear. "Why? Why'd you do this to me?"

Catherine could not answer – not enough air in her lungs. While he continued to constrict her movement with one arm, Elias grabbed the nape of her neck with his other hand and kissed her cheek.

"You betrayed me," he said. "Just like my little Joey. You remember what happened to my little dog, don't you?"

Catherine nodded. In her mind, she saw a helpless puppy, eyes bulging, lungs screaming for relief – a little animal who slowly morphed into...her.

"I didn't..." she tried to speak in between uncontrollable sobs. "I'm sorry."

He seized her neck with both hands and pulled her face up to his, forcing her to stand on the tips of her toes. He held her there, nose to nose, for a few moments.

"Joey had to be punished."

Elias started to squeeze.

"And so do you!"

His powerful hands tightened, slow and methodical, closing off her windpipe.

Catherine gasped for air and clawed at his hands. The pressure increased and the sadness in his eyes gave way to anger, then unadulterated fury.

Catherine pounded on his forearms. She heard Gabe's panicked voice.

"Elias!"

A vein bulged in the middle of her head. Her face turned dark pink. Snot bubbled out of her nose. Water trickled from her eyes. The world grew blurry.

"Dammit, Elias!"

And still the pressure.

She saw Ayita's face – smiling…angelic. The youngster's image grew steadily darker, blurring at the edges as a cloud of unconsciousness settled on Catherine. She offered a brief, wheezing prayer, and felt peace fill her as if she were a bucket dipped in a deep well.

She saw her father beckoning to her from the other side.

A rifle cracked...

...the tension around her neck disappeared...

...air rushed back into her lungs accompanied by a spasm of coughing. She landed hard on the ground.

Gabe held the smoking long gun in his hands.

"Dammit, Elias! Stop! What the hell are you doin'? We're supposed to take her back alive."

Elias pried his gaze from Catherine's convulsing form and leered at Gabe. "I know what the colonel said."

Gabe exchanged uncomfortable glances with the other men. "So, what are you doin?" he asked.

Elias grinned like a parson greeting parishioners at the church door. "Just lost my head, that's all. Nothin' to get your britches in a wad about."

He looked down at Catherine. She was breathing in long heaves as her natural coloring returned. Ugly red welts marred her neck. He held out his hand – a gentleman assisting a lady over a wet spot in the road. "My apologies. Sometimes I forget my own strength."

Catherine took his hand only to avoid further wrath. She shook free and wobbled but refused to fall. She saw Gabe exhale in relief.

Salal was curled in a ball, his arms clutching his legs. Manjusha, stifling sobs, looked at her with eyes pleading for forgiveness.

Elias stepped closer. "You okay?"

Catherine nodded.

"Good," he said.

Then he hit her so hard with his fist that she didn't feel its impact before the world went completely black.

CHAPTER THIRTY-EIGHT

Thomas wanted to rush over to the body, but the fear of being ambushed gave him pause.

He was just getting the Cherokees started on their last three miles back to Fort Newnan when he heard the two gunshots, one from a rifle, the other from a pistol fired a few minutes after the first. The gunshots themselves weren't a cause for concern. Thomas figured it was either hunters or a drunken shooting contest. He did not give the noise a second thought until Waya rushed up to him.

"Those shots came from the direction where my people are escaping," he said. "There's a clump of trees we've been using as a meeting place."

"You sure?" Thomas asked.

"I'm sure." Waya glanced around. "There's more. Jeevan told me he can't find his wife and if that's not enough, I can't find Catherine or her friend, Salal."

Thomas studied Waya for a minute.

"Where exactly is this rendezvous point?"

"I'll show you," Waya replied. "I'll just—"

"No, best if I go alone."

"I can get you there faster."

"No. It'll raise too many questions, you know that. Just tell me where it is."

Waya gave the directions and Thomas called Roe.

"You're in charge," Thomas said. "Get these people back in good order."

"Where you goin'?"

"I am going to see what the gunfire was about."

"Why bother? Prolly jus' a couple of hunters."

"I just want to take a look."

"Why don't you send someone else?"

"No. I'll go. We've got hundreds of Cherokees out here and God only knows who's running around in these woods. I just think it is a good idea to see what the gunshots were about."

"Take Bond with you."

"No. I can travel faster by myself. Just take the people back to the fort."

"Yes, sir."

Thomas scanned the throng of Cherokees hoping to catch a glimpse of Catherine. Then he headed into the forest.

Silo made good time despite the low branches and fallen logs. When he came to the clump of trees Waya had described, he scanned the area for any sign of another human being. He waited, barely breathing, for several minutes.

The forest was quiet.

He clicked and touched Silo's flank with his boot.

Less than fifty yards later, he saw a body lying face down in a clump of tall grass. He slid from the saddle and unsheathed his rifle.

Careful, old man, he thought. *You've seen this ambush before.*

Thomas crept along the ground careful not to make noise. The closer he got, the more familiar the body looked…thin…feminine arms and legs…long hair.

Catherine!

Panic-stricken, he raced across the remaining distance, dropped to his knees, and rolled the body over.

It was the petite young man Thomas had seen hanging around Catherine – her friend Salal. The gaping hole in the side of his head removed all doubt about the cause of his demise. Thomas touched the powder burn.

Pistol. Close range.

Relieved and not the least ashamed by it, Thomas searched the area.

If Salal is here, Catherine must have been with him. Why now? She wouldn't run a few days ago.

Thomas hunted for thirty minutes for any other bodies. When his search turned up empty, he remounted and moved along a small trail next to the trees. He rode with deliberation, scrutinizing every print on the ground and broken branch. When it was apparent the trail was leading back to Fort Newman, he touched Silo with his spurs.

Thomas raced through the front gate of the fort, then reined to a stop at a crowd gathered around the far end of the corral. An unusual mixture of soldiers and Cherokees were struggling to get a better view of whatever was happening.

Silo parted the crowd as he trotted towards the action.

"Why Captain Edwards," Colonel Morse said, "you're just in time."

From atop his trusty horse, Thomas could see a makeshift stage. His heart sank.

"In time for what?" he asked.

"For our little trial, of course."

Colonel Morse pointed to Gabe who was stepping onto the platform with Catherine in tow.

"This little girl here stands accused of duplicity."

Catherine's hands were scraped, swollen, and shackled. The wrist irons were rusted and looked ridiculously large around her small wrists. She walked with a slight limp. She'd obviously been beaten. Thomas began to calculate how many soldiers he could kill before they brought him down – how many, beginning with Morse.

Elias stepped next to Silo. "Best be takin' that pistol from ya, Captain." He grinned. "Just to keep it from going off, accidental."

He slipped Thomas's pistol from its holster and pulled the rifle from its scabbard. "And don't even touch that saber."

Thomas never took his eyes from Morse. "Duplicity?"

"Yes, duplicity. She was helping one of our prisoners try to escape. Duplicity, plain and simple."

It took every ounce of concentration for Thomas to keep his voice calm. "She was helping someone escape?" He looked around. "Where is this person?"

"It doesn't matter, Captain," Colonel Morse replied. "What's important is who's been helping this little girl. It's impossible to think she's been acting on her own."

"Charges require proof. Where is it?"

"Reports," Morse said.

"From whom?" Thomas reminded himself to stay measured. "Desperate people will say anything to gain favor."

"That's true," Colonel Morse said. He walked past the captain and pointed at Catherine. "However, we caught this little one in the act. And with the rash of escapes as of late—"

"You're pinning a lot on her," Thomas said.

That's it, he thought. *Detached...dispassionate...reasoned.*

"Perhaps. Or perhaps she's part of a larger conspiracy."

Thomas released a sardonic laugh. "You have quite the imagination."

"Maybe I do, Edwards, but I would remind you I am still a colonel and therefore deserving of your respect."

Bypassing a response, Thomas dismounted. He handed the reins to Roe and walked toward the colonel. By the time he was within six feet, Elias was on the platform next to Catherine.

"Let's go back to the beginning," Thomas said. "You said you caught her helping someone escape?"

Colonel Morse sighed. "We did."

"How?"

Colonel Morse looked up at Elias on the stage. "Go ahead. Might as well tell him."

When Elias grinned, he resembled a wolf at dinner time. He stepped past Catherine and pointed to the assembled crowd.

"'Cuz there were so many of you running off, I had to find out what was going on," he said. "So, I…ah…convinced one of your own to betray you all."

Murmuring swept through the corral. Another smile from Elias.

"That's right. And there's more than one. I have others. Right here as I speak."

Whatever trust ran amongst the residents of the corral dissipated in a matter of seconds.

Thomas was unmoved. "Still waiting for your proof," he said.

Elias held onto the captain's gaze for a moment then placed two of his fingers in his mouth and whistled.

"Here's your proof."

Two men walked up the steps and dropped Salal's body on the stage.

"Don't bother actin' surprised, Captain," Elias said. "My boys saw you. They were hidin' whilst you wuz skulkin' around. Soon as you hit the trail, they scooped up this…ah…this sissy man and hightailed it down here."

A collective gasp rolled through the corral.

For the first time, Catherine moved. She shied away from the corpse.

"This delicate creature here," Elias continued, "he thought he could run from us. Well, now you all can see what happens when you try that."

Elias stepped closer to Catherine and smoothed her hair back off her face revealing her busted and swollen lips.

"Apparently, this is the one to talk to if you got any inclination to escape," he said.

Thomas's hand reached for his empty holster.

"So, you caught someone on the run. Who says this young woman had anything to do with it? I want to talk to whomever it is."

Morse sneered. "And people in Hell want cold water, Captain. We caught her in the act, plain and simple. We have over a dozen witnesses." Thomas looked over at Catherine. There was no fight in her sunken eyes.

"So, what are you going to do with her?" Thomas asked.

Colonel Morse shuffled up the two steps of the stage and waddled over to the middle of it. When he nodded, Elias raised his pistol to Catherine's temple.

"Listen up!" Colonel Morse delivered his announcement with all the flourish of a Shakespearean actor. "I know the majority of you can speak English, so I know you all will understand what I'm about to say. This woman here is accused of facilitating an escape. That is a crime against the government of the United States, a crime punishable by death!"

The colonel got the reaction he wanted – shock and terror.

"I sentence this woman to die tomorrow *unless* the individuals who have been helping her come forward. If you come forward, the resulting executions will be quick and respectable."

Morse looked directly at Thomas.

"If no one steps up, I will personally peel her skin off one piece at a time until someone confesses, or she succumbs to her injuries. Either way, I don't care."

Colonel Morse held the captain's gaze for a few moments before turning back to the crowd.

"You have twenty-four hours."

CHAPTER THIRTY-NINE

Thomas waited several hours after Colonel Morse's ultimatum before trying to talk to Catherine. He wanted to get her as far away from the fort as possible but there was no way to do that without causing even more problems.

Acid churned in Thomas's stomach as he mounted the stairs to the platform where Catherine was chained to a post. A private stepped in front of him.

"No one sees the prisoner, sir," he said.

Thomas never raised his voice. "Stand down or die, soldier."

The private lowered his rifle and stepped to the side.

Catherine tried to rise but her chains were too heavy, and she was obviously exhausted. She reached for Thomas, but he refused to get close enough to touch.

"I'm sorry," he said.

Catherine looked down, dumbstruck by the unexpected rejection.

"They're watching," he said. "Elias and Colonel Morse. We have to be careful."

Catherine nodded. "I'm scared," she said. "They know about Ayita."

"How?"

"Elias knows about Manjusha and Jeevan's children. She's the one who told Elias about me. It only makes sense that he'd know about Ayita."

"Does he know where they are?"

"Yes. He threatened Manjusha with selling her children."

Thomas didn't know how to respond.

"What's going to happen to my little girl?"

Thomas squared his shoulders. "I swear on my honor as an officer, nothing will happen to her. Or the others."

Catherine looked away.

"I'm sorry I got you into this," he said. "My arrogance and stupidity did this."

"No, I chose this."

Thomas put his arms behind his back and walked past her. He turned his back to the guard and whispered.

"I'm going to get you out of here."

"What? How? You can't...They'll find Ayita for sure and—"

"I won't let 'em do that."

"Where would I go?"

"Miriam's."

"No. Elias will be ready for that."

"He's not expecting anyone to help you escape."

"You don't know that. Besides, what about Ayita?"

Thomas began to pace, to anyone watching he was an officer interrogating a petulant prisoner.

"They were bluffing."

Catherine jerked her head towards Sala's body. It was beginning to smell.

"I don't think so," she said. "It's all a trap! Holding me here, on a stage. Threatening me with Ayita. Giving my accomplices twenty-four hours. It's all a trap. You're foolish if you can't see it. And I think you're wrong about Elias." Her voice croaked from lack of water. "Helping me escape is exactly what he's expecting. He might not think it'll be you, but he's always one step ahead. He'll catch us, and when he does, he'll take pleasure in killing us."

"Did he ever mention Ayita?"

Catherine took a deep breath. "No, but—"

"If he knew about her, he would've used her to get information from you just like he did to Manjusha. He wouldn't threaten you like this."

"I can't be so sure," Catherine said. "My daughter's in danger and there's nothing I can do about it."

Thomas removed his hat and ran his fingers through his hair.

"I'll tell them it was me, then," he said. "I'll tell Colonel Morse I was the one who let those people escape and you had nothing to do with it."

"They know that's not true," Catherine said. "They caught me helping Salal and who knows what Manjusha told them. If you say anything they'll just—"

"There's no way on God's green earth I'm going to sit by and do nothing," Thomas said. "I'm not going to let Colonel Morse get his hands on you. It's simple, I'll turn myself in."

"Like hell, you will!"

Thomas and Catherine jumped. Roe had mounted the platform and was standing with his arms folded across his chest.

"I'll kill you myself before I let that happen," he said.

Roe walked past the guard.

"Best it you quit listening to anythin' here, boy," he said.

The private scurried to the farthest corner of the platform and stood post. Roe looked at Thomas.

"Go on," he said. "I'll stop ya when you say something asinine."

A coyote howled in the distance, a wailing cry of discontent that mirrored the scene on the little platform.

"If no one steps forward by tomorrow, Elias won't kill you," Thomas said. "He'll torture you."

"I won't talk."

"Maybe," Thomas said, "but it won't matter. Once he gets bored, Elias will start killing your friends. He will find out what he wants one way or another."

"The captain's right," Roe said. "Elias is a cold-hearted bastard."

"And if I run, Waya, Leotie, Jeevan, Manjusha, all of them with their children, will have to go with us or Elias will punish them."

Roe looked at Thomas.

"She's right, Captain. We leave anyone behind, they'll suffer."

Thomas sighed. "The first thing we need to do is figure out how to get those kids."

"I have an idea," Roe said, "but it'll take some luck." He thought for a moment. "The kids are at Fort Hetzel, right?"

"You know they are," Thomas replied.

"I think we can extricate 'em from their situation."

"How? First and foremost, we need a letter from the commander of *this* fort requesting the transfer of those specific three children before Fort Hetzel would consider letting them go. Then that letter needs to be presented by an officer—"

"We can do all that," Roe said.

"What do you mean?" Catherine asked.

"We need a letter from the commander of this fort, right?" Roe asked.

"Right," Thomas replied. "You expect me to waltz into Colonel Morse's tent—"

Roe beamed. "For a smart guy, Captain, you sometimes lack analytical acuity."

"Pardon?"

"No one in his right might would go to Morse. But Captain Dorsey'll do about anything when he's drunk, which is most of the time."

"And I can deliver the letter to Fort Hetzel," Thomas said.

"Surprised you figgered that one out your own self," Roe said, but his smile outweighed the sarcasm.

Thomas paced for a while. "There is no way I can get to Fort Hetzel and back before tomorrow evening."

"It wouldn't matter if you could," Roe said. "Finding the children won't save Catherine. We gotta face the fact that you ain't gonna be able to get the kids *and* rescue Catherine at the same time."

"So, what do we do?" Thomas asked.

"I'll take her," Roe said. "While ye're getting' the kids from Fort Hetzel, I'll facilitate her escape."

Catherine's eyes were pleading. "What about Manjusha and Jeevan?"

"Them too."

Thomas shook his head. "I cannot ask you to do this, Roe. Your career will be over. You will undoubtedly face charges—"

Roe held up a hand. "Captain," he said, "Thomas…we've been together a long time. Sure, we had a dust-up a day or so ago, but that happens in the best of families – and among the closest of friends. I ain't sittin' on my saddle sores while you throw *your* career away and this young lady gets killed. Not my style and I ain't altering my life now."

"Roe, I won't allow—"

"You won't *allow*? Since when have you been able to control me?" Roe laughed. "Begging the captain's pardon, but I do what you tell me to do out of *respect* for you, not fear."

Roe began talking to himself. "Won't allow...ain't heard nuthin' quite so funny in a while now...won't allow. Geez."

Thomas wanted to put up an argument, but he knew the sergeant too well.

"All right then," Thomas said. "No one on earth I trust more than you."

"Not like you have a plethora of considerations," Roe said.

He had not quit laughing.

CHAPTER FORTY

"What's this?" Captain Dorsey asked.

"A request for a prisoner transfer," Thomas replied. "There are three young children being held at Fort Hetzel. Their parents are being held here at Fort Newnan."

Dorsey dropped the letter on his desk. "Why are you bothering me with this?"

"It's a situation that was brought to my attention, sir. I'd take care of this myself, but it requires the signature of the commanding officer."

"So, I'm the commander now?" He sat back in his chair and poured a shot of whiskey. "Tell me, Captain Edwards, why should I give a hoot in hell about the savages' children?"

Thomas looked at Captain Dorsey's distorted reflection in the window. "You ever fire your weapon in anger, sir?"

"What's that have to do with the price of corn in Kentucky?"

"Just answer the question."

Dorsey tossed back his drink and poured another before slouching in his chair.

"I have. Probably seen as much action as you."

"Seen some awful stuff, haven't you?"

Dorsey stared at the translucent liquid before it disappeared in his maw. "Stuff I wouldn't wish on my worst enemy."

"I can tell."

"How's that?"

"Your eyes, Dorsey." Thomas let his response hang in the air for a moment. "And the whiskey."

"Maybe I just like to get drunk." Captain Dorsey spun the empty glass. "I don't hear anything about you drinking. How do you deal with your demons?"

Thomas chuckled. "Who says I don't drink? Maybe I'm just better at hiding it."

"Maybe so. So, what's your point?"

"Just that I know you've seen a lot of terrible things this world has to offer."

"And?"

"And this is your chance to make a bad situation better. How often do we, as soldiers, get a shot to do that?"

Captain Dorsey uncorked his bottle with exaggerated deliberation. "I'm a drunk, Captain. And now, I am a piss poor soldier. But I'm not stupid. I know when I'm being manipulated."

"Just a chance to clear your conscience."

Dorsey's laugh reeked of stale whiskey, tooth rot, and spoiled meat. "My conscience, Captain, can be located several steps behind my sobriety."

Dorsey waved an unsteady hand at Thomas. "I used to be like you – thought I could make a difference."

"What happened?"

The bottle pinged up and down on the edge of the glass as Dorsey poured. "Wasn't just one thing." He put the glass up to his nose and inhaled. "It was a thousand little nicks and cuts. They chipped away at the human being inside of me. It's the price you pay when you're in command of hundreds of men during a war after you've quit caring why you're fighting."

He swirled his drink with a stubby index finger, then licked the whiskey from his fingertip. "And bastards…taking orders from unadulterated bastards. Bastards who've studied war but never seen one – bastards who've never heard a fourteen-year-old flag bearer screaming for his mommy just after he realizes his leg is gone but before he understands he's going to die – bastards who give orders to kill everything that moves, man, woman, child, and dog."

Captain Dorsey closed his eyes, trying to unsee the scenes rolling through his head.

"I don't know what you've seen," Thomas offered. "I don't know what you've had to do. But I do know what we can do right here."

"You do realize they're all going to the same place," Dorsey said. "When it's all said and done, they will all be back together."

"Yeah, but those children – six, four, and two – they are lonely and frightened. The trip will be a lot easier with their parents. Then there's the parents' anguish."

"So, you want to get those kids out of one hellhole and bring them here?" Dorsey looked up as if he'd suddenly realized he was not talking to himself. "I'm sorry, Captain, where are my manners? Would you like one?"

"Why not?"

Dorsey reached to the windowsill, blew dust out of a second glass, and filled it halfway. "One of my corporals makes his hooch," he said. "His uncle's recipe. Probably doubles as a good paint remover."

Thomas took the glass and examined it for a moment. He raised the glass, then emptied the contents in one long swallow. The whiskey burned all the way to his bowels.

He coughed.

"My compliments to the chef," he said.

"What about the girl?" Captain Dorsey asked.

Thomas felt his stomach twitch.

"What girl?"

"The one Colonel Morse has chained up outside and is planning to use as a taxidermy class. You know exactly which girl."

"None of my concern," Thomas said.

Dorsey howled and doubled over. "Edwards, you are a hell of a horseman, a fine shot by reputation, a gentleman, a scholar, and one atrocious liar." He took a moment to recover. "But you are willing to let her die?"

Thomas shrugged.

Captain Dorsey chuckled.

"What?" Thomas asked.

"You are a heroic son-of-a-bitch. I see it in you. No way you let a beautiful woman like that die. Especially, at the hands of a devil-like Colonel Morse."

Thomas sat up straight and adjusted his uniform. "Are you willing to help me with these children or not?"

Dorsey tipped the bottle. Three pathetic drops fell into his glass. He looked like a child who'd lost his puppy.

"Not sure I want to get involved with you and Colonel Morse. Less sure I want to sign a piece of paper that brings those kids to this hellhole." He looked down at the orders for a moment. "Maybe we should send their parents over to them."

"Look Dorsey, I don't have—"

"Save it, Edwards," Dorsey said, "I'll sign your order on one condition."

"Name it, sir."

"Walk over to that cabinet and bring me another bottle of this hooch."

§§

Colonel Morse sat up out of his sleep and gasped for air. He was drenched in sweat and trying to escape the same nightmare he'd had every night for several weeks. A mysterious woman haunted him, lurking in the shadows of his mind – never recognizable but never out of sight.

Did she call my name? he wondered.

The first few nights she chased him through the woods until he reached a cabin. He awakened. On the fourth night, the cabin turned into his boyhood home, but he could not open the door. She drew closer – he pounded on the door. No one came. The woman reached for him, and he screamed himself awake.

Tonight was the first night he heard her say anything.

"Colonel Morse?"

Morse jumped. The voice was outside his tent. He propped up on an elbow.

"Enter!"

A young man ducked under the flap, stood, and saluted.

"Private Rhodes, sir."

"What is it, Private?"

"It's Captain Edwards, sir."

"What about him?"

Rhodes cleared his throat. "You wanted to know if he was up to something."

Colonel Morse struggled to shake off his sleep. "Yes. Yes." He swung his legs over the side of his cot with a grunt. "What's going on?"

"Sir, Captain Edwards mounted his horse and rode off with a couple other men."

"And the girl?"

"Still chained on the platform, sir. Appears to be asleep."

"Captain Edwards didn't try to rescue her?" Morse struggled to light an oil lamp. Rhodes stepped over, snapped his knife over a flint, and sparked the lantern to life.

"No, sir," Rhodes said. "He and Sergeant Bickford was talkin' to her earlier in the evening. Then the captain rode over to Captain Dorsey's cabin. He stayed there for a little while, then went back to his tent. I thought he was done for the night, but next thing I know, he headed out."

"Which way did they go?"

"North, sir. Northeast."

Colonel Morse rubbed his forehead.

"Find Elias."

"Yessir."

While Colonel Morse got dressed, he ran the area's geography through his mind.

East is where Edwards marches the Cherokees. That's where Elias caught the girl. Only thing to the north is Fort Hetzel. That's where Lieutenant Hatten is – or is he a captain?

The tent flap rustled.

"You asked for me, Colonel?"

Morse buttoned his top button, then marveled at the ridiculous hat perched on Elias's head.

"Captain Edwards left about an hour ago."

"That's why you woke me?"

"He left with a few of his men!"

"So…they went for a ride…maybe scoutin'."

"No, it's something else."

"What makes you think—"

"He headed northeast! Don't you see?"

Elias shook his head.

Morse exhaled. "Northeast, toward Fort Hetzel."

"So?"

"And he went under cover of darkness." Morse strode across the tent, then back. He wrung his hands. "He's up to something."

"Or it's nothing."

"Are you challenging me?"

Elias rubbed his face with his hand and blew out a long breath. "Okay…so, what do you want to do?"

"Stay here and keep an eye on that girl…." Colonel Morse paused for a moment. "That girl…"

Is she the one – the woman in the dreams?

The colonel began to pace once again. "That girl…" he mumbled. "Edwards is going to Fort Hetzel to bring someone who will stop us from killing her."

"Why there?"

Colonel Morse could not make the pieces fit.

"Wouldn't he stay here to keep an eye on her?" Elias asked.

Colonel Morse chewed on a dirty fingernail. "He saw Captain Dorsey earlier in the evening. Maybe…" He trailed off frustrated by the mystery of the captain's actions.

"Wouldn't he jus' send one of his men to Fort Hetzel?" Elias asked. "Why go himself?"

Colonel Morse's anger spewed like steam from a teakettle. "I don't know, dammit."

He raked his hand along with his small dining table. China and silverware smashed and clanked on the floor. He put both hands under the table and flipped it while he screamed.

"Dammit, Elias. The man is planning a coup with Dorsey and Lieutenant Hatten. Bastards!"

Elias was going to correct Hatten's rank, but Morse would not stop shouting.

"Private Rhodes!"

The young private burst into the tent. "Yes, sir."

"Alert Sergeant Parkinson. Tell him to get my men ready. We're going after Edwards. Everyone assembles outside my tent in ten minutes."

"Yes, sir."

"Why don't you let me go after that son-of-a-bitch?" Elias asked.

"I want to get to him before he reaches Fort Hetzel and gets Lieutenant Hatten all riled up. Me, not you."

Elias couldn't stand it any longer. "He's a captain."

"What?"

"Hatten – not a lieutenant—"

"Oh, yes, yes, yes, Captain Hatten. Captain Edwards is sure to use what I did to Captain Hatten against me. He was there when I put a sword to Hatten. I'm sure he'll remind him of it."

"Captain Edwards wasn't there, sir."

"What? You sure?"

"Yessir. It was a small squad. We only had a sprinkle of officers and Edwards wasn't one of 'em."

Colonel Morse waved his arm. "Doesn't matter. Edwards must be stopped."

"You sure you don't want me to go, Colonel. Perhaps you need more rest."

Colonel Morse squinted. "No," he said. "Edwards is wily. He'll try to sway you. He can be very convincing, that Edwards – all good looks and boyish charm and family influence. No, no…I need to be there, so everyone will hold fast. I want you here in case someone tries to help that Cherokee witch escape. She has the evil eye, you know – she can cast spells – she can—"

Morse broke off and began examining the handle of his saber.

"Damn fine sword, isn't it? Given to me by George Washington himself after the Second War against the British. Commended me for the bravery he did – gave me this sword. Would have made me a general except they plotted against me. They all hated me for my battlefield acumen – my grace under fire."

Elias chose not to mention that Washington died thirteen years before the war Morse was referencing. He also knew the colonel had never seen action in the conflict.

Old man's sun is settin' in the west, Elias thought.

"If you're not back before her twenty-four hours are up, what should I do?" Elias asked.

Morse snapped back to the present. "The woman. If I'm not back…turn her skin into a shawl."

CHAPTER FORTY-ONE

"It's a bit slower in the dark, sir," Private Bond said.

"It's fine, Private," Thomas said. "That means it'll be hard for anyone trying to follow us." He turned and looked behind them, half expecting Elias to appear. "Let's just keep a steady pace."

Both Bond and Ratliff answered in unison. "Yes, sir."

"Remember what I told you two," Thomas said. "If we get caught, or when this is all over, I ordered you help me."

Private Ratliff studied the captain for a moment. "I'm with you on this, sir. My pa would understand. He was against the relocation of the Cherokees to begin with and was none too happy about his son being forced into this detail. I think he'd be proud of what we're doin'."

"I appreciate that, Private." Thomas looked up at the sky. "I sure hope someone in command feels the same way."

§§

Colonel Morse tied his saddlebag and struggled up into his saddle. A horse and rider pulled alongside.

"Took you long enough, Sergeant," Colonel Morse said.

Nathan Parkinson clenched his teeth. "Sorry, sir," he said.

"How many men do we have?"

"Including you, twenty-eight, sir."

"Good. That deserter Edwards only took a couple of men, so they won't put up much of a fight."

Colonel Morse looked over his men. Most were bleary-eyed having managed only a few hours of sleep after a full day before being rousted in the middle of the night.

"Men, we have a deserter and possible usurper on our hands. It's been reported that Captain Edwards deserted his post here at Fort Newnan a few hours ago."

The men exchanged dubious looks.

"He's on his way to Fort Hetzel to gather more troops. He plans to come back here tomorrow and overthrow my authority. I imagine he thinks the Indians will seize the opportunity and rise up against us. We have to stop him, elsewise there may be widespread insurrection."

The colonel scanned the shadowed faces.

"Do you understand what this means?" he asked. "We could have a revolt on our hands. Thousands of Cherokees could take up arms against us. We cannot allow that to happen!"

"Am I understood?"

A resounding "Yes, sir" echoed in the night air.

§§

Catherine knew Elias would go after Thomas – she'd been warned. But hearing the horses thunder away into the gloom of a moonless night terrified her. Though she could not see anything, she knew Elias's hat would be bobbing up and down near the head of the pursuit team. And she knew what would happen when he caught Thomas. Her chains rattled when she shifted into a seating position.

Ayita, what did I agree to?

Elias slithered onto the platform. "Well, we are alone again, ain't we?"

Catherine gasped and scrambled to her feet as best she could. She wobbled in her weakness and her voice quavered. "What are you doing here? You...you are not...you should be..."

Her dry throat seized in a fit of coughing; she sagged to one knee.

"Where else should I be, lover?" Elias asked. He moved closer, somehow making no noise despite the haphazard construction of the structure. "Been too long."

Catherine could not move – a bird locked in fear by the sight of an approaching snake.

"A man can't have his woman grow cold in her passion towards him, now can he?" Elias took off his jacket and placed it on the edge of the steps. The guard was nowhere to be seen. She knew Thomas was gone. Roe was somewhere finalizing the escape plans.

Elias's voice echoed in the gloom. "This ain't what I had in mind. I had everything set up last time – for our reunion, you know. I had fires in our glade all set up – ten of 'em in fact, one for each day we were apart. But you betrayed my trust."

His smile faded.

The feeling returned to Catherine's limbs. They moved in concert. For every step Elias took forward, Catherine moved back. Elias looked at the chain.

"Ain't got a lot of slack left, honey," he said. "That chain's pretty taut."

Catherine tried to move only to discover he'd been right. The links strained tight.

"What's wrong?" Elias asked. "Ain't it proper etiquette for a man to call on his lover ever' so often?"

When he finally got close enough, Elias reached up and caressed Catherine's cheek. She erupted.

"Proper etiquette disappeared when you raped me," she said.

Elias raised his eyebrows.

"Oh, so you know the word etiquette. And, what it means, apparently."

"I know a lot of things."

Elias chuckled. "I know a few things myself." He reached out for Catherine's hand.

Catherine tried to pull her hands away, but the chains wouldn't allow it. The corners of Elias's mouth twitched as he watched her struggle.

"Aw, c'mon, lover."

"Stop calling me that."

"Why? Saving yerself for someone else?"

Elias seized her raw throat and pulled her face to his.

"I don't plan to share you with anyone. What's mine, is *mine*."

Catherine spit in his face.

Elias sent her sprawling with a stinging backhand. Catherine cupped her cheek in her hands and glared at Elias who wiped the spit off his face with a black handkerchief.

"I wonder," he said, "do you think any man would be interested in you if they knew you were a whore?"

Catherine stood and swung at him, but he caught her wrist and slowly bent it back until he forced her onto her knees. She screamed in pain while Elias pulled her by her wrists until they were face to face.

"Do you think yer precious Captain Edwards would mind that I had a taste of you first?"

Catherine's expression changed from anger to surprise.

Elias giggled like a mischievous schoolboy.

"So, you do have feelings for the good captain."

Elias was within inches of her face. No longer redolent of mint, his foul breath made her queasy.

"So, tell me, lover. If the good captain feels the same for you, why'd he leave the night before you're to be executed? I'd think he'd stick around and try to help you."

Catherine bit her tongue to keep from speaking.

"Maybe he doesn't have feelings for you after all," Elias said. "Or, maybe he found out about us."

Elias placed his cheek onto hers and swayed back and forth as he hummed an eerie song known only to him.

"Should we tell him about us, lover?" Elias asked. He was still dancing. Catherine remained immobile. "I think we should. But how? That's the question." He hummed a few more bars. "Maybe it'd be best if we told him together. What do you think?"

Elias pulled away just enough to look directly into her eyes.

"Or…maybe we could just show him."

Catherine began to struggle in his grip. "Let go of me."

Elias cackled.

"Oh, keep scrappin'," he said. "I love yer fightin' spirit." He smacked his lips. "It's so delicious. When I'm on top of you, I see the fire in yer eyes. It doesn't get any better than that."

Catherine swung her leg up toward Elias's groin, but the chains kept her from striking him with any significant amount of force.

"Whoa!" Elias said. "Well, now, that's gonna cost you."

He threw Catherine down and flopped on top of her. Catherine moaned from his weight. Elias slimed his tongue from the base of her neck all the way up to her ear.

"When you strike out at me like that, it hurts my feelings, lover," he said. "Don't like hurt feelings."

She could feel him wrestling his pants off while tugging at her dress. She fought as much as the chains allowed. Then…

"Elias! Elias!"

Elias looked up at the man flat-handing the platform. "Can't you see I'm busy?"

"Sorry, but you gotta come quick. Buddy and Randy are dead – one of Dorsey's men too."

Elias rolled off Catherine and yanked up his pants. "Is this some kind of joke?"

"No, sir. It's true. They're dead."

Elias looked at Catherine.

"Later, lover," he said. "Don't be going anywhere now."

§§

Elias's strode across the camp, frustrated and angry.

"You couldn't wait three minutes?"

"Sorry," the other man said. "It's dark. Didn't know you were… ah…courtin' until I got right up on ya."

Elias struck the man in the shoulder with a closed fist. "If you'd been any closer, you'd have been part of the group, you nosy son of a bitch." He took a few steps. "Tell me what happened."

"Don't know exactly. They had little arrow-like things in their necks and they were all puffy—"

"Poisoned darts," Elias said. "Cherokees hunt small game with 'em. Did the darts come from the corral?"

"Don't think so, sir. None of the men were near the Indians."

"Show me."

The young man led Elias to the far end of the camp. Two bodies lay motionless on the ground their necks and faces swollen as if by a thousand bee stings. A group of soldiers encircled the corpses.

Elias knelt down next to one of the bodies. "How many are dead?'

Sergeant Singleton's weather-beaten face looked tired and perplexed. "Three, total."

Elias shook his head. "Hell's fire. Didn't know that stuff would kill anything larger than a muskrat. You ever seen anythin' like this?"

Singleton bobbed his head. "Years ago when we wuz fightin' the Creeks. We had some Cherokee warriors helpin' us out. They shot tiny darts out of a bored-out cane stick."

He plucked a dart from the neck of one of the bodies. "This is what they look like."

Elias took it and leaned towards the firelight.

"Hand-carved," he said. "Don't recognize the markings." He looked at Singleton. "They kill Creeks with these?"

"Yep. They swole up the same way. But it ain't efficient. Cherokees used these things mostly to frighten the others when they were outnumbered. Or if they needed to kill a few, quick and quiet. Them Cherokees can shoot them darn things from just 'bout anywhere. I seen one of 'em knock as squirrel out of a tree at about fifty feet."

"Damn," Elias said. "Most of these blue bellies can't hit the broad side of a barn if they were standin' inside it." He turned over one of the bodies with the toe of his boot. "How long they been dead."

"Can't say for sure. We found the first, one of yer men, 'bout an hour ago. The dart came out when he fell, so it took us a while to figger out what happened. Then, they got one of my guys. Found the dart in his neck. And when the third man was found, we figured out what was goin' on."

Elias turned the dart in his fingers a couple of times while he muttered to himself. "You think more than one man did this?"

"Considering how accurate those Cherokees can be, one of 'em could do a lot of damage all alone," Sergeant Singleton said. "But whoever did it would know we'd be mighty peeved. Maybe some old guy just wanted to get under our skin."

Elias's eyes turned to flint. "Or maybe someone wanted to distract us."

Singleton's face contorted. "From what?"

Elias shot to his feet.

"The girl," he said. "Somebody go check on the girl!"

CHAPTER FORTY-TWO

The moment Elias disappeared with the other soldier Catherine curled into a ball. She could not stop shaking. She'd never known it was possible to feel excruciating pain simultaneously with... nothing.

She heard a voice – a whisper – "Catherine" – persistent – "Catherine" – urgent – "Catherine!"

Roe was next to her.

"We need to get going," he said. "He'll be back soon."

He unlatched the chains around Catherine's ankles. "We created a little diversion, but he'll figger it out soon enough. Let's go."

When Catherine stood, she was too dazed to notice her dress fell off her shoulders and collected at her feet. Roe swooped down and pulled her dress up, but the rags slipped again. Desperate, Roe looked for anything with which to cover her.

"This'll have to do," he said.

He pulled her dress up then draped Elias's jacket around her shoulders to keep it in place.

"We have to go," he said and grabbed Catherine's hand and led her towards Ticket. Catherine shuffled behind him, unseeing, unfeeling, unknowing. When they reached the horse, Roe interlaced his fingers and offered a boost.

"Up you go," Roe said.

Catherine did not move.

"Where are the others?"

"They're down the road, waitin' fer us," Roe said.

"I'm not going without them."

"They're gone. We sent them on ahead. We gotta go, little lady."

Catherine shook her head. Roe fought to keep his voice soft and even – a trainer easing a balky filly to the starting line for her first race.

"Captain Edwards is riskin' his career to save your hide – to help you and your little girl. Things are in motion. If you don't go with me, it's all for naught."

Catherine continued to examine the dark.

"He'll find me," she said.

"Yep," Roe said. "Captain Edwards will find you and the others."

"Not him." Catherine began to shake. "The other one."

Cognition came slowly for Roe, but it did come. "You mean Elias."

"Yes."

"Not going to lie. He's gonna try. He's powerful, evil. Something's wrong with that man. But the captain, well, he *needs* you to go with me."

Catherine looked at Roe's face. Through the perpetual series of smudges, she saw a portrait of desperation. The painful concern etched across his visage snapped her into the moment.

"What's wrong with Thomas?

"He ain't himself," Roe said. "Snappish…petty…disconnected. He's drinkin' way more than he should. He's lost something – he's lost faith."

"In what?"

"In everything… the Army… humanity … himself…God."

"I'm not responsible for that," Catherine said.

"Didn't say you wuz. Don't see no culpability in you at all. But I know he needs you."

Roe studied the shell of what was once a vibrant and courageous young woman. She looked haggard – worn like an abused boot – terrified.

"Do you recall the first time me an' you met?" he asked.

Confused, Catherine met Roe's eyes

The only sounds came from the night.

"Did you ever ask yerself how I knew it was you? How I knew to bring Thomas to you and introduce you?"

She shook her head.

"I knew it was you, 'cause I'd seen ya before – hundreds of times. He draws you, you know – from memory – almost every night. Has pages and pages of renderings. Sometimes he gives you short hair. Sometimes you're younger. Sometimes it's just the face. But one thing never changes."

"What's that?"

"Your eyes – the windows to your soul." Roe leaned in to get Catherine's full attention. "The same ones I'm lookin' at now."

Catherine met his gaze.

"He's never forgotten you," Roe said.

"I've never forgotten him."

He put his foot in the stirrup and mounted Ticket. Before she knew it, Catherine was behind him. Her head collapsed onto his shoulder. Roe checked all sides, then flicked the reins. Ticket understood the subtle instructions and walked quietly through the gate. They did not speak again until they were in the trees.

"He never stopped loving you," Roe said. He heard a croaking sound. He could not tell if Catherine was mocking or surprised.

"Then why did he leave me?" she asked. She did not want to cry but the tears paid no attention and fell like silent rain.

"You told his father it was over. Broke his damn heart."

Now she gasped.

"I never said that. His father told me that Thomas didn't love me."

Roe's chuckle was harsh, an accusation and condemnation. "That sorry bastard," he said. "Sounds just like something ole

Clinton would do. Told you the captain was done with you – told Thomas the other side of the coin."

The moon came out just in time for them to duck under a low-hanging branch.

"Does Thomas know?"

"You think he'd be curled up in a jug of rock gut if he did?"

They rode in silence for the next few miles. They came to a small clearing. Waya, Leotie, and the trio of children for whom Catherine acted as surrogate embraced her.

Manjusha stood at a distance, aloof and hesitant. Catherine inclined her head and offered a brief wave of forgiveness.

I would have done the same to save Ayita, she thought.

Three soldiers trotted into the clearing on horseback. Stifled shrieks erupted from the group. The women shielded their children. Waya looked for a weapon as a half dozen more soldiers arrived.

Roe's voice remained calm. "It's okay. It's okay! They're with me."

A small caravan of wagons pulled into the little clearing. There were rags covering each wheel. The horses' hooves had been similarly muffled.

Roe pointed to the wagons. "Get in. These men are going to take you to the captain's land. They're my best – trustworthy. They volunteered to help."

Catherine tugged at his sleeve. "Won't the wagons leave a trail for the soldiers to track us?"

"Yes," Roe said. He pointed. "Get into those two. They are going where you want. The others will go in different directions. They're loaded with rocks – all the wagons will leave the same depth of track."

Waya smiled. "You think like a Tsalagi."

"A high compliment, indeed," Roe said. "Now, git!"

Waya turned to the others. "Come, Walks the Sky wants us in these wagons. We will be with him by the day's end."

§§

"Dammit!"

Elias slammed the empty shackles onto the platform. "How could you let this happen?"

Gabe cleared his throat. Elias struck the young man's jaw with the force of a sledgehammer. Gabe landed in the dirt and groaned.

"Shut up! Just shut up!"

Elias surveyed the area. "Damn moon ain't helping any. Can't see nuthin'."

He looked around. The other men on the platform stayed conspicuously out of reach. Gabe staggered up the stairs.

"You didn't need to hit me," he said. "I didn't do—"

Elias lunged at him but restrained. "Damn right you didn't. Catherine's gone."

A voice from below crept atop the platform.

"Ain't the half of it, boss."

Elias glared into the gloom. A squat man with a pockmarked face was looking at him.

"What's that mean, Bert?" Elias asked.

"Indians is gone."

Everyone on the platform took a step back – just in case. An odd serenity scrolled across Elias's face. The calm before the storm. His voice was low and feral.

"Bert, my hearin' must be bad. Sounded like you just said the Cherokees were gone."

"Yep."

"How many of 'em."

"Best I can tell, about fifty."

"What about the little crew Captain Edwards shepherded around – you know, Catherine's little friends?"

"Them too."

Everyone braced for an explosion, an attack. Instead, Elias sat. He reached into his shirt pocket and extracted a cigar. After he lit it, he smoked. Everyone looked at Gabe.

"Ah, boss?" Gabe said.

Elias looked up. "Yes."

"What you think we should do?"

Elias stood, dropped his cigar, and smashed it with his booted toe.

"You mean after I turn every last one of you into a gelding?"

Several of the men involuntarily covered their groins.

"Sure, boss. After that."

Elias straightened his hat and scanned the group of men.

"How's this happen?"

Bert thumped up the stairs.

"We ain't been exactly sharp-eyed the last few weeks, Elias," he said. "You know, we have a few runaways, but most of them Indians is too worn out and hungry to do much of anything. When those two boys got killed tonight, most of us ran over there to see what was going on."

"You mean the three or four of you who were sober enough to stand, right?"

Bert hung his head. "Ain't much else to do 'cept gamble and drink. You know that."

"So, for all you know, the Cherokees have been slipping out all night."

"Best we can tell."

"You track 'em."

Bert rolled his tongue around in his mouth. "Can't."

The dam broke. Elias slammed his hand into the post to which Catherine had been chained. He stomped his foot and unleashed a profanity-laced tirade. He screamed into the face of every man on the platform and tried to kick those who were gathered around it. He whirled to face Bert.

"You are the best tracker at this fort. Hell, you're one of the best in the whole damn Army. What do you mean you can't track 'em. They must have left enough signs for a blind man to follow."

Bert's laughter was so unexpected that Elias backed up. "That's just it, boss," Bert said. "There are too many signs. Can't make heads or tails of 'em. Like you said, they've been slipping out for a while – ever since sundown would be my guess. And they made no attempt to hide their tracks. Looks like some of 'em even dragged their feet. They headed in all sorts of directions. They is tryin' to confound us – footprints going every which a way. Ain't no way to tell who went where until it gets light and by then, the closest will be miles away."

"I'm surrounded by idiots," Elias said. He placed his pistol under Bert's chin and cocked the hammer.

Gabe took a step forward. "Elias, he don't deserve that!"

Elias bit his lower lip and nodded several times. He un-cocked the pistol and slowly lowered it into his hostel.

"You're right, Gabe," he said. "He don't deserve it."

He drove his knife hilt-deep into Bert's abdomen.

"Shootin's much too good for the likes of him."

Bert crumpled. Elias howled with untethered malevolence.

While Bert gurgled and lurched, unattended, Elias wiped the
blood off of his knife with a black handkerchief, then looked around
licking his lips as if savoring the impenetrable darkness. He pointed
at Gabe. "Find five men sober enough to stay on a horse. Send them
out in different directions. On foot, most of those savages ain't gone
more than a few miles. You find any, you tell them to get back to the
fort. They'll do what you tell 'em – they is sheep. If one of you finds
the big group – the group with the woman – do not lose track. When
you don't come back, we'll know, and we'll be there straightaway."
He looked around.

"You incompetent asses think you can handle this?"

No one dared to speak.

"Good – now git!"

The men could not disperse quickly enough. After they were
gone, Gabe bent over Bert's body.

"Leave him," Elias said.

"This is bad," Gabe said.

"Mebbe," Elias said. "But it ain't the worst thing."

Gabe looked at his bloodstained hands. "What's worse than this,
boss?"

Elias scratched his groin and lit another cigar.

"Damn Indian woman stole my favorite jacket," he said.

CHAPTER FORTY-THREE

Half of the sun was on the horizon when Thomas and Private Ratliff crested a ridge. They looked back over the valley they had traversed. Thomas peered through his telescope.

He took his time scanning the trail then flinched when he saw a cavalry brigade appear from a copse of trees.

He handed the glass to Ratliff. "Tell me what you see, Private," he said.

Ratliff moved his lips as he counted.

"Twenty…twenty-eight mounted soldiers, sir," he said. "And I'd bet my monthly whiskey ration that's Colonel Morse at the head of the column. I reckon he's about three-quarters of an hour behind us."

"I was sure Elias would be the one tracking us down," Thomas said. "Morse must have heard I'm going to Fort Hetzel. And I bet he's afraid I'm going there to cause trouble for him."

"Do you know anyone at Fort Hetzel, sir?"

"Not personally, no. But he wouldn't know that."

"Worried ye're after his command, sir?"

"Probably, but that's not my intention."

Ratliff passed the telescope. "Well, reality and Ol' Cutthroat don't run in the same circles very often, sir."

Thomas's head snapped to the side. "What did you call him?"

"Nothin' you ain't heard before, Captain. Everyone out here knows about Morse."

Thomas slammed his palm on the saddle horn. "I've put everyone in danger, haven't I?"

Private Ratliff shook his head. "I can't speak for the civilians, sir, but I can speak for all the soldiers under your command. We'll follow you into the mouth of hell, sir."

Thomas looked back at the young private. "Well then, we better get going. Ol' Cutthroat looks like he has no intention of slowing down."

§§

"Sir, we have to give these horses a rest," Sergeant Parkinson said.

Colonel Morse's eyes never left the horizon.

"Sir. Sir! We have to stop. The horses need rest."

Colonel Morse looked at him, confused. "What?"

"The horses, sir. We need to give 'em a rest. We've been running 'em for too long."

"No! We can't stop. We have to catch that traitor before he reaches Fort Hetzel."

"Sir, even Captain Edwards will have to stop and rest his horses after a while."

"Good. That'll give us time to catch up with him."

The colonel leaned forward in his saddle and dug his spurs into his horse's flanks.

"Colonel! Sir! This is madness! We must stop, sir!"

Colonel Morse spurred his horse once again. This time she raised her head, whinnied, and jerked her head around, breaking the colonel's concentration.

"Sir! We have to stop!"

Colonel Morse turned around in his saddle. The other horses' heads were low; their breathing was labored.

"Very well," he said. "We'll stop here for a short rest. A very short rest. But if Captain Edwards gets away, it'll be your necks!"

§§

The sun had finally crested the horizon when the fourth rider, David Norlander, could be seen racing back to the fort from the west.

"That settles it," Elias said. He lowered his telescope. "They're headed east." He immediately turned his horse. Frustration tinged his voice. "We should've headed east hours ago!"

Elias and Gabe had spent the interim investigating the escapees. Though he brandished his knife a few times, Elias never used it out of fear of being overrun by the remaining Cherokees. With Morse gone and five riders sent out, there were not sufficient soldiers left in the fort to combat an uprising.

The only thing Elias learned was that Captain Edwards had a grandmother living somewhere east of the fort near Dahlonega. Interesting, but not sufficient proof to charge towards the rising sun.

"What about Norlander," Gabe asked. "Shouldn't we wait fer him?"

Elias looked out at the tiny silhouette of David gradually getting bigger. "No. We've wasted enough time. They've got about a four-hour head start on us." He paused with one foot in a stirrup. "Actually," he pointed to one of the men, "you wait for him. Get him a fresh mount and the two of you catch up."

"Yes, sir."

Elias turned to another man. "You – yes, you with the crooked teeth – ride to Fort Hetzel. Tell the colonel what's going on. If he ain't already heading back here, tell him that Edwards has a grandmother near Dahlonega and we're heading that way. We're gonna need help."

"Yes, sir."

Elias mounted his horse. "Now, gentlemen, I'm going to get back what rightfully belongs to me."

§§

Thomas snapped his telescope closed. "I don't see them. But Morse is still comin', make no mistake about that."

Bond and Ratliff nodded.

"Private Bond," Thomas said. "Don't wait on me to talk to the commander. Go and get those kids."

"Yes, sir." Bond headed towards the Fort Hetzel corral.

Thomas handed his telescope to Private Ratliff.

"I want you to stay here at the gate and keep a look out. The moment you see the colonel, come find me. I figure once he crests that hill, we've got maybe twenty minutes before he gets here. So, timing's important."

"Yes, sir."

Thomas turned Silo in the direction of the commander's tent.

Fort Hetzel wasn't as dirty or disorganized as Fort Newnan, but it carried the same stench of human waste and death. Thomas got a few curious looks as he made his way through the rows towards Captain Hatten's tent, but no one tried to stop him.

Twenty-five feet from the commander's tent, a young soldier ran up and saluted.

"State your business, sir."

"I'm Captain Thomas Edwards, assigned to Fort Newnan. I was sent here on official business regarding the Cherokees in your custody."

"Is the commander expecting you, sir?"

"No."

The private looked around and scowled.

"Is there a problem?" Thomas asked.

"Ah, not sure, sir. Captain Hatten was planning on riding around the fort today to check the outer fortifications and to inspect the corral."

"Has he left yet?"

"Yes, sir. Just left. I might be able to catch him. Do you mind waiting, sir?"

"Seems I have no choice."

"Can I get you some coffee sir? Just made some."

"No. It's imperative I speak with Captain Hatten. It's of considerable importance. And time is of the essence."

"Understood, sir. You can wait outside of his tent there, and I'll go fetch him."

"Very good. Please hurry."

"Yes, sir."

§§

"I recognize where we are, sir," Sergeant Parkinson said. "We're not far from Fort Hetzel now."

"Wanted to catch that scoundrel *before* he got to Hetzel." Morse said. "I don't want any interference from Captain Hatten." He pointed at Parkinson. "Remind the men that Captain Edwards is a fugitive – a traitor and a deserter. He's not to be killed, however. He's to be arrested on the spot and taken back to Fort Newnan. I'll deal with him there. Anyone aiding and abetting Edwards should be viewed in the same light."

CHAPTER FORTY-FOUR

Thomas paced outside of Captain Hatten's tent trying to come up with alternate plans when he spotted the young private approaching with another man riding at an intolerably slow pace. He wanted to run over and ask them to hurry, but military protocol and prudence dictated he stand firm and wait.

As the two riders got closer, Thomas flashed a nervous smile and greeted the commander with a perfect salute.

Captain Hatten looked confused as he halted his horse in front of the unexpected visitor.

"Good morning, sir." Thomas said.

"Good morning to you," the young commander replied and saluted back. "Captain Edwards, is it?"

"Yes, it is, sir."

Captain Hatten smiled broadly, slid off of his horse, and walked over to shake Thomas's hand. He was a tall, slender man with red hair, freckles, and green eyes. His every movement radiated confidence.

"I wasn't expecting any visitors today," he said. "I'm sure Private Parks already told you."

"He did. And I want to apologize for not sending a request beforehand."

Captain Hatten waved him off. "No need for that." He gestured toward his tent. "Come on in. It'll be a bit more comfortable in here. Private Parks, please bring Captain Edwards and me some coffee."

"Yes, sir."

Captain Hatten held the tent flap for Thomas, then followed behind while he removed his riding gloves.

The captain's tent was simple but well organized.

"I understand you're coming from Fort Newnan."

"Yes, sir."

The pleasant expression on Captain Hatten's face turned a bit more serious. "How's Captain Dorsey these days? I heard he's been bitten by the whiskey bottle and hasn't been able to shake it."

"Sorry to say that what you heard is true, sir."

"That's a shame. He was a good man."

Captain Hatten motioned toward two chairs sitting adjacent to one another.

Private Parks arrived with the coffee and some bread and jam – a luxury Thomas hadn't enjoyed in a long time. He suddenly realized how hungry he was but felt he couldn't waste any time eating.

"What I need to speak to you about is of a serious matter, sir," Thomas said. "I must also tell you that time isn't on our side."

"I deduced as much since you obviously rode all night to get here. How can I help you?"

"It's funny you asked about Captain Dorsey, I'm here on his orders."

"Orders for what?"

Thomas removed the papers from his coat pocket and handed them to Captain Hatten who immediately set his coffee down and read them. Thomas watched Hatten's eyes scan the paper.

Precious seconds ticked by.

"It says here, the ages of the children are six, four and two," Captain Hatten said. "Is this accurate?"

"Yes, sir. I'm afraid it is."

"How can this be?"

"They were separated from their parents during the roundup, sir."

"What?"

"Yes, sir. Their parents are being held at Fort Newnan."

"I don't understand. These children are so little. So young."

"And they aren't the only ones, thanks to the Georgia militia."

"Are you sayin' this isn't an isolated incident?"

"Exactly, sir. There are several children at Fort Newnan right now without their parents."

Captain Hatten sat back in his chair. "My God, I had no idea." He read a little more before lowering the papers to his lap. "I never paid attention to the names on our rolls. I just kept track of the numbers." He turned to Thomas. "We need to fix this."

"I agree, sir. That's why I'm here. Trying to fix one situation at a time."

"I'm glad you brought this to my attention." Captain Hatten turned toward the opening in his tent. "Private Parks!"

"Sir?"

"There are three young children in our corral without their parents. I need you to find—"

"That's not necessary, sir," Thomas said. "I took the liberty of sending one of my men to get them as soon as we arrived."

"That's awfully presumptuous of you."

"I had to take a chance, sir. I didn't know what kind of man you were, so I thought if you were hesitant to okay the transfer, when you saw the children, you might be more willing to agree."

Captain Hatten studied Thomas for a moment. "I understand what you're saying, but I don't like it. Feels like you're trying to put one over on me, Captain."

"Not at all, sir."

Private Ratliff burst into the tent. Captain Hatten shot up to his feet. "What's the meaning of this?"

Thomas stood. "This is Private Ratliff, sir. I had him stationed at the south gate as a lookout."

"A lookout for what?"

"Not what, sir. But whom."

"Okay, *whom* was he looking out for?"

"Colonel Morse, sir. He's followed us all the way here."

"Did you say Morse?"

"Yes. Lieutenant Colonel Jeremiah Morse," Thomas said. "And he's due here any minute."

Thomas looked over at Private Ratliff who nodded, assuring the captain there was little time.

"Cutthroat Colonel Morse…" Captain Hatten said to himself.

Thomas nodded.

"Why would he follow you here? How's that crazy old man wrapped up in this?"

Thomas drew to attention. "Colonel Morse has the mother of one of those children under lock and key. He plans on killing—"

"I don't need to hear any more," Captain Hatten said.

"But, sir—"

"I know that snake well enough to deduce that you're trying to protect an innocent person. Morse's reputation for insanity is far from exaggerated."

"You know him, sir?" Thomas asked.

Hatten sipped his coffee. "I served under him. I was there when he was busted down to Lieutenant Colonel."

Thomas's eyebrows raised.

Captain Hatten stepped to the threshold of his tent and looked towards the southern gate.

"I was a lieutenant under his command a few years back," he said with a sigh. "I'm not proud of it now, but back then I was in charge of a…kill squad that the Colonel loved to use down in central Florida. Sometimes we were used as a decoy, other times to cause havoc, creating fear among whomever it was we were fighting. Anyway, one night there was a small village near where we were on patrol. An outpost. Mostly missionaries and their families – just godly people trying to preach the gospel to the natives. Well, because they interacted with the Seminoles, Ol' Cutthroat thought they were aiding them, helping them out with food, water and telling them about our military tactics. He was so convinced that he ordered us to slaughter the entire village. Men. Women. Children. He didn't care."

Thomas glanced over at the Parks and Ratliff. The young men were standing, their eyes bulging, their mouths agape.

Thomas looked back at the commander. "Did you—"

"I did not," Hatten said. "I refused to order my squad to go through with it, but I couldn't stop the colonel. When I tried, he gave me a gift I still carry."

Captain Hatten looked up at his audience. He unbuttoned his shirt. An ugly pink scar ran from his navel to the base of his throat.

Thomas gasped. "Oh, my good Lord, you're the one. I always thought it was a myth!"

§§

Hatten dipped his quill into an inkwell and signed the orders. He sprinkled pounce[2] on it and handed it to Thomas who checked it, rolled it, and put it in his satchel.

"I honestly don't know how that crazy old man was still allowed to wear a uniform," Hatten said.

A young soldier came running into the tent.

"Sorry, sir," he said as he came to attention. "There's a Colonel Morse demanding to see you. He's got a bunch of men with him."

"He hasn't entered the fort, has he?" Captain Hatten asked. He buckled his sword and slipped a pistol into his holster.

"No, sir," the young man replied. "Sergeant Rose is holding them there. Rose said something smells funny about all this, so he sent me to get permission before he let the colonel into the fort."

Hatten squared away his belt. "Run ahead and tell Rose to keep him there. I'll be right behind you."

"Yes, sir."

"What are you going to do?" Thomas asked.

"Stall," Hatten said. "We don't have time for the whole story, Captain, but if you have Colonel Morse's ass hairs standing on end, you've got my support. I'll try to keep him busy while you find your man and get those kids out of here. Head out to the north end of the fort. The forest begins right there. It will give you some cover. You can circle back around south towards Fort Newnan."

---

[2] A fine powder (usually ground cuttlefish bone) used to dry ink.

"Thank you, sir."

Thomas didn't feel the need to explain they weren't headed back to Fort Newnan.

Before Thomas and Hatten were ten feet out of the tent, they could hear the argument at the south gate escalating.

Morse's voice echoed throughout the camp.

"Sergeant, get the hell out of my way or I will shoot you where you stand!"

Rose refused to surrender any ground. "You can try, sir," he said.

Captain Hatten clenched his teeth. "That arrogant bastard." He stuck out his hand. "God speed to you."

The two soldiers shook hands.

"And to you, sir," Thomas replied. "Thank you for everything."

Captain Hatten nodded before racing to his horse and leaping onto it without slowing down. He made a beeline to the gate.

Private Ratliff pointed. "There's Bond."

Bond had all three children with him. When Thomas rode up, he immediately knew Ayita.

She has her mother's eyes.

Even though the southern gate was close to two hundred yards away, Thomas and his compatriots could hear the commotion. Thomas could make out men trying to force their way into the fort. Some of Hatten's men were trying to pull the riders from their mounts. Morse caught sight of Thomas and began to gesticulate like a bird with a broken wing. His voice boomed.

"There he is. Traitor! Deserter! Someone arrest that man!"

"There's going to be gunfire soon," Thomas said. "We've got to go." Soldiers in the fort who were unaware of the situation stumbled from their tents in various stages of undress. Some grabbed weapons – some struggled to put on their pants. Chaos rolled through the fort in a mighty wave, increasing in intensity as the conflict at the south gate got worse.

Thomas grabbed Harsha, the youngest, and placed her in the saddle in front of him. With the poise of a seasoned professional, Private Ratliff put Kavi, the four-year-old, in his saddle and spurred for the north end. About the time Bond settled Ayita in place, they heard the first shot.

"Let's go, Private!"

Bullets sliced through the air.

"Get on the damn horse, Bond!"

Harsha and Ayita started crying.

Private Bond managed to regain his composure. He scrambled onto his horse and wheeled in pursuit of Ratliff.

Morse and a handful of his men broke through the blockade and were firing at will.

Like salmon swimming against the current, Thomas and his men sped through the flow of soldiers running towards the ruckus. Bond's panic returned. He screamed above the din.

"I can't believe they're shooting at us!"

Thomas shot a glance over his shoulder as he spurred Silo to go. The melee behind him was just short of a pitched battle. To his relief, he saw that more men were fighting each other than were involved in his pursuit. His blood ran cold when he heard Harsha shriek.

He looked down. To his surprise, the toddler had her hands in the air and her head back. She was squealing with delight as the wind whipped through her long hair. She pantomimed a rider, her arms going up and down as if controlling Silo's reins.

The tree line loomed in front of them. Just as they passed the first pine, an explosion to Thomas' right-hand side sent pain radiating through his skull. He clutched Silo with his knees to keep from falling. He felt the familiar sensation of blood trickling down his cheek from his brow. His vision blurred. He slowed Silo.

A bullet splintered a small tree. Splinters embedded into Thomas's face just above his right eye.

Thomas looked to see if Harsha had been injured. She stared up at him with an ear-to-ear smile. Her brown eyes were wide with wonder as she looked at the curious man who was giving her a horsey ride. Other than a few tiny pieces of wood in her long black hair, there were no signs she was riding through a dangerous assault.

Private Ratliff pulled up from his lead position after several hundred yards. Bond and Thomas reined up beside him.

"Why are we stopping?" Thomas asked.

"Sir, your eye," Ratliff said.

"Never mind. I'm fine," Thomas said. "Why are we stopping?"

"You don't hear that, sir?" Private Ratliff asked.

Thomas took a deep breath and listened.

"That's cannon fire."

CHAPTER FORTY-FIVE

When the first cannon had erupted to his right, Morse flinched and tugged the long rifle a little. He saw the tree next to Thomas's head explode instead of the skull under the fleeing captain's hat.

After the first shot, Captain Hatten rushed at the battery but couldn't stop two more volleys.

"Cease fire! Who the hell ordered that barrage?" Thankfully, his men weren't trying to hit anyone, they were just trying to startle Colonel Morse's men.

His face purple with rage, Hatten stood nose to nose with Morse.

"You are a crazy, paranoid old man. You are not fit to dig privy pits much less wear the uniform of a United States Army officer. If I shot you right now, no court-martial would find me guilty. Just what in the name of all things sacred is your problem, Colonel?"

Morse seemed confused – a naughty puppy unsure why his owner is yelling at the mess he made on the rug. He pointed towards the trees with a trembling finger.

"That man is a fugitive – a deserter. You, Captain, have obviously been helping him all this time. You have been plotting against me – with him."

Hatten stepped back. "I met Captain Edwards for the first time this morning when he delivered signed orders from Captain Dorsey."

Colonel Morse hocked, then spit. "Those orders are null and void; Captain Dorsey is unfit to command."

"The orders looked official to me, Colonel. Do you have orders overriding Dorsey's?"

"I don't need any damn orders! I'm a colonel and if I want to, I will burn this fort down to the ground! Do you understand me, you insignificant pissant?"

With calm deliberation, Hatten drew his sidearm and leveled it at Morse's head.

"It will be the last order you ever give, you arrogant bastard," Hatten said. "The only thing keeping me from splattering your brains all over the ground is my oath as an officer. Now, take your men, and your corpulent ass back the way you came. Otherwise, my men, and I will be forced to defend ourselves and this fort."

Colonel Morse studied the steely, green eyes of the young commander. He blinked several times as if awakening from a nap, then looked at his sergeant.

"Prepare the men to return home," he said. He saluted with excessive formality. "Captain Hatten, I apologize for any inconvenience my unannounced arrival caused you or your contingent. By any chance, did Captain Edwards mention his intended destination?"

Captain Hatten lowered his gun. "I have no idea where he is going…sir. I assume he is headed back to Fort Newnan."

422

Morse took the reins of his horse from an aide and huffed his way into the saddle. Once astride, he straightened his hat and jacket. "Very well, Captain. We will depart."

§§

Thomas could feel his pulse throbbing around and inside his right eye. Whenever he looked anywhere but straight ahead it felt like a hundred needles were piercing his eyeball. "We need to stop," he said.

Ratliff and Bond slowed their mounts, then stopped.

Keeping a hand on Harsha, Thomas climbed off of Silo and stretched his legs and arms before assisting the child to the ground.

"Water?" she asked.

Thomas smiled at her and grabbed his canteen. He knelt down and showed her how to drink from it. Once she understood what it was, she smiled at him and took a drink. The two of them shared the canteen for a few minutes and watched Ayita and Kavi walk around near the other two soldiers. When Harsha was finished drinking the water she smiled at the captain once more.

"Ouch," she said and pointed at the captain's face.

"Yes, ouch."

Private Ratliff appeared with some rags. Despite Thomas's protests, he cleaned the wound and removed as many splinters as he could. While Ratliff took care of the captain, Private Bond played with the children and watched for any sign of pursuit.

"Do you think Morse made it through the fort, sir?" Ratliff asked.

"Don't know," Thomas replied.

"What do you think he'll do?"

"Again, I don't know. He could be heading back to Fort Newnan but who knows. We'll just have to be prepared for anything in these woods."

"Yes, sir."

Thomas watched Ayita while he and Ratliff spoke. He could not get over her resemblance to Catherine. The child had the same skin tone, the same luxurious black hair, the same eyes.

I'm getting her back to her mother, he thought – *no matter the cost.*

§§

"Do you think he came here just for those young'uns, sir?" Sergeant Parkinson asked.

"Seems that way," Colonel Morse said. "But why? And why now?"

There was a subtle commotion among the colonel's men who'd been waiting for the colonel to decide on a route. A lone rider weaved his way towards Morse. He saluted and mumbled what must have been his name.

"What is it?"

"Elias sent me with a message, sir. The Cherokee woman has escaped."

Morse slapped his hat against his knee. "Mother of God. What's going on back there?" He glared at the messenger. "Can I trust anyone to do their job?"

The man swallowed hard. "It's Captain Edwards, sir. He got 'em all out."

Colonel Morse threw his riding gloves onto the ground. "I leave for one day and all hell breaks loose. Weren't you people supposed to be watching them?" He pointed to his gloves. His ever-attentive aide returned them. "I assume Elias is tracking them as we speak?"

The man nodded. "Going to Dahlonega. Edwards got family there."

Colonel Morse appeared to search the heavens for divine guidance. When no voice sounded from above, he turned to Sergeant Parkinson. "Of course, of course. I should've realized what was going on. It's all starting to make sense now."

Sergeant Parkinson looked at the rider and rolled his eyes. Morse did not notice.

"Good work, young man – excellent work. You've earned yourself a battlefield promotion. I'm going to make you a captain."

Parkinson coughed and spoke quietly. "The man's a civilian, sir."

Morse thumped his saddle horn with his palm. "Precisely Redfield. Making sure you are on your toes. Now, young man, get a fresh horse and race to Dahlonega. I want you to deliver a message."

CHAPTER FORTY-SIX

"Can it be fixed?" Roe asked.

Sergeant Bollinger slid out from underneath the rear end of the wagon. "Nope," he said. "Axle snapped clean in half. Ain't never seen anything like it."

Roe exhaled a string of profanity. "We must've exceeded its capacity."

"Don't know about that," Bollinger said, "but when she hit that hole, sumbitch busted like a dry twig. It's built cheaply as hell – it's a wonder it lasted this long."

"Army life," Roe said.

"Ain't that the truth," Bollinger said. "Built to haul Cherokee. I'm sure some fat cat back East is smokin' fancy ceegars and sippin' good whiskey courtesy of the Quartermaster's Office."

"That's for damn sure."

Roe rubbed his face and sighed.

"We're about an hour away from where we're supposed to meet Captain Edwards along the Little Amicalola Creek."

Roe saw a small cloud of dust in the west making its way towards them. It was no doubt his scout heading back to let them know Elias wasn't far behind.

"Looks like we're gonna have to make a stand sooner than I hoped."

The two men walked towards the front of the wagon where everyone else was gathered around Waya.

"We can't outrun Elias or Morse, so we're gonna have to make a stand. Get the extra rifles we brought along and all the ammo and firing caps you can find."

"Yes, sir."

Roe stood on a stump and addressed a small sea of expectant faces.

"You all will carry on eastward," he said. "Don't worry. We can load up the second wagon and we've got enough rifles for every man here, soldier and otherwise. My men and I will stay here and stage a delaying action while the rest of you civilians escort your families east."

Roe turned to his men. "We knew this was likely gonna happen at some point along the way. Might as well be now."

Waya and Jeevan stepped forward.

"Please, let some of us stay and fight," Waya said.

Roe shook his head. "Absolutely not. Out of the question."

"Please, there's still a long way to go, and if any soldiers find us wandering out here in the forest, armed and in an Army wagon without a military escort, they'll surely kill us. Send some of your men with our women and children to protect them and let some of us stay and fight."

Different scenarios bounced around in Roe's head, none of which he liked, and all of them involving gun battles and bloodshed.

"All right," he said. "Sergeant Bollinger, take nine of your best men and go with these civilians. Keep heading east. That'll leave me with an even dozen."

"You'll need more than—"

"No, I won't. We've got the element of surprise on our side. Elias ain't thinkin' 'bout anything but runnin' us down. The last thing he's expectin' is for us to turn and fight."

Waya stepped forward "But—"

"Listen, while I appreciate yer enthusiasm, war is my specialty," Roe said. "Ye're gonna need as many men with the families as possible. We don't know what's happened with Captain Edwards, and Colonel Morse is probably running around with his own folks. Be prepared for trouble along the way."

"What about Elias and his men?" Waya asked. "They're skilled warriors, you'll need more of us—"

"There's nothing more to discuss," Roe said. "Get your people in that other wagon and get going or all this talk won't mean a darn thing."

"Sergeant Bickford!"

Roe turned to see his scout trying to catch his breath. "Report."

"Elias is about fifteen minutes behind."

§§

Elias had never been a jealous man.

When he wanted something, he simply took it. Money, food, authority, it didn't matter. It was just a question of his will over another's, a battle he'd always won. His rapacious nature had become a habit, second nature, a subconscious act. He truly didn't know what it felt like to want something and not get it.

However, he never wanted someone's heart until now.

Women were objects to be taken. He had one and moved on. "Love-making," or whatever euphemism women wanted to append to the carnal act, was a physical activity intended for pleasure and stress relief. It happened – and then, it was over.

At least until he met Catherine. Even her current betrayal, something he would ordinarily punish with lethal force, didn't bother him. Catherine was headstrong; she possessed a coltish resistance to authority.

I'll break her, Elias thought. *Then she will be mine.*

The first of several bullets whistled just past Elias' head. He automatically dove from his horse with little regard to how he'd land on the unforgiving ground. Shaken, Elias scanned the area. Several of his men lay on the ground clutching at wounds.

Thunderous bursts of gunfire cascaded from too many directions for him to track. The relentless noise pounded Elias's brain. He experienced momentary – and uncharacteristic – disorientation. He low crawled until he reached the edge of the woods. Once he secured his position behind a fallen tree, he looked to return fire.

When the assault ended, Elias and three others rallied in the trees. They left their compatriots in the road.

"Dammit, where'd they come from?" he asked.

Gabe slid in next to Elias with a sizable wound on his left arm. "Holy shit. They just started firing from everywhere. Both sides of the road."

Elias assessed the situation. Horace would not stop screaming.

"They cut us down! Shot us like dogs. Took Billy's head clean off. Oh God, Oh God!"

Gabe was no less panicked, but his voice was quieter. "What do we do?" he asked. "What do we do?"

Elias swallowed hard and looked off towards the southwest and safety. A thought came to his mind, but the concept was so foreign, it took a while for the word to pass his lips. It was a word for lesser men – an order only issued by cowards.

"Retreat," he said and grabbed Clyde, the man nearest to him. "We retreat."

§§

Thomas stared at the abandoned, broken-down wagon.

"I don't understand what's going on," he said.

Earlier in the day, they got turned around several miles outside of Fort Hetzel. Eventually, Thomas found the northernmost point of what he believed was the Little Amicalola Creek. Not wanting to stop and tend to his eye, he headed south hoping to rendezvous with Catherine and the others as planned.

They stopped more frequently along the way than Thomas wanted, but the children just couldn't ride as long as the seasoned soldiers. Thomas tried to be patient. During the breaks, he observed Ayita from a distance, a way of getting to know Catherine's world a little more. She was a lot like her mother, and it didn't take long for him to develop deep feelings for the little girl.

Even with the many stops, Thomas felt they were making good headway until a little past noon when the eruption of gunfire echoed in the distance.

"That could be them," Thomas said.

They rushed towards the sound of battle, ducking branches, and holding tight to the children until the fracas ended as abruptly as it began. Thomas reacted to the sudden silence by pulling back on Silo's reins and coming to a complete stop. The others followed suit; they all waited to see if the fighting would resume. It did not. The unexpected stillness hanging oppressively over the forest.

Thomas looked back at Private Bond. "What do you think?"

"Bein' so quick and the way it sounded, I'd hafta say it was an ambush."

Thomas nodded and drew out his pistol. "Question is, who ambushed who?"

The two young soldiers pulled their weapons as well and fell in line behind the captain who took up a much slower pace. They rode a little more than a half-mile through the trees before stopping several yards short of a main road.

"I know this road, Captain," Ratliff said.

"You think this is the road Roe would use coming from Fort Newnan?" Thomas asked.

"Has to be," Private Ratliff replied. "Can't imagine any other route."

Thomas looked down at Harsha who gazed at him and smiled.

"Thank you for being so quiet," he said which made her look at her brother and smile even more. "I'm going to go take a look," he said.

Thomas dismounted before handing Harsha to Private Bond. The captain crawled on his stomach to the edge of the forest where it met the road. The road was empty but obviously well-traveled.

Too many tracks to tell if Roe came this way, Thomas thought.

There were no travelers – no signs of the gun battle. He crept back to the others.

"We should continue on east," he said. "Even if we're ahead of Roe's group, I'm sure we'll run into them eventually. Let's stay off the road in case we come upon whoever was shooting. I'm guessin Elias, God help us. I really hate not knowing where that snake is."

He put his hand up to his eye and checked to see if the bleeding had stopped. "The good thing is he won't be expecting *us*."

"Let me check on that, Captain," Private Ratliff said.

"No, I'm fine. Let's push on. I want to find out what the shooting was all about. Once we do, then I'll let you take a look at my eye."

They rode on for five minutes or so when Private Bond snapped up in his saddle and pointed towards the road. He whispered to Thomas.

"Holy crap, Captain, look!"

Eight bodies painted the dusty road with black splotches. Anxious, Thomas slid off Silo and motioned to Bond.

"Stay sharp – mind the children," he said. He pulled his long rifle from its scabbard, then made his way to the edge of the forest. He opened his telescope to inspect the bodies some fifteen yards away. Relief washed over him.

None was female.

Then, a further realization.

They're all Elias's men.

Nearly euphoric, Thomas stepped from cover. None of the dead had so much as drawn a weapon.

Ambush.

Thomas inspected each corpse and was disappointed not to find Elias among the casualties. He followed a blood trail into the woods on the other side of the road. A body slumped against a fallen tree.

Gabe.

Thomas made his way back to Bond and Ratliff.

"Elias's men," he said. "Every last one of them. Ambushed. Roe did good work."

"How many?" Private Bond asked.

"Eight in the road – one in the trees."

"Please, tell me Elias was one of 'em."

Thomas shook his head. "We're not that lucky."

Thomas settled onto Silo behind Harsha. He pointed east and clicked. Silo moved without further encouragement.

"Keep your eyes sharp and your weapons ready," Thomas said. "We know Elias is around – and nothing's more dangerous than a wounded animal."

They followed the road for a quarter of a mile before it went down a hill and that was where they came upon the abandoned wagon, a myriad of footprints, and a single wagon trail heading east.

"Busted axel," Private Ratliff said as he crawled out from underneath the wagon. "Broke clean in half."

"That explains the ambush," Thomas replied, looking back up the hill. "But where'd they all go?"

"Seems like they kept headin' east," Private Bond said as he came back from that direction. "I found prints from horses, humans, and the second wagon."

Thomas stared down the road. "Why do I feel like we're being watched?"

"Elias is out there somewhere," Private Bond replied. "He's prolly watchin' us right now."

At that precise moment, gunfire erupted from the direction everyone seemed to have gone.

CHAPTER FORTY-SEVEN

Colonel Morse rubbed his eyes and tried to focus. Sergeant Parkinson touched him on the arm and pointed into the direction of a group of Cherokees sitting in a clearing.

"You see what I see, Colonel?"

"Thought I was seeing things, Sergeant," Morse said.

"I count ten soldiers with 'em," Parkinson said. "No sign of either Edwards or his little toady, Bickford."

The colonel counted nine Indians. "I only see a few rifles with the savages, but we must assume every male is armed."

Sergeant Parkinson nodded.

"Spread out," Colonel Morse said. "We'll surround them and end this nonsense."

"Yes, sir."

As the sergeant was relaying orders to the other men, Colonel Morse continued to study the misfit group in a small glade.

Is this the meeting place? Will Edwards be here soon? Maybe we should wait and grab them all up at once.

The idea of waiting disappeared the moment a familiar-looking woman came into view.

Morse recognized her eyes.

That's the one who cast the spell on Elias. The woman from my dreams.

Colonel Morse grabbed Sergeant Parkinson's arm. "It's her."

The sergeant motioned for the colonel to speak more quietly.

"That's the one we had chained back at the fort. How is she here? I was planning on skinning her when I got back. That witch must be stopped."

Parkinson took a step back. He had not realized witchcraft was involved. He regained his composure and motioned for his men to get into position. Once set, he signaled Morse, who advanced with the confidence of a debutante making an entrance at a grand ball.

An explosion to the colonel's left covered him with a warm, wet, oozing mess. Sergeant Parkinson fell into the colonel's arms with most of his head and face missing. His inert body knocked Morse over, saving him from a fusillade that whistled just over his head.

With Parkinson's lifeless body on top of him, fog coated Morse's mind. The noise and smoke confused him. He heard shouts and screams but could not locate their source.

"Why was it happening?"

Someone grabbed the colonel and shook him. "Colonel. Colonel. Are you okay?"

Colonel Morse looked down at the hand holding onto his jacket, unsure of what it was. His eyes followed the arm up to the shoulder and into the face of a concerned young soldier he thought he recognized.

"You okay, sir?"

"Yes, yes, I'm fine," Morse said. The sound of his own voice cut through the miasma in his head. He shoved the hand away. "I will not be pawed at, thank you."

Still partially trapped by Parkinson's corpse, Morse began to shout.

"The traitors are everywhere. They are all in league with Captain Edwards. They.... must... all ... die!"

He was not sure how he had failed to identify so many disloyal men, but he had no doubt he would wipe them out. He pushed Parkinson's bloody carcass to one side, stood, and fired.

§§

The Crossroads

Roe dropped down below a tree stump to reload his rifle, frustrated he just missed Colonel Morse and hit Parkinson instead.

"Too bad, mate," he said. "You chose the wrong side."

Still, Roe was irritated. He just missed Morse – and earlier it was Elias.

Ye're losin' yer edge, old boy, he thought.

After the wagon axel broke and Roe sent Sergeant Bollinger on his way with the Cherokees, Roe and his men had doubled back up the hill and just past the bend in the road. He was concerned Elias would suspect something if he saw the disabled wagon sitting at the bottom of the hill and eliminate the element of surprise.

Roe situated his men a few feet off the road on both sides.

Once in position, Roe instructed his men to select one specific rider in Elias's posse. No two shooters were aiming at the same person. If all thirteen of them hit a different rider, they had the potential of taking out almost all of Elias's men on the first volley.

"Don't fire until I give the signal," Roe had said. "And before any of you even think about it, Elias is mine."

Satisfied his weapon was ready, Roe eased into a firing position and locked his sights on Elias who was looming larger on the road. Roe's voice was low and confident.

"Steady now, boys," Roe said. "Steady."

Roe shut out the rest of the world and concentrated on the area just slightly left of the center of Elias's chest. The sound of twelve horses galloping grew steadily. He waited until the ground shook. Roe slowed his breathing and relaxed his arms. He waited until he could see Elias's blue eyes.

Calm and collected, Roe exhaled and squeezed the trigger. Just as the firing cap exploded and the barrage began, the horse the young one was on – the one they called Gabe – stepped on a rock and pitched left. The slug intended for Elias's black heart plowed into the boy's arm.

Roe's men fired. Elias's men dropped, one after the other. Elias, Gabe, and two other men squirmed their way into the woods.

Roe's men pinned Elias down behind a small ridge. It was impossible to know if they were injured or dead as there was no returned fire. After several volleys, Roe heard a man's voice calling for a retreat. Roe ran out onto the road, followed by a couple of other men. They fired at anything they saw moving.

Then nothing.

Silence.

Roe held his breath and waited.

"Should we go after 'em, sir?" asked one of the other men.

Fighting every instinct and choking back the thrill of battle, Roe shook his head.

"Let them go," he said. "We need to catch up with the others."

Roe and his men mounted their horses and raced east. After riding at full speed for several miles, they saw no trace of Bollinger and his group. Roe signaled for a halt.

"Something ain't right," he said. "No way they've gone farther than this. Not enough time. Some of 'em are on foot. Let's double back."

After a while, they spotted the second wagon hidden in the brush on the north side of the road. One of the scouts examined the site.

"Boots and bare feet," he said. "No sign of a struggle and the wagon is still in operatin' condition."

"What in tarnation is goin' on?" Roe asked.

Leaving their horses alongside the road, Roe and his men headed into the woods. Before long, they spotted a group, but not who they were expecting. Lurking behind a stand of twisted pine trees, Colonel Morse and his men were in the process of surrounding Bollinger and the Cherokees. They were so focused on the target they had no clue Roe and his men were on their eastern-most flank.

"Same rules, boys," Roe said. "Pick one target per man. We kill as many as possible in the first volley." He smiled. "Anyone wants to guess who gets Morse?"

As soon as Parkinson fell, Bollinger and the Cherokees scrambled for cover. What was left of Morse's men fired in every direction – some at Roe – others at Bollinger, the Cherokees, and the children. Roe watched with horror as the frightened Cherokee youngsters took cover behind rocks and logs.

God forgive me, Roe thought.

§§

Twisted Pines

When the first shot sounded, Catherine dropped to the ground and pulled as many children as she could grab down with her. She tried to shield them with her body.

The firefight escalated. Bullets scythed through the leaves. Dust clogged the air. Catherine could taste the gunpowder. Terrified shrieks from the children mingled with the screams of men who were hit.

The gunfire rose and fell as men volleyed, then reloaded.

Catherine took a chance and peered around for her friends. Leotie and Manjusha were on the ground, their bodies covering children.

A slight breeze cleared the air enough for Catherine to make out the outline of Jeevan. He was shooting over a tree stump close by her. After he fired, he shrank down to reload. He motioned for her to stay low. She complied and hunched over the children while praying for the madness to stop.

From behind, Catherine heard someone bellowing. "Don't shoot – don't shoot."

Roe dove to the ground next to her.

"Keep still," he said, "We've got to get all of you out of here."

Jeevan squeezed off a shot and was answered by a spray of bullets that splintered his meager shelter.

"They'll charge any minute," Roe said. He reloaded and fired twice within a minute. "They'll overrun us. We—"

Waya tumbled in beside him "Kanuna's been killed. Mohe's wounded shot clean through the shoulder. There are too many soldiers."

Roe nodded. "Time to go."

Jeevan's eyes glowed with the ferocity of a cornered bear. "No," he said. "We stay, we fight."

"We stay, we die," Roe said. "We're outnumbered and outgunned."

"We can't keep running," Jeevan said.

"You have to," Roe said. "If Morse overwhelms us, he'll skin your children while you watch. God knows what he'll do to your wife before he kills her."

Another withering sheet of lead carved through the air over their heads. Roe brushed debris from his sleeve.

"Now! You gotta go. Now!"

CHAPTER FORTY-EIGHT

Thomas watched Roe's predicament from a small hill just above Twisted Pines.

How in the world did the colonel track Roe and the others down?

Private Ratliff appeared from behind a tree. Thomas motioned for him to get down. When the youngster hunkered next to him, Thomas asked. "What the hell are you doin' here?"

Transfixed on the battle raging below, the young man did not respond.

"Private!" Thomas demanded. "Where are the children?"

Ratliff stared past Thomas – through Thomas – at nothing. The young man's voice trembled.

"Never been… never seen anything… horrible…blood and guts everywhere."

Ratliff leaned to the side and emptied the contents of his stomach. Thomas waited. Then he patted him on the back and offered a canteen. Ratliff chugged water, then rinsed his mouth. When he looked up, his embarrassment was obvious.

"I ran to find you, sir. Not much of a soldier, am I?" Ratliff said. He wiped his mouth.

"Happens to everyone, son," Thomas said. "If you ever get used to it, it's time to quit. If you ever decide you like it…"

He trailed off.

"Then, you're Elias, right sir?"

"Right."

Thomas put his hand on Ratliff's shoulder. "Where are the children?"

"They're…they're back at the road. Hidden like you wanted them to be."

"Then why are you here?"

"It's Elias, sir. Showed up out of nowhere. I watched him almost shoot Sergeant Roe's horse." The boy shuddered. "What kind of monster kills a beautiful animal? Anyway, he didn't on account of the heard shootin'. He scooted into the woods about half-mile yonder."

He pointed. Thomas looked around for any sign of the man in black then shifted around so his back was more to the battle, allowing him to see if anyone was coming from the direction of the road.

"He weren't alone," Private Ratliff added. "He had two other men with him. I was afraid they'd come up behind you. Ambush you. I had to warn you, sir."

Thomas patted the young man on the arm. "Okay. You did fine, son." He scanned the area. "They could be anywhere. We've got to work together. Watch each other's backs."

Ratliff looked too frightened to move. The boy swallowed, dug the butt of his musket in the ground and used it to hoist to his feet.

"I'm a cotton farmer's son, Captain," he said. "Forced into duty. I don't belong here."

"Can you watch my back?" Thomas asked. "Can you do that?"

He waited for any kind of response.

"Private!"

Private Ratliff's head snapped up.

The look on the young man's face made Thomas think he was going to run.

"I need to know," Thomas said. "Can you watch my back? I've got to be able to trust you."

Private Ratliff knuckles blanched as he squeezed his musket. He looked as though he was going to throw up.

Thomas looked at the young man's musket and something about it made him smile.

"What are you doin' with this thing, anyway?" He tapped the musket with his knuckle. "We need to get you a real gun. A Kentucky Rifle is what you need. This big beast is only good if you're shootin' something five feet away. It's good for volleys, not much else."

The alarm in the young man's eyes began to dissipate "Only gun I got, sir." A proud smile creased his face. "Don't talk about Ole Earl here. He and I was the best shot in my county three years runnin'. I'll stick a round-up a turkey's tight bunghole from seventy feet — and that ain't braggin'."

Thomas nodded his head in respect. "That's good. That's real good, son. I'm gonna let you prove that. Can you watch my back? And I'll watch yours."

Private Ratliff raised his chin a little. "Yes, sir."

Thomas patted him on the shoulder and spun back around to the gun battle. He saw a man in all black about twenty yards away. Without hesitating, he raised his rifle and fired. The man fell over.

Thomas looked at Private Ratliff and raised his gun a little. "That's what you can do with a Kentucky rifle. Now, cover my behind with your cannon."

Thomas ran off towards the man in black, checking in every direction along the way. He felt a little cheated. He'd shot so quickly he had not had a chance to savor the moment when he killed Elias.

When Thomas got up to the motionless body, he drew his pistol, then kicked. No movement. Thomas slid his toe under the man's shoulder and flipped the body.

It was not Elias.

Name was Norlander, I think.

Mid-curse Thomas ducked when he heard a thunderous roar. He went for his pistol as he turned, but he could not get it from the holster before another black-clad man fell into him – dead. Thomas sluffed off the body and looked up the hill. Ratliff was holding up his musket in triumph.

Ratliff raced down the slope.

"Told you, Captain. Hit that sumbitch right twixt the ears, I did. Never knew what hit him. Only wish I could have seen his expression when—"

Ratliff's head turned to jelly just before he fell into Thomas's arms.

§§

Elias lowered his rifle and watched the young man collapse into Captain Edwards's arms. He chewed on the unlit cigar in his mouth.

"Well, at least one thing went my way today. Next time, I get you, pretty boy," he said under his breath.

He was still irritated with himself for giving the order to retreat at the crossroads. After the command, he fled for several minutes without stopping, running faster than he cared to admit. He found a good hiding place and stopped, surprised to find no one in pursuit. He took advantage of the situation, secreted himself in some brush, and waited while he reloaded his new Colt revolver that required partial disassembly. He fumbled a little, irritated by his trembling hands.

"C'mon, dammit," he said through tight lips.

He glanced around expecting someone to descend upon him, but no one ever came. Sweat poured off his brow but he finally managed to get the gun reloaded. He fastened the last piece in place. The loaded gun gave him some comfort, but his hands still shook.

After twenty minutes of waiting for an enemy that never came, he headed back towards the road with the unfamiliar feeling of unease. About halfway back, Elias found Horace's lifeless body. He had several gunshot wounds, but the death blow was a shot in his back. He'd been running away.

Coward!

Furious, Elias continued only to find Clyde a few minutes later. The bullet hole in his back reinforced Elias's disgust.

Elias returned to the spot where he'd last seen his men alive. Gabe lay where he'd been left. When Elias rolled the body over, he saw a gaping exit wound.

"Worse than I thought. Sorry, kid," Elias said. "But you showed some grit – some real grit."

Unconcerned about the bushwhackers who had waylaid them, Elias meandered out onto the road where he stood among the dead for several minutes bouncing his pistol off the side of his leg.

He felt strange. Hollow. Alone. There was no anger – there was no sadness.

Hoofbeats sounded from around the bend. He cocked his pistol and aimed. Two riders, horses in full lather, veered around the turn. They were dressed in all black. One of them had stayed at Fort Newnan waiting for the other to return from chasing one of the many rabbit trails left by the Indians.

What are their names?

"What the hell happened?"

"We came as fast as we could. We heard shots."

Daniel...and John. No, that's not right. David...David Norlander and Orson Sipes.

Elias snapped into action. He looked once more at his dead compatriots then whistled. Within moments his horse, Absinthe, appeared. He hoisted himself aboard.

"Let's go," he said. "I'll explain everything on the way."

The ambushers had not made any effort to hide their tracks. Elias raced ahead of his men. When he passed an abandoned wagon, he nodded in understanding.

They couldn't go anywhere. They had to make a stand.

He paused for a moment, checked the signs in the dirt, then popped his mount on the rump with the reins. The horse shot forward. Two miles later, Elias spotted a number of horses tethered at the side of the road – Army horses. Elias recognized one of them.

Ticket – belongs to that bastard Roe.

Craving instant retribution, Elias dismounted and walked towards the horses while keeping a constant lookout for the riders. When he pulled his pistol and put it to the side of Ticket's head, he could clearly see visions of his men being slaughtered.

He was just about to pull the trigger when he heard gunfire over a series of low hills. Elias holstered his weapon and backtracked west, back up the road to where the shooting was the loudest. He lead Norlander and Sipes into the woods and, ultimately, to their deaths at the hands of Captain Edwards and Private Ratliff. After he watched Norlander and Sipes die, Elias took great satisfaction in putting a bullet in Private Ratliff's brain.

Captain Edwards dragged the young man behind a tree. He thought he was well hidden as he hovered over the dead body of Private Ratliff, but he was more exposed than he ever could know. Elias reloaded his rifle and took aim at the captain. A simple pull of the trigger. It would be so easy. An exquisite kill.

But something forced its way through the ocean of anger and madness that was bursting the seams of Elias's mind. It was slow and quiet. An idea. A better way to get back at the captain. Death was too simple, too quick, too easy. Instead, there was a way to rip his heart out, crush his soul and when that was over, the captain would beg to be killed.

Elias howled in delight.

All I got to do is find Catherine before Edwards does.

CHAPTER FORTY-NINE

Still shaken by Ratliff's death, Thomas moved next to Roe, and leaned against a tree out of the line of fire.

"Captain, is that your blood?"

Thomas raised his hand. "Not now. I'm fine." He forced the image of Private Ratliff dying in his arms to the back of his mind. "Where do we stand?"

Roe spit. "Peaches, Captain – just peaches. We're pinned down and outnumbered two to one."

"Casualties?"

"We lost three. Wounded, I don't know."

"The civilians?"

"One wounded. And one...dead."

Thomas's head snapped toward Roe.

"Not her," Roe said. "One of the men, Kanuno or Kanuna."

"Kanuno." Thomas replied. "Where are Waya, Jeevan? All the others?"

Roe pointed to Thomas's head. "What happened to your eye?"

"Later."

The stump behind which Roe crouched took a trio of solid hits.

"Where's the civilians?" Thomas asked.

"I told 'em to run, head to Dahlonega. All the men, Waya, Jeevan, all of 'em are armed. I figured we can keep the colonel's men busy for a while. Give the others a chance to make it."

"Who did you send with them?"

"Sergeant Bollinger and Phillips. That's all I could spare." Roe glanced out at the enemy and looked back at the captain. "There's something else."

"What?"

"As soon as Bollinger and the civilians left, Colonel Morse took about a dozen men and took off."

A bullet nicked Roe's ear. He swatted at it – nothing more than a troublesome insect.

"What do you want to do?" he asked. "We're overmatched. Ain't got no big guns – ain't got no avenue of egress. We gotta fight. We need a damn plan."

Thomas reloaded. He told Roe about the exchange he had with Elias's men and about Private Ratliff.

"That no good…" Roe trailed off. "Ratliff was a good kid."

Thomas nodded.

"So, where's Bond?" Roe asked. "Did you get the kids? Did you get the girl? Ayita?"

"They're hiding, not far from here."

Roe took aim and scanned for a target. "They're dug in like a tick on a dog's backside over there. Can't get a good fix."

He settled back in between the tree stump and bullet-riddled tree. "You need to go after him."

"Who?"

"Elias. If we're all going to die, I want to take that piece of dirt with us. You can't let him get his hands on Catherine."

"What about you?" Thomas asked. "You can't fight the colonel's men alone."

Roe chuckled. "Even with you here, it's only a matter of time before they—"

A shower of bark and dust fell on their heads when a half dozen bullets struck the stump.

"The boys and I will keep 'em busy as long as we can," Roe said. Before Thomas could object, Roe slapped his captain on the shoulder. "Now get out of here."

"You just assaulted an officer," Thomas said. He was fighting tears.

"I'll happily stand court-martial later," Roe said. "Now, go get that woman. Take her and that little girl to your family's land. Spend whatever time you have left making them happy." He ducked again. "Now, with all due respect, *get the hell out of here.*"

Roe raised and aimed. "Go!" He fired, dropped the rifle, picked up a brace of pistols, and fired one at a time. Thomas bolted for the road, unsure if he could find Catherine...

...unsure if he would ever see his friend again.

§§

"No," Leotie said.

"Take the pistols," Waya said.

"No! It's a terrible idea."

"There are too many of them," Waya said. "We cannot outrun them. We have to stay and fight, slow them down, so you can get away. Take the pistols, and the children, and run."

"Why, so they can track us down and kill us farther up the road?" Catherine asked.

"No, you'll stay in the forest," Waya said. "Hide, cover your tracks."

"We should *all* use the forest to run," Catherine said. "We have to stay together."

"Kasewini, listen to me," Jeevan said. "We have many advantages right now. The biggest one is the soldiers are not expecting us to stop and fight. Our resistance will surprise them."

"They will still come after us," Waya said. "We will have to run, hide, attack, draw their fire, and ambush again. We cannot do that with the children here."

"We need to know you're safe," Jeevan said. "We will drive them back if we can – if not, we will try to draw them away from you. By the time they find your trail, you will be in Dahlonega."

"If this is such a good plan, why do we need the pistols?" Leotie asked, fighting back the tears. She knew deep down no matter how many questions she asked or how hard Kasewini protested, it wasn't going to change the men's minds. "We need *you*, not guns."

Waya grabbed his wife and embraced her. The children joined in the hug. "You must believe I don't want this," he said. "But a terrible situation forces us to make a terrible decision."

He held onto his family for as long as he could.

Sergeant Bollinger busied himself with making sure all of the long rifles were loaded and ready to fire while the families said their goodbyes. He also made sure each man had enough powder and ammunition for the upcoming battle.

Sergeant Philips appeared, winded and startled. "The colonel's about three minutes behind me with close to a dozen men."

"Sorry folks, it's time," Sergeant Bollinger said. "We've got to get into position if we're gonna stand a chance."

Catherine grabbed Waya's strong, caring hands that once helped her father, and kissed them. Deep down she'd always known how much he meant to her but facing the possibility of losing her dear friend was almost more than she could tolerate.

"Do you think he's waiting for us?" Catherine asked. "Thomas, I mean, with Ayita. Do you think he got her and is waiting?"

Waya smiled. "I'm sure of it. You'll see your daughter again." He looked over at his wife and children then back to Catherine. "Please, take care of my family. I want to see *them* again."

§§

457

Thomas stepped out onto the road and whistled for Silo, who grunted but stayed where he was hidden, exactly as he was taught.

Thomas followed the sound and soon found Private Bond watching over three little ones who had managed to fall asleep in spite of all the noise.

"What the hell's going on?" Bond asked. "Elias rode up with a couple of men and headed into the woods. Next thing I know Ratliff followed and left us here. Then Elias comes back out, furious at the world, gets on his horse and rides off." Bond looked Thomas up and down. "You've got more blood splattered over you than before – fresh blood. Ratliff?"

Thomas took a knee, pulled out his canteen and handkerchief and wiped what blood he could off of his face and hands. He explained all that transpired and what was happening as they spoke. Private Bond jumped to his feet and grabbed his rifle.

"We can't just let 'em die. Those are my friends over there. We gotta try to save 'em."

Thomas grabbed the young man's forearm. "We can't leave these children. If we go and get killed, what's going to happen to them? We can't leave them alone in the woods." He let go of the private's arm and looked into the distance. "Roe would never forgive us if something bad happened to these children all because we were trying to save him."

Private Bond glared at Thomas, then took a knee.

"Your job is to get these kids to my grandmother," Thomas said. "Understand? Nothing else. Get them there and she will do the rest."

Bond's knuckles went white against his rifle.

"Do you understand?" Thomas asked.

Private Bond raised his head, a deep scowl entrenched on his face. "Yes…sir. I understand."

"Good. No matter what, you're to stay with them. Wait until… this battle's over and the colonel's men leave. They're surely going to head east to catch up with the colonel. Let them go. Then find a way to my grandmother's land. Lay low for a day or stay hidden in the forest for as long as you can. Just get them there."

"What are you going to do?"

"I have to find Elias and stop him. If I can do that, maybe I can help Catherine and the others."

Thomas watched Ayita sleeping the sleep only the innocent know.

"And maybe," he said, "just maybe, the Lord willing, this little girl can be with her mother again."

§§

Private Cannon wheezed and caught up to Roe.

"Why are we running, Sergeant? I know there are only six of us, but I thought the captain wanted us to stay and fight."

"He did," Roe replied. "And we are. But he said nothin' 'bout just sittin' around waitin' to be obliterated. We're gonna make 'em chase us for a while. If they're gonna kill us, they're gonna have to earn it."

For the first time, Roe noticed how young they all seemed, about the age he was when he first joined the Army. They were all covered in dirt, soot, and blood.

Young men of courage.

"We're gonna die, ain't we?" It was Anderson. "I don't mind dying for my country, but this don't seem right."

"What do you mean?" Roe asked.

"We're dyin' for nothin', Sergeant."

"Meaning?"

"My pa fought the British. My uncles died doing the same, fightin' for their families, their country. But me? I'm gonna die for some Indians. Hell, don't know but about three of their names."

Roe knelt down, removed his hat, and wiped his brow with his shirt sleeve.

"What do you suppose dying for your country means, son?"

The young men looked at one another unsure of how to answer.

"What about standing up for innocent people, so they can live in peace?" Roe asked.

"It ain't the same," Anderson said. He threw back some water. "My mother, my sisters ain't gonna gain from this. I ain't keepin' 'em safe by dying out here."

Roe rested the butt of his rifle on the ground. "You think those guys tryin' to kill us are good people?"

"No, but...how's me dying gonna change that?"

"What would you rather do, son?" Roe asked. "Captain was right. Lettin' a nation of people starve to death ain't what soldierin' is about. Morse and Elias is killin' them folks just as sure as they put a gun to their noggin's."

Roe studied the scratches on his rifle for a moment. "Been doin' this a long time. Fought with and against a lot of Indians – come to respect 'em. We told the first lie to the Indians about hundred years ago," he said, "and we kept lyin' – became our second nature. We promised *this* would be the last time we took their land – at least until we wanted more. We been pushing these people around since the first booted white foot stepped onto the soil of this great land. I don't think it's—"

Cannon interrupted. "I think I hear 'em coming, sir,"

Roe stood and checked his rifle. Satisfied, he looked every young man in the eye. "If you die today, you'll be dyin' to defend the soul of this nation. And you will make your family proud."

CHAPTER FIFTY

Catherine held a branch up while the children scurried under it and down the narrow path.

"Keep going, keep going," she said. "Don't look back, keep going."

Catherine had taken the lead after saying goodbye to Waya. She was the only one emotionally capable of shuttling the others away from their loved ones. Everything in her heart told her to stay, but when she heard Colonel Morse and his men getting closer, she knew it was for the best.

She led the families east as Waya suggested, never allowing them to stop. The children flinched with every shot – the women fretted when the firing stopped. Catherine kept driving them to move ever faster.

The children looked exhausted and bewildered. Catherine wanted to hug each one of them. She wanted to tell them everything was going to be fine.

But how could she ask them to believe something she didn't believe herself?

§§

Sutton's Hollow

After Elias watched the young soldier die in Captain Edwards' arms, he went back to the road, climbed upon his horse, and headed east in search of Catherine. To avoid another bushwhacking, he stuck to the woods on the south side of the road. After less than two miles, he heard shots.

They stopped as abruptly as they started.

A few minutes later he heard the telltale echoes, this time from a slightly different direction.

"Hit and run," he said. "Clever."

He crested a hill and pulled out his telescope. Even from a distance, he could pick out Morse's corpulence. The colonel was making indistinct circles with his sword. He looked more like a drunken band leader than a battlefield commander. Bodies lay strewn around the colonel.

Elias scanned the trees. He saw occasional puffs of discharged powder but could not get a solid fix on any position. As he suspected, whoever was nettling Morse fired, moved, reloaded, and fired again. No two shots came from the same place.

Elias replaced his telescope and imagined himself in the situation.

"Wouldn't want a lot of gear. Guns, ammunition, powder, maybe a little water. No horse – that would slow me down in the trees. And I wouldn't want anyone with me."

He spurred his horse toward the carnage, head low, full speed. The chances of anyone hitting him at the gallop were minuscule. More shots – these farther west.

They're trying to lure Morse to chase 'em, he thought. *They want the colonel as far away as possible from the children...and the women.*

The colonel had already left the scene, abandoning the dead and wounded. Elias looked to the west. He heard shots and saw the remnants of discharges floating off through the air. He pulled his hat low over his brow, pointed his horse to the east, and put spurs to flanks.

§§

Colonel Morse was incensed. He bellowed over the sound of the fire.

"Stand and fight, you cowards!"

A self-appointed "genius" of tactics, Morse kept looking for a flank to attack, a redoubt to charge. He wanted a flag-waving, trumpet-blaring assault on a fixed position – a fixed position he could not detect.

A shot knocked his hat from his head. Another killed the soldier to his immediate left. Morse thrust his calvary saber into the air.

"Damn cowards!"

Then it came to him.

"The Indians can only move that fast if they are unencumbered by women and children. They have been moving steadily westward."

Morse signaled to two riders closest to him. The trio set off at a gallop and left the others to fend for themselves. The wind whipping across his hatless, hairless head reminded Morse of the cavalry charges he'd always dreamed of leading.

The children are in this direction, he thought. *And if I can find the children, I can find the witch!*

CHAPTER FIFTY-ONE

Thomas knew better than to step into the clearing. Years of warfare had honed his sense of danger to a keen edge. He knelt in a thicket and waited. He sipped from his canteen and kept an eye on the opposing tree line.

He'd just replaced the cork and picked up his long rifle when Elias stepped into the clearing, pistol in hand. The tall hat seemed even more incongruous in the middle of the woods than usual, but the menacing look on Elias's face was intense and lethal. Thomas held his breath and tried not to move.

Elias stared straight at the thicket concealing Thomas for a long time before he scanned the rest of the area. He scrutinized every shadow, every low-hanging limb, anything that might be an enemy or a place of hiding. Finally, he crouched and studied the very tracks Thomas had been following.

Thomas raised his rifle with agonizing deliberation. He rested the stock against his shoulder and centered the sight on Elias's chest. Having cocked the weapon earlier, he slipped his index finger around the trigger and steadied his breathing.

Elias shifted just enough to expose the broadest part of his back – a perfect opportunity. Then…

"Lay the rifle on the ground, Captain. I've got three guns aimed at your head."

Thomas closed his eyes.

Morse!

When he opened his eyes, Elias was disappearing into the bush on the other side of the clearing, completely unaware of his razor-thin brush with death.

"Damn it to hell!"

Colonel Morse laughed. "You just might get your wish, Captain. Now, drop your weapon and stand up. Slowly!"

Thomas dropped his rifle and stood. When he turned, he was face to face with the business end of a pistol.

"Nice piece, isn't it, Captain?" Morse was drooling a little in his excitement. "It's an 1836 Asa Waters Pattern Pistol – .54 caliber. It will turn your head into a dugout canoe if you so much as break wind."

The colonel was flanked by a couple of young soldiers, neither of whom looked like they had a grasp of the situation.

"Why don't you shoot me then?" Thomas asked.

"Don't tempt me," Colonel Morse replied. "But I will derive far more pleasure watching you twitch at the end of a rope." He gestured to the young man on his right. "Keep him here. Don't let him move a muscle."

The colonel pulled the other soldier to the side and whispered directions into his ear before sending him off into the woods.

Colonel Morse leveled his pistol at the captain again. "Private."

"Yes, sir."

"You saw where Elias went?"

"Yes, sir."

"Find him. Tell him to meet me at the cabin. He'll know what you mean."

The young man looked at the colonel and back at Captain Edwards.

"Don't worry, I have this one under control," Colonel Morse said.

The soldier lowered his weapon and looked at the captain with a hint of regret in his eyes. He offered a slight nod before running after Elias.

"All right, Captain," Morse said. "Let's go back to the road and collect that horse of yours. Fine animal. I'm going to enjoy riding him after you hang."

§§

Although she knew the children needed to rest, Catherine hated the idea of stopping. She felt she needed to get them as far away as possible, but when they came upon a creek bubbling its way through the forest, she couldn't tell them no.

It wouldn't have mattered if she had.

The children raced past her before she could protest and, once she felt the sensation of the cool water going down her own throat, she found herself sitting on the bank delighting in the children's momentary happiness.

"You have to be quiet," she said.

"Speaking of quiet, I haven't heard any gunfire in a while," Manjusha said as she sat down next to Leotie and Catherine.

"Could mean anything," Leotie replied. She had noticed the silence earlier and had been trying to convince herself that the men were still alive. "Maybe the men have hidden from the soldiers. Knowing my husband, he's probably driving them mad trying to find him." She reached out and patted Manjusha on the leg. "They're going to be all right."

Catherine stood and adjusted Elias's jacket. She shuddered when she remembered the original owner. "I am going to go follow the creek for a little and see if I can find some food. We have to consider the possibility we will be sleeping under the stars tonight on our own."

"You are probably right," Leotie said. "Look for a cave or outcropping – something to give us some shelter where we can rest."

Catherine shook her head. "Just a few more minutes and then we must be on the move. We need as much distance from the soldiers as possible."

She watched the children for a few moments before following the creek to the southeast. No, she didn't want anyone to go with her. Yes, she would be fine, and everyone needed their rest.

The creek babbled along, twisting and turning its way through the trees before it opened up a little more.

As she followed the creek, Catherine searched for seeds, roots, or stems to eat. If they were lucky, she might find some nuts, anything to give to the kids

Not far from where the creek widened a little more, Catherine found an area teeming with roots the children could eat. She considered going back and getting everyone but decided it might cause too much noise, so she gathered as much as she could carry, stuffing the pockets of Elias' jacket before filling up her arms. Satisfied she had enough for everyone, she headed back. Catherine hurried along the creek bank with a sense of accomplishment. The day had turned into a nightmare; this little glimmer of hope would brighten everyone's spirits. The children were safe for the moment and, as much as she hated leaving the men, she believed their plan to divert the soldiers would allow her and her charges to get to Miriam's land.

She could hear the children splashing in the creek just around the bend. They were a bit too loud. Catherine quickened her pace and chastised herself under her breath.

"I should have reminded them we are still being fol—"

A calloused hand covered her mouth; a rope-like arm encircled her. She dropped everything. Elias's voice hissed in her ear.

"Come with me and I won't kill the children," he said. "Make a sound and I'll pick my teeth with their bones."

Keeping his hand over her mouth, Elias dragged her backward for several minutes.

Catherine considered biting his hand until she felt the barrel of a gun against her temple.

"I'm gonna take my hand from your mouth. If you make a sound, it will be your last. Then, I'll go back for those brats. Understand?"

Catherine nodded. Elias loosened his grip and let her take a step away from him. He pointed to a deer trail that wound through the trees and pushed her ahead.

The longer she walked, the more her anger built. She could smell Elias's stench, the mingled odors of whiskey, blood, and weeks of sweat. Every little shove he gave her along the deer path grated her insides. She recalled his nauseating attempts at romance – his brutal assault. Bile rose in her throat; rage throbbed into her temples. She stopped moving and whirled.

"Why don't you just shoot me now?"

Elias stepped back slightly, conflicted by the instinct to punch her and the desire to embrace her.

"I don't want to kill you," he said. "You're all I have left."

His abject misery startled Catherine. Her mouth dropped. She stared at his despondency, confused – no, baffled.

"What did you say?"

"You're all I got left. My men are gone. Morse is probably dead, not that I care. You are my future. You will be why I get up every morning. Our love is going to save me."

He was staring at her, but she could tell he saw nothing. She looked around and saw a fallen branch – about four feet long – broom-handle thick. She stooped, snatched up the club, and smashed it onto Elias's hand. The Colt spewed fire and noise and dropped to the ground.

Catherine spun completely around and lay the branch against Elias's temple with all her might. The man grunted and clutched at his head as his hat flew into the brush at the side of the path. Catherine raised the stick again and slammed it into Elias at the base of his neck, then sprinted down the path as fast as she could.

She had only one thought. *Get away.*

Fifty feet down the path, she stopped.

I have no place to go where he will not find me. Even if I elude him, he will kill the children.

When she turned, Elias was strolling along the path and dusting off his hat.

He stopped an arm's length away and swiped at the blood trickling across his brow.

"I'm sorry," she said.

His eyes reflected no soul. His voice carried no emotion. "Not yet, you're not."

CHAPTER FIFTY-TWO

The small, one-room log cabin looked like it grew out of the mountain. The cabin was built next to a towering boulder and surrounded on two of the remaining three sides by fully mature white pines, which provided a natural shelter from bad weather and high winds.

The location was perfect for hunting, leading Thomas to wonder why the place had been abandoned. He dismounted.

Not a bad place to die, he thought.

Letting his hand run along with Silo's buckskin as he walked, Thomas stepped in front and stroked his horse's nose.

"You've been a good friend," Thomas said.

Silo nickered and blew warm air down Thomas's neck. The captain laughed in spite of the situation. He took Silo's head in both of his hands, studying the bottomless eyes and remembered. "I don't know what I would have done without you," Thomas said. "Goodbye, my friend."

Silo began to grunt and stomp his feet.

Colonel Morse dismounted and leveled his pistol at Silo. "You either get that beast to calm down or I'll put a bullet in him."

Thomas refused to acknowledge the colonel directly. Instead, he patted Silo one last time.

"Easy, boy," he said.

Silo cut his eyes at Morse and stood like a statue.

Tired and frustrated by the entire day, Colonel Morse shoved the captain towards the cabin. "Get going."

The sunset display had begun. Varying shades of yellow-painted the western sky. Thomas admired the celestial artwork and breathed in the scents of summer and the crisp smell of pine trees. He could hear a trickle of a small brook somewhere in the distance, a little stream going about its daily work of carving into the earth a little at a time while no one noticed or appreciated its toil. The cabin itself was the only unnatural thing for miles.

Wonder how long it will be before someone finds my body. Or will they ever find it?

A woman's scream from inside the cabin broke the silence. With an instinct born of combat and a life of service, Thomas made a quick step for the door.

"Stop," Morse said, "or I'll drop you right here."

Thomas, still facing the cabin, let out a low snarl. "Before this is over, I'll kill you, old man."

Colonel Morse laughed. "Maybe. We'll just have to see." He put the barrel to the back of Thomas's head. "Now move!"

Thomas stepped for the door. His eyes scanned the area in search of a weapon. When he reached the latch, he paused.

No other sounds. I wonder if the woman who screamed was killed in there.

He closed his eyes in dread.

"Go on in," Colonel Morse said. "What are you afraid of?"

Thomas opened the door. A thin line of light partially illuminated a pitiful room full of cobwebs, broken furniture, and…Catherine. She was bolt upright in a wooden chair. Elias stood behind her holding a rope that was looped around her neck.

She gasped when she saw the blood-soaked bandages wrapped around Thomas's head and the blood on his uniform. Elias tugged on the rope – an owner calming a rambunctious dog on a leash. When he saw Catherine's concern for Thomas, his jealousy reached the boiling point.

"Get in there." Morse shoved Thomas through the opening and shut the door. Thomas regained his balance in time to feel the barrel resume its position against his skull.

"One false move and I'll happily pull this trigger."

Thomas glanced back at the colonel who was looking in Catherine's direction as if he was seeing a ghost.

"What…what is she doing here?" Morse asked.

"She's my woman now," Elias replied. "She goes where I go."

"She…she shouldn't be here," Morse said. "She's a witch. A witch who killed my family. Trapped them in a cabin just like this one."

"What are you goin' on about?" Elias asked. "You ain't right in the head, Colonel."

Thomas considered rushing Elias – then he saw the knife. Elias held a ten-inch, bone-handled blade. It hung in his hand like an extra appendage. It gleamed in the meager sunlight. If Thomas charged, he had no doubt Catherine would be dead before he took his second step.

"I know a witch when I see one," Morse said. "You must get her out of here."

"I brought her here," Elias said. "She's *my* prisoner. And she'll be leaving with me."

Thomas's gaze moved from Elias back to Catherine. She had fresh cuts and bruises on her face. She was obviously tired and frightened, but the pleading look in her eyes is what bothered Thomas the most.

"So, what *are* we doing here?" Thomas asked.

Colonel Morse looked at Thomas like he was surprised to see him there. He opened his mouth to answer when the door burst open and a large man in civilian clothes walked in holding a pistol out in front of him.

He spoke like someone comfortable with being in charge. "What's the meaning of this?"

Backlit by the setting sun, the man's face was shrouded in shadows. He moved into the room with deliberate, calculated steps passing from the darkness of the doorway into the faint light of the room – and of recognition.

Thomas had never been so grateful to see his father's face.

CHAPTER FIFTY-THREE

"I don't think I can do this," Private Bond said out loud.

He plopped down next to Ayita and ran his fingers through his hair, unsure of what he was going to do. He'd just managed to avoid a catastrophe when the children woke up at roughly the same time, all three hungry and thirsty. Luckily, he had his canteen to offer and, while they shared it with one another, he managed to find some roots he thought might be edible.

But that was this one time. He still had a long way to go and what did he know about taking care of children?

He exhaled long and hard before realizing he was being watched. Bond slowly turned his head and met the concentrated gaze of a six-year-old little girl.

Ayita studied him with beautiful, curious eyes making him feel vulnerable while causing him to smile and run oddly short of breath at the same time.

"We're going to be okay, right?" he asked.

Ayita smiled and kept chewing on a root.

He considered taking the children back to Fort Newnan, but he had promised the captain to escort the young'uns to the family property in the east. Besides, they were at least halfway to

Dahlonega at this point. Going back would be just as difficult as going forward.

All he had to do was avoid Elias, Colonel Morse, and a passel of soldiers all of whom were trying to recapture the children and kill anyone who'd aided in their escape.

No problem, Bond thought.

The battle on the other side of the road had ended about ten minutes ago. He heard shots somewhere in the distance, but he had no idea who was involved. He debated whether to sit or to move.

This is so damn confusing.

Bond buried his face in his hands. His commander was gone – somewhere. His friends were dead. He was alone.

He dove and covered Ayita when he heard the sound of boots crashing through the undergrowth. Just across the road, over a dozen men burst through the tree line. Bond drew his pistol. He held his index finger over his lips. The children, though confused, understood the motion, and froze in place – standing. Momentarily paralyzed by indecision, Bond started to reach for the closest child when he recognized a familiar dirty face.

"Roe!" Bond stood. "Here. We're here." He scurried towards the road with his hands in the air, just in case.

"Private, where are the children?"

Roe no sooner got the question out of his mouth than the three little ones came out of the woods, trailing behind Bond-like ducklings.

Private Bond lowered his arms. "How did – Captain Edwards said you were outnumbered. I thought—"

"I thought so too," Roe said. "But then these boys showed." He gestured to eight men at the end of his line.

Roe had sent out four decoy wagons from Fort Newnan at the beginning – two men per team – all designed to confuse Elias and Morse from the start. When their ruse was discovered, they returned to the fort, then headed east in case Edwards or Roe needed help.

They came up behind Morse's men who were so intent on polishing off Roe and his squad that they had not posted any rear guard. They were cut down in short order.

Roe gestured back towards the west. "Get your horses and join us up the road. We got more work to do. Maybe we can turn this things around yet."

§§

"I asked a question," Clinton said.

He took another step forward. Thomas couldn't take his eyes off of his father who was always larger than life but who dominated the cabin in an almost comical fashion. The gun in his massive hand looked small, like a toy. Clinton' gaze fell with a quiet disdain on Colonel Morse.

"I want to know what the hell's going on here," Clinton said. He pointed his pistol directly at Catherine. "And what's *she* doing here?"

Morse shrugged. "She's Elias's little plaything. Ask him."

The withering look passed to the man in black.

"Well?" Clinton asked.

"Who the hell are you?" Elias asked.

Clinton exchanged glances with Morse and began to laugh. "You should take the time to get to know who employs you."

Elias's eyes widened. He glanced at Morse who nodded.

"Then you can tell me what *I'm* doing here," Elias said.

Clinton looked at Elias with more disdain than if his oversized boot had stepped in something foul, "You're here to tell me what happened at Fort Newnan today. And you," he turned to Thomas, "wipe that look off your face. For the love of God don't tell me you haven't already figured all of this out. I thought you were supposed to be a bright lad."

The tumblers fell. The pieces came together. He opened his mouth to reply but was met by Clinton's raised hand. The older man, apparently unafraid of vipers, had drawn to within a few feet of Elias.

"And while you are at it, kindly explain to me why the only supply chain that's broken down in this entire region is the one you and that sorry blob of a colonel over there are running."

Thomas stepped forward. "How'd you know we were here?"

Clinton tilted his head, annoyed by the interruption, but he never took his eyes from Elias. "You can thank the colonel for that. I was on my way to Fort Newnan for an explanation regarding the supply line when the colonel sent word of the recent fiasco. I got several messages throughout the day today. The last informed me the colonel would be bringing you here (he pivoted to look at Thomas) – son."

"Explains why he did not kill me."

Morse scoffed. "The *only* reason, you pampered ass."

Clinton's fist cracked into Morse's jaw. Morse crumpled in the corner.

"You broke my teeth."

"Shut up you fat bag of shit."

Clinton picked up the colonel's sidearm and stuck it into his belt. He wheeled toward Thomas, his face full of parental disapproval.

"If you had just done what I told you—"

"Wouldn't have hurt to know the truth,"

"Which is?"

"That you are stealing supplies from the government, the ones intended for the Cherokees."

"You were never to be read in on any of that."

"Then what was I supposed to do?"

"*Your damn job!*" Wounded elk roar with less violence than Clinton Edwards. "You were supposed to report to Fort Newnan and follow orders. Now everything is flummoxed."

Thomas grinned without humor. "You lie down with dogs..."

"At least these two dogs always delivered," Clinton said. "A job well done. Profitable. No headaches." He turned his body more towards Thomas but didn't bother to lower his gun. "You think I'd entrust my son's career to just anyone? There was too much at stake."

"Too much what?"

Clinton's voice changed. Now he was a patient instructor, explaining something mysterious like butterflies to a four-year-old child. "Money, son. Money, power, influence, prestige, position – everything you need for a future in this country." He exhaled his exasperation through clenched teeth. "Weren't you listening to anything I said in my office? There are millions of dollars at stake, more money than fifty people could spend in a lifetime. All you had to do was be a good boy – take care of a simple assignment – escort a gaggle of savages from here...to there. But it's not too late. Let these men protect you, show you the ropes. You will be richer and more powerful than you can ever dream."

Thomas's anger reached the boiling point.

"So, now you are telling me about my dreams?"

"I don't give two hoots in hell about your dreams, boy," Clinton said. "They do not matter to me at all."

Having made his final point, Clinton turned back to Elias. "You still haven't told me what she's doing here."

"She's with me," Elias replied.

"With you?" Clinton asked. "What does that mean?"

"She's mine."

"She doesn't need to be here," Clinton said.

"Well, she's stayin'."

Clinton raised his pistol. "You dispatch her, or I will."

Thomas inched toward Catherine while the two fighting gamecocks assessed one another.

Elias's pointed his knife at Clinton. "Like hell, you will."

Catherine was less than a yard away.

"You sure she's worth dying for?" Clinton asked.

A blank look of despair painted Elias's face. "She's all I have," he said.

"What?" Clinton asked.

Though still clutching the rope around Catherine's neck, Elias seemed dissociated from everything in the room. His voice was hollow – his stare was vacant.

"They're all gone...all because of your money."

"Who's gone?" Clinton was as lost as everyone else.

"Gabe…Norlander…Sipes…little Joey…every last one of 'em. Dead at the side of the road or buried in my back yard."

Clinton spoke over his shoulder. "The man's gone 'round the bend," he said. Then, to Elias. "Let's focus on what's important."

Elias shook his head as if clearing water from his ears. "And what's that?"

"My money!"

Elias clucked his tongue. "Heard you wuz greedy."

"You say that as if I should be insulted." Clinton scanned the stupefied faces in the room and laughed. "You people. You all slay me. Tell me, what else in this world opens doors…no, kicks doors down? Money! What do you think every war ever fought on this earth was ever about? Political Ideology? Ha! Why does the lion rule the jungle? Why does everyone fear the lone wolf? Because they *take* what they want."

"They were my friends," Elias said.

"Friendship is a useless endeavor," Clinton said.

"And you are a worthless piece of shit," Elias said.

He lowered his knife. He walked past the others and opened the door, leading Catherine by the rope around her throat. He looked at Clinton.

"Those guns ain't worth anything if ye're 'fraid to use 'em. Lucky for you the tables weren't turned. I'd had killed you without a fair thee well."

Elias walked out with a wide-eyed Catherine in tow.

"Colonel," Clinton said, "make sure he understands his job isn't over. And make doubly sure he knows to get rid of that damn woman!"

Morse clutched at the lone windowsill and staggered to his feet. Blood and saliva dripped from his busted lips. His left eye was already swollen shut. But he nodded and waddled from the cabin.

Thomas stepped for the door. Clinton continued to hold the gun – aimed.

"I'm not finished with *you,* yet," he said. "We need to talk."

"I don't want to talk."

"Well," Clinton said, "I didn't mean converse. I don't care about anything you have to say. I am going to tell you what to do."

"And if I don't? What if I walk out that door like Elias?"

Clinton's laugh was harsh, mirthless, and intimidating. "You think there is anywhere you can go where I cannot find you? I know everything that happens in this state. Hell, I know everything about what happens in this nation."

"Do you?" Thomas asked.

"Indeed, I do, boy."

Thomas stepped to within three inches of his father's sneer.

"Then tell me what happened to my grandfather, you son of a bitch."

CHAPTER FIFTY-FOUR

Growing more afraid of being alone, Colonel Morse slipped several times trying to catch up with Elias. When he drew abreast the top-hatted figure, the colonel slurred his words.

"Leave her here," he said, feeling like an unwanted child chasing after a friend.

Elias continued dragging Catherine.

Wretched Cherokee witch, Morse thought. *You haunt my dreams – you complicate my life.*

"That's an order," Morse said.

He wiped uncontrollable sputum away from his lips.

Elias spit his response over his shoulder. "You have no control over me, old man."

"You don't need her. Leave her. We'll go to the fort."

When Elias spun, Catherine cried out in pain as the rope cut into her flesh. Elias made no acknowledgment.

"Go back? To what? There's nothing there. They're all gone. All I have is her."

"Nonsense! That woman has bewitched you. Can't you see that?"

"I have nothing, you hear me! Nothing! My men are dead. Most of yours have been slaughtered. There's nothing left."

A drumbeat of pain engulfed the colonel's head. He looked around at his surroundings as if lost.

"Liar!"

Why did I shout? he wondered.

Catherine recoiled a little from the colonel's outburst. Elias took a step forward. "What the hell's goin' on with you?"

Embarrassed, Colonel Morse cleared his throat and pulled at his jacket. "What…what I meant to say was – there are the Cherokees." He took a deep breath. "Yes, we have responsibility for the remaining savages."

"No, *you* have the responsibility," Elias replied.

"If you don't help me, they'll win," Colonel Morse said. When he looked over at Catherine, the witch from his dreams, a wave of panic brought with it a tsunami of pain just behind his eyes. "We can't…we can't let them get to the cabin. We must get there first."

"Colonel, what's wrong with you?" Elias asked. "You haven't been making sense for days."

Colonel Morse blinked.

"We…we have a job to do," Colonel Morse said.

"My job wasn't to escort those people. My job was to track 'em down, keep 'em in line and watch over the supply lines. And I failed. Don't happen to me much." Elias lowered his head – a schoolboy standing before a demanding headmaster. "So, I'm startin' over. I'm takin' this woman and starting over."

Colonel Morse did not intend to laugh but he could not help himself. The lunacy of the situation suddenly hit him.

"You…starting over. What? A little cottage in the woods…a small farm. Children? With *this* vixen? It's not a fantasy, it's a waste. Even you could do bet—"

He would have finished his insult, but he could not talk with Elias's pistol jammed between his gums.

"You're a mad dog, Colonel," Elias said. His eyes were slits of rage. "I put down mad dogs."

He jerked his pistol back when Morse started giggling. As soon as the barrel was out of his mouth, the colonel began to sing. "You… can't…walk…away…you…are…a sol-dier."

Morse had his hands over his head – a child at play singing with friends in a field – not a care in the world. Elias moved away. "Where…are…you…going…to…go…Elias?"

"You got the pox – something's in your brain, Colonel. You ain't right in the head."

§§

Ten minutes had passed since Elias walked away. Morse was still dancing in the trees, alone, singing to himself.

"Where are you going to go?"

He spread his arms wide, tilted his head back, and looked up at the sky as he spun round and round, feeling free as a child in a field of flowers.

"Where are you going to go?" he sang over and over again. "Where are you going to go?"

He was captivated by the twirling treetops. Turning and turning, they circled above his head and merged into one, enormous green spire. Faster and faster. Round and round they turned. He discovered that the faster they twirled around, the closer they got to him. Closing in, closer and closer until he could almost touch them. He spun, faster and faster, sang louder and louder until the trees finally knocked him over.

He collapsed to the ground. Nausea set in. He continued singing in a whisper.

"Where are you going to go, Elias? Where are you going to go?"

The treetops slowed, separated, and settled into their rightful places just above him in the ever-darkening sky.

He thought he might be sick.

The ground – lying here is making me sick.

He attempted to stand but stumbled and fell. He perched on all fours and laughed. Then he howled.

I am the wolf!

"Where are you going to go?"

Elias did not answer. The Indian witch did not answer.

"Answer me, dammit – where are you going to go? What are you thinking, Elias?"

Bile surged from his mouth. It splattered when it hit the ground. Morse groomed the back of his hands like a cat, then rolled onto his back.

"My guests, my guests," he said. "I must not neglect my guests. Lionel, tea, please. Dammit, where are the sweetcakes? These people will think I was reared in a barn."

The sky changed colors…black to flashing yellow…a lovely magenta…indigo. He lolled to his side and vomited again.

"Don't forget the honey," he said.

He took a few breaths to calm down and poured all of his concentration into standing. After stumbling a few times, he finally made it upright, although the trees still vibrated all around him. He flogged dust from his trousers.

"Where can you go, Elias? he asked.

Still no answer.

The colonel turned, slower than before, and scanned the darkening terrain for Elias and the witch.

Why do all the trees look the same? Can't find anyone.

He spoke again. There was comfort in the sound despite the mumbling. At least he did not feel as alone.

"I like fields – open fields – not as claustrophobic. Fields are nice. Except the Indians can get you there, in the open field." Morse crouched to hide from the savages no one else could have seen.

"They chase you down, slice you open, and leave you there after they make you watch them slaughter your family."

Without warning, he saw his painting – unfinished – exposed for the world to see – naked in its incompleteness.

"My painting!" He was wailing. "I must go back and finish my painting!"

There's no place to hide in an open field. Can't make it to the trees!

"I have only one choice – kill the Indians – kill them all. Then they can't kill my family. They can't hurt mother or father – they can't do those things to my sister."

He saw a young girl – early teens – brown hair (always pulled back), hazel eyes, a perpetual smile. He saw the savage behind her – on top of her. He saw the gaping yawn of her severed throat.

Why does my head hurt? It has hurt for months. Pressure – noise – always pressure and noise – brass bands don't make this much noise. Cannon fire does not make this much noise. My sister's screams did not make this much noise.

"Where are you, Elias?"

The colonel looked to the left and to the right.

"Elias, you sneaky scoundrel." He giggled at the thought of Elias playing such a silly kid's game.

The colonel spun as fast as he could, hoping to catch Elias sneaking up on him. He whirled in the opposite direction eager to beat Elias at his game.

He's cunning. He's shifty.

Another rotation and the world tipped on its head as vertigo set in and the colonel collapsed. The trees passed judgment on him from on high.

Why are they staring?

Now they were helping him up. No, wait. Those were hands, the hands of a person. No, many hands – many people.

Dark hair. Dark faces.

Indians!

"It's you," the colonel said. "You finally came to finish the job you started years ago when I was a defenseless boy in a field."

Colonel Morse struggled to free his arms, but he could not move them.

"Get the rope." He heard in perfect Cherokee dialogue.

"Elias!"

Morse felt something burning his neck – chafing – rough, prickly.

A rope.

The treetops came closer. Breath came in choking gasps. The pain in his neck grew intolerable. Momentary pain on the left side of his throat. Then warmth ran down his neck and chest.

And then the world grew darker and colder…

…until everything went black.

§§

Leotie began to cry watching Manjusha being reunited with her children. It had been almost two months since she'd seen her littlest ones. Now, quite unexpectedly, they were right in front of them. The children looked bewildered and tired, confused about what was happening, but as soon as they saw their mother, all other concerns disappeared. The moment the soldiers set the little feet on the ground, the children raced to the outstretched arms of their weeping mother.

"Oh, my babies," Manjusha said over and over again. "My babies. It's so good to hold you again. Mamma missed you so much."

Manjusha buried her head in her children's arms and wept.

Her oldest children looked on with a mixture of confusion and sadness on their faces until their mother motioned for them to join her. They wasted little time getting to her and their siblings.

Leotie had to turn her head to keep from falling apart. She was worried about Waya and the other men. And though she was witnessing a reunion, she knew everyone still had a long way to go before any of them was safe.

Leotie walked over to the little girl standing all alone next to a young soldier. "You must be Ayita."

Ayita's head barely moved.

"I am Leotie. I know your mother, Kasewini."

Leotie saw the girl's lips move but had to bend over to hear anything. "Where is she?"

The eyes, Leotie thought. *The eyes belong to Catherine.*

"She went on ahead of us," Leotie said. She motioned for her daughters to come over. "We'll catch up to her later. In the meantime, I'd like you to meet my little girls."

She introduced her daughters and stepped back, hoping their presence might comfort Ayita a bit.

Roe pulled Leotie aside. "Where are the men? Where are Waya, Jeevan and the others?"

"They told us to stay here," Leotie replied. "When we told them Catherine disappeared, they went to look for her. They told us to stay here until they returned."

"Where's Colonel Morse? We found the rest of his men back yonder a ways, all of 'em dead or close to it. But no colonel."

"I…we don't know," Leotie said.

"What happened back there?"

"Jeevan told us that they ambushed the colonel. Then they split up and ran. They hid, attacked, and ran again. They wanted the colonel to chase them. It worked for a while and then the colonel stopped. They didn't know why or where he went. Waya told me that when the colonel left, his men fell apart. Completely disorganized. That's when Waya and the others landed the killing blow to all of them."

"But not the colonel?"

"No, Waya and the others let him go. They picked up our trail and found us. We stopped here for water before they caught up. Kasewini went to look for food." Leotie looked down at her hands. "She never came back. One of the men found…" She could not finish.

"I'll do all I can to find her," Roe said. "I promise you." He gently grasped Leotie's arms. "Now, what did they find?"

"Signs of a struggle just beyond the bend in the creek. She was dragged away."

"Bear?"

"No – human."

Roe looked into the woods. "Elias."

Leotie nodded but said nothing more.

Roe pointed east. "We have to get you and your people to Dahlonega, even…even if we can't find Catherine. Lord only knows if more soldiers are coming from the fort. He looked at Ayita.

"She's riding with me," he said. "Come hell or high water, that little girl is going to see her momma again."

§§

The sun slept. The only light in the cabin came from a small candle Clinton pulled from his saddlebag. Anchored in a makeshift stand of tallow, the taper added faint illumination to the gloomy surroundings.

"Say that one more time before I strangle you," Thomas said.

"I had Oscar killed," Clinton said. He could have been commenting on the weather.

Thomas twitched to rush his father. Clinton raised his pistol.

"Easy, boy," he said. "I didn't pull the trigger, mind you, but he went down on my order."

"I knew all about your letter – your plea for him to rescue you from the Academy. I put in a lot of work to get you in that school. I was not about to let him waltz in and destroy everything I had built."

A sudden calm eased its way through Thomas – the assurance of knowing what to do.

You're going to die, old man, he thought.

He relaxed and let Clinton continue his sneering monologue.

"How do you think I felt when it became apparent my son was too soft for the military – too coddled – not tough enough? I always despised the way Oscar babied you. And when I heard he was on his way to get you out of the academy that was the last straw! He needed to be eliminated from your life once and for all."

"You son of a—"

"Oh, come now, Thomas. You can do better than settling for cursing me. But I guess Oscar won that battle long ago. You are weak – you are afraid of a challenge – you don't want to hurt anyone's feelings."

Shock waves of guilt seized Thomas.

"Damn it to hell, boy," Clinton said. "Are you crying? Jesus Christ and his traveling band of minstrels, you are softer than I thought. Pathetic!"

"I weep over Oscar's death," Thomas said. "I promise I will not over yours."

"That doesn't bother me one whit," Clinton says. "I'll be gone, having lived a great life. All that matters is the here and now."

Thomas blinked the tears away. "Speaking of which…what happens now."

"You go back to Fort Newnan and do as you are told. Morse will not utter a word of your little…ah…indiscretion. Things will proceed according to plan."

"And if I refuse."

Clinton waggled the gun back and forth. "The bears will have a wonderful breakfast surprise."

"So, if I do what you say and keep my mouth shut, what happens to Catherine?"

"I think you and I both know what Elias plans to do."

"Oh," Thomas replied. "I meant after I kill him."

Clinton exhaled a lung full of exasperation. "Never thought I would have to deal with her again."

"Again?" Thomas flinched in anticipation of what he now knew was coming.

"Remember when I came to get you just before you went to the Academy."

Thomas did not respond.

"I told that wretched gold digger you did not want to see her anymore. I explained how it was a fling – a frolic – a laugh. A young buck in full rut."

"She wouldn't have believed you."

"Well, what doubt she had was erased when I intercepted letters she sent to you in the Academy and sent them back to her, unopened."

Thomas's voice barely registered. "Why would you do that?

"She's a damn full-blooded Indian, son."

"So is my grandmother."

"And no one took Oscar seriously either. I've hidden your mother's background for a long time. Was so damn glad when you didn't come out of her womb with dark hair and red skin."

Thomas spread his arms.

"This is the best target you will ever get," he said. "Do it now or look over your back for the rest of your unnatural life."

Clinton's finger tensed for a moment, then fell from the trigger.

Thomas walked out of the door and mounted Silo.

"Did you see which way they went, old friend?"

Silo bolted for a trail. Thomas hung on.

Catherine, I am coming. I will find you if it's the last thing I ever do.

CHAPTER FIFTY-FIVE

Catherine collapsed for the third time. Elias jerked at the rope.

"Get up!"

She looked at his twisted, angry face and felt her mind shutting down. She knew he was frightened; she feared what he might do. She stayed on the ground.

"I swear if you don't stand, I'll leave you for the wolves," he said. "Now get up!"

He wrenched her wrist. She would have screamed but she felt his knife against her throat.

"Quiet-like," he said.

Catherine pushed off the ground, swaying like a drunk.

"Let's go."

The sun was gone. The moon, if there were one, had not risen above the treetops. Catherine felt her way along while her mind raced.

Where is Ayita? Did she make it to Miriam's? Does Elias know where she is?

Her body felt like it belonged to someone else. What little hope she had managed to retain left her one drop at a time.

"I have to rest," she said. "I'm so tired."

"We've got to put some distance between us and that cabin," Elias said.

Catherine thought of Thomas alone in the cabin with his father. Her heart ached.

Will he find out the truth? Will he know I never wanted to leave him?

The questions running through her mind kept her moving.

"Where are we going?" she asked.

"We're not heading east, I guarantee you that," Elias replied. It was the first time Catherine had ever heard uncertainty in his voice. "South maybe. Out of Georgia for damn certain."

Catherine's legs locked. Elias jerked her arm. She screamed. He struck her in the face.

Catherine put her head back and melted into the cold embrace of the earth.

Elias straddled her torso and raged into the night. "Get up, dammit! Get the hell up!"

§§

Catherine!

Thomas slid off of Silo and headed towards the scream. He stumbled over rocks and roots and still he ran. A tree branch raked his injured eye – and still he ran. He ricocheted off an oak and into the ground, his breath expelled from his searing lungs – and still he ran. He careened through the stygian darkness driven by love and a lust for blood.

He heard a second cry and veered left. The tree spread just enough to allow a solitary beam of moonlight to illumine…

…a body dangling from the end of a rope.

Thomas reached for a pistol that wasn't there, then walked forward to inspect the body of Lieutenant Colonel Jeremiah Morse. Dried blood from a puncture wound in his throat painted a ghastly river of gore just below his swollen, blue face.

A brutish voice shattered the grim quiet.

"Get up, dammit. Get the hell up."

Thomas looked once more at the grizzly corpse, then plunged into the darkness.

§§

Elias grabbed a fistful of Catherine's hair.

"I said get up! You're gonna learn to obey me, woman." Catherine felt nothing except for the cold creeping up from her ankles. She was covered in sweat, a result of the forced march through the humid evening, but she felt like winter was invading her body. Try as she might, she could not stand. Breath came in great heaves. What little vision she had was blurry. Elias let go of her hair and reached for his knife.

"I really hoped things would end different, lover."

§§

Thomas's lungs and thighs burned, but thoughts of Catherine propelled him through the trees. He stopped and listened for even the slightest sound.

There!

He burst into a clearing when the moon shone with the glare of fifty candles. Elias was standing over Catherine with his arm raised to slash Catherine with his knife. Thomas charged and bowled him over.

The knife flew into the air.

Thomas flailed at Elias, a wild series of savage blows to head and body. Elias took the punishment, then unloaded a haymaker to Thomas' jaw. Thomas's heart pounded like a drum signaling attack. He slammed his foot into Elias's knee.

Elias howled and crumpled but when Thomas closed, Elias threw an uppercut into the captain's groin. Thomas collapsed like paper in a rainstorm. Orange starbursts exploded across his vision; he rolled over and retched. He started to curl into a ball, then remembered...

Catherine.

He rose to his knees and braced for an attack. It never came.

Thomas squinted his one good eye and looked for any sign of the man in black. Nothing. He heard Catherine move and looked at her. Her face was tight with horror.

"Look out!"

Thomas felt a burning pain across the middle of his back at the same time he heard retreating footsteps. He dropped to one knee and fought against his racing pulse and rising nausea. Elias's laughter bounced off the trees. Thomas could not pinpoint a location.

Thomas screamed into the forest.

"What's wrong, Elias? Can't face me man to man? Have to run and hide like a coward?"

Thomas stabbed his blade into a nearby tree and hoisted up to his feet. All the while, he scrutinized every shadow. He heard the footsteps a moment too late. Elias's blade scythed across his back once again.

Thomas bellowed, releasing weeks of pint-up frustration.

The voice echoed all around. "What's wrong Captain? Got a little back pain?"

Rage pulsed through Thomas' body; it masked the pain – a little. He turned in a slow, tight circle.

Footsteps!

Thomas turned and caught Elias under the armpit. He flipped the attacker over his shoulder and began to unload punches

Right...left...right again. Thomas's knuckled screamed in protest as they smashed into Elias's face, but Thomas continued his assault until his arms burned. Thomas pulled back his right arm to deliver an overhand punch.

Elias shifted slightly. His movement combined with Thomas's fatigue caused the captain to miss and lose his balance. Elias whipsawed his legs and knocked Thomas onto his back.

When he hit the unforgiving ground, all the air rushed out of Thomas's lungs. He gasped for breath and tried to find his footing. He managed to get as far as his knees.

He looked up.

Elias stood, three feet away. He held a thick limb over his head.

"I'm gonna beat you senseless, Captain," he said. "Then you can watch me screw this woman while you die."

Elias reared back to deliver a blow.

Suddenly, he gasped and stood up straight, back arched. His eyes registered surprise and pain at the same time. He threw a hand over his shoulder, groping, searching for the source of his agony.

A piercing war cry split the night at the same time Elias's own knife slit his throat. He gurgled, then fell on his face in the dust.

Catherine stood behind him. She wiped the blood from the blade but did nothing about the crimson stain on her face.

She walked to Elias's twitching body and spit.

"Go to hell, you son of a whore."

CHAPTER FIFTY-SIX

Thomas rushed to Catherine who doubled over, knee to the ground. He knelt beside her and would have embraced her – except she shuddered when he touched her. In the blaze of the moon, he could see a river of blood running down her leg from under the black jacket she clutched ever closer. He stroked her hair.

"Let me see," he said.

The gaping wound reminded Thomas of things he had seen on the battlefield – terrible things – gruesome things – fatal things.

"Oh God, no."

Catherine's eyes, the deep orbs he had seen in his mind every day for the last seven years, locked onto his with an expression of peace and acceptance.

"I'm so sorry," she whispered.

Thomas closed his eyes and prayed to a God he was not sure was there. When he opened them, Catherine's face was the most beautiful sight he'd ever seen.

"My father…he lied to us – "

Catherine placed her finger on his lips. "I know. I know everything."

Thomas kissed her. She responded, tenderly at first, then with an intensity springing from years of denial. Her arms locked around his neck.

"I love you," he said. "I never stopped loving you."

"I know." She caressed the side of his face. "And I never stopped loving you."

Shouts echoed through the trees.

"It's Roe," Thomas said. "I'd know that voice anywhere." He pulled away a little – but not much. "We're here. Hurry!"

Catherine studied his face as if looking at it for the first time.

"Walks the Sky," she said. "Will you come visit me on one of your excursions?"

"The only reason I will ever study the sky again will be to look for you," he said.

Pain washed all the color from Catherine's face. She squeezed his hand until the wave passed. When she gathered herself enough to look at him, there was less light in her eyes.

"Ayita?"

Thomas managed to smile. "She's fine. Elias and Morse can't touch her."

"Thank God." Catherine closed her eyes for a moment then looked back up at Thomas. "You must promise me something."

"Anything."

"Do not be bitter."

Thomas stared at her. Her voice was faint but firm.

"Do not harden your heart, I need you to be there. I need you to —"

Roe and a dozen panic-stricken men burst into the clearing. Roe set Ayita on the ground. The child rushed towards Catherine.

"Mamma! Mamma!"

Thomas boosted Catherine a little and pulled the jacket across the wound. Ayita barreled into Catherine at full speed. Catherine released a sound, the closest thing Thomas had ever heard to pure joy.

"Oh, my baby girl." Catherine wept. "My beautiful, beautiful baby girl."

"Captain?"

Roe was looking at Thomas's hands and the pool of blood around Catherine's feet. Before the sergeant spoke again, Thomas nodded towards Catherine and shook his head. Roe removed the hat from over his dirty face with the reverence of a priest conducting the sacrament.

Only Thomas heard the mutter. "Dammit!"

Roe twisted his cap in his hands, looked at mother and child once again, then walked away into the shadows.

Catherine pulled away from Ayita, whose clothes were now stained with her mother's blood. She cupped her daughter's face with her hands and looked into her young eyes.

"My beautiful girl. I'm so sorry I let those men take you from me. I'm so sorry."

Ayita wept. "Not your fault, Mamma. They were bad and strong."

"I am sorry," Catherine said.

Ayita hugged her mother again.

Catherine held her daughter for as long as she could, but time, precious time, was slipping away.

"I have to go, baby girl," she said.

"Go where, Mamma?"

"I'm going to go be with your father. And your grandfather."

"Where are they?"

Catherine swallowed hard. "They are all around us. You cannot see them, but they are always here. If you close your eyes and listen hard, you can hear them."

"Grandpa used to tell me that when we walked the tall grass."

"Yes," Catherine replied.

"Can I go with you?" Ayita asked.

Catherine blinked hard. "Not this time sweetheart. You have to stay here and help our people."

Ayita's chin began to sink but Catherine held it in place.

"I want to go with you, Mamma," Ayita said. "I don't want to be without you."

Catherine pulled Ayita close. "You will never be without me. I will always be here, I promise."

"Who will take care of me?" Ayita asked.

Catherine looked at Thomas. "This man. This is my friend, Thomas."

Thomas managed to smile.

"You sent him to get me, didn't you, Mamma?"

"Yes, I did."

Catherine took Thomas's hand and placed Ayita's inside of it. "I was hoping the two of you will take care of one another when I go."

Ayita looked at Thomas and saw something in his eyes that made her feel safe.

"I will, Mamma," Ayita said.

Catherine's hand fell to the earth. Her head slipped to Thomas's chest. And the light in her eyes faded peacefully into the eternal night.

EPILOGUE

Thomas stared at his reflection. He liked his suit – added a little gravitas to his aura – and looked better than a uniform. His fingers traced the scars around his right eye then poked at the flecks of gray around his temples.

Not bad for a man turning forty soon.

He straightened his vest and adjusted his tie before walking to his mother's bedroom door. He knocked, then opened it without waiting for an answer.

"Is it bad luck to see the bride before the wedding?" Thomas asked.

"Come on in." Despite her advancing years, Louise Edwards had never looked more radiant. Her high-necked gown set off with imported lace at the collar and organdy cuffs, combined with her perfect posture to form a portrait of grace and elegance.

"Besides," Louise said, "I think the bad luck attaches to the groom, not the father of the bride."

Louise turned to Leotie and Manjusha. "Come on ladies, let's give them a moment."

"Of course," Leotie replied.

"I will make sure the men are ready," Manjusha said.

Thomas held the door. Each one squeezed his hand as they passed. Louise hugged him and pecked his cheek.

When he stepped in, his throat constricted, and his eyes watered. Ayita stood in the middle of the room in a gown Louise had insisted on making herself. The young woman's face glowed with a vivacity Thomas had only seen in one other – her mother Catherine.

"You look beautiful, dear. Absolutely stunning."

Ayita smiled and opened her arms for a hug.

Sixteen years had passed since the night in the forest, an event of which they seldom spoke but one they remembered every day.

"How are you doing?" Ayita asked as she pulled away.

"I'm doing well," Thomas said.

"You are a terrible liar, Thomas Edwards," Ayita said.

And he was, but he knew his heart and soul had mended. He had drowned himself in alcohol for the first three weeks following Catherine's death. Then, one day, when he reached to hug little Ayita, she recoiled.

"You smell," she had said. "And your eyes look like the soldiers who took me away from mamma."

He had not had a drink since.

"Do you think she'd be proud of me?" Ayita asked. She looked at herself in a full-length mirror.

"No," Thomas said. "She *is* proud of you. Remember, she is with you every day. So are Jishnu and your father."

Thomas held her gaze until he felt he would burst into tears. Embarrassed, he cleared his throat and stepped away.

"So, explain to me again why you needed this," he said.

He meandered over to a small table and picked up the ear of corn he had brought Ayita earlier in the day at her request. It was encircled by a red ribbon.

"It's a Tsalagi tradition. That's my clan's color, the Aniwahya, the Wolf Clan, but you knew that already. The bride presents the corn to her husband as a symbol that she will be a good wife. She will share her harvest with him. The husband offers his wife a ham of venison showing he will provide meat for the family."

"Doubt I will be handing out a lot of hams as wedding gifts in the future."

Ayita punched him on the arm. He feigned great pain. "I did not realize you were from separate clans."

"Yes. Kavi is from the Ani Tsiskwa clan. Some call it the Small Bird Clan or the Eagle Clan. Their color is purple."

Thomas nodded.

"Kavi will be a good husband," Thomas said. "If not, Jeevan and I will make a ham out of him."

They embraced.

"Do you need anything else?"

Ayita looked around the room. "No, I think I have everything."

"Okay, then," he said. "I have something to give you."

519

He closed her hand around a leather bracelet.

"Your mother made this for me years ago. Now it's yours." He could feel his self-control slipping. "Now I will leave you be and send the ladies back in to help you."

"Father?"

"Yes?"

Ayita took Thomas's hand in a vice-like grip. "Thank you," she said. A tear trickled towards her jaw. "Not just for today but for…for everything."

Thomas took a stuttering breath. "It has been my honor to watch you grow up into such a strong, young woman. I've loved every minute."

Ayita swiped at her cheek. "You have to go now, or I will never make it through this day."

Thomas hugged her one more time, then opened the door. Two women virtually fell into the room. Thomas burst into laughter.

"She's all yours," he said.

Leotie and Louise smiled.

"Where's Manjusha?"

"She went home to make sure Jeevan had Kavi ready," Leotie replied.

"All right," Thomas said. "I will see to the comfort of our guests."

Louise brushed Thomas's damp face. "Are you okay, son?"

"Nothing millions of fathers have not already survived," he said.

He could hear the noise from the gathering increasing by the minute. "I am simply full of pride." He felt his jaw tighten. "Pride... and memories."

Louise squeezed his hand. "We are both truly blessed." She sighed and looked out the window. "I have to be honest. For a while there, I wasn't sure I was going to survive your father's disappearance. That was a long year and a half or so. But selling everything and moving here to Dahlonega with mother and helping you raise Ayita have been wonderful. I could not ask for anything more."

Thomas instinctively looked away. He had never told her the truth about Clinton – the schemes, the duplicity, the murder of her father. Though her fable-ized memories of Clinton threw sand in Thomas's emotional gears, he deemed it best for her to remember her scab of a husband as a good, hard-working man.

And when Clinton's body was found in a remote cabin in the middle of the woods, Thomas paid a pretty penny for the report bearing the phrase "self-inflicted gunshot wound" to evaporate. For the rest of her life, Louise Edwards publicly believed that retired Colonel Clinton Abingdon Edwards had died on a hunting trip somewhere in his beloved Georgia mountains.

"Thomas?"

He smiled as best he could. "Just missing Catherine," he said.

"She's here, right?" Louise said. "Isn't that what you just told Ayita?"

"Honestly, mother. Eavesdropping is bad enough. Self-conviction is worse."

Mother and son embraced, each with their own secrets, each hoping the other neither knew nor suspected what they both knew or suspected.

"If you would like, I will go with you after the party,"

Thomas nodded. "I'd like that."

He never missed a day of visiting Catherine's grave. He stared out of the front window and remembered.

The day she died, Thomas and his charges marched with the resolution of those who circled Jericho to ensure they would reach Miriam's in time for a proper Cherokee burial before twenty-four hours lapsed. For a little over eight months, Thomas lived quietly at Dahlonega.

Then, late one afternoon, a small contingent of cavalrymen trotted up the drive. Miriam answered the door. The officer, hat in hand, bowed deeply. He was young, handsome, and stained by the grime of the road.

"Are you Miriam Madison, grandmother of Captain Thomas Edwards?"

"I am," she said. "If you are looking—"

"Begging your pardon, Madam," he said, "I am Captain Nehemiah Gilyard of the Sixth Cavalry Division of the United States Army currently deployed at Fort Newnan, Georgia. I fear I have grim news."

"Go on," Miriam said. She hoped Thomas would have the good sense not to appear from the next room.

"With your kind permission," Gilyard said, "I will summarize the official report to spare your delicate sentimentalities."

"My daughter was married to a soldier," Miriam said. "As you stated, my grandson is a soldier. I assure you I am well prepared for whatever you will tell me."

Gilyard cleared his throat. "An official report was filed by one Sergeant Dearborn Roland Bickford III and verified by Captain John Dorsey, recently retired. It recounts how, after learning of the abduction of three Cherokee women and several children by Colonel Jeremiah Morse and a civilian scoundrel named Elias Watkins, who intended to sell the victims into slavery or to use them – pardon my directness, Madam – for their own nefarious and prurient purposes, Captain Thomas Edwards led a rescue effort. The victims had previously been placed in the safekeeping of your son at Fort Newnan. He took it upon himself to free them. There were numerous skirmishes along the way. I am pleased to report that both Colonel Morse and Elias Watkins were killed. Their skeletal remains were discovered in a heavily wooded area. They had been...ah..."

"Ravaged by wild beasts?" Miriam asked. She struggled to keep from smirking.

"Ah…yes ma'am. Apparently, Colonel Morse, having taken leave of his senses and all manner of military decorum, determined he would pursue your son. In the process, the colonel tried to seize control of Fort Hetzel from which he was forcibly ejected by Captain Arthur Hatton. The Bickford account corroborates the report from Captain Hatten."

"My, oh my," Miriam said. She coughed into a handkerchief to stifle a giggle.

Gilyard's face took on a visage of official mourning. "It saddens me to report that in the performance of his duty, Captain Thomas Edwards perished. His…ah…even after an exhaustive search…his remains were never recovered. All parties laud his superior leadership and his gallantry. In light of which…"

…he turned to an aide who handed him a box.

"In light of which, the United States Army has commissioned me to deliver to you this medal for meritorious service and to inform you that Captain Edwards has been promoted posthumously to the rank of Major with all the rights and privileges appended thereto."

Miriam bit the inside of her mouth. "There being none of any tangible nature inasmuch as my grandson is apparently no longer on this mortal coil."

"Ah, no ma'am…I mean, yes ma'am…I mean, I am so very sorry for your loss, and I convey to you the heartfelt sympathies of a grateful nation."

Gilyard and his small retinue of men snapped to attention and saluted. Miriam nodded gravely and thanked them for their efforts.

"Under more pleasant circumstances, I would invite you gentlemen inside, but given the devastating nature of your communique, you will understand if I choose to grieve alone."

She decided not to mention that she recognized the medal as one repurposed from the War of 1812.

Gilyard shifted like a man wearing ill-fitting shoes. "There is one more matter, ma'am."

"Yes?"

"Reports are that you have a small settlement of indigenous people on your land."

"I do," Miriam said. "My late husband and I worked with the Seminole people in Florida. We brought a number of them back with us. They have their own farms and homes and families."

"Yes, ma'am," Gilyard said. "Well, since we were told that Morse and this Elias character were headed east to sell the Cher—"

Miriam did not have to feign her wrath.

"Young man, are you suggesting I purchased the women and children Colonel Morse and this Elias kidnapped? Do you think I have Indian slaves here?"

The captain backed up a few steps and raised his palms. "Lord no, ma'am. We never found them, and I was just thinking—"

"No sir," Miriam said, "you were not thinking at all. My dear Thomas wrote me regularly about the deplorable conditions at Fort Newnan. There was no food…there was no water…there was no housing. Men, women, and children corralled like animals and sleeping in their own filth. He also told me there was no roster. The Army had no idea who was in its custody because no one ever bothered to ask. No telling where those unfortunate waifs went but it could not be worse than the hell you and the Army created. If you want to check my land, go ahead, but since you have no information by which to check anyone's identity, if you attempt to remove any of my friends, I will go upstairs, get my grandson's old shotgun, and fill your backside so full of birdshot that you will not sit properly for months!"

The men behind Gilyard sniggered. Gilyard shot them a quick and threatening glance. He spoke as he backed off the porch.

"Very well, ma'am," he said. "We will consider this matter closed and allow your courageous grandson to rest in peace. Again, my deepest sympathies to you and yours. Ah…God bless the United States."

When Colonel Gilyard turned in his report, Major Thomas Edwards was listed as "deceased." No one from the government or the Army ever called on Miriam again.

Thomas chuckled and turned from the window.

"I better get out there, before Roe's brood of kids destroys the place." He looked back at Louise. "It's a good day."

"It is," Louise replied and went back into the bedroom to help Ayita.

Once outside, Thomas laughed. Roe was wrangling a herd of eight children, each more rambunctious than the next. Thomas couldn't believe the man who once commanded men in combat could not control a brood of tykes.

Roe saw Thomas approaching and threw up his hands. "Sorry, they're a bunch of rascals."

Thomas shook his friend's hand. "Not to worry. They're just having a little fun." He looked over at a beautiful woman twenty years Roe's junior. "I hear Luyu is expecting again."

Roe let go of a wry smile. "She is," he said. "I have no idea how that keeps happening."

"You better figure it out or pretty soon you will be stocking your own cavalry regiment."

The old friends embraced again.

After returning to Fort Newnan and filing his report, Roe and what was left of the captain's men were sent to Fort Cass in Tennessee, a primary emigration depot for the Cherokee removal. Several months later, in November, when thirteen contingents of

Cherokees crossed Kentucky, Tennessee, and Illinois, Roe went with them.

Once Roe reached the Indian Territories, he stayed and reunited as many children with their parents as he was able. He met and fell in love with Luyu, whose name meant Wild Dove. She could not resist his boyish charm – and she still could not quite get his face clean. They married and lived with her family in the Indian Territory until she gave birth to their third child.

"You ever gonna start a family of yer own?" A favorite question of Roe's as of late.

Thomas shook his head and held Roe's youngest son upside down by the ankles.

"I think Ayita would understand," Roe offered. "Catherine would, too."

Thomas nodded. "They would."

Thomas swung Roe's youngest from side to side before letting him down.

"It just doesn't feel right," Thomas said. He looked at the community who called his grandmother's land their home. "I'm quite content with my life as it is."

Roe stood next to his friend and looked at the gathering as well. "It is a good life here. I'm indebted to your grandmother for lettin' me move onto her land with my family. Indian Territory ain't no place to raise a family."

"Excuse me, Master Thomas."

Rigton's back was bowed from years of caring for horses, but his smile was radiant.

"Sorry to interrupt," Rigton said. "But would you be so kind as to help an old man whose fingers won't cooperate."

He held up a bow tie.

Thomas smiled. "Certainly, my friend."

"I ain't worn this suit since, well, since the day I married Clarebelle," Rigton said with a satisfied sigh.

"I believe you're right," Thomas replied. He remembered how happy the two of them were on their wedding day.

Rigton and Clarebelle followed Louise to Miriam's land and married shortly thereafter. They built a one-room house not too far from the main house and lived as free newlyweds until she died four years later. Heartbroken after her funeral, Rigton couldn't bring himself to live in the dwelling they once shared, so, with Thomas's help, he emptied it of their possessions and burned it to the ground.

Thomas helped Rigton build a new home where he spent his days watching the corn grow and keeping an eye on Roe's children, who lovingly referred to him as "Uncle Rigs."

"There you go."

Thomas stood back and admired his handiwork. Rigton adjusted his suit and stood as straight and proud as his old back would let him.

"Oh, my, look how handsome you look," Miriam said as she walked up next to Thomas. "Rigton, you look splendid."

Rigton smiled and bowed his head to her. "Thank you, ma'am."

"Looks like everyone is here," she said to Thomas. "I think it's time to get started, don't you since you are the father of the bride?"

Thomas nodded and smiled.

"Rigton, would you escort me over, so we can get the wedding fire started?" Miriam asked.

"Be my pleasure, ma'am."

Rigton offered his arm and they leaned on one another as they made their way across the uneven ground.

"Guess I better get these future outlaws settled," Roe said. He patted Thomas on the arm. "Talk with ya later."

"Sure thing."

§§

That evening while the wedding party was still going strong, Thomas stole away to visit Catherine's grave. He thought about asking his mother to join him, but when he saw her surrounded by friends, laughing and telling stories, he couldn't ask her to leave.

Thomas knelt next to the rectangular slab of slate marking Catherine's resting place and brushed away a little debris. With the music celebrating Ayita's new life resonating in the distance, Thomas ran his fingers over the letters spelling out Catherine's Cherokee name.

"Ayita's all grown now," Thomas said. "A bright young woman. Beautiful, inside and out. She'll make a good wife and mother if she chooses. I think Kavi is a good match for her. He is a good man and comes from a good family."

"So very nice of you to say," Jeevan said.

When Thomas jumped, Jeevan apologized. "I'm sorry," he said. "I didn't mean to startle you."

"That's okay," Thomas replied.

He got to his feet.

"Is it a bad thing for both fathers to be missing from the wedding party?" Thomas asked.

"Doubt they notice."

They stood next to one another looking down at Catherine's grave and listening to the music.

"This day would not have happened except for you," Jeevan said.

"Why do you say that?"

"If you had not forgiven my wife after we came here," Jeevan replied, "we would have left. Who knows—"

Thomas began to protest, but Jeevan laid a gentle hand on his arm.

"You cannot imagine Manjusha's guilt," Jeevan said. "It was tearing her apart. She felt responsible for everything that happened. Probably still does."

The moonlight glinted off Catherine's marker.

"Manjusha was so afraid at the beginning, so lost when our children were first taken from us," Jeevan said. "To lose your children the same day you are forced out of your own home at gunpoint was a horrible experience. We did not think we would ever see them again. The conditions at Fort Newnan increased her fears. She thought things might get better if she informed Elias about the people running away and Catherine helping Salal escape." Jeevan took a deep breath. "But, when Kasewini was caught and… everything that happened to her, Manjusha realized what she had done."

Jeevan shook his head.

"Catherine never said an unkind word to my wife about it. She knew – and she never said a word."

Thomas could not have spoken even if he wanted.

"Manjusha scarcely slept for the first year we were here. Guilt ate at her like worms. All the deaths were on her head. I did not know what was wrong until she told me. I told her to let it go, but that was not enough. That is when she went to you, my friend."

"I only did what anyone else would do."

Jeevan shook his head. "No, Thomas, you did not. It is only human to want vengeance. And you would have been justified to banish us from your grandmother's land. But you forgave her – you forgave her in front of everyone. You called her your 'sister,' and

532

then you blessed our son's love for your daughter. You saved her life
– you saved my family."

"That was such a terrible time for all of us," Thomas said. "We
have to forgive ourselves for the choices we make, and we have to
forgive one another. You and I both know it's what Catherine would
have done."

The moon shone, the music echoed, the night sang its lullaby,
and the two men stood, lost in their thoughts of the past.

"She saved *my* life," Thomas said. "Catherine. Not just by
killing Elias. Her faith saved me. Her belief in goodness when
everything was so terrible – when I did not have faith in myself. She
saved me from self-destruction – then Ayita did."

His breath made a long plume in the night air – a trail of pent-up
emotion. "Without them, I would not be standing here."

A branch cracked. Both men whirled – each had clenched fists.

"There you two are," Ayita said. "Manjusha has been looking all
over for you, Jeevan. You better get back to the party or you'll be in
trouble."

Jeevan laughed. "That's my cue to go." He touched Ayita's
hands and smiled before walking away. "Don't stay away too long,"
he said. "I believe you owe your new father-in-law a dance."

"Only if you promise not to step on my toes this time," Ayita
said.

She stood next to Thomas and watched Jeevan leave. After a moment or two of reflection on her mother's gravesite, she turned to Thomas. He was searching the stars.

"Is she up there?" she asked.

Thomas took her hand and placed it on his chest.

"And here as well."

"I hate to interrupt," Kavi said, "But some of the guests with a long ride home are leaving. We should say goodbye."

"Go," Thomas said. "I am fine – I will be there in a moment."

"Okay."

Ayita kissed his cheek and walked away with her hand in Kavi's.

Thomas stared until they disappeared into the darkness; he could not shake the thought he was losing a part of Catherine.

Inevitable, he thought. *Life moves on.*

Thomas put his hands to his lips, then touched Catherine's marker.

"See you tomorrow, Kasewini," he said.

He walked back towards the celebration of a new life – a new love – a new family. He knew his beloved would be waiting for him amongst the stars the next time he walked the sky.

THE END

ACKNOWLEDGMENTS

I'd like to go back to the beginning of this journey and thank Michael Neff with Algonkian Writers Conference for being excited about the title, *Walks the Sky*, and helping me flush out a solid plot for the story. I learned a lot in our short time together.

The story would probably still be a complete mess if I had not taken the Author Salon course offered through the Algonkian Writers Conference. It was a lot of work but valuable. I recommend it to any writer who wants to improve.

I'd like to thank Sam Severns for holding my hand as I chopped my original tale down from 220,000 words to a more manageable number. Working with you was a pleasure and I wish all the best to you and your family.

Thanks to the Paper House Book Publishing Company, more specifically to Tiffany Sears for being patient with all of my questions. Mo Raad for his amazing skill at cover design. Steven Kelly, for his help designing my website, and Gerald Mcraney, for the video trailer. It has been a fun process and you all made it easy.

A *huge* thank you to Arthur Fogartie, defender of puppies both real and fiction. You managed to whittle the manuscript from 120,000 words to a lean 98,000 and made it a better story in the process. I appreciate your honesty, humor, and willingness to go through eight rounds of edits with me. I learned a lot working with you and though we didn't agree on everything, we were never disagreeable. I'd like to think I made a friend during this process and hope to work with you again in the future.

Jeff Owen was an encouraging force at the beginning of my journey. I appreciate your kind words and willing ear more than you'll ever know.

David Rasbold – you plowed through my work at the *very* early stages when I couldn't see where the stairs were leading. With your help, we took each step one at a time in faith.

A special thanks to Carole Rhoades Thompson. You have been a cheerleader from the beginning and probably the only one who read my bloated 220,000-word original piece. Looking back, I'm not sure how you survived. Ha. I appreciate your honesty from the beginning and your constant support along the way. There were times when I doubted myself and this story, but your faith in it helped me keep going.

Tracy Spihlman – you took on just about every role a writer could want or need: beta reader, editor, cheerleader, sounding board, and shoulder to cry on. You and Jeff held me up. There are not enough words. Thank you, thank you, thank you!

Family is essential in any project. Mom and Dad, Ron and Betty Habeck, I never question your love and care. You are always there when I need you. I love you.

My sister, Rhonda Deleuran, introduced me to writing at a very young age. You did it when we were kids and I wondered if I could do it too. Thanks for all the "rah-rahs," feedback, and help.

Many thanks to Cassandra Torres, my other sister, for reams of information about the Native American culture. If you got tired of my bouncing ideas, you never let on. You helped me to define a clear path.

The credit for the great title, *Walks the Sky,* goes to my brother-in-law, Bill Torres. Wish I'd thought of it first.

To my in-laws, Rev. Gerald & Dr. Jane Calaway – words cannot convey my deep appreciation for your willingness to read and reflect on my efforts. Your readiness to babysit when I wanted to sneak in a few extra hours at the keyboard was invaluable.

Thank you to my younger daughter, Jaryn. Your hugs and kisses while I was writing on a Saturday morning, or as you went to bed and I stayed up to write this story, kept me going. You inspire me. I love you to the moon and back.

To my older daughter, Bekah -- you are blossoming as a writer yourself. Thank you for being my sounding board from time to time and listening to my boring stories. I'm so happy to have someone with whom to talk character and scene development. I love you a bushel and a peck.

Jaynanne, my wife – where do I begin? Without you, this story would never have been started, let alone finished. You bought my first laptop and told me to quit talking about stories and to start writing. You've encouraged me to take classes and go to conferences, write stories, and helped me decide being an indie author was the way to go. None of this would be possible without you. You are a cherished life partner. I don't know how I got so lucky. You make me want to be a better man. I love you with all of my heart – now, always, and forever.

And I thank God. Without him, nothing is possible!

ABOUT THE AUTHOR

Ron Habeck lives in Godfrey, Illinois, with his wife and two daughters. He teaches clinical dentistry at Southern Illinois University School of Dental Medicine. He began his research into *Walks the Sky* nine years ago, which stemmed from a desire to bring a new perspective to the tragedy of the relocation of the Cherokee Nation ("The Trail of Tears").

Ron is currently working on a second novel and has others for which he is doing research. In his leisure time, he enjoys spending time with his family, traveling, playing sports and board games, and going to the movies. He also loves to cook whenever he gets a chance.

Lightning Source UK Ltd.
Milton Keynes UK
UKHW022005151221
395612UK00003B/155